ROUGH MUSIC

ROUGH MUSIC

Robin Blake

severn
House

This first world edition published 2018
in Great Britain and 2019 in the USA by
SEVERN HOUSE PUBLISHERS LTD of
Eardley House, 4 Uxbridge Street, London W8 7SY.
Trade paperback edition first published
in Great Britain and the USA 2019 by
SEVERN HOUSE PUBLISHERS LTD.

British Library Cataloguing in Publication Data
A CIP catalogue record for this title is available from the British Library.

ISBN-13: 978-0-7278-8851-8 (cased)
ISBN-13: 978-1-84751-975-7 (trade paper)
ISBN-13: 978-1-4483-0191-1 (e-book)

Typeset by Palimpsest Book Production Ltd.,
Falkirk, Stirlingshire, Scotland.

In memory of Janet Waugh 1923-2018

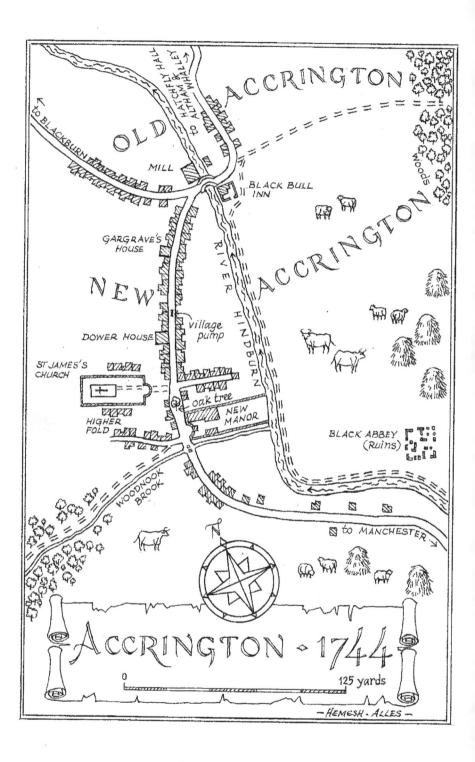

PROLOGUE

At the beginning there were just three conspirators, but like a wine spill on a tablecloth the disturbance spread and soon most of the village had caught the stain. Two of the three were brothers – Simon and Charlie Stirk – and the third was Harry Hawk, a discharged soldier who had returned from the French wars. It seems to have started when they were drinking together one Friday evening at the Black Bull Inn. Billy Whist, the blind fiddler, had been sawing away at his instrument and singing obscene ditties to amuse the company, but now he had stopped. In the relative quiet that followed, the three companions found they were overhearing the talk at the next table, where John Gargrave was complaining vehemently at his wife's domineering ways.

Gargrave was a small tub of a fellow, fifty years old with a round stomach and a fringe of wispy ginger hair around the back of his bald pate. Anne, his thin and wiry wife, was certainly a forthright woman with a tart tongue. She made no secret of her views, not just on her husband and his short-comings, but on any theme of village life and in a voice that could be heard on most days of the week. Listening to the latest list of Gargrave's grievances, it seems that the Stirks and Hawk were moved not to pity Gargrave but to despise him.

Billy Whist was feeling his way from room to room and from table to table, soliciting coins in payment for his concert. As he approached the Stirks, one of them called him to come and sit down. They poured ale for Billy and began questioning him closely. It was out of this conversation that an enterprise was shaped, to be put into effect during the following Sunday.

On Saturday morning, then, the Stirks went down to see the carpenter Peter Castleford and obtained from him a stang, a stout beam eight-feet long that looked something between a thick plank and a gatepost. The brothers carried this stang to a place where they met Harry Hawk, who tested its size and weight and helped with nailing the seat of an old stool to it halfway along.

By now it was Saturday afternoon. They put the stang away in a place where no one would disturb it, and went around the village speaking quietly with every young apprentice, servant and farm labourer they met, explaining what would come to pass the next day following Divine Service, and what each man and girl should do to ready themselves to take part.

The next day, when it was past noon, the Gargraves heard a cats' chorus of hooting, hollering and whooping from the street outside their house, accompanied by birdscarers' rattles, bull bells, wooden spoons drumming on pots and pans, and farting sounds blown through pie funnels. Amidst the cacophony there was one real musical instrument, the fiddle of Billy Whist, who sawed away with demonic and discordant fury. Charlie Stirk conducted this performance, waving his arms and jumping up and down to the rhythm of the clattering, and from time to time he would stop, cup the side of his mouth with his hand, and give out a wolfish howl.

All at once, as Gargrave appeared at the window, the lads took up a rhythmical chant:

> *What's to do? What's to do?*
> *Find the shrew!*
> *Bang-bang! Bang-bang!*
> *Bring out your wife to ride the stang!*

Gargrave opened the window. 'What's this fooling, boys? Don't you know it's the Sabbath? Leave us in peace, won't you?'

The chanting stopped and Simon Stirk stepped forward.

'We will not leave you in peace, John Gargrave,' he said. 'Not until you tell your shrew wife to come out and listen with those flapping ears of hers. She must listen and take what's coming.'

The crowd at his back cheered.

'My wife? What possible business can you have with my wife? Be off with you, I say.'

He began to close the window, but Simon Stirk – the elder of the brothers – stepped up and grasped it by the frame. At the same time, his brother and one or two others rushed forward and lunged at Gargrave, catching hold of his clothes, and without ceremony hauled him out through the aperture and into the air. Dragging the protesting Gargrave back to the road, they threw him down into a water-filled wheel rut – it had stormed and rained heavily in the night – then clustered around and gave him a kicking in the ribs, arms, legs and back, and even planted a few well-aimed blows in his face and on his bald head, while the rut water splashed and sprayed around him. Then they hauled him up and supported him on his legs.

'What do you say now, Gargrave?' Stirk challenged him, thrusting his face towards his victim's and pointing at the house's front door. 'Do you bring out your wife to the threshold or take another kicking? We've heard you whining of how you are pecked by Mistress Gargrave's sharp beak. We heard you on Friday night at the Black Bull, wishing you could stand up to her. We're here to help and you cannot change horses now.'

Muddy water dripped from Gargrave's clothing and blood ran from his nose and lip. Dazed and bewildered at the force of the assault, he tried to assemble his wits. He looked back at his house, and saw the form of Anne Gargrave peering down from an upper window.

'I, ah, didn't mean it, you know. I mean to say, I couldn't let you abuse my wife, not in any way. Besides, you have bruised me, you know, and, well, my wife is indoors and means to stay there, but perhaps she would hear you from the window, if you have anything to say. Indeed, she surely *will* hear you.'

Stirk looked at Gargrave with what the latter would call mad eyes, and scoffed at him.

'From the window? Don't be so soft, man. The old bitch must come outside. She must sweep her threshold. If you do not produce her, we must go inside and fetch her out.'

He pointed to the front door and, taking the hint, his brother stepped up and tried the handle. No one within had thought to turn the key, and the door opened easily. Moments later, a few of the company went into Gargrave's hall and up the stairs. A shriek was heard from above as they seized Anne Gargrave, who they found on a ladder trying to climb into the attic. They grasped her ankles and mercilessly pulled her down, and then bundled her into the hall and out to the road. When they released her, she spun round to face them spitting defiance and disdain.

'You blackguards! How dare you lay hands on me! In what way have I ever offended you?'

The elder Stirk took up a position in front of her, legs apart and thumbs in his waistcoat pockets, and addressed her in a mock-judicial voice, though at the same time barely containing his laughter.

'Mistress, you are hereby charged with keeping a sharp tongue and meddling in other folks' affairs. And of beating your husband, which you must not do, you know, even if he is as weak as an old man's stream of piss. It follows that if John Gargrave cannot rule you, then it must be done by us, his and your kindly neighbours.'

The company laughed. Their numbers were growing now as news of the disturbance spread around the village, with women as well as men coming out of their houses to join the to-do. While her tormentors were still guffawing, Anne Gargrave took advantage of her guards' inattention and broke away and began to run. She had not gone twenty yards when easily and almost lazily they caught up with her and brought her back by the ears to stand opposite her own threshold – the place where her punishment would begin.

'Get that skirt off her – and the bodice,' said Simon Stirk.

'No, no!' Mrs Gargrave screamed, turning towards the lookers-on. 'Husband! Friends! Will no one put a stop to this filthiness? Call yourself men? Have you not the stomachs and spines to aid a defenceless woman? Help me! Help me!'

But no one stirred as the boys laid hands on her. They stripped off her outer clothing and tore away her cap, so that she stood in her shift with her grey-streaked brown hair hanging down to her shoulders. Then the stang was brought forward and the victim's wrists were tied. She struggled briefly and then suddenly abandoned all resistance, allowing herself to be sat astride the stool that was nailed to the beam. As they hoisted her up high, a cabbage stalk arced through the air and hit the side of her face. As if this were the signal, the chant '*Ride the stang! Ride the stang! Ride the stang!*' now went up.

So they started up the street, led along by Billy Whist and his guide. This was a boy who held a pair of leather-covered batons, which operated partly as the shafts of a cart and partly as steering reins, one being attached to each side of Billy's belt. Barking instructions to this boy and playing his whining unharmonious tunes incessantly, Billy pranced and capered ahead of the mob, followed by the band of five or six men banging their pots and pans and dancing in jig-like patterns around the puddles and ruts. The beam carrying Anne Gargrave came next, shouldered by four strong youths, and just behind it stumbled the bleeding John Gargrave between the Stirk brothers, who made sure he kept up by whacking him from time to time around the buttocks.

The chanting and jeering mob followed them down the street, still growing in number until they reached the village pump, which stood in its round of grass in the middle of the street. Vegetable missiles, as well as wet clods and cowpats, were flying around, many striking Anne Gargrave with full force, so that by the time they reached the well she was streaked with mud and manure about her shift and face. A bucket was produced and water pumped into it, whereupon it was hung from the stang.

Up the street they went, past the narrow alleyway that led to St James's Church and then the manor house, where Squire Thomas Turvey looked out at the scene in dismay through the leaded glass of his windows.

'Oh dear! Those poor people. I should go out there. I should try to put a stop to this.'

'No, father, no! I forbid it.'

His daughter sat beside him in the chair mounted on truckle wheels that Peter Castleford had fettled up for her. He had pushed the chair up to the window so that she too could see what was going on.

'Is that Harry Hawk amongst them?' she said.

'Aye, so it is. I don't like to see one of my men engaging in such rowdiness. I really ought to go out and remonstrate with those lads.'

'You'll never stop them by yourself. And what if you're attacked and killed? What will happen to me, left on my own?'

He told himself she was right. This was near a riot. To quell it would require a magistrate with the militia at his back, and the militia could hardly be obtained at less than three days' notice.

'Very well, my dear,' said Turvey.

He sighed to express his powerlessness (and his relief) and stepped back from the window. 'Better to stay out of sight for the time being, I think, for fear that our looking-on might signal approval.'

The mob by now had carried Mrs Gargrave to near the end of the village, where a brook that crossed the street was traversed by a line of stout stepping stones. They wheeled around an oak tree that stood nearby and paraded her back past the manor house, then past the well and back to her home again. Here Charlie Stirk held a brief whispered consultation with Whist, then ordered the victim to be dragged down from the stang. Her eyes were shocked and her mouth was a round O as she was pulled to the threshold and forced down on her knees, receiving a few solid kicks in the process.

'You shall scrub your threshold now, Mistress, or suffer the consequences,' Stirk told her.

The bucket of water was placed at her side and someone handed the woman a scrubbing brush. But though she held the brush in her hand, Anne Gargrave did not move. All under-standing had been knocked out of her. Simon Stirk came and knelt beside her, and grasped the hand holding the brush.

'You must do it, Mistress. You must scrub, like this.'

He forced her hand down until the brush landed on the doorstep, and began to force it around in the circular motion of scrubbing. The assembled company, gathering round to watch, began a new chant.

'*Scrub-a-dub and empty the tub!*'

But after less than a minute, Charlie stepped forward and pulled his brother out of the way.

'That'll do,' he said. 'It's time for this shrew to ride the stang again.'

Abruptly picking up the bucket, he voided it without

ceremony over Anne Gargrave's head. She flinched and squealed like a porker as the cold water soused her. Then he led her back to the waiting stang.

'No, boys, no!' cried John Gargrave. 'You'll not make her do it again.'

'We'll make the two of you do it,' shouted Charlie Stirk in glee, and with several others laid hands on Gargrave and mounted him on the stang. There not being room on the stool seat for the two of them, he sat planted painfully on the beam itself back to back with Anne, but would have rolled off it had they not been bound together with several turns of rope around their chests and bellies.

So the 'music' began again and the whole performance was repeated, only now the crowd's excitement had risen to a new pitch as they followed the stang carrying both husband and wife down the street and around the oak tree once more. They bayed and cheered as every egg, rotten vegetable and clod of earth found its mark, in particular when the woman was hit. Anne's shift now clung wetly to her bony frame, translucent enough where not covered in filth to show patches of bare pink skin beneath the wet cloth. Now one of the older village women came out of her house and stood in their path with arms wide.

'Will you not stop this foolishness?' she shouted. 'Haven't you had enough of tormenting this man and woman?'

Two lads ran forward, lifted her by the armpits, and removed her to the side of the street.

On their second return to the Gargraves' house, both husband and wife were tumbled from the stang, untied and dragged to the doorstep. This time, while Anne was set to scrubbing the stone, several of the young men opened their breeches and pissed into the waiting bucket, which was then emptied over her head as before. A minute later, she and her husband had been remounted on the stang and were being paraded yet again the length of the street, while the discordant orchestra marched ahead of them banging and rattling. Far from tiring at the repetition, the mob was more frenzied than ever.

The whole procedure was repeated twice more, but at last it ended. The Gargraves were tumbled one final time from the stang, having had to be supported for the last stretch by lads running alongside and holding them, or they would have fallen off into the street. Now, as the crowd began to disperse, their victims lay together face down in the street unmoving, for three minutes or more. Finally, John Gargrave stirred, getting himself to his hands and knees, and started to crawl towards his door. The servant, who had been watching in terror from a window, saw him moving and came out to assist his master, hauling him to his feet and in through the front door.

Anne Gargrave still lay in the road, her face down and her body unmoving.

ONE

When I learned that Elizabeth was carrying our child, all I wanted was for the contentment to continue *ad infinitum*. This euphoric glow bore me through each day of business, and in the evening home to Elizabeth, where we would sit together by the fire, and over our supper and later in bed, where I would babble out my happiness to her and read passages aloud, from books in my library, of love and dreams. I did not feel like a grey-templed forty-three-year-old lawyer, but a rapturous foolish lad.

It wasn't until I held our baby Hector for the first time in my arms – which was in the spring of the year 1744 – that those impractical emotions were displaced by new considerations. In essence, I now regressed from the dreamy disposition of a moonstruck youth to the obsessive practicality of a schoolboy. Now, I wanted to know every possible factual detail of Hector and his infantile existence. What was that spongy spot in the top of his skull, and that rash on his bottom? How was he best winded? Why did he smile or frown like that? How soon would he grasp, laugh, crawl? When would he know me, hear my voice, speak my name?

All this proceeded from my simple delight in Hector's very existence. But slowly, after the first month of his life, my curiosity as to the unfolding facts of babyhood began to alternate with an ineffable feeling of dread. I was possessed by the thought that all too often apparently whole and healthy babies fail to thrive. The life in them dwindles and dwindles until suddenly it is gone, and there is nothing to do but hold a funeral. The fragility of the little vessel containing the life and soul of my son haunted me. Every cough or sneeze he gave, every runny nose and fit of bawling, awoke in me this fear of losing him.

Elizabeth, though fifteen years younger than me, had a wiser and more placid head. She rocked the baby in her arms or gave him her breast (she wouldn't think of a wet nurse) while enduring my questions and doubts with good-humoured patience. But sometimes she could not answer them in terms that gave me any satisfaction.

'Little Hector is well, Titus,' she would insist. 'Look how strongly he sucks and how loudly he yells. Leave well alone, and do not take alarm when there is none to be taken!'

But I could not leave well alone, so I pestered instead my scientific friend Luke Fidelis who, being a doctor of medicine, I expected to give me the definite answers I craved, though childless himself. He told me that in many cases no one could be sure of the question: this authority thought one thing while that one thought another, and no final determination could be made. And running to my library to consult old and previously trusted authors proved equally unedifying.

My hypochondriacal obsession with Hector's health grew even worse one hot still evening in June, when the smell of manure and decay hung dangerously in the air of Preston. I had met Luke Fidelis by chance at the old bridge at Walton-le-Dale while riding back from Higher Walton, having taken witness statements in the matter of the death of a brewer. This foolish fellow had fallen from a ladder while attempting to clear birds' nests from the eaves of his grain store. When I told Fidelis, who was riding in the opposite direction, of my business he said that the brewer deserved his fate, as birds' nests should not be interfered with at this time of year.

'And what takes you down this road,' I asked him, 'when all honest men are heading home to their suppers?'

'An outbreak of disease at Bamber Bridge,' he said. 'Paralysing Fever. It may be a dangerous development.'

Bamber Bridge lies a few miles to the south of where we were, along the old road south.

'I have not heard of that. What is Paralysing Fever?'

'A sickness that comes on like an ague but then affects the legs and arms with grave *sequelae* in some cases. Many recover but a few, particularly the children, are left permanently crippled. In the worst cases the disease destroys the lungs' ability to draw breath, and so they die very quickly.'

'That is dreadful. What can you do, as their doctor?'

'Little enough. It appears to be a kind of contagion and spreads especially among infants after the age of six months. I fear it may come in time to Preston.'

My ride home, up the rising road that leads from the bridge to the eastern bar of the town and then along Church Gate, was a fearful one. *After the age of six months!* That was just the age of our son. With every snort of my horse I imagined a new horror. That my precious boy would fall sick and never walk again; or that he would walk but be unable for ever to use his hands and arms; or even that he would be seized by a paralysis of the breath and so suffocate.

By the time I drew level with St John's Church and turned towards the yard where my horse was stabled, I was in a state of acute distraction. If Preston were to be struck by such a mortal disease, I must make sure at all costs that Hector was not affected. He must be taken away to safety.

My wife was calm, as usual, on hearing this news. But I could see that even she was a little alarmed by it.

'If it is safer for Hector to leave the town, then that is what we should do, my dearest. He may go to my parents, I am sure.'

'But they live only four miles away. He must be removed much further than that.'

'Where then? We cannot just set off like vagabonds, without a destination. No. I would like to have the particulars of this danger from Luke's own lips before anything is decided.'

'I've told you exactly what he told me, in every detail. Don't you believe me?'

'You are inclined to exaggerate any danger where Hector is concerned, Titus. It is a loving impulse, I know, but I want to be assured for myself.'

'Very well, I'll take you to him first thing in the morning. What he has to say is frightful, and when you hear it I am sure you will beg me to take you and Hector as far away from this town as possible.'

It had been more than half a year since Luke Fidelis left his lodgings in Fisher Gate and become a householder in his own right. His new home stood on the Fylde Road, a little way outside the western bar. I rapped the knocker and Luke came to the door wearing an apron. The sleeve-savers on his arms were spotted with black stains.

'We are making up a tar salve. Come in.'

The house was filled with the smell of hot pitch. Luke led the way through the hall to its source, a room overlooking the stable yard that he had had equipped as a doctor's laboratory. Over the fire a pot stood on the trivet, guarded by a pimply youth – his apprentice, Joe Peason – who assiduously stirred it with a wooden spoon. A slight popping sound could be heard as the thick black mixture gently bubbled. Fidelis crossed to the pot, and sniffed it. He lifted it off the flame and set it to one side.

'Keep stirring until it is cold,' he told Peason, then peeled off the sleeve-savers, used one of them to wipe his brow, and beckoned Elizabeth and myself to follow him. 'Come through to the parlour. It is too warm in here for consecutive thought.'

'Luke,' I said as we did so, 'tell Elizabeth what you spoke of yesterday when we met at the bridge. The contagion in Bamber.'

'The Paralysing Fever? I have not previously come across any cases here in England, though I read of some in Holland during my time studying at Leiden. The disease is described in passing in Professor Boerhaave's writings.'

'Is it a contagion, then?' asked Elizabeth.

'I don't know if it is really passed on by the touch. It may be through food, or perhaps by some breathable miasma.'

'How does it show when one falls sick?'

'A sweating fever, great pain in the head, and bodily pain too, but not very specific. Soon enough great weakness in the limbs and muscles. Adult patients usually recover. Some children, especially small ones, suffer a rapid death. And in rather more, there will be crippled and withered limbs for life.'

Elizabeth's closed fist touched her mouth.

'Oh! How terrible! Does it spread quickly?'

'Not as quickly or as virulently as the plague – certainly not. In its communicable aspect I would compare it to the smallpox.'

Elizabeth drew in a sharp breath.

'Like smallpox? Please deal plainly with me, Doctor. I am a mother now, and must know. You tell us this disease is particularly serious in children and it has appeared in Bamber. Will it come to Preston? And if it does, how much danger is Hector in?'

Fidelis shrugged.

'I am afraid that it might come here, but these matters are impossible to predict. If it does, then yes, he would be in a degree of danger. All infants in Preston could be prey to it. There will have to be precautions, such as—'

'There is only one possible precaution,' I burst out. 'We must leave this town, and as soon as we can.'

Elizabeth put a staying hand on my arm.

'But where shall we go, Titus? Where?'

'Somewhere with as few people in it as possible,' I told her. 'Some forsaken place nobody has heard of, from where nobody comes and to where nobody goes.'

'Then where, Titus?'

The answer came later the same day in the form of a note in the hand of Luke Fidelis.

Dear Cragg,

I have been turning over in my mind your determination this morning to quit Preston with your wife and child while there is any danger of the Paralysing Fever breaking out here. I understand your apprehension for little Hector and, though I am not sure it is strictly necessary, there is no doubt that if you do retire to some remote country place you will certainly obviate any risk of infection if a serious outbreak of this sickness comes. Furthermore, far from seeing any other danger in such a remove, I think a stay in the green and healthy country-side would do nothing but good to your little fellow during these hot days of summer.

I therefore have a suggestion. I know a village – extremely remote and unconsidered, but lying less than twenty miles from here – where a Dower House has recently become available after the death of the householder, Mrs

*Entwhistle. She had been my patient for three years or
more. I also know from her son-in-law, the Squire of the
place – I last saw him two weeks ago when I attended
my patient's funeral – that he wishes to put a new
tenant into it as soon as possible. It is a small Dower
House in the centre of the village, a few minutes' walk
from his Manor House. The village is sparsely popu-
lated. It lies in a delightful valley with surroundings
entirely rural and I believe it will be very suitable to
your needs.*

*I have already written to him on your behalf. His name
is Thomas Turvey. I will tell you as soon as he replies.
As you will guess, the Turveys adhere to my own Roman
Catholic religion, which is why I attend them.*

I was anxious, impatient, but there was nothing I could immediately do. The brewer's inquest was to be held on the following
day, and several other business matters needed my attention.
I got down to work with Robert Furzey, my clerk, but however
deeply I tried to immerse myself in these legal tasks I surfaced
continually, wondering how soon Mr Turvey would reply and
wishing that Fidelis had been more specific about where exactly
the man lived.

The jury at Higher Walton took a sympathetic view of the
death under inquest. God – who is so often identified as the
agent of such fatalities – was found blameless. So, after some
caustic evidence given by his wife, was the ladder. The brewer's
brain, she told us, had been pickling for years in fermentation
fumes, and there had been many previous falls, stumbles, cuts
and bruises. The jury therefore found that there could be no
other verdict than 'Death by falling, while the balance of his
body was disturbed.'

The audience was beginning to file out, and the jurymen to
chatter amongst themselves in a congratulatory way, when I
heard one of them say something that almost stopped my heart.
They had touched on why one of the reserve jurors – who
had not been needed and so had not come to my attention –
had never appeared.

'He was taken sick,' said one. 'All of a sudden, with an
ague. And now he can hardly walk. His muscles have wasted.'

An ague? Hardly walk? My blood seemed to chill. I was
sorting the inquest papers before handing them over to Furzey
for safe keeping, but now I dropped the papers and crossed
to the group of jurors.

'Did someone say this man is suffering from an ague?'

'Aye, it's Michael Greenhalgh, Mr Cragg. A fever, shivering,
which the doctor called an ague. I heard it from the wife.'

'And you said he could not walk?'

'He couldn't. The doctor said—'

'Which doctor was that?'

'Oh, Dr Kettle, from here. He said he'd never seen the like
of it.'

'Surely he's treated an ague before?'

The man gave me a pitying look.

'I mean that Michael couldn't walk, Sir. Not that he
lacked the strength to walk, but that he couldn't move his
muscles. He couldn't shift his legs. It were exactly like the
strings were cut.'

Yesterday Fidelis had spoken of the outbreak being in
Bamber Bridge. So was it now, today, in Walton?

'Had Greenhalgh been in Bamber Bridge in recent days, by
any chance?'

The jurymen merely shook their heads, or shrugged. Happen,
but none of them knew.

But one thing was certain: Walton was two miles nearer to
Preston than Bamber Bridge. And if Greenhalgh really had
caught this Paralysing Fever, then the disease might indeed
be on the move.

There's a passage in the Roman poet Lucretius's *The Nature
of Things* of such importance to him that it occurs twice: in
Book III and again, word for word, in Book VI. It is about
fear – baseless, unreasoned, disproportionate fear that grips the
mind and will not let go. Was my fear for Hector of such a
kind? It was not, I knew, entirely without foundation, at least
in the case of this new and threatening infection. Item one, the
Paralysing Fever had certainly appeared in our neighbourhood;

and item two (as I had on Fidelis's authority, which I trusted), it was specially destructive for little children. But was my fear out of proportion?

That night I went into my library, opened my copy of Lucretius's peerless poem and found the passage on fear. Such apprehension, he writes, may keep us awake in the night but it is not necessarily scattered or dissolved in the warmth and clarity of the dawn. The light of the sun alone does not melt our fears; that is done by knowledge and understanding of the inner working of nature.

Disease, which we are all subject to in our faulty fallen natures, is the most pernicious of all sources of fear. I think I know all about myself, but only when I feel a pain in the pit of my belly do I realize how little I really know. I become helpless in face of it. I cannot see it, cannot account for it. I am like a child trembling at night, afraid of what is beneath the bed. My pain is likewise formless, malevolent. It appears seemingly from nowhere, and if it does not grow it may just as mysteriously disappear. Then I forget it – until it appears again.

I cannot see into Hector's body any more than into my own. But facing my infant crying, I am really more helpless than when the pain is my own, as I am unable to question him or reason with him. He cries and cries and cannot say why. It is nothing but wind, of course, and soon he lets it out and is smiling again and gurgling. So what purpose is served by that transient pain, when it is no different from the pain that threatens disease and may presage death?

But if we ever understand the coming and going of pain and reveal the secret springs and levers of disease inside us, will we be truly less afraid? Lucretius thinks so; I do not. A pain still hurts, however well understood. And death is still final, come to that.

Two days later, Fidelis brought me Mr Thomas Turvey's reply to his enquiry. It confirmed that he had not yet tenanted the Dower House and would gladly grant us a lease for a period of three months, renewable by agreement. Moreover, having so recently been the abode of his late mother-in-law, it was now immediately inhabitable without needing any repair or furbishment.

'That is very good news and I am determined to take it,' I told my friend when he had read the meat of the letter aloud to me. 'But you have told me little about this beautiful place of refuge in its rural valley. Where, for instance, is it?'

'Almost due east from here. I can ride there in less than four hours.'

'And what is its name, this demi-paradise?'

'Its name is less pretty than its surrounding country.' Fidelis smiled, with that practised enigma that he liked to exercise.

'And what is it?'

'You will not have heard of it. It is called Accrington.'

TWO

To get to Accrington from Preston had meant a whole day's journey. For to carry a tot that distance on horseback in blazing heat, with a packhorse in tow, required many halts and dismountings. Yet even before our destination had come into view I had made up my mind that it would be a delightful country retreat. The valley along which we approached the settlement was that of the River Hyndburn and consisted on both sides of rich green pasture, with woods higher up the slopes forming a screen against the barren gale-swept moors on the heights above. The green, pastoral topography of the valley was entirely agreeable and its air was pure and healthful.

We came up to it from a northern direction, where the last town we'd seen had been Whalley, having paused there to look at the ruins of the famous abbey. Nearer to Accrington we'd struck the Hyndburn's crystalline stream, flowing against the direction of our travel. The road – if you could call it a road – ran along the bank of this small river until it reached Accrington and then carried on southward towards Manchester. It was a scarred and potted ancient way, much too narrow and rough for carriages.

'It cannot have been improved since William the Conqueror,' said Elizabeth caustically.

'Well, it's the shoddy state of this road that makes Accrington so fit for us,' I pointed out. 'The road is so bad that hardly anyone goes there.'

Elizabeth sighed.

'I feel like the town mouse on her way to visit her cousin the country mouse – little knowing what to expect.'

'Don't worry, my dearest. We will adopt the ways of country mice while we are here. Our life will be wholesome and we shall enjoy it.'

Towards mid-afternoon a few cottages had appeared by the

wayside, after which we passed a pair of stately gates with a lodge cottage besides. Half a mile after this, two tall, solid buildings appeared up ahead, which proved to mark the two ends of a stone bridge – one a flour mill, on the far western bank of the river, and the other, on the near side, the Black Bull Inn. It was at the inn that we asked for Mr Turvey's residence.

This was called New Manor, though it was not new at all but an ill-kempt ramshackle place that had not seen prosperity for at least three hundred years. Here we learned that Turvey was up on the moor seeing to his beehives, and so we had a long wait in the dark stone-flagged hall, which at least had the virtue of being cool. This soothed our boy to sleep. We were offered no refreshment by the old servant, who said her name was Sukey.

At last our new landlord arrived. The Squire was a tall man and large in every direction, including his head, which seemed particularly massive. His chin had a deep cleft in it. He gave every indication of pleasure at our arrival.

'The County Coroner and his lady – by all!'

Thomas Turvey wore an extraordinary wide-brimmed straw hat with fine-mesh netting falling from the brim, jerkin, gloves and gaiters of leather, and countryman's clogs. His padded coat was old, and his leather breeches had several times been patched and mended.

'We are right honoured, Sir, to have a man of your standing coming here. The Coroner himself! In Accrington! It is . . . Well, I might almost say . . .' As he cast around for the word, Turvey took off one of the gauntlets and scratched his backside.

'Come, come, Sir,' said Elizabeth. 'We are modest people and not at all grand, you know. Shall you show us the house we are to live in?'

She wasted no time in courtesies, as Hector was now red-faced and bawling in her arms. He needed a feed.

'Ah yes, of course!' said Turvey. 'It is not five minutes' walk. You may leave your horses – you'd best stable them here with us.'

We gave our mounts into the care of a desultory-looking

youth, who would install and water them before bringing the
packhorse and our luggage to us. Turvey led us across New
Manor's unevenly cobbled weed-strewn forecourt and under
the gatehouse. Here he dodged into a room on the ground
floor which, looking in after him, we saw was a storehouse
for clothing, gloves, hats, netting – everything for the beekeeper.
The room was fastidiously tidy, with a row of hooks for each
set of bee armour and baskets hung from the wall containing
more beekeeping apparatus.

Turvey had divested himself of the padded bee suit and
hung it on its peg with the others.

'I like to keep everything to do with my bees in its place,'
he said when Elizabeth remarked, by way of conversation,
how tidy the room was. 'The hive itself is a very finicky place,
you see. I like to emulate it as far as I can.'

He led us into the village street and up to the Dower House,
one of the dwellings lining the left-hand side of the street. It
was not a magnificent dwelling, being deficient in all points
of modern amenity. But as Turvey had spent no more lavishly
on his own house, it was clear that the difficulty had not been
any lack of concern for his wife's parent but shortage of ready
cash.

Apart from the hall and stairs and a passage which ran to
the scullery at the back of the house, the ground floor was
taken up entirely by a flag-floored room that stretched from
the street at the front to the yard at the back. It had a casement
window looking on to the street, an oak settle, and four spoke-
backed chairs around the fire, two of which were armchairs.
'One for each of us,' said Elizabeth. The rear of the room
contained a cooking range, a vast oaken sideboard, and a door
leading into the scullery beyond. In between, making a dividing
line between the two parts of the room, stood a heavy dining
table. A long clock, a pair of blanket chests and a moth-eaten
tapestry wall-hanging completed the furnishings.

Turvey took us upstairs and showed us the front and
rear bedrooms – whose bed-hangings were in no better condition than the arras below – and then the two attic rooms that
formed the servants' quarters.

'There has been only the one maid here in recent times,'

Turvey told us, 'and she scooted back to her people in Yorkshire after my mother-in-law died. Shall we look for someone in the village to serve you, Mrs Cragg?'

Elizabeth shook her head.

'No thank you, Mr Turvey. Our girl Matty will join us from Preston the day after tomorrow. She is all I need, and I will shift for myself until she comes.'

'Well, we shall make sure food is sent over from our kitchen until she arrives, shall we?'

'That would be extremely obliging, Mr Turvey.'

'And for water, the house has its own well at the end of the yard, a great benefit. The water is sweet, you will find. So that leaves only the, ah, sordid side of the matter, Mr Cragg.'

'I'm sorry, Mr Turvey, you elude me.'

Turvey coloured slightly and shifted his feet.

'The, um, cash consideration, you know.'

'Of course, Mr Turvey! I am sorry. You mean the rent. I have it with me, of course.'

The lad had arrived with the packhorse, so I would have quickly been able to retrieve my purse from the baggage. But Turvey held up his hand.

'No, no. Later will do. You must sup with us this evening and we'll do all then.'

Turvey was standing at the front window, his bulk excluding much light.

'You know, Mr Cragg, it is a lucky chance that you happen to have come amongst us at this moment.'

'Oh? Why is that?'

'Well, there has been a very serious matter and we are baffled to know what to do.'

But before he could go on he was interrupted by a sharp rap at the window, and he opened it to see what was the matter. A gaunt-looking fellow with a dog in tow and a shepherd's crook in his hand was dancing up and down outside and pointing.

'They're a-swarming, Mr Turvey! Up on slopes o' moor. I've just come down from it. A massive swarm!'

'What? My bees swarming? The devil they are!'

'Aye. You better shift yoursen, or you'll lose thousands of 'em.'

Ungainly in his hurry, Turvey stumbled out into the hall and opened the door. He had some rapid discussions with the messenger and then returned to us.

'I am suddenly called away,' he said. 'There's a swarm, just like the old saying.' He wagged his finger good-humouredly. 'I'm blaming you, Mr Cragg!'

'You puzzle me, Mr Turvey.'

'Don't you know it? *When strangers arrive, the bees leave their hive.* I've never known it come true until now. I must go. The matter must be seen to without delay. Shall we expect you at the Manor at half past seven? Good! Until then.'

The door slammed behind him.

'A good man, but very rustic,' I said. 'Are you glad we came to Accrington?'

Elizabeth said, 'I won't know that until I know Accrington, Titus.'

'I already feel good about it. A quiet village, governed in the old way by a Squire who the people look up to but who is also one of them: a piece of old England. It'll make a peaceful sojourn and we will discover how refreshing it is to live simply.'

Elizabeth gave me an indulgent smile.

'If you say so, my love, though in my experience no village is entirely peaceful, or simple, however small and antique.'

A little later we were sitting at the dining table with pens in our hands. Elizabeth was writing a letter with instructions to Matty, who would be coming out from Preston with the jagger Peter Wintle and his cart, while I sat with pen in hand hesitating in front of a blank sheet of paper on which I intended to write a list of books for Matty to bring.

'I cannot decide which books to ask her to fetch,' I said. 'Besides, I fear she won't find what I specify.'

'Matty can read a book's title perfectly well,' said Elizabeth. 'And the book itself, in most cases. I taught her how to read myself. But consider how books would weigh the cart down and take up needed space. We want more important things.'

'More important things than books?' I asked indignantly. 'What things?'

She tapped her letter.

'Tea, coffee, wine, soap, caustic, Fuller's earth, vinegar, greens from the garden, dresses for me, suits for you, shirts, stockings, your best wig, writing paper, sugar, a ham, pickles, my sewing box and stuff for new bed-hangings – and a lot more of things besides. I wish we could bring Hector's cot over, but it will never fit on the cart. So while, as you know, I do love reading, bedding, clothing and food are more important, after all.'

'Books are food,' I argued. 'For the brain.'

She laughed.

'Are you afraid your brain will starve here for lack of them?'

'It might.'

'You will be able to borrow some from Mr Turvey, perhaps.'

'Turvey?' I scoffed. 'You've seen him. He's a bumpkin. He won't have any books.'

'How can you say, until you ask?'

I laid down my pen. Perhaps after all there would be reading matter at New Manor.

'Very well, I'll leave Matty be and tonight we'll see what New Manor has to offer.'

'His wife may be partial to literature.'

'Does he *have* a wife? None appeared when we arrived, and none has been mentioned at all.'

'I suspect he has one, or why would he have removed his mother-in-law into the Dower House?'

'So why have we not met her?'

'She may be ill or insane,' said Elizabeth, 'and so must be confined.'

Instead of my reading list, I wrote to Furzey with some legal instructions that had come to mind since we parted. Twenty minutes later we had finished, folded and sealed our letters.

'I will go and see what we can do with them,' I said.

'I want to come,' said Elizabeth.

'What about Hector?'

'He shall come, too. I'll carry him in the sling.'

So we set out, all three, along the village street to see what postal arrangements this primitive place had to offer. The line of buildings on either side descended in gentle steps towards the bridge. These were a mixture of simple thatched and wooden dwellings joined to each other in rows of six or seven, interspersed with shops also of the simplest kind, usually with a side alley leading through to a yard and outbuildings and workshops. Elizabeth noted the site of the bakery and the dairy, and I that of the smithy.

There were no front gardens to any of these buildings, so the people sitting outside their doors, on stools or low benches to enjoy the evening sun, did so in the street itself. I greeted several as we walked past. One, by way of reply, spat. Two brown and wrinkled old women put their heads together to pass a remark, and then cackled with laughter. Most just watched us morosely, ignoring both my tipped hat and Elizabeth's friendly smile.

'What horrible impoliteness!' she said, adjusting the baby's weight in the sling. 'But I suppose they will get used to us.'

The inn proved to be a warren of little rooms, at the centre of which were the kitchen and the tap room, where we introduced ourselves to the hostess and tapster, whose name was Jane Malkin.

'Aye,' she said in reply to my question. 'We've a post rider that comes and goes by with a satchel. That's every day but the Sabbath. One day he's from Manchester going to Preston, and next the other way. Staying long, are you?'

'A few weeks. No less, and perhaps more.'

She took our letters, saying they'd go the following day at about ten and be in Preston three or four hours later.

'That's good,' said Elizabeth. 'Matty will have my instructions with just enough time to do the packing. We are lucky that she's such a capable girl.'

As we made our way through the maze that led to the street door, a woman of forty or fifty, plainly but respectably dressed, accosted us in one of the narrow passages, blocking our way, with hands on hips appraisingly.

'Art tha Cragg?' she demanded.

'I am.'

'Coroner Cragg?'

'That is correct. May I ask your own name?'

'I'm not afraid to tell you. Susan Bacon. Have you come on purpose here to spy on us?'

'Of course not. What gives you that idea, Mistress Bacon?' She shook her finger.

'Just know this. We'll not be spied on and judged by a bumtrap from Preston, whether or not he brings his wife and babby. We'll do us own judging, and we give not a fart for Lord Derby. He's done nowt for us here, nor has anybody at the Duchy. I say, not Lord Derby nor anybody.'

We edged awkwardly past my accuser, left the inn, and started back up the street, once again under the eyes of the villagers.

'I wonder what Susan Bacon thinks a coroner does?' I said in a low voice. 'That I act for Lord Derby as some kind of police agent such as they have in France?'

Elizabeth laughed.

'She is a tartar, Titus. Those are women of a dangerous age: their beauty is less than it was, but their tongues are so much sharper. What did she call you? A bumtrap? We must make them see you otherwise.'

'But can it be that there's never been a coroner's court in the neighbourhood? Don't tell me there's never been a suspicious death here!'

'I suppose they have short memories.'

'More likely they just keep any troubles to themselves. That woman said as much. "We'll do our own judging." What an insular place! Have they not even a magistrate here?'

'As the local Squire, that should be Turvey – but as a Catholic he's debarred from the Bench.'

Back at the Dower House, I held the baby in my arms, rocking and playing with him while Elizabeth knelt beside the great sideboard, going through the crockery she'd found there.

'I shall feel the want of my library while we are here,' I said.

She heaved a pile of plates out and on to the floor and began inspecting them one by one.

'But as we were saying before, you may be surprised at what books can be borrowed here.'

'I don't mean the books, I mean the room. I mean the chair, the writing desk, the privacy.'

'Oh! You mean, where will you go to escape from us women?'

'I mean, where will I go to write and read and smoke? Where will I write my journal?'

'You will have to muck in with us, that's all.'

She pointed to the fireplace, at the other end of the room, and its surrounding furniture.

'You can write in the armchair. Your journal book is big enough, so you can rest it on your knee. I shan't stop you.'

'You might creep up behind and read over my shoulder.'

She made an expression of mock distaste.

'What? Your review of everything you've done in the day? That would be too long and tedious. You tell me the pith of it, which is enough. You're welcome to have the fireside armchair to yourself – for your pipe, your writing, and your reading.'

'If I ever find any reading,' I said gloomily.

When she had looked over all the crockery and found only a few unimportant cracks, she took Hector back and crossed to a chair in order to feed him.

'Why not see if you can get that clock going?'

It was a clock made in the last century with a brass face atop a tall case of oak. I opened the case door and peered inside. There were the hanging wires with pulley wheels looped into them, but no weights attached at the bottom. It was impossible to be sure what lay in the depth of the case but something glinted, so I knelt and reached down. I felt the two solid-brass cylinders lying there, and brought the first of them out and then the second. But I had felt something else. And when I reached in again, my fingers closed around the leather covers of what could only be a book.

'The house is not completely destitute of books, it seems,' I said. 'I have found one in the clock.'

'A book? That's curious! You'll have something to read now.'

'It is sure to be only a collection of sermons.'

I brought the book out. It was an octavo volume quite nicely bound in calf. I flipped it open and read the title page:

TRAVELS into several Remote NATIONS of the WORLD In FOUR PARTS.

'Well, I was wrong,' I said. 'I have found a book worth reading.'

Elizabeth was sitting back in the chair, her eyes half closed, in that state of semi-trance that appears in women giving suck.

'What gem of literature have you found, then?' she said.

'A fascinating, many-faceted one, my darling.'

'And written by?'

I read the author's name out to her. '*By Lemuel Gulliver, First a Surgeon, and then a Captain of several Ships.*'

'Oh! Is it *Gulliver's Travels*? That's much better than sermons. What's it doing in the clock?'

'I don't know, or care. It is good reading.'

'Haven't you read it before?'

'Of course I have. But this is not a book to read only once. I'm not sure that six readings would exhaust it completely.'

THREE

New Manor stood at the opposite end of the village street from the inn and the mill. One wall of the house abutted the street itself, while on the opposite side the windows looked out on gardens and orchards that stretched down to the river bank, and then across the stream to the land beyond – fields of hay and pasture that rose up towards the dark-green band of woods – and, above these, to the purple hue of the moor.

Having dealt with 'the cash consideration' in what he called his business room, though it was more like a storeroom for guns and old boots, we now stood in the leaded bay window of the Chamber Major (as Turvey called New Manor's largest room), looking out at this prospect. It was spacious, panelled in oak, and had plaster courses covering the ceiling in a pattern of diamonds connected at their corners by angular knot-patterns or by carved bosses. The fireplace was like a monument in carved stone, and the walls were adorned with weapons, heads of stags and portraits of Turvey ancestors in ruff collars. These splendours of another age were now, however, much chipped, tarnished, mouldy and generally dilapidated.

Standing between Elizabeth and me (Hector had fallen asleep and was in the care of the wrinkled retainer named Sukey), Turvey pointed out a group of ruined walls visible on the far bank of the river, a little upstream of us. They were the remaining stones from an earlier dilapidation – what had been a monastic establishment long ago. The ruins were not extensive (a modest affair compared to the great abbey at Whalley we had seen earlier in the day), but they spoke eloquently of the antiquity and lost grandeur of the place.

'There is an even better view from upstairs. You must come up and see my dear wife's room.'

He led the way up a broad oak staircase and on to a gallery that stretched from one end of the house to the other. At each extremity of the gallery was a large window whose leaded lights were set with heraldic shields showing the coats of arms of the Turveys and their relations. One looked over the village street, while the other enjoyed a long view of the river's course and the distant moors in which it arose. Tom Turvey led us down the gallery towards the latter end. It was hung with more recent portraits of Turvey men – some armoured, others in wigs – interspersed with women in flowing silks. As we passed, they all seemed to glance down at us in supercilious pride. Turvey stopped beside one of these canvases, which from the costume of the handsome woman depicted was the most recently painted of them.

'Mr Cragg, Mrs Cragg,' he said, indicating the picture with a flourish of his hand. 'May I have the honour of presenting to you my dearest wife, Henrietta?'

Involuntarily I began to bow my head, as if acknowledging the presence of a real person. I immediately checked myself, but there was something about New Manor that made the unreal seem real and the inanimate animate. But that was absurd! It would have made this a house of dreams or ghosts, whereas in fact it was made of solid old walls standing on solid foundations.

Turvey opened the door at the far end of the gallery and we passed through it into a chamber containing a bed with carved posts and hangings of good damask, though faded and moth-eaten. A set of linen and a dress were laid out on the bed, and on the dressing table beside the window were pots of powder and face paints, cut-glass perfume flasks, and a tortoiseshell brush, comb and mirror. There was also a jewellery casket.

'She has the best outlook this house affords,' observed Turvey, standing at the window. 'The pasture and forest with the moors above, and the river flowing below.'

He waved his hand high towards the distant skyline.

'It rises up there in those fells. My own room looks out on the street.'

'And your wife,' said Elizabeth. 'Is she from home at present?'

Turvey let out an exaggerated sigh.

'She is these last seven years dead, Mrs Cragg,' he said softly. 'I keep her room exactly as it was and cannot do otherwise as I feel her continued presence here, watching over everything. She would not like any change.'

He crossed to the dressing table and flipped up the lid of the jewellery casket. He picked up a necklace that appeared to be of white pearls graduated in size.

'Her favourite,' he said fondly.

'Are you not afraid to keep such valuables in the house unused?'

'Oh, they are not very valuable you know. Paste and glass for the most part, you see.'

He snapped shut the casket lid and turned away from his wife's dressing table.

'And now to dinner, my friends. Let us go down.'

The so-called Chamber Minor lay at the other end of the house, beneath Turvey's bedroom. It was here that the family ate its meals, on a table which tonight had four places laid ready. At one of these, to the surprise of both Elizabeth and myself, a curiously misshapen child sat in a bath chair waiting for us. She seemed to me about nine, but I was misled. She was in fact twelve, though with the childish appearance often seen in invalid cripples.

'My daughter Thomasina,' Turvey announced proudly. 'As ladylike as she is beautiful.'

Thomasina Turvey's face tightened as she frowned.

'Oh Father, don't!' she said. 'You know I detest it when you speak like that.'

The food was a dry, scrawny broiled fowl, with a thick gravy and black bread, followed by white cheese just a little penetrated by a blue mould.

'I had the hen killed on purpose,' Turvey told us. 'It's not so usual we have real meat at table; but it's not so usual we have visitors, neither. There's eels and good trout from the beck, which is everyday meat enough for us.'

Turvey produced no wine, and to wash this feast down we drank honey beer in pewter tankards. Hiding as best I could the difficulty I had in swallowing this disgusting sweet-sour liquor, I asked if it was produced at home.

'Of course it is!' said Thomasina, who was an alert child with the bright eyes of a bird. She was not afraid to speak up. 'We are beekeepers, you know.'

'So are we, back in Preston,' said Elizabeth. 'We have hives on our garden patch.'

'Indeed? How many?'

'Just two.'

Thomasina smiled complacently.

'We have fifty hives. Most of them are up on the moor now, working the heather.'

'Is that where you were summoned to today, Mr Turvey?' asked Elizabeth. 'Didn't you have to put on your bee armour again?'

Turvey chuckled.

'Armour, you call it? Well, I suppose it is armour in a way – helmet, gauntlets and greaves being armour – but it would put quite the wrong idea into your head. Keeping bees is not a campaign of war. You want bees to know you and like you, as being family. So you've to be gentle and familiar with them. If you are, they'll rarely attack you. The special gear is as much to make you recognized by them as to protect you against them.'

'You were called to a swarm, you told us,' Elizabeth said. 'I hope you did not lose it.'

Turvey grimaced.

'I did that, and in the worst possible way. By the time I got there the swarm had gone off my land and settled on the property of another man.'

'Oh dear. He will let you have the swarm back, though?'

'That he will not – or not willingly.'

'How disobliging. Who is he?'

'Father will not mention his name,' said Thomasina, 'or have it mentioned in this house. He lives at Hatchfly Hall, at the other end of the village, on the Whalley road.'

'Yes, I believe we passed its gates on our way.'

Turvey drained his glass.

'Have we all finished?' he said. 'Right, Mr Cragg and I will
take a glass of port here. Would Mrs Cragg be kind enough
to wheel Thomasina next door, as the Coroner and I have a
particularly serious matter to go over?'

We had been served at supper by Sukey's grandson, the
drooping youth – Danny as he was called – that I had last
seen taking charge of our packhorse. He now reappeared with
a dust-caked bottle and two stem-glasses.

The bottle was opened, and we poured ourselves glassfuls
of a thick, brown aged liquor. Turvey seemed in no hurry to
get down to whatever business he wished to discuss.

'My household is greatly reduced in the seven years since
my wife's death,' he said sorrowfully. 'She had the management
of the money, you see, and good she was at it.'

He tapped his wig.

'Not me. No head for figures and too soft at bargaining.'

'Your girl is a bright child.'

'Aye, she is her mother's daughter right enough. She's
already beginning to keep my accounts for me. I thought for
a while that I should seek a new wife: I have no son and am
the last in the male line, you know. But though I miss it terribly,
having a wife, I simply didn't know how to go about finding
myself another one. I know what I want, but find myself forever
mistaking what women want.'

An awkward silence followed this confession, which I broke
with a businesslike question.

'So, what is it you want to speak to me about, Mr Turvey?'

'Ah yes! A most regrettable incident occurred here last Sunday.'

He told me of the events that had happened in the village
street of Accrington just two days before our arrival – the
public punishment of Anne Gargrave for being a shrew and a
gossip, and her resulting death.

'We saw it all from this very window,' said Turvey in conclusion. 'The whole procession coming past, led by Billy Whist
playing his fiddle like a madman. Mrs Gargrave's body lies now
in the church. She was to be buried this week, but knowing you
were coming I have persuaded Gargrave to wait the funeral.'

I took a sip of port while I considered what to say.

'That is a terrible tale and a deplorable event,' I said. 'There is no measuring the cruelty of a mob. As for the body, you have done right. It will have to be inquested before burial, of course. Who is the magistrate here?'

'The one whose name I cannot mention.'

'And has he arrested the guilty parties?'

'No.'

'Why on earth not?'

'I suppose he chooses not to. I cannot act officially myself; and our other magistrate, Colonel Walmesley, is sadly reduced by age and does not go abroad. All I have been able to do is dismiss one of the ringleaders from my employ.'

'Who was that?'

'A former solider named Harry Hawk, who was my assistant beekeeper. But cannot you as Coroner initiate criminal proceedings?'

'Not directly. However, I act independently of the Bench and, following an inquest, may recommend a prosecution. My decision holds force – great force. I shall instigate an inquest here without delay. It seems to me that Mrs Gargrave's death demands justice, if we can obtain it.'

'I am glad to hear that. Anne Gargrave adhered to the same religion as myself, you know, and we are not in general accustomed to having the benefit of justice. How will you conduct the inquest?'

'My usual procedure is to gather witness statements, beginning with the first finder. When I have determined who are the key witnesses, I appoint a jury of qualified men and set a date for the hearing, which must be held locally and as soon as possible. At the hearing, the witnesses speak and the jury deliberates on the cause of death, after which, guided by me, they bring in a verdict.'

'You must go careful, Mr Cragg. It is boggy ground you cross, and there are men here who will make it their business to try to sink you.'

'I cannot be intimidated, Mr Turvey. I assure you of that.'

Turvey drained his glass and stood.

'Perhaps it is time to rejoin the women.'

*   *   *

As we made our way to the Chamber Major, we heard music coming from another room that gave off the corridor. Turvey opened the door and showed me what he called his music room, a parlour containing an old spinet on whose much chipped and yellowed keyboard Thomasina was now playing for the entertainment of Elizabeth. The instrument was missing a few of its strings and needed tuning, but Thomasina Turvey did not care, playing on and on with little refinement but much spirit to the end of the piece. We applauded, none more loudly than her father, who fairly battered his hands together in his zeal.

'Isn't that grand? She's a musical treasure, is my little Thomasina.'

We heard infantile mewling from the corridor and Sukey came in with Hector, who had been asleep, under her eye, in the kitchen. Now, having awoken, he was demanding his mother. In an hour it would be quite dark, and Elizabeth said it was time we left New Manor to spend the first night of our stay at the Dower House. We said our goodnights and made our way into the street.

It was a still, warm evening and a number of Accringtonians were out enjoying the twilight air. Elizabeth had quieted the baby, but he would inevitably begin to bawl again unless he was soon fed, so we hurried down the street towards our house.

'Well, we have solved the mystery of Turvey's wife,' whispered Elizabeth as we went.

'Yes. It's pathetic to see that room frozen in time except for the work of the moths. All that is left to him is his wife's clothing and a collection of false jewels.'

'Oh, they weren't all false, Titus!' said Elizabeth. 'We did not see the entire collection, but unless I am much mistaken that necklace was made of true pearls of excellent quality.'

'But he said—'

'I know. Perhaps he doesn't know.'

'Or seems not to.'

'I cannot imagine why he would pretend. So what particular matter was it that he wanted to talk about over your port?'

'A most unexpected thing,' I murmured. 'It seems I have coroner's work to do here.'

'What? Here in Accrington?'

'Yes. An unpleasant business.'

I said no more until we were within doors. Elizabeth sat in one of the spoke-backed chairs and immediately began to feed Hector, while I closed the shutters and lit candles. Then I sat down and told her the whole story of Anne Gargrave's death, just as Thomas Turvey had related it to me.

'But why did they go to such extremes?' she cried when I had finished. 'The woman may have been a shrew, which is a failing, but no cause for murder.'

'The people here evidently see the matter otherwise. This stang-riding is no doubt a traditional sanction, centuries old. That she died at the end of it is likely to be considered here as unintentional, in essence an accident.'

'Then you must make them reconsider, Titus. These young men who started this are responsible. A woman has lost her life because of their actions, whether or not they meant it. They should be punished for manslaughter, at the very least.'

The candlelight flickered around the room, illuminating and in turn hiding its corners and crannies.

'Indeed,' I said. 'Though to my way of thinking there might even be more to it than manslaughter. They might have planned it. There might be a deliberate murder in this.'

For want of a cot we had pulled out an empty drawer from the sideboard, made it into a crib for Hector, and set it down on his mother's side of the bed. He would be comfortable enough.

'But you *will* see about a real crib for him in the morning, Titus?' Elizabeth pleaded. 'He cannot sleep in a drawer for all the time we are here!'

I promised that I would. And then the thought of our son, and the reason we had come to this scarcely furnished house, brought to mind an idea I had had earlier.

'Little Thomasina Turvey,' I said, settling beside my wife in bed. 'She is a strange one. Sharp as a bodkin in her mind. Was she born a cripple? I wonder because another possibility occurred to me while we were with them.'

'I know just what you're thinking,' she said, 'because the same thought occurred to me. And while I was trying to find a tactful way to ask her, she simply came out with it. "I know what you want to know," she said, "and the answer is I was not born like this. I had the Crippling Ague as an infant, and it left me misshapen and without the power to walk." I said that the will of God is sometimes hard to understand. She answered only with an ironic laugh and said she was tired of the subject and would play some music for me: she is old beyond her years, that one.'

'The Crippling Ague! Is that what she called it? Well, its effects seem to me very much like those of Fidelis's Paralysing Fever.'

'I asked her if the disease is still found here in Accrington, but she said she hadn't caught it here but in Warrington while she was staying with her grandparents. Nothing like it has been heard of in Accrington.'

I sighed with relief.

'That is just as well, or our whole reason for being here is undermined.'

We faced another whole day before Matty would arrive with Wintle's cart and, as none of the promised food had arrived from New Manor, I took the responsibility of fetching milk, butter, cheese and bread, and finding a source of fuel, of which I carried home a sack and ordered a further three hundred-weight for delivery. Then I set and lit a fire under the range.

'Doing all these unaccustomed tasks, I feel like Robinson Crusoe before he found his man Friday,' I said.

'Shall I then play the role of the goat on the island?' said Elizabeth. 'I do produce milk, after all.'

'You make a very beautiful nanny goat, and Hector is your kid.'

'Who needs somewhere to sleep, don't forget. That is your next task, Titus.'

So I set off to find the workshop of the village carpenter, from whom I intended to commission a bed for the baby. Two or three that I asked in the street for his name and whereabouts pretended not to hear me; one bent-backed old man scowled and swore by way of answer. Eventually a child rolling his hoop told me that he was Peter Castleford, and that his yard lay a little way from the village, beside a tributary which flowed into the Hyndburn at the southern end of the village.

I fully expected to have to overcome the same reserve, or rather hostility, in my dealings with Castleford. I was wrong. He proved a generous and intelligent man of about thirty-five who greeted me in friendly terms.

'I'm happy to meet you, Mr Cragg. Not everyone in the village has said the same, I hazard.'

'They have not, Mr Castleford, and I am glad indeed to hear a friendly voice.'

'They'll come around. They are not used to changes, new faces. They see every stranger as an enemy.'

'But you do not?'

'Oh, I've seen the world, Mr Cragg. Ten year a ship's carpenter, I was, until this happened.' He moved his long leather apron aside and I saw that he stood on a wooden leg. 'A prosthesis – that's the fancy word for it. I made it myself, of course.'

'Do you wish you were still at sea?'

'Well, I feel shipwrecked out here, I do. I was born in the village, but I went to sea as a boy when the press gang came through, so a ship's been longer my home than my parents' cottage was.'

'You were pressed as a boy? That is illegal.'

'No, not pressed, but when the sailors came here I left with them. I was full of dreams of seeing the sea. I wasn't disappointed.'

We settled the business of the baby's cot quickly enough. Castleford made a sketch of a neat cradle on rockers, which looked just right, and soon we were shaking hands on a price. He said that, as this was Thursday, he could finish the job by the end of the week. My child would sleep in his own purpose-made bed on Saturday night.

'I have heard of the terrible event here on Sunday last,' I said carelessly, before leaving. 'A woman died, I am told.'

Castleford frowned.

'They went too far. I am not against the old country ways, but they went too far.'

'Did you see it?'

He shook his head.

'No, I was away that day at my sister's at Altham. But two lads, the Stirk brothers, came by and had a stout beam from me on the day before. Could be it was that they used for their stang. Any road, I have a box ready for the poor woman when it's time.'

So we parted and I returned to the Dower House with Castleford's sketch of the new cradle.

'Our kid will have sweet dreams in that,' said Elizabeth.

New Manor had at last sent down some supplies – greens and root vegetables – and so we had a simple village dinner of pottage, bread and cheese. When we'd finished, I rose from the table and prepared to go out again.

'I am going to the church,' I said. 'I need to see the body of this poor woman.'

FOUR

'Hey! What the devil are you about?'

The Church of St James stood behind the village street, in a close with cottages ranged around it. It was reached through a passage between the street's houses at the same end of the village as New Manor, but on the opposite side. The church was old and small, with windows for the most part plain-glazed, a stubby tower and a simple wooden porch. I had just entered this porch and was rattling the locked door when I was hailed by the voice of a woman hurrying up the church path behind me. I turned. She was trailing a long-handled spade behind her.

'The church'll be closed till Sunday fortnight when the Reverend Rishton's preaching.'

I judged her to be sixty, a wiry figure in working clothes – a practical buffin skirt, drill shirt and domed, wide-brimmed straw hat.

'Who am I addressing, Madam?' I asked.

'Who is addressing *me*?' she said, propping her spade against a tombstone.

'My name is Titus Cragg, County Coroner, and I am looking into the death of Anne Gargrave, whose body I believe lies inside this church.'

The woman stepped back in surprise and looked me up and down. Her frown cleared. She smiled, bright-eyed.

'Frances Nightingale, at your service,' she said touching her hat. 'I act as churchwarden here. I am glad to meet you, Sir. You're at the Dower House, now vacated since the late Mrs Turvey's mother moved into the graveyard here. Am I right?'

'Yes, my wife and I will be tenants there for a few weeks. That I am in Accrington so hard upon the decease of Anne Gargrave is happenstance but, from what I know of it, an investigation is essential, as it was a violent end. Do you have the church key with you, Mrs Nightingale?'

She unhooked a ring with several keys from her belt and stepped past me to open the thick nailed door.

It was a plain interior: simple benches in the nave, a single aisle separated by a line of columns, and a heavy lectern standing before a bare altar. Once there had been figures carved into the columns' capitals, but these had been chiselled away by zealous Protestants long ago. All other reminders of the church's distant Romish past had been similarly expunged.

'There is a crypt – this way.'

Frances Nightingale led me to a corner doorway and a narrow stairwell down to a cool, dry basement lying immediately under the nave. She fumbled with a tinderbox while I waited in the dark until she had lit a candle, and only then did I get a sense of the space. It was at most thirty-foot square and must originally have been a burial vault, though it was now used as a vestry and for the storage of books. In the centre of the space was a table, and on it the prone form of a human figure lying under a blanket.

Mrs Nightingale hung back near the foot of the stairs as I lifted the end of the cover and brought the candle close to Anne Gargrave's dead face. She had a high brow, a prominent nose, and thin lips. Her hair was straight and gathered tightly in a bun underneath. With my thumb, I slid up an eyelid. Grey eyes, but dull; it was impossible to tell how they might have been in life.

These were her permanent features. In addition, her face was bruised and scarred with wounds.

'Do you see these?' I said.

Uncertainly, the churchwarden approached and looked.

'These are grievous wounds,' I said. 'Did you witness the assault?'

'Some of it. When they passed my cottage in procession, I came out and tried to stop them. But there's not much a weak old body can do when a crowd of youngsters has its blood up.'

'I'm curious about this stang ride. Is it a custom in these parts? Is it inflicted often?'

She shook her head.

'Not in this village. I've heard of it being done over in Yorkshire, in the more faraway parts. Not here.'

'So how did the young people know what to do? The provision of the stang, and the banging of pots and kettles? They must have wanted details. Where did they get them from?'

'I've an idea about that. There's a man called Billy Whist, a blind fiddler that's lived here for years and reckons he knows all the old customs. He was there on the day, playing his fiddle while others rattled and bashed their pots and pans.'

'Yes, I've heard mention of Billy. I am hoping to speak to him. But tell me, was a doctor called to look at Anne Gargrave after it was over?'

Mrs Nightingale shrugged.

'No one saw the need. She was beyond medical help. The usual women cleaned her up and she lay in her own house until next morning, then she was brought here. I was told the next thing would be the funeral. A grave plot's been chosen and we were to start digging this morning.'

'Then you may put away your spade,' I said. 'The next thing will be an inquest, not a funeral.'

For now, there was nothing more I could do, and we ascended with some relief into the daylight. Thinking I should speak to the incumbent priest about my plans, I asked the whereabouts of the vicarage.

'There is none, Sir. We're not a parish here, never have been – just an occasional chapel, as they call it.'

'A chapel of what parish?'

'We are part of Altham curacy, which is in the Parish of Whalley, so we're very small beer. The curate, Mr Rishton, preaches here once a month at most, and comes over to bury folk. But if you want a christening or marriage you've to go to him. He doesn't much care for this place and we don't much care for him, if you want to know the truth, though he's all we've got in the clergy line.'

'You said you act as churchwarden? That is most unusual, for a woman. I take it this is not an official post then?'

'It should be. But no man would do it, so I stepped up five years ago – just for the time being, they said. The time is still being, and they've never appointed a wage for me. I'll die acting as churchwarden for gratis, no doubt of that.'

'Yet you do all the churchwarden's duties as they should
be done. Why won't they pay you?'

'There are three reasons in all.'

She counted them off on her fingers.

'One, I am not Accrington-born, as I come from Clitheroe.
Two, they are too mean to pay the wages. And three, I'm a
woman – who cannot be churchwarden in the first place, never
mind that I am. More fool me, you might say, to go on with
it. But someone has to, don't they? I suppose it is malfeasance
on somebody's part, though I doubt it is a tort. I doubt I can
gain recompense.'

'You're probably right, but I'm interested that you put it
like that. You are familiar with legal language, Mrs Nightingale?'

'Am I not! After thirty-two years married to the clerk of
Mr Gilbert Holden of Clitheroe, Attorney-at-Law, I'll say I'm
familiar with it. I even did my husband's writing when he
wasn't well enough – he was often an invalid, was my poor
Georgy.'

This was encouraging. Mrs Nightingale had shown none of
the hostility towards me that I had met elsewhere in the village.
She was also intelligent. Perhaps I had found a new ally and
source of information, one who lived in the village but wasn't
quite of it.

'Is Mr Nightingale living still?'

'He passed away five winters ago.'

'I'm sorry. But Mrs Nightingale, I wonder if you would do
me the honour of dining with my wife Elizabeth and me at
the Dower House.'

Her face brightened.

'That's right hospitable, Mr Cragg. When were you
thinking of?'

'Would tomorrow be suitable?'

'It would.'

'I think you dine early in these parts, but I will expect you
at one o'clock. One last thing. Would you tell me where John
Gargrave lives?'

I called in on Elizabeth and found her in the wash-house with
her arms up to the elbows in suds. Before I could escape again,

she detained me and next thing I was in the yard pinning the baby's napkins on the line to dry, which I hoped no one saw me doing. When I came in again, I told Elizabeth of my viewing of the body, my meeting with Frances Nightingale, and my invitation to dine. Of course, she thought immediately of the practical difficulties.

'Oh, Titus, what can I possibly give her?'

'I'm sure she isn't particular, but anyway you are an excellent cook.'

'Even the best cook's no good without good food.'

'I like your pottage.'

'I can't give her that!'

'A fish then. They have fish all the time, Turvey said.'

'But where do I get it from?'

'Go and talk to Sukey at New Manor. I'm going out again. I'll be an hour – or not so long if he can't or won't see me, which is possible.'

'Who do you mean?'

'John Gargrave. Before this enquiry goes any further, I must hear his side of the story.'

I walked briskly down the street, almost as far as the mill. The Gargrave house was one of the better ones in Accrington. It boasted rooms on either side of the front door, and was higher by a storey than the cottages on either side. The thatch was in good repair, and the paintwork fresh.

A servant came to the door and told me Mr Gargrave was not well and seeing no one. I insisted that he tell his master the County Coroner was here, holding an inquest into the death of Mrs Gargrave. This information made all the difference and I was ushered into the parlour, where I found a man a little older than myself, a round figure but with a grey complexion and a haunted demeanour. He wore a day-cap but I could see the edge of a bandage underneath it and traces of facial injuries not unlike those I had just seen on his dead wife.

A quick survey of the room told me Gargrave was fairly prosperous – a cut above the majority of Accrington men who made their living by labouring on the land or by handling horses and farm animals. This house was certainly an advance on the Dower House. It contained well-looked-after furniture and was more modern, being divided up on the ground floor between a parlour, where we were now, a dining room across the passage, and a kitchen in the rear. On the other hand, there was no evidence of recent fashion. There was little use of plaster except on the ceiling, while the walls conformed to the old-fashioned taste for wooden panelling.

I bowed, introduced myself, and repeated why I was there.

'You're wasting your time, Mr Cragg,' he said wearily.

'I am often told that, and it rarely proves true. It is pure chance that I am here, but it's a happy chance for you, Mr Gargrave. If I had not come to Accrington, I doubt anyone would have bothered to call a coroner to look into your wife's death. She would have gone into the ground with no one the wiser about how and why.'

Gargrave shook his head sadly and spoke in a hoarse voice.

'She was murdered. So, nearly, was I.'

'Well, if that's the case—'

'It *is* the case.'

'Then an inquest is the way to prove it, at least in the first instance. If it can establish guilty parties, they will be sent for trial.'

Gargrave raised his finger and wagged it from side to side.

'Mr Cragg, you don't know who you are dealing with. They close their ranks.'

'So who are they? Why did this terrible thing happen?'

'It happened because they hate me and they hated her.'

'Yes, but who are *they*?'

He did not reply. Nor did he look at me. His eyes were fixed abstractedly on a framed embroidery that hung on the wall – a sampler. It showed letters from the alphabet in the form of capitals and lower case, but only four letters in all – A M D G – repeated over and over.

I had not been invited to sit, but I took a chair and brought it close to Gargrave's. I knew I must try a different approach if I were to penetrate the man's mask of grief, fear and shock. So I started to tell him about myself, my family, my work in Preston and then in the county, the cases I had inquested, the successes and failures, and the opposition I had in many cases run into and sometimes succeeded in overcoming. I told him of the poisoner I had unmasked in Garstang who had killed three members of his wife's family without arousing the slightest suspicion; of the boy at Ormskirk accused of rape and murder who, when I looked into it, had proved to have been five miles away when the crime was committed; of the child found dead in Chipping, where I knew one of the parents had done the deed but didn't know which.

'I couldn't solve it until I discovered the murderer's secret motive, and the existence of others standing behind that murderer guarding the secret. There were a few moments of grave danger when I made that discovery, for when men – or for that matter women – see the spectre of the gallows looming above them they are capable of any desperate act. I do this job not because it is safe, not for the entertainment, and certainly not for the money or the glory. I do it because – as your very agreeable churchwarden said to me earlier at the church when I asked her why she does that job without pay – someone must. It's needed. So, coming back to my reason for being here, if I don't look into what happened to your wife on Sunday last, who is to do it? Who is to bring meaning to her decease, if not me? I am needed to do it, I want to do it, and I shall do it. You must help me.'

As I spoke, I noticed I increasingly caught his attention, until he was following me word for word. Now I paused and waited. I knew that I would find this business extremely hard to conclude, if not impossible, unless I had Gargrave with me. But I knew equally that I could not force it.

For half a minute nothing happened. Then he turned to me and for the first time managed a pained smile.

'Very well, Mr Cragg. How can I help?'

'For the moment I have a few questions, that is all.'

'Ask away.'

To begin, I sketched for him what I had been told of the attack on him and his wife and asked him if he remembered it differently in any way. He shook his head.

'No, Mr Cragg. But I don't remember any of it well. It's all very muzzy in my mind. But what you say sounds right.'

'Then tell me a little about yourself. What is your work?'

'I am factor for all the lands hereabouts belonging to a nobleman whose main estate is in the south.'

'You mean the south of England?'

'I do. He has never visited his farms here, and I doubt he ever will.'

'Who is he?'

'He is Lord Petre.'

'Tell me now about Mrs Gargrave. How long were you married?'

'Twelve years.'

'You have no children?'

'We had a son and a daughter. We lost him before he was two. She at the age of ten.'

'I am sorry.'

'It was God's will, as I must believe.'

I indicated the sampler on the wall.

'Is it your daughter's?'

'Yes.'

'It is beautiful work. Now, if you please, a little more about your wife. What was her character?'

'She was . . . She was . . .'

Suddenly he was thinking with more energy. It was as if no one had ever asked him such a question before, as if he had never even thought about it and was now seeing it as a question of the greatest significance – which, in fact, from my point of view it was.

'She was strong-willed, and she wouldn't bend. I could never win an argument with her or get her to do something if she'd made up her mind against it. We had many battles, but mostly in the end I would let her have her way. I was exhausted by it all. And it made so much discord in the house, especially with our daughter—'

He pulled up in mid-sentence, then collected himself.

'With our daughter not being well, I suppose I allowed Anne to rule the roost. I had my job to do outside the house, and I did it well. But here at home, I couldn't . . . I just couldn't . . .'

Now he broke down, pressing his face into his hands while sudden tears coursed out between his fingers and sobs shocked his body. When, after a few moments of this, he raised his face again it was contorted with anguish.

'I know the fault was all mine. I could not rule my wife. I was hen-pecked. Why else would they have brought that accursed stang to our door?'

'I don't know for certain why they did that, Gargrave, though perhaps I shall know in time. But I feel sure those who abused you acted out of malice. You yourself said, when I came in, that "they" hated you. So what grudge did they bear, the ringleaders? How were they so possessed by hatred?'

'The Stirk boys, you mean?' He took a couple of deep breaths, forcing himself to be calm. 'I've known them since they were children. I can't think of any reason why they'd do this. They are not thinking men; no particular philosophy or belief guides them. But I do remember their eyes on that day. There was a light there, a mad light, or a devilish one maybe. I don't know if it was hatred, but they were possessed by something.'

'Might it not be a matter of religion?'

He raised his head.

'No. As I just said, the Stirk boys are not religious people.'

'But many use religion as a weapon, I find. You follow the old faith, against which there is much ill-feeling in some quarters. But if it is not religion, maybe the source of your suffering was economic. You are a large employer in the area. Do the Stirks work for you?'

'Oh yes, they have done. The labouring class get their money where they can – this estate or that estate, they're not bothered. This pair have done field work for me on day rates, just like they've worked for Mr Turvey and Mr Horntree.'

'Mr Horntree?'

'Of Hatchfly Hall.'

'Ah! So that is his name. Well, is there any grudge the Stirks might hold as a result of having worked for you?'

'Not that I can think of.'

'What about the other man, Harry Hawk?'

'He's a tenant of ours. An ex-soldier. He rents a small farm up on the high moor that's part of his Lordship's estate.'

'So he's a farmer?'

'Not much of one, not on that property. He hires himself out as a labourer, just like the Stirks.'

'Is there any reason why he might persecute you?'

'We had a small disagreement recently about the rent. I increased it and he came down here and said he couldn't pay. There were some hard words said. Happen that was the reason.'

'Finally I would mention the fiddler, Billy Whist. He seems to have led this vile procession up and down the street.'

'I would not bother with him, Mr Cragg. He is a low, foolish fellow.'

I rose from my chair.

'Mr Gargrave, I shall leave you but you will hear from me again. In the meantime you must not take any guilt upon yourself for what happened to your wife. You must bear up.'

Before leaving Gargrave's house I had a brief word in the hall with his servant, a solemn middle-aged man who told me his name was Gerald Piper. I asked if he had been the person who brought the body of Mrs Gargrave into the house and he told me he had.

'Then you will be first finder for the purposes of the inquest,' I told him. 'I will require a full statement from you, which I propose to take tomorrow. Would you be kind enough to attend on me at the Dower House at eight o'clock?'

Some of the heat had gone out of the air, but the late afternoon remained sultry. Leaving Gargrave's house, I headed for the Black Bull, where I ordered a two-gallon keg of beer to be delivered to the Dower House. Then I strolled to the bridge, where I leaned on the parapet and looked down into the green-tinged depths below. Midges and waterflies had begun to assemble for their evening flight and, to judge by the occasional concentric ripples breaking the surface, one or two were being taken by fish. That was what an inquest enquiry was like, as often as not, I thought. Like the ripples accompanying the death of one of those waterflies, the effect of a human death radiates outwards, with many in the vicinity feeling it for good or ill, until it exhausts itself. The death of Mrs Gargrave would surely be no exception.

Two young men, with a long-legged dog trotting behind

them, were approaching the bridge. They both walked in the same way, an insolent go-to-the-devil gait, with a forward pitch of the body, a splaying of the feet and a bending and bouncing about the knees. They had a number of thin wires slung over their hunched shoulders, with wooden pegs tied to one end and the other ending in a running loop. I recognized these straight away. They were gin traps, exactly like the ones I'd learned to use on Preston Moor when I was a boy and the sight of them gave me an idea.

'I say!'

They stopped as one and regarded me moodily.

'I see you're out after rabbits. Might even bag a hare, eh?'

One looked at the other.

'Gentleman wants to know if we're going to break the law, Sim.'

The other smiled slyly.

'Aye, Charlie. But why would we ever risk it when a man can find his sen bein' sent to America?'

'Well we wouldn't would we, bein' law-abiding folk as we are.'

Living in a town, one is inclined to forget the Game Law, which entirely forbids the poor to take game of any kind. Hastily I said, 'Well, I make no accusation, of course, but if you do happen – by chance of course – to have a good-sized rabbit or hare hanging in your larder tomorrow morning, I'd be very glad to buy it off you. I could offer sixpence.'

Their eyes widened. It was probably twice what they would normally get even for a big buck rabbit. The one called Charlie looked hesitantly at the other. They were tempted. I reached into my waistcoat pocket, found three pennies and proffered them.

'Why don't you take threepence on account? The rest would be payable when you deliver the animal to me at the Dower House.'

The two put their heads together for a moment and then Simon stepped up and snatched the money from my palm. Greed had overcome their caution.

'We'll see, mister. Dower House, you say?'

I nodded and they slouched off. It was only as I made my

way up the street that I connected the names Charlie and Sim,
and realized I had been face to face with the Stirk brothers.

'I don't like it,' said Elizabeth as she planted Hector firmly
in my arms. 'From everything you've told me, this is a pair
of poachers and ruffians and we should have nothing to do
with them.'

I rocked the baby and for a moment was rapt, looking
into his pure-blue eyes.

'But I can't have nothing to do with them. They were in
on the death of Anne Gargrave and will be an important
part of the inquest. Besides, with luck they'll bring us a fine
rabbit in the morning to feed Mrs Nightingale and make
you very happy.'

Elizabeth tightened her lips, a sure sign I was doing
something wrongly.

'Don't rock him so vigorously, Titus. And we don't need
a rabbit. I've been to see a villager who fishes a pool of the
river a little way upstream, and he has promised to bring me
some trout in the morning.'

'The rabbit will keep a day or two if need be.'

Once we were in bed – Elizabeth sewing as she sometimes
did before sleep, and I making a start on *Gulliver* – I attempted
a diplomatic *démarche*.

'I shall look for somewhere other than this house to conduct
the business of the inquest.'

'I would be glad if you can,' she said, seeming to relent
for now she allowed me a smile. 'Anyway, I don't see how
you will hold it without Furzey. He can scarcely be here
before Saturday and, knowing him, more likely the middle
of next week.'

'I can manage without him.'

'How?'

'Somehow.'

FIVE

Friday morning dawned clear and bright, promising another hot day. I opened the street door to allow air through the room and found four trout gleaming on the threshold. Elizabeth was delighted with them, and a little triumphant.

'No sign of your rabbit, I see. But my trout are bonny enough for our dinner today, specially as it is Friday. I got an extra one for Matty. I hope she will arrive with the cart before dinner.'

Breakfast was interrupted by Gerald Piper, come as requested to give his statement. As soon as the table was cleared, I sat him down with pen, ink and paper.

'Now, Piper, you must write in your own words how you found the body of your mistress, Mrs Gargrave.'

He nodded, dipped the quill and seemed about to write. I waited. Piper looked at the blank page, and then at the pen, and then at the paper again. His brow creased. He sighed.

'Don't tell me you can't write, Piper,' I said at last.

'Oh no, Sir. I can write, of course I can *write*.'

I gestured at the paper.

'Then please.'

After a brief scratch of his head with his free hand, Piper bent over the sheet with pen poised once more. His face assumed a look of purposeful strain, like a man sitting at stool. But still nothing happened and he sat up again. He leaned backwards and squinted at the table as if trying to see the task from a new angle.

'You can't write, can you Piper?'

'I can. I can write a list. I can write any old list you might want. I can't just write . . . this sort of thing.'

'You mean a narrative?'

'That's right. What you said. I can't do that.'

'It's easy. Just put it down as you might say it.'

'I don't know how to begin it.'

'It would be usual to start with the date of the event in question, as "On Sunday last, being the tenth of June . . .""

He wrote with considerable labour as follows:

On soomday lass been the tent of joon.

I picked up the paper and clicked my tongue.

'I know it's not right,' said Piper. 'But I can't keep the proper letters in my head when it comes to writing down.'

'Very well,' I said, sitting and plucking the pen from his fingers. 'You tell me and I'll write.'

And so we proceeded, eventually cobbling together in half a page of script the simple story of how Mrs Gargrave's body was found. Elizabeth had been right: I was in urgent need of a clerk.

I sent Gerald Piper on his way and walked to the workshop of Peter Castleford, who showed me the work in progress on the baby's bed. I told him that, with the weather as it was, I was concerned about the state of Mrs Gargrave in her underground chamber and had decided it would be best to box her up. Would he bring the coffin that he'd made to the church? He said he would.

'An hour from now,' I said. 'And in the meantime, would you give me directions to the house of Billy Whist the fiddler?'

'He lives at Clayton's Quarry, a little way out of the village.'

Clayton's Quarry lay down a track off the lane that led westward towards Blackburn from the bridge. Billy Whist lived in what may have been a quarryman's hut, for its situation was enclosed on three sides by ragged cliffs from which stone had once been hacked. This cottage now looked, from the outside at least, little better than a hovel. The roughcast walls were a piebald of moss and mould, and tarred planks had been nailed across the single, unglazed window. The thatch was dishevelled, as if in sore need of a comb, and the chimney was a ragged, blackened snapped-off stub of earthen bricks.

I knocked at the door and heard a voice.

'There's no lock on the door!'

I went in. At first, after the brightness of the day, the gloom was Stygian. But as my eyesight adapted, enough light winked through Billy's primitive shuttering to reveal an unexpectedly well-swept and orderly room. Billy himself occupied a rush-seated chair by the fireside and a young lad of perhaps twelve sat behind him on a broad window ledge. A book was open on his knee, the print illuminated by the bars of light. I must have interrupted a reading aloud.

'Who is it that's entered our house, boy?' said Billy, his head turning this way and that.

The boy said nothing and I answered for myself.

'I am Titus Cragg, Billy.'

'Cragg the Coroner, does he say?' said Billy. His voice had that nasal tone which seems always to insinuate more than it says. 'We heard he'd come to Accrington. Let him state his business.'

'My business is the death of Anne Gargrave,' I said.

'Oh, aye?'

'I am looking into it and hope you can help me.'

'How can I help him look into it, me? I'm blind.'

'You were playing your fiddle while she was made to ride the stang. It was after that she died. I wonder why you did so.'

'I play my fiddle on many occasions.'

'Tell me why on this one.'

'Because Anne Gargrave had a nasty tongue in a flapping mouth. Will you put out a seat for our visitor?'

The boy laid the book aside and jumped down. He fetched a chair from beside the far wall and pulled it across the floor until it stood close to Billy Whist. I took the opportunity of strolling across to the window and noting the title of the book. It was a surprise.

'I see you are reading Milton's *Paradise Lost*,' I said. 'A substantial poem.'

I sat down, noticing for the first time that Billy's fiddle lay across his lap, and that he continually caressed its neck as one might stroke a cat.

'It is *the* poem, the only poem. We read it continually. When we come to the end we start again.'

He threw his head back and quoted:

A Dungeon horrible, on all sides round
As one great Furnace flam'd, yet from those flames
No light, but rather darkness visible
Serv'd only to discover sights of woe.

'A startling conceit, is that. "Darkness visible." There's only a blind man could think of that. Which Milton was, of course. But let us continue. What was Mr Cragg saying?'

'I want to know who instigated Mrs Gargrave's punishment, Billy, and I was wondering if it was you.'

'Instigated?' The fiddler angled his head back towards the boy, who had resumed his place on the window ledge. 'Is he saying Billy Whist instigated something?'

'Stirred them up,' I went on. 'Gave them the idea. I have heard that when they'd got her out of her house, and mounted her on the stang, you led them down the street and back again, several times, playing your music.'

Plink-plink. Billy's fingers plucked sharply at a fiddle string.

'Led them?' he said. 'Does he think blind men lead? They are led themselves. Nor do we instigate – we are instigated against. Mr Cragg must know that.'

'But wasn't it you that gave the whole idea to the Stirk brothers, Billy? I've heard tell that such a thing as a stang ride has been unheard of in Accrington since anyone can remember. So from whom did they know how the thing is done?'

Plink-plink.

'Billy?'

Billy grunted and shifted in his chair, turning his sightless head upward and a little to the side.

'The blind fellow is not an ignorant fellow. He knows a thing or two.'

Plink-plink.

The obliquity of his replies was beginning to annoy me.

'So you are confirming that *you* gave the young men the information? It was you that told them what to do?'

'Like the man is saying, they wanted to know about the old country way of chastising a shrew. I told them.'

'Did you tell them also to chastise John Gargrave equally with his wife?'

Billy Whist's face assumed a sardonic smile, and he spoke in a voice like a proclamation:

> *Thus it shall befall,*
> *Him who, to worth in woman overtrusting,*
> *Lets her will rule.*

'That's Milton, is that, and it's good enough for me.'

'It wasn't good for the Gargraves, was it?'

'It was good for Accrington. It was cleansing. We here are not Accrington-born, but we owe Accrington our living. We must prove ourselves friends to Accrington, true friends. Or if not, starve. That is all we did.'

He picked up his fiddle, tucked it under his chin, and began to play a dirgelike tune. I had heard enough, and with a sense of rising disgust rose and went to the door.

A true friend of Accrington, I thought, letting myself out. And with a friend like you, there is no call for enemies. I was glad to leave that gloomy place, and as I picked up my pace the mournful music diminished behind me and was lost in the wind.

I went straight to New Manor, where I found the Squire in a state of bother, his great frame quivering with suppressed anger.

'It is intolerable, Cragg,' he said. 'The man has seen me off his premises, with his men pointing firearms at me.'

'Do you mean Hatchfly Hall?'

'Most certainly I do. I went there at first light yesterday to sneak in and collect my swarm of bees before anyone was out and about. I needed to go, you see, because what they do is they cluster for several hours overnight, on a tree branch usually, and then take off again next day to find a permanent home. It's during the clustering phase you've got to nab them, before the warmth of day gives them the signal to go off again. Once they do, there would be no knowing how far they might fly. I would probably lose them entirely somewhere in the woods.'

'But what happened?'

'I never got near the bees. I never even got through his gate. His men were waiting for me with guns. Said their master told them I'd be coming and that I was to be warned off.'

'I hold no brief for Mr Horntree, Turvey, but you cannot steal on to his land secretly, you know.'

'I don't see why not, if it's to collect my stolen property. They are my swarm of bees, and he's got them and what is more intends to keep them.'

'How do you know?'

'The bees clustered on a branch in his orchard and, as I now know, he's had the swarm knocked down and collected. He means to keep the bees. I suspect they're in a hive by now. That is theft according to me. I told his men I'll take their master to court and have my bees back with interest. And now he's had the effrontery to fire *this* back at me.'

He handed me a letter addressed to himself. It was dated on the previous day.

> *Sir, I have been informed of your ill-advised threat to take action in the courts claiming a swarm of bees. Those bees have now assaulted and stung me and members of my household. I hereby advise and warn you that I shall take an action against you in the Sheriff's Court for these injuries unless you discontinue your suit and pay me the compensatory sum of 10 gns.*
> *(signed) Grevel Horntree*

'What do you think of that Cragg?'

'Are you asking my legal advice?'

'If you care to give it.'

The truth was that I could not be sure what I thought, but it looked like a knotty dispute and Horntree was arguing it with some cunning. If the bees were no longer his, Turvey's suit was lost. If they were his, he must pay compensation or himself be sued in turn by Horntree. Either way, Turvey was the loser.

However, I said I'd look into the question if he promised not to take any precipitate action. He sighed, clearly not yet relieved of his agitation.

'Very well. I suppose it is a consolation that the swarm is safe and not living in a hollow oak five miles away. As for that man's demand, naturally I shan't pay his ten guineas.'

He scowled.

'I *can't* pay, come to that! Now, what can I do for you, Cragg?'

I put to him my problem about business premises for the enquiry into Mrs Gargrave's death.

'I need to interview witnesses, and the Dower House is quite unsuitable. Where can I go instead?'

'Well, you can have my gatehouse if you like – the upstairs room. It was last used for an apple store, so it's dry, though dusty. Would you like to see it?'

He took me outside, across the courtyard and up the narrow stairway let into the arch on the right side of the gate. The gatehouse looked distinctly ruinous from the outside but its room, stretching twenty feet in length over the gate itself, was well lit; its window glass was unbroken, and its timbers solid. It contained a pair of collapsible tables, a number of old chairs, and three tiers of shelves or racks around the walls for apples. The fruit's scent faintly and pleasantly filled the room.

'Yes,' I said. 'It is rough and ready, but will do very well, I think. I will make use of the tables and some of the chairs, if you agree. It might even do for the inquest itself, I fancy.'

'Oh no, Cragg, you must have my Chamber Major for the hearing itself. It has greater gravity.'

'That is very obliging of you, Turvey. In the meantime, this will be very useful to me as a business room.'

'I'll have the boy sweep it out.'

'The County will of course pay for its use, as well as the Chamber Major. Shall we say three shillings and sixpence?'

Turvey's eyebrows arched and he scrubbed his hands together in nervous pleasure.

'Oh! My word! That's very generous, Cragg.'

'It is your due. I'll start using the room at once, if I may. Can you oblige me with some writing materials?'

I spent the next half hour composing a summary of Turvey's dispute with Horntree over the swarm of bees. This I enclosed in a note to Furzey instructing him to look up the precedents in case law. I was just on the point of adding a request that he pack a bag and make his way to Accrington as quickly as he could to act as my clerk in the inquest, when I paused. Furzey hated to receive an order. He would inevitably prevaricate, and his complaints over having to travel so far at my behest and stay away from his mother would plague us extremely. I'd told Elizabeth that somehow I would hold the inquest without him. But how?

All at once the complete solution came to me. The more I considered it the more I liked it – so, instead of ordering Furzey to Accrington, I sealed my letter and took it straight to the Bull, just in time to catch the postman. Then I returned to the church, where I found Peter Castleford, with the coffin, in conversation at the door with Frances Nightingale. She unlocked and we brought the box in. What air there was in the crypt smelled musty and a little sweet, not disagreeable but telling us that the process of bodily mortification was under way. Castleford and I heaved the corpse into the simple coffin he had provided and closed the lid. I knew I couldn't delay a close examination of the body for much longer, with at the very least a full list and measuring of the wounds. But I was so much used to doing it with my friend Dr Fidelis that I felt quite reluctant to face the task alone.

Once the carpenter had left us, Mrs Nightingale and I walked together to the Dower House for our dinner. She was dressed a little more formally today.

'I am tickled to be able to wear the taffeta,' she said. 'It is not often I have occasion for it.'

'You look fine in it, Mrs Nightingale, and I hope you have an appetite. My wife is baking some fine juicy trout straight from the river. But before we reach the house I have a request or, if you prefer, a proposition for you.'

She looked at me warily.

'Please go on.'

'It isn't out of curiosity that I am holding this inquest. As Coroner, I am bound by law to hold one. But I have a difficulty. My clerk Robert Furzey is in Preston. He has considerable business in hand and I could not expect him to be here to assist me before the middle of the week. However, with this

heat and its effect on the dead woman's remains, I can't wait
the hearing that long. It must be on Monday – that is the latest
I can allow.'

'I follow you so far, Mr Cragg, but I haven't yet heard your
proposition.'

'Very well, it is this. Please will you act as my clerk, Mrs
Nightingale?'

'Your clerk? Me?'

'Before you say anything more, let me finish. It is essential
that the statements or depositions in the case are written down
and that the hearing itself is recorded. I might at a pinch be
able to write the statements, but I cannot both conduct and take
the minutes of the inquest. You are a literate woman and have
long familiarity with the law and can write a legal hand. Also
you know the affairs of this village, which will be of great
assistance to me. I think you are the only possible person for
my clerk.'

'But I'm a woman, Mr Cragg. Would it not cause a scandal?'

'Why would it? If St James's Church can have you as
churchwarden, then I can have you as my clerk. The big difference is that I propose to pay you. What would you say to a
fee of four shillings?'

'Well, Mr Cragg, I would do it free of charge. But as you
are so handsomely offering, you have found yourself a very
willing clerk.'

'Good. We shall start work this afternoon, and the first job
is to lay our hands on a sufficient supply of paper, ink and
sealing wax.'

Elizabeth took to Frances Nightingale at once and she
to Elizabeth, and I felt sure the women would be good friends.
Elizabeth was surprised and then delighted when I told her
who I had engaged to act as my legal writer.

'You have much relieved me, Mrs Nightingale,' she said. 'I
was afraid I would have to be Titus's clerk.'

'You must call me Frances, my dear,' said our guest. She
was at ease in our company and we in hers.

The trout were tasty and we soon reduced them to their
bare bones, with much talking as we did so. We spoke for

some time of Thomas Turvey, and his way of conducting the
squireship of New Accrington.

'He has terribly impoverished the estate, has Turvey,'
Frances told us. 'Of course there is the double taxation which
takes a severe toll on all papists. But even allowing for that,
he's never held firmly to any plan, not even for the mending
of the land, never mind its improvement. The seasons go round
and every year the yields are less and the amount of cheating
he endures is more.'

'Do his tenants cheat him?'

'Yes, and his suppliers. A lot of people cheat Tom Turvey
when the opportunity arises. It's such a pity. But he doesn't
care, it seems. Mind you, it doesn't arise so often now he's
grown that much poorer.'

'He cares for his crippled daughter, though.'

'Oh yes, she's all he cares about, really, and the bees. He
has a passion for those little beasts that overrides all other
business. It is where he goes wrong. The man thinks only of
honey and nothing of money.'

'I can believe it,' I said. 'He's consulted me over a legal
embroilment that he looks likely to get into with Mr Horntree
of Hatchfly Hall. It's over some bees that have swarmed
from Mr Turvey's land on to that of Mr Horntree, who won't
give them up. But there is an older feud than this between
these two gentlemen, I believe.'

'They disagree about everything, always have ever since
Horntree came north to occupy the Hatchfly estate. The two men
are opposite poles by nature and will never be reconciled.'

'Tell us about Grevel Horntree, then. I have not met him.'

'He is rude, high-handed and aggressive.'

'You do not much like him, I suspect.'

'I am not alone. He is generally disliked. I mean his person
is – his money is popular, though. He has made a success
of his inheritance and grows steadily richer as Mr Turvey
grows poorer. Horntree's dairy herd is excellent, they tell
me, and he produces the best cheese anywhere in the neighbourhood. He has pigs and sheep, all thriving, and he's got
a few fields under cultivation, which is rare in these parts.
So there is always more work to be had with Horntree than

with Turvey, and a lot of the villagers depend on day labouring.'

'So he is the true power in Accrington now?'

'Turvey has the advantage of his heredity. The Turveys have been here more than two hundred and fifty years, which still carries some weight. But Turvey is pitied more than he is respected, his condition is that reduced. Grevel Horntree is on the opposite path. He's on the rise.'

'But there is a third influence in Accrington,' I said. 'Lord Petre, who is a considerable landowner here, is he not?'

'That is so.'

'What of his representative, Mr Gargrave?'

'Gargrave is nothing remarkable. He does his job well enough. Was always at odds with his wife, though, and I think the truth is he took the loss of his girl Amy very badly.'

'It's hard to know what to make of this attack on the Gargraves. There should be more to it than the unpopularity of his wife.'

'There may not be. This here is a retarded bit of country when it comes to the position of women, as I should know.'

'Is Grevel Horntree married?' Elizabeth asked.

'Oh yes, but Mrs Horntree is rarely seen out. She is young – much younger than he is – and a great beauty. And Horntree is said to be so jealous that he hardly ever lets her leave the estate. She has been seen in church and from time to time goes riding, but otherwise she is more or less invisible.'

Elizabeth had just finished clearing the table when there was a small disturbance in the street outside. I had been listening for the sound of a cart drawing up, and felt sure this at last was Wintle with Matty and our baggage and traps.

'I think it's them! They've made very good time.'

I hurriedly left the table and went to the door, which I pulled open expecting to see Matty on the threshold, with her shining smile. Out of sheer surprise, the smile of greeting on my own face fell instantly away.

'Well, Titus,' said Luke Fidelis. 'I've come all this way, through intolerable heat and dust, and you don't seem very pleased to see me.'

SIX

The opposite was true, but I would not have admitted it. 'I hope you're not expecting your dinner,' I said. 'And by the way, I've got work for you.'

Elizabeth joined us at the door, exclaiming at the unexpected sight of Fidelis, who stepped back and gestured behind him at the laden cart, which was only now drawing up.

'I took it upon myself to escort your goods from Preston. I could not have forgiven myself if some footpad took a fancy to your belongings on the way.'

'You are extremely kind, Doctor,' she said. 'But, you know, we are glad to see you for your own sake – as we are to see Matty!'

She slipped out and handed Matty down from her place sitting next to Peter Wintle.

'Matty, dear! Has it been an uncomfortable journey?'

She ushered Fidelis and Matty into the house while the girl chattered away about their adventures on the road and exclaimed over Hector. I introduced Frances Nightingale to Fidelis, then went into the scullery for beer, ham and cheese to augment the one remaining fish. When I returned bearing the tray, the two were chatting like old acquaintances.

Fidelis, Matty and Peter Wintle sat down to eat and drink while I wrote a hasty letter to Furzey to go back with the cart. Fidelis, who intended to stay for the night, rode to the Black Bull to arrange accommodation for himself and his horse while we unloaded the baggage and transported everything into the house. After I paid Wintle, he set off on his journey home, and as the empty cart rattled away Fidelis returned.

'You claim you have work for me to do, Titus,' he said. 'I'd better do it today, or not at all, for I go back to Preston first thing.'

'Good, because it wants doing today. You have your medical bag?'

'Never go without it.'

'There's a woman I want you to see professionally.'

'You introduce me to so many patients Titus for which I'm grateful, truly. On the other hand, they are always stone dead so can't pay me a fee.'

'This one is no exception. But she will interest you.'

'Then I am at your disposal.'

A few minutes later we were walking towards the church, with the acting churchwarden's keys in my hand.

'Let us try an experiment,' I said. 'Suppose I tell you nothing about the circumstance of this death. You will then be able to draw your conclusions without prejudice.'

'What would you like my conclusions to concern?'

'The usual things. How she died. Was it disease or mischance? Was it deliberate?'

'An act of God or an act of man, then?'

'Precisely.'

We heaved the coffin up the crypt steps and brought it to the side aisle of the church, where there was plenty of light. A table that stood there was cleared of stacked hymn books, and the body heaved on to it. Then I locked the church door and we set about our task. Fidelis had done similar examinations for me many times, and he went about his job swiftly. My own part was to help him to strip off the clothing – she was wearing an ordinary dress – and then to idle around, as I did not like to see him cutting and then sewing up again. Concentrating hard, he would say little but perhaps hum a tune. Unlike me, Fidelis was musical.

I stood for some time in front of the Ten Commandments, trying to reckon which of them were likely to have been broken in the puzzle of Anne Gargrave's death. Idolatry and image-making might have been charges brought against the poor papist Gargraves, but could not be laid at the door of their persecutors. The Sabbath had undoubtedly been desecrated. Killing looked rather likely, as did blasphemy and false witness. Nor was it impossible that adultery might be part of the conundrum. But the last commandment against covetousness was the one I thought about most. Were those who persecuted the Gargraves merely enjoying the pleasure of bullying and humiliating other human beings? Or was there some other motive?

'I've finished and she's sewn up again,' Fidelis said at last.

We dressed Anne Gargrave again, with all the difficulty that is impossible to understand for anyone who has never tried to dress a corpse. Then we replaced her in Castleford's box and manhandled it down to the crypt.

'The dry air down here will slow the mortification,' said Fidelis as we returned to the church, where we fetched buckets of water and cleaned the table and the floor around it.

'So, Luke. What did you find?' I asked, when I had locked up and we were walking towards the lychgate.

'Later, Titus. I shall go to the inn now and write my report while all is fresh in my memory. I invite you to join me there for a glass and a little supper later on, when we can talk it over. Agreed?'

I went now to the gatehouse, where I hoped my clerk would be awaiting me. She had said she would bring a store of paper that she had at home and some ink, so we would be able to get started on preparations for an inquest. I was determined to hold it in four days' time and to do so, as discussed with Turvey, in New Manor's Chamber Major.

I found her as businesslike as I could have hoped. The most important matters when preparing for a hearing is the list of witnesses – which I needed to compile myself – and the list of jurors, who had to be selected, as dictated by tradition, by the Headborough, or constable, of the parish of which Accrington was a part.

'Give me your opinion. From where will our jurors be drawn?' I asked Frances.

'Around Altham, most likely. John Gubb, the constable there, is a lazy, doddery old fellow. He won't cast his net too far from home.'

'That might be better than having them from around here. What is the feeling between the people of Altham and Accrington?'

'Altham looks down on us as a poor relation, though God knows it's not the Garden of Eden itself.'

I dictated a letter to Gubb formally requesting that he raise the necessary jury for the following Monday, which Frances wrote out in an excellent legal hand.

'There is a boy, Roger Eales, who is a reliable messenger,' she said when the letter was sealed. 'He'll have this over the hill in less than half an hour.'

Fidelis was sitting alone in one of the many small parlours and snug rooms that comprised the ground floor of the Black Bull Inn. He was writing at a table before the window – it was still light enough to see – with a pewter jug of beer beside him. As soon as he saw me, he drained the jug, cast sand on the paper, and jumped to his feet.

'Ah, Titus! You will join me in a walk in the evening air?'

'You have drawn up your conclusions? I am hoping to hear them.'

Fidelis picked up the paper that lay on the writing table, folded it, and presented it to me with a bow of mock formality.

'But won't you give me the pith of it?'

'Let us walk in the air and I shall.'

Leaving the inn, we didn't cross the bridge into New Accrington but continued along the road towards Whalley. I explained to Fidelis the difference between the two townships.

'I can't say that the old looks at all older than the new,' he observed. 'Both are primitive enough to be antediluvian.'

However that may be, Old Accrington was a lesser place than New Accrington. It amounted to a dozen dwellings grouped around the Black Bull, the mill and the bridge, with a few more scattered for a quarter of a mile along the road and others even more scattered around the slope of the valley above. Most of these homes were squalid cottages, their windows without glass, their roofs a disorderly thatch, and their children ragged and barefoot.

'As we agreed, you told me nothing in advance about this woman,' said Fidelis as we set off along the rutted road. 'However, I estimate her age to be about forty years and deduce that she was either married or a widow, as she was wearing a wedding band. Her hands and feet are moderately calloused, telling me she is not quite a lady, but above the labouring class. She has given birth. Her inner organs seemed healthy, as did her mouth, though there were some missing teeth. At some point her collarbone was broken and ill set, but this was an old injury, probably from childhood.

'There were, however, a great number of fresh wounds, mostly to or about the head, with cuts and contusions and fractures to the right cheekbone and eye socket. I also found many bruises on the arms, flanks, upper legs and buttocks, and in some cases the skin had been broken. There are also a couple of broken ribs on her left side. All these injuries appear to have been inflicted close together in time. I conclude that she had been severely beaten in a single attack lasting several minutes.

'Unfortunately, the body had been washed after death, so any accidental traces on the skin – which might have told me a little more about her death – were absent. I have reason to think she died towards the end of the morning, or perhaps late in the evening.'

'It was the former. How on earth do you know that?'

'I looked inside her stomach. She had not dined.'

'Do you have an opinion about the cause of her death?'

'It is more than an opinion, Titus, and perhaps you will be surprised by it. She drowned.'

'Drowned?'

'Both her nostrils were clogged with dried mud, and there was mud in her throat and a little in her lungs. I am fairly sure she drowned in a pool of liquid mud. Does that conform with what you already know?'

I was about to give him an account of the cruel stang ride to which Anne Gargrave had been subjected when we were interrupted. We had walked for a little less than half a mile and come to a great pair of stone gateposts beside the road, forming the entrance to a house whose roof we could see another half mile from the road. There was a woman standing in this gateway, a widow by her appearance, her face contorted by agitation.

'Oh, Sirs!' she called out as soon as she saw us. 'Thank

God you have come. We need the doctor. A lady is sorely
ill and I am fearing for her life, as she doesn't reply or open
her eyes.'

'Where is she?' I asked.

She pointed to the lodge cottage that stood inside the gate.

'Here in my house, Sir.'

'And where is your doctor?'

'At Haslingden, Sir, on the Manchester road.'

'There's no need to send to Haslingden,' said Fidelis. 'I am
a doctor. Please show me in.'

She led us into the simple lodge, through the room at the
front, and into a darkened bedchamber beyond. Fidelis immediately threw open the shutters and rich evening sunlight
flooded in. A young woman lay fully dressed on the bed with
her eyes closed. Here and there on her face were what I took
to be bumps or injuries of some kind – one or two of them,
pinkish and puffy.

Fidelis sat beside her on the bed and made a rapid examination, feeling her pulse and looking into her eyes. He touched
her forehead, sides, hands and feet. He spoke to her, but she
made no response beyond a few moans. He put his ear to her
chest.

'How long has she been like this?'

'She came here at about midday, Doctor. She said she felt
faint and had a megrim, and asked if she could rest here for
a little. I took her inside and put her to lie on my bed. She
slept, but when I went in to her half an hour ago I couldn't
rouse her.'

'And what is she? A wayfarer? A stranger?'

'Oh, no, Sir, not a stranger. It is Mrs Horntree, from up
the Hall. She said she had been out walking in the grounds
when she felt poorly.'

'That may be an understatement.'

He leant over her again and rapidly patted the back of her
hand. There came no response.

'Does she cough? Has she been feverish over the last days
or weeks, perhaps? Or feeling any pain?'

The lodge-keeper, who had told us her name was Peggy
Stirk, shook her head.

'I don't know that she did, Sir. I go up to the Hall every day to do the cooking and washing and the like, and I seen her walking around just normally this morning.'

'With no sign of illness?'

'No, Sir. As I said, just as usual.'

'And the swellings on her face? Is that her normal state, also?'

'No, Sir. It makes her look bad.'

Fidelis lifted her hand and felt the pulse again.

'What is her given name?'

'Flora.'

'And what you call "the Hall" is Hatchfly Hall?'

She nodded.

'I live here in the gatehouse. The Hall is a little way up the drive. You would be able to see it clear but for the trees in the way.'

'So why have you not sent for Mr Horntree to bring her back home? Why solicit the help of two strangers if her husband is at hand?'

'Because when she came in the house, before she lay down, she told me express that on no account was I to send to him.'

'How strange. Did she tell you what her purpose was in coming down to the lodge?'

'She said nowt, only what I've told you. Then she lay down, and when I came back to her she'd fainted in a half swoon.'

'The very best thing we can do for her immediately is give her good nourishment. Have you any soup, or thin gruel maybe?'

Peggy Stirk shook her head.

'Then we must get something nourishing from the inn. Titus, will you carry a message there?'

Through all this, the object of our attention had lain still, oblivious, her shallow breathing being her only sign of life.

'I will fetch something back,' I said.

'Broth if possible, but bring eggs anyway. And I need my medical bag. Will you get it from my room? Now, Peggy Stirk, you must have some milk in the house. Would you be so kind as to warm some for me?'

I left them and hurried back along the road towards the inn.

* * *

Half an hour later I was walking back towards the lodge cottage of Hatchfly Hall, carrying Fidelis's medical bag. Following me was the potboy from the Black Bull. In one of his hands was a pail filled with beef broth and in the other a paper bag of eggs.

Arriving at the place, we found a change. Beside the cottage door stood a roughly made chair equipped with carrying handles fore and aft, and lounging nearby were two young men who I guessed were the appointed chairmen. I recognized them at once as the brothers I had met at the bridge, from whom I thought I had acquired a rabbit for my table. Seeing me turn in at the gate and approach the cottage door, they exchanged a few words *sotto voce*, followed by a snort of laughter. This did not perturb me greatly, as an angry voice now made itself heard inside the cottage.

'How dare you, Sir? You wander on to my property from the public road and immediately begin to trifle with my wife. It is intolerable, and I am dubious of its lawfulness.'

Evidently the sick woman's husband had come down to bring her home. I heard Fidelis's voice replying, but its tone was low and I did not catch the words.

'You *say* you are a doctor,' went on the other. 'For all I know, it is a pretence and you are only a contemptible and low-born blackguard. Where is your wig? Your bag of tricks?'

At this I pushed open the door and went inside, closely followed by the boy.

'Here is Dr Fidelis's medical bag,' I said. 'I don't have his wig, but I will vouch for his having one, as I have seen him wear it many times. We have also brought sustenance for the patient.'

Grevel Horntree, whom I confronted with this information, was a solidly built man of about my own age. His hair was black and abundant, his cheeks glowed, and his eyes flashed dangerously as his anger rose.

'What's this? Another stranger butting on to my property! What the devil are you doing here, Sir?'

'I bring broth for your wife.'

'Good God! Have you the impertinence to bring charity food to my house?'

'I believe this is Mrs Stirk's house.'

'Only by my grace and favour. And my wife is no one's patient unless I choose to call a doctor to her.'

We were in the parlour, into which the outside door directly opened. I handed the bag to Fidelis, then turned back to Horntree.

'I am Titus Cragg of Preston, at your service. I believe you are Mr Grevel Horntree.'

Instead of replying, Horntree went to the cottage door, wrenched it open, and shouted.

'Simon! Charles! Come here at once.'

The two brothers appeared at the door.

'Show these men and the boy off the premises.'

Fidelis and I exchanged a glance.

'If I may remind you, Mr Horntree,' Fidelis said speaking rapidly, 'your wife's health should be a matter of concern. I believe I can help her, and—'

Horntree shook his fist convulsively at Fidelis's face.

'Be damned with you! Get out of my sight!'

Fidelis said something in a low voice to Peggy Stirk and stalked out into the air. I nodded curtly to Horntree, who continued to regard me pugnaciously, his fists clenched by his side. Outside, the two brothers followed us to the gate and stood there for a while, arms crossed, watching as we walked down the road towards Accrington.

SEVEN

It was past eight o'clock and the light was beginning to fade when Fidelis and I reached the Black Bull. Walking down from the gates of Hatchfly Hall as far as the bridge, he had told me a little about the young woman, Flora Horntree.

'I first caught sight of her last year when I was staying in the village to consult on the illness of Mrs Entwhistle. It was just the once. I was on this road in the evening, thinking my own thoughts, when there she was in the park. She was taking the air alone and looked, I thought, exceptionally alluring. I fancied that on seeing me in the road she twirled her parasol.'

'She was not playing the flirt today. Do you think her condition serious?'

'Perhaps. The swellings on her face, the megrim and her fainting fit might all be symptoms of some internal disease or contagion. I cannot at this stage identify it and so have no positive ideas for her treatment.'

'Horntree is excessively protective of his wife. I don't believe he will ever let you near enough to treat her. Love affects some men violently like that.'

'Do you call it love, Titus? Well, it is passion of a kind, certainly. You have seen how quick he is to anger. I suspect he is a tyrant of jealousy, Titus. If he were to accept a medical opinion on his wife, it would entail giving a doctor access to her, which he cannot do. He is driven to possess her utterly, entirely, and to the exclusion of all other men.'

'There may be other explanations.'

'True. He may know quite well what ails her.'

We had come to the nub of our discussion. I voiced what was in both of our minds.

'Because he inflicts the ailment himself.'

'Just so. He beats her.'

'He would no doubt call it chastisement: that keeps him within what is lawful.'

'But he may not actually take a stick or a fist to his wife. There are subtler ways of giving a beating.'

'Such as browbeating.'

'Precisely. I would like to challenge him on the question, but more immediately I must ensure that Mrs Horntree recovers her health.'

'Have a care, my friend. Horntree is adamant you shall not see her, or even come near his house. If you ever broach the matter of ill-treatment, he may lose all reason.'

'I too can be adamant. And when a woman needs my help – a beautiful and sensitive young woman, by the way – I shall do whatever is in my power to render it.'

'You will not be returning to Preston in the morning, then?'

'It's out of the question. I must stay and put right whatever is amiss in the house of Grevel Horntree.'

We had arranged that Fidelis would not hazard Mistress Malkin's food at the Black Bull, but would sup with us at the Dower House. First, however, he had further letters to write in time for the postman to Preston who came in the morning. We therefore parted at the inn, Fidelis promising to come to us within the hour.

Making my way up the village, I reached the house of Frances Nightingale, who I found sitting in a wicker chair beside her door, smoking a pipe and enjoying the warm evening. I asked if she had had any success in raising a jury for the inquest, at which she rose and went inside, emerging a moment later with a second wicker chair and a new pipe. She invited me to sit.

'You have caused much excitement in the village, Mr Cragg,' she said, handing me the pipe and gesturing at her tobacco jar, which stood on the ground between us. 'An inquest here in Accrington? Such an event has never been known, not in the lifetime even of those that can remember the last century.'

'But there will be no inquest unless we raise a quorum of jurymen.'

'There will be no difficulty there. I've had a note from Gubb, with a roster of fifteen names. Tomorrow he will serve them with notices to report for duty on Monday. He is quite confident of a dozen answering – for, as I told you, this inquest is stirring everybody up, and plenty of folk want a box seat and a say in the outcome.'

'Good. Then all we need are our witnesses. The first finder I have identified as Gerald Piper, the servant to the Gargraves.'

'There's no shortage of witnesses to the death, Mr Cragg. The question is, can you get any to speak.'

'What we want most of all is testimony from those that started the mischief. According to what I've heard, that would be the Stirk brothers. They appear to work at Hatchfly Hall, but where do they live?'

'In the Hatchfly gatehouse, with their mother.'

'Ah! The widow's their mother? What happened to the father?'

'Went away when they were small and never came back. She affects to be a widow, but she can't be sure if he's alive somewhere. The boys grew up lacking a firm hand, which is very apparent. For ever in trouble, they are.'

'How long has Mrs Stirk been in service at the Hall?'

'She came there as a wet nurse to a child of the previous owner, above twenty years ago and long before I came. She already had the two boys, I reckon, and was still nursing her youngest, Charles. When Grevel Horntree bought the place, Peggy Stirk stayed on. Nowadays, she does their cooking and laundry as well as keeping the gatehouse.'

'And Simon and Charles? What do they do?'

'Farm work.'

'For Horntree?'

'Yes, but they're not particular. They'll work for anyone who'll hire them.'

'So they are not dependent exclusively on Grevel Horntree for money.'

'They do most for him. They live in a house he owns. Their mother works for him. That makes doing his bidding important to them.'

'The reason I ask is, as I've been told, Horntree is an ambitious, improving landowner. He might see much advantage in his local rivals – such as the well-run estate of Lord Petre – going downhill, as it were. If, for instance, Lord Petre's factor were to be attacked in some way and become unable to do his work well.'

'I see what you're getting at, Mr Cragg. But there were many besides the Stirks at the stang ride on Sunday. And their prime target was Anne Gargrave, not her husband.'

'Yet there seems to be some agreement that the brothers named were among the instigators. I can't help wondering, were they put up to it?'

Consideringly, Mrs Nightingale and I drew and blew our smoke several times into the soft, still air. A cloud of it hung before our eyes, slowly dissolving while gnats and flies fussed around the periphery.

'Grevel Horntree is more rough than smooth, I grant you,' she said at last. 'But would he commission such an attack? Would he have such blood on his hands? He is a wealthy man of some standing. No, that woman was liked by few in this village and, if you ask me, so many are guilty for the killing that it will be hard to see the wood for the trees.'

The Dower House when I reached it was permeated with the rich smell of pastry and meat.

'Rabbit pie for our dinner on Sunday,' said Elizabeth. 'I was taking Matty around the village, showing her where to find the mill, the dairy, the bakery and all, and when we returned there was a fine big buck rabbit lying on the doorstep. And look, it had a note pinned to it.'

She showed me a scrap of paper on which was written 'Threepence to pay' in badly formed letters.

The pie filling was simmering on the stove and giving a rich gamey smell. I took a spoon and dipped for a taste.

'That's tasty.'

Fidelis arrived an hour later and insisted on seeing Hector, whom he pronounced to be as bouncingly healthy a baby as he had ever seen.

'He is, isn't he?' said Elizabeth, and a flush of pleasure pinked her cheeks.

Later, as we sat down to eat our supper of cheese and bacon, I told my friend why the house smelled of rabbit stew.

'I'll be seeking out the Stirk brothers to pay them their

money. I must also discuss the death of Mrs Gargrave with
them. It seems they were much involved in it. Peter Castleford's
told me that on the day before they obtained a beam of wood
off him.'

'You can see them tonight at the inn,' Fidelis told me. 'They
arrived there just as I left and I'd be surprised if they were
not there still.'

'Then I will come back with you.'

As we navigated our way through the ground floor of the inn,
with its intricate system of corridors and rooms, we found
some areas empty and others – mostly the larger ones – full
of customers singing and conversing. When we entered the
fullest of these, the hubbub drained away and all faces turned
towards us. Even though not a word was spoken, it was then
that I understood the truth of what Frances Nightingale had
told me: that the village might pretend to indifference towards
me, but was in reality agog at my arrival in their midst. Mrs
Gargrave had just died. Now, only a week later, I would be
holding a coroner's inquest into the death, with attendance
open to all. This prospect, for the moment, was Accrington's
only subject of conversation.

We enquired about wine and were told there was a quantity of what Jane Malkin called Rhenish. This was for the
benefit of travellers, since there was no call for wine among
the local folk. We commanded a bottle and some tobacco
and found a small parlour which we had to ourselves, though
every passing patron and servant stopped at the open door
to look us over.

'We are the objects of general curiosity,' said Fidelis.

'Yes, an attraction. Only a visit by a group of players would
bring more excitement.'

'They have a singularly violent notion of play themselves,
it seems.'

'The Stirk brothers will enlighten us on that, perhaps.'

'When the wine comes, shall I ask for them to be sent
to you?'

'No, let them trot along by themselves, which I'm sure they
will. They won't miss the opportunity to get another threepence.

But let's have two more glasses and extra pipes. We'll try the effect of treating them.'

We sat in high-back chairs on one side of the table, leaving a settle on the other side for our guests.

'Tell me in the meantime how Mr Turvey is,' Fidelis said. 'I mean to pay a visit to New Manor tomorrow.'

So after Jane Malkin had brought our bottle and pipes, I gave him a full account of our evening with the Turvey family.

'Thomasina in particular made a strong impression,' I said.

'Yes,' Fidelis agreed. 'Her body may be wasted, but she possesses an irrepressible spirit. What do you make of Turvey?'

'He has suffered many blows in life. I wonder that a man of evident vigour is content to lead a celibate life.'

'He is consoled, no doubt, by his bees and his daughter.'

Our discussion went no further, for now the two poachers slouched into the room, with the older of the two, Simon, in the lead, while Charlie rested his back against the door cheek and began biting his nails, insolently content to leave the talking to his elder brother.

'Hello, Stirk,' I said. 'The rabbit will make excellent eating. I have tasted the meat and it's good.'

'You shouldn't of eaten it yet. For best, it should be let hang three or four days, then eaten.'

I took out my purse and shook it gently to let him hear the clink of coins.

'I have your money. But before I give it to you, take a little wine with us, won't you? You know Dr Fidelis, who you saw earlier at your mother's house.'

The idea of trying something so novel as wine proved irresistible to the Stirks and Simon sat down on the settle, with Charlie beside him. My invitation had taken some of the insolence out of them, and now they nodded to each of us in an approximation of politeness. After watching me pour the ruby liquid like a couple of thirsty spaniels, they took up their glasses almost at once, taking deep gulps as if it were beer. Then, as the flavour hit their palates, their eyes popped in surprise.

I leaned forward to emphasize what I had to say next.

'Now, I may have come to Accrington to enjoy some

leisure, but I cannot ignore my duties as Coroner, which means when I come across a questionable death I must look into it. The end suffered by Mrs Gargrave was very questionable, wasn't it?'

They exchanged an uncomfortable glance.

'She must have been sick all along,' said Charlie.

'Yer, she must of bin goin' to die any road,' added Simon.

'So you don't think it was the stang business that did for her?' I said.

'That were just a bit of fun. Nowt meant.'

'Who planned it?'

Glancing at each other again, they answered by shrugging and pouting.

'Oh come, come,' I said. 'You mean to tell me you don't know? Really?'

Both shook their heads.

'You see it happens that I've spoken to Peter Castleford. He's making a baby-cradle for me. And he told me that you, the two of you, went to him last Saturday and obtained a beam of wood from his yard. What was that beam for?'

Both men looked uncomfortable. They picked up their glasses and took another gulp of wine.

'Just for a bit of work at home,' said Simon.

'What bit of work?'

'For a post in our mother's garden.'

'I saw no post when I was there today.'

'That's cause we didn't use it. It were borrowed off us.'

'Borrowed? Was that for the stang? Was this beam the stang on which you and others paraded the Gargraves up and down the street? Tell me straight.'

'Aye, that's right.'

'So who borrowed it from you?'

Charles looked at Simon, then mumbled, 'It were Harry Hawk.'

'Hawk? The returned soldier?'

'Aye.'

'Is he a friend of yours?'

'Not a friend. We know him.'

'And did he talk you into taking part in this stang ride?'

'He did. It were all his doing. His idea. He'll tell you.'

'So it wasn't Billy Whist's idea?'

Simon laughed abruptly.

'Billy? Half-crazy, he is.'

'But he knew how to do it, didn't he, Sim?' said Charlie. 'He told us what we needed.'

'Oh, aye. He told us how it was done. With the stang and that.'

'What was the purpose of it, though?' said Fidelis in sudden interruption. 'Apart from the exercise of wilful cruelty, why pick on this unfortunate woman?'

'They needed a lesson, Harry says. She were a nag and he couldn't act like a man, but more like a babby.'

'Aye,' added Simon. 'She commanded him, stead of him commanding 'er, is what Harry says. He were a soldier and knows who should command.'

'Is this such a crime, though, that a woman must die for it?'

Charles reached for the bottle and without apology sluiced more wine into his glass.

'Like we said, that were an accident or else she had a bad heart.'

'Aye,' said Simon, taking the bottle from his brother's hand and filling his own glass. 'It's not the ride that killed her. It were only a bit of fun an' a bit of a lesson at same time.'

The wine had loosened their tongues and at the same time inflamed their manly pride. Charles seemed particularly fired up.

'When I get a wife,' he declared forcefully, 'I don't want her filled up wi' ideas like Anne Gargrave's, tellin' me to do this an' tellin' me to do that, like she's the master.'

He looked to Simon, who nodded in agreement.

'Me neither.' He jerked his head back and let out a hoarse guffaw. 'I'd sooner marry my dog.'

'So though you fully share Mr Hawk's strong views on the duties of a wife, you're saying that the whole idea for making the Gargraves take a stang ride was Hawk's?'

'Aye,' they both said in unison. 'You talk to Harry Hawk,' Charles continued. 'Not us. The whole thing were his idea.'

He shook his finger.

'Harry Hawk, that's who.'

'Where shall I find him? Where does he live?'

'On side o' moor.'

'Does his house have a name?'

'Old farm called Gunwright's Heath. Tumbledown place.'

I had the next link in the chain of my investigation and, as it did not seem profitable to let the conversation run any further, I rose and dug out my purse. At which point Jane Malkin came in, hoping to serve us another jug of Rhenish. The Stirk brothers stood up awkwardly but did not yet shape to leave, in case more drink might come their way.

I opened my purse and dribbled three pennies on to the table.

'Here is the balance of your money, boys,' I said.

As soon as the brothers had seized the coins, the landlady bundled them out.

'You shouldn't have any business with those young harum-scarum lads. You cannot trust them.'

'Our business is the death of Mrs Gargrave,' I said, 'as I think you know, Mistress Malkin. We understand they led the way in organizing this stang ride.'

'Is that what they've told you?'

'No, on the contrary. I am merely trying to establish the truth. Do you know who those boys associate with? Their particular friends?'

'They come in here – when they have money, mind – and I seen them many times with that Harry Hawk, him with the face all torn up. There's not many will drink with him – but the Stirk boys will, long as he's buying.'

'Thank you, Mistress. I will say good night.'

EIGHT

Early the following morning I called at Frances Nightingale's house to ask her to come with me on inquest business, and to bring her inkhorn and paper.

'It's for taking witness statements, I'm guessing,' she said. 'I hope so.'

'Who's the witness, and where at?'

'Harry Hawk. I've been told he lives at a farmhouse called Gunwright's Heath. Do you know it?'

'Oh aye, two or three mile above Old Accrington, on the moor. A desolate sort of place.'

'So you can show me the way?'

She led me through the village and across the bridge but, instead of turning left along the main road, we walked straight ahead past the Black Bull Inn and along a packhorse road between stone walls that headed straight uphill towards the moor. We crossed the belt of pasture that covered the lower part of the hillside, until the enclosing walls ended and the track plunged into the woods above. The warm, dry weather still held and the woods were wonderfully cool and green, haunted by pigeons and, from time to time, a cuckoo. Deer bolted as we approached, leaping away through the bracken until all we could see of them were their bobbing white scuts.

As we climbed, pausing from time to time to catch breath, Mrs Nightingale told me all she knew about Harry Hawk.

'The man divides opinion hereabouts. Nobody can even settle on his right name. When he came back so sudden from war, for quite a while people would talk of nothing else.'

'And why the division of opinion?'

'Well, it's a fact that Harry Hawk did go from these parts for a soldier. But trouble is, he was listed as killed in the battle – or that's the word that came back from the army. So you can imagine everybody's surprise when this fellow appeared, some months later, claiming to be him, large as life and not killed at all.'

'I suppose such mistakes often happen – in the fog of war, and so on. Surely there can have been no doubt about whether it was him?'

'There can have, Mr Cragg, because you couldn't recognize him, you see. Had half his face mangled, and his voice was different as well. And what's more he wasn't the same character. The Harry we all knew was a pleasant, laughing boy; this fellow was sour and gruff and professed to hate all mankind.'

'How did his family greet him?'

'This is what was so strange. His wife, she welcomed him with open arms. But there were other folk that called him an impostor.'

'Who do you mean? His parents, his brothers and sisters?'

'Hawk didn't know any parents – the original Hawk, I mean, if I can call him that. He was taken by Grevel Horntree into his household as an infant – a foundling.'

'Well, well! There's that name again, Grevel Horntree. He keeps cropping up wherever I turn. I met the man yesterday, and it wasn't a pleasant encounter.'

'That wouldn't surprise me, or anyone that knows him.'

'How did he come by the child, though?'

'Some say he was Horntree's bastard, others that the kid had been left on his doorstep in a basket. My husband's employer acted as Horntree's attorney but even he didn't know the truth about the child. We did know that Harry was never allowed to take the proper name of Horntree, though he came as a boy to Hatchfly with Horntree and was treated much as a son. Until they had differences.'

'They quarrelled? Over what? You told me young Harry had a happy temperament, not a quarrelsome one.'

'So he had. He was as sunny as Horntree was saturny, and that's why they clashed. Folk will tell you the two of them fell out over something or other every other day, though when the break came it was as bad a grudge as you may find.'

'What happened?'

'It was when Harry was twenty. He eloped and married, and Horntree didn't like his choice of girl.'

'Who was she?'

Frances was breathing hard from the climb. She leaned against a fallen tree by the side of the path.

'She was Mr Horntree's servant. Rosemary is her name. So you may see why he was angry.'

I didn't, not entirely. For a son to seduce one of his father's servants has never been a rare thing. Marriage would be another matter, but Harry was a foundling boy taken into the household. He hadn't the status of a son, so why should Horntree oppose his choice?

'And after the elopement?'

'Two weeks later they came back as a married couple and, as Mr Horntree had entirely broken with him and barred him from Hatchfly, Harry took her to live up here. It is rented off Lord Petre's estate.'

'On a lease by arrangement with John Gargrave?'

'Yes, and then he joined the army.'

'Why? He had a new wife.'

'And a babby on the way, by then.'

'So why would he leave them?'

'You shall have to ask him. But it was shortly after he left that Mr Horntree got himself the wife he has now. So when Hawk came back, all at Hatchfly had changed.'

We resumed our climb and as we went along I told Frances what had happened at the lodge cottage of Hatchfly Hall and of the condition of Mrs Horntree.

'Dr Fidelis is concerned for her health, as am I.'

'Perhaps she is abused, Mr Cragg. Mr Horntree is known to give way to angry outbursts.'

'There is some considerable gap between their ages. Where did she come from?'

'Who knows? Horntree went off somewhere and brought the girl back with him. They do say she's not Lancashire. And not even North Country, from her speech.'

Reaching the top of the woods, we emerged on to a wide expanse of moor that rose to the skyline. It was abundant with heather and grouse, and there were no doubt a few nesting curlews and snipe here and there. Just ahead, beside the track, which took a course up to and over the horizon, was a group of beehives enclosed by a fence of white palings. I strolled up to them. The insects were hurrying in and out through small doorways near the base of their straw houses.

'Mr Turvey's bees, I take it. Is this his land?'

'The track is a boundary line. Mr Turvey's estate – or the bulk of it – is on this side, where the hives are, and Mr Horntree's lies on that. The bees are brought up here in season because they love the heather blossom, which they turn into their most succulent honey.'

'They are certainly industrious creatures. If the human race could be induced to work so hard, it would double or treble its production.'

'But then it would be a race of slaves, Mr Cragg,' said Mrs Nightingale.

'Is that what bees are – slaves? Or do they give their labour freely for the good of the hive? How can we know?'

I looked again to the horizon and turned to take in the full width of the moor.

'This is a wild enough place. The bees seem at home and contented here, but they have little in the way of neighbours. Which is our direction?'

Frances pointed to a solitary farm that was about two miles distant, reached by a path branching off the packhorse road.

'There is Hawk's house – Gunwright's Heath.'

For a few minutes, as we entered a dip in the path, we lost sight of Gunwright's Heath Farm, and when it reappeared we had left Turvey's land and entered Lord Petre's. What we now saw was a house, a byre and a barn built around a cobbled yard in solid stone blocks, in which a few chickens scratched about. Charles Stirk had called Gunwright's Heath tumble-down, and the outhouses were certainly ruinous, with holes in their roofs and, in the case of the barn, an open cleft running down one of the end walls. Nor was the place in best repair. Its roof was lichened and there were broken and missing slates. The guttering sagged, the downspouts were kinked, and the wood of the window frames rotted. But rough wooden scaf-folding, clinging to the house's front, and a few new slates piled at the foot of the ladder alongside showed that somebody had been attempting repairs.

As we approached, we heard a steady CLACK-CLACK-CLACK from inside.

'Somebody's weaving,' said Frances.

As soon as I knocked, the percussions ceased and a woman came to the door, her pale face drawn and with strands of hair escaping untidily from her headscarf. I guessed she was aged about twenty-five.

'Mrs Hawk?'

'Yes.'

I removed my hat.

'I am Titus Cragg, the County Coroner, and I'm looking into the unfortunate death of Anne Gargrave, that occurred down in New Accrington last Sunday afternoon. This is Mrs Nightingale, whom I have engaged as my temporary clerk.'

'What's it to do with me that you've traipsed all the way up here?'

'It's your husband that I am hoping to speak to.'

'He's not here. He's got a day's ditching over behind Altham.'

'May we have a word with you, in that case?'

She hesitated, then pulled the door wide.

'You must bide a while. I have to use the time to work while my boy's asleep. He'll waken soon and then we can talk.'

We entered directly into a large room containing a dresser, an oak table and a variety of chairs, and a fireplace in which a blackened pot simmered over burning embers. A few more pots were ranged on a shelf along the chimney breast. In most homes these would have been the essentials of the room, but this was a weaver's home, dominated by the presence of the loom. It was of the modern kind, one of those broadcloth looms that employ Mr Kay's ingenious fly-shuttle. The sound of the shuttle resumed. It was a bullet shape that spooled out the weft thread as it hurled itself from side to side, banging into the box, or end stop, at each end of its run. To watch a weaver working such a loom is to marvel at the cleverness of the machine and the endurance and dexterity of the operator. At the same time, it is quite impossible to hold a serious conversation. I looked at Frances and she shrugged.

My clerk laid out her writing materials on the table and sat down to wait, while I took a tour around the room. The walls held no pictures, but a small number of books were arranged in a row on the projecting beam above the fire. I had a look through them and found mostly sermons, though one was a somewhat dilapidated book of poems.

I did not hear the baby's cry but Rosemary Hawk, with a mother's ears, caught it immediately. She left off operating the loom at once and bustled into the inner room, emerging with the young one in her arms, a sleepy child of eighteen months or so. She sat on one of those low three-legged cottage-fireside stools that is called a cracket, and began to unbutton her dress, revealing an elegant neck and, round it, a silver chain from which hung an oval silver pendant, her only piece of jewellery so far as I could see. Suddenly aware that I was staring, I quickly turned my gaze towards the window as Rosemary Hawk continued to slip her buttons in order to nurse the child.

'Please, take a chair Mr Cragg,' she said. 'And you, Mrs Nightingale.'

She seemed perfectly at ease giving suck in our presence.

'That is better,' I said, sitting in an armchair on the opposite side of the fireplace. 'I mean, it's quieter. We may talk now?'

'Of course. I do not mean to be unmannerly, but you see I must use every minute that I can on the loom if I'm to complete my twenty-four yards of cloth for the wool factor when he comes on Monday. If not, I shan't be paid or get my next week's supply of thread, which will put all out of kilter.'

'I imagine your domestic economy depends upon regular production.'

'Twenty-four yards a week, that is my contract and I get good enough money. But we have to keep it up. We've much to pay back on the borrowed money that bought the loom and there's little to spare. It is better since my husband came home, but only a little.'

'You must have been hard pressed during his absence in the army.'

'I was.'

She did not enlarge on the matter, however, but only moved the child to the other breast.

'May we talk about last Sunday in the afternoon? Were you here? Were you working the loom?'

Mrs Hawk looked shocked.

'On the Sabbath, Sir? Don't you know that I am a clergyman's daughter?'

She gestured to her tiny library.

'When I wasn't looking after my son, I was reading Dr Andrewes's sermons.'

'Where was Mr Hawk?'

'He went to Accrington.'

'To the church service?'

'No, there was no service. Church is only once a month here.'

'What did your husband go for?'

She shook her head.

'His own business. He didn't tell me.'

'When did he return?'

'Late, but it wasn't dark. Maybe eight o'clock.'

'And he didn't tell you what he'd been doing?'

'He told me he'd seen Mr Gargrave and his wife made a mock of.'

'What was his feeling about that?'

'He was glad. He hated that Gargrave witch. She was a cross-patch, and she spread that spiteful story about Harry not being Harry. But of course he didn't know she'd died until later.'

'Did he not feel any responsibility for that?'

'Not him. Said it was an accident and never intended.'

'Harry is much changed since he came back from the army, I am told.'

'Well, his face has lost its beauty, as everyone can see, but that's not the only way he's different – his hair is turned white and he is angry and sad by turns. It's the army did that, and the fear of war. There are days he won't say a word from morning till night. That's hard on me and baby.'

'So why did he go into the army? You had just set up house, and he knew he would soon be a father. Why did he leave?'

'It was for the money, Sir. We had just got the loom, but the weekly repayments to the moneylender were great and I could not earn money until I was able to weave. "Nowt learned and nowt earned" – as those damned collybists say. Harry'd send me a shilling a week from his army pay to give the moneyer.'

'You heard Harry had been killed in battle?'

'Aye. The worst day of my life.'

'Yet it was a mistake, and he came back to you after all.'

She rocked her child, who had slipped off the nipple and was dozing contentedly. Looking at him, her mouth slipped into a momentary smile.

'Oh yes,' she said. 'He came back.'

She put the child down, closed her dress, and stood.

'I will get on, now, Mr Cragg. The wool factor's a hard man and we are still paying the moneyer.'

She seated herself on the operator's bench, and the room was again filled with the percussion of the fly-shuttle and the bang of the batten. As Frances Nightingale collected together her writing materials (she had been dutifully taking notes of what Mrs Hawk told us), I shouted a goodbye above the noise and we left.

'It is unfortunate that we couldn't speak to Hawk,' I said as we made our way along the moorside track. 'But we have not wasted our time. His wife told us much.'

'She bears her misfortunes with courage,' said Frances.

'You noted she is daughter to a clergyman? She was not meant to waste her life on a cottage weaver's bench.'

'She was a servant before she was a weaver. Her family must have fallen on hard times.'

'Which she is unlikely to admit. Harry may tell us more about her, if we can ever catch up with him.'

'Look in the Black Bull this evening. He drinks there with the Stirk boys. It would save us the trouble of climbing back up here, any road.'

'I will, and in the mean time I am going to Hatchfly Hall. Mr Grevel Horntree was Gargrave's competitor and I can't get rid of the suspicion that he lurks somewhere at the back of all this.'

Being able to descend the woodland road much more quickly than we had gone up it, we were soon back at the Black Bull.

'I shall go on my way home now, Mr Cragg.'

'Are you not coming to Hatchfly Hall?'

'No, and you should take care yourself, Mr Cragg. He is a difficult man to have to do with.'

So I walked on alone, covering the half mile to the gates of Hatchfly Hall in another ten minutes.

NINE

G revel Horntree's home gave me a surprise. Coming up to it, past the screen of trees that had mostly hidden the house, I saw that it was a three-storeyed gentleman's residence built, I guessed, no more than thirty years before. Its windows were ample, and the whole of the so-called ground floor was in fact raised above the ground, so that the front door was reached by climbing a fan-shaped flight of stone steps flanked by elegant balustrades. I had never imagined I would find such civilized architecture in the vicinity of the unkempt and unimproved village, whose only other notable house was Turvey's ancient and ruinous seat.

As I approached the front entrance, I heard a scraping sound and some high words. Somebody was being roared at as a blackguard and hell-damned lecher who should go back to whore-biting and pox-mongering and a catalogue of other low practices. A moment later the door itself was flung open and a man was propelled through it as by a kick. He stuttered for a moment at the top of the steps, then pitched down them, bouncing painfully as he went. The door slammed as I went over to pick up, and dust off, my friend Luke Fidelis.

'Are you injured?'

'Somewhat bruised, but nothing broken. Don't commiserate, please. I knew quite well what might happen if I ran the risk.'

I led him away until the belt of trees was again between us and the house.

'Tell me exactly what happened, Luke,' I said, sitting him down on a stone bench beside the drive.

'A bare quarter of an hour ago,' he said, wiping away the blood that was seeping from a nostril, 'I was giving Peggy Stirk instructions about what food she should give Mrs Horntree for her better health. I'd gone to the back door, hoping to avoid Grevel Horntree, but he happened to come into the kitchen while I was there and, in a passion, he hauled

me through to the hallway and told me I was not welcome
in his house.'

'Did you see Mrs Horntree? I take it she was the object of
your visit.'

'She was. And, no, I did not see her. When I asked after
her well-being, Horntree wouldn't discuss his wife, let alone
allow me to go in to her. He only swore at me.'

'I am sure violence is in his blood,' he went on. 'As the
old doctors would have it, he is choleric by nature. Of course,
I deliberately stoked up his ill humour by answering his
gratuitous insults with rebukes of my own. My tongue ran
away with me, I fear, and I told him I thought he mistreated
his wife.'

'Great goodness! You did not!'

'He came at me with a great roar, hurled me to the wall,
then wrapped an arm around my neck and dragged me out
through the front door, whereupon he put his boot to my backside and propelled me down the steps. By Christ, he's strong!'

Fidelis rubbed an evidently bruised knee.

'How odd that a man with such a jarring temperament should
live in such harmonious-looking a house.'

'Harmonious? Perhaps. But the climate of the place is soul-
less. Inside it feels cold. It repels even this summer's heat,
just as he repels visitors.'

'I suppose he wants his privacy. Which is a reasonable
desire, however unreasonably expressed.'

'I don't agree, Titus. To cut oneself off is not reasonable in
an outlying place like this – not unless a man is mad or hiding
something. In all truth, I cannot decide the case of whether
Horntree is a criminal or nothing more than a misanthrope.'

'He may be neither. And he cannot be truly cut off, even if
he does desire privacy. The man is a successful landowner and
he appears to manage his own affairs. He is obliged to deal
with the world, or he would have no income.'

We set off down the drive towards Mrs Stirk's lodge cottage
and Fidelis asked what had brought me into the dangerous
zone of Hatchfly Hall.

'I want to know why the Gargraves were picked on for the
punishment of the stang.'

'Why should Horntree know about that?'

'We heard evidence last night that Hawk, the man Horntree adopted as a boy, was the ringleader. They are estranged now because Hawk stole away with one of the Hatchfly servants. But I suspect Horntree may still tell us something. Mrs Nightingale has praised his success at working the estate. He is ambitious for its prosperity, and seems to have been putting pressure on Turvey to "cooperate" with him, which won't happen. Turvey hates him. I wonder if Horntree found that Gargrave would no more cooperate than Turvey would, and so found a way to punish him for it.'

'Cooperate in what?'

'Some agricultural enterprise? An improvement project? I don't know. Of course the direct causes of Anne Gargrave's death is naturally to the fore in this inquest. But I want to know the background. I learned a little of it from Mrs Hawk this morning.'

In deference to Fidelis's bruises, we went slowly. So by the time we reached the Dower House I had been able to describe my visit to Gunwright's Heath in full, with Fidelis listening attentively.

'So, a pretty young woman came to Hatchfly Hall,' he said, 'and when she fled the nest was immediately replaced by another. Interesting.'

'She was not exactly replaced, Luke. Rosemary Hawk was a servant, Flora is a wife.'

'Hmm. There is not always a great deal of difference, though, is there?'

No sooner had Matty pulled off my boots and I'd got settled by the hearthside than Elizabeth handed me a letter from Preston, addressed in the hand of my clerk, which had arrived in the late morning. I broke the seal at once.

Dear Mr Cragg (wrote Furzey),

 I write in reply to your enquiry regarding the legal ownership of a swarm (examen) of bees, though I have not found it an easy matter to look into, and was required to expend much time on it, which would have been more fruitfully spent in profitable activity. However, what I have gleaned is as follows.

All fully domestic animals (domitae naturae), such as fowl, pigs, horses and milk-goats, are in their essence beneficially owned. On the other hand, truly wild animals (ferae naturae) may be deemed to be property only so long as they are held in captivity. The status of half-tamed beasts (mansuefactae) – deer, for example, and fan-tailed and tumbling pigeons, ornamental peacocks and indeed honey bees – is not limited by strict captivity. Should such a creature stray, it may continue to be property if, on the one hand, it intends to return (this is called its animus revertendi) or if, on the other, it has been followed and kept in view by its owner.

In sum, your client will have difficulty in proving his title to the examen unless he can show that the bees possess the animus revertendi and, or, he has kept them in his sight with a view to recapture. The other party's suit, of course, will also succeed or fail according to the same criteria, but applied in reverse.

I remain, etcetera, Robert Furzey, Clerk at Law.

I read Furzey's postscript describing the mischiefs of the spaniel Suez, whom we had left in Furzey's care, and refolded the letter.

'I have some news for Mr Turvey,' I said to Fidelis. 'If you are calling on him this afternoon, then I will come with you.'

We found Tom Turvey in a shady spot in his yard, dozing in a basket chair. I picked up a book that had fallen from his knee and glanced at it. It was *Melisselogia: Or the Female Monarchy* by the Rev. John Thorley.

'Good afternoon, Cragg,' said Turvey, opening his eyes. I returned the book to him.

'Ah, yes! A new treatise on beekeeping which I received only yesterday from the bookseller in Manchester. A thorough mixture of good sense and nonsense, I find. At least this fellow Thorley understands that the hive is led by a female – even Shakespeare was wrong on that point, you know. You have read *Henry the Fifth*? Some men quickly become irrational when instructed that in bee society the females do all the working and fighting. The males are forbidden all business except a single act, which in the end only one of them actually performs. Women have no quarrel with this notion, I find, but men do not like it and so won't believe it.'

He laughed delightedly and clapped his hands together.

'I am glad to see you are a reader, Mr Turvey,' I said. 'I am a great reader myself and have been wondering if you have a collection from which I could borrow.'

'Oh dear, Cragg, I must disappoint you. I read only on beekeeping, and there are no other books in the house.'

Turvey stood up and shook hands with Fidelis.

'Dr Fidelis, may I say what a pleasure it is to see you again, Sir. Your care for my late mother-in-law was a right good lesson in the art of medicine.'

'I regret I could not save her.'

'No, no! Don't distress yourself. Her time had come.'

'I have some news from Preston,' I said. 'We have looked into the law on bees and I regret to say the matter is very doubtfully in your favour.'

I handed him Furzey's letter.

'However, if you wish to pursue the matter, let us consult further on it. Now, I wonder if I may have the loan of your servant, Danny? I need his help preparing the Chamber Major for Monday's inquest.'

Turvey gave the cover of the letter a painful look, as a lover views a letter from a spurning woman. Then, abruptly, he tucked it into a pocket.

'Of course, of course! There are various benches around the place, which you can use for your seating. I will send him to you. Meanwhile I shall take Dr Fidelis in to greet my daughter.'

For an hour Danny and I worked hard, setting up a table behind which I could preside, then bringing benches and setting them in rows for the jury and public. After an unfortunate incident at Preston during the previous year, I now made it my practice to provide for precautions against fire at all my inquests. I told Danny to bring as many buckets as he could, fill them with water, and place them at intervals around the room. We had been working for an hour, and had got the place as nearly right as I wanted it, when Elizabeth arrived carrying a small vase and a bunch of summer flowers.

'I've come to see your courtroom, Titus,' she said. 'And I bring flowers from the Dower House garden to brighten it up. Is it not traditional for the judge to have a sweet-smelling posy under his nose, to alleviate the smell of the crowd?'

I put my nose to them and inhaled, and as the floral perfume filled my head I heard through the window that faced the house the whindling sound of Thomasina Turvey's spinet in the next room.

We returned for our supper at the Dower House, where Matty greeted us. She had the babe in her arms and an excited look on her face.

'It's here!' she said. 'The baby's bed is here.'

We went up to the big bedroom, where Matty had asked the carpenter to deposit the cradle. It was exactly as Peter Castleford had shown me in his sketch – a rectangular oaken box standing on curved struts by which the whole cradle could be rocked. Over one end was an arched cover, like a hood, to shade the baby's eyes.

'Oh, how beautiful!' exclaimed Elizabeth. 'Hector will like it very much I am sure, and might even sleep all through the night in it.'

'You men!' said Elizabeth, after we had eaten. 'You cannot sit still for half an hour but you must be away to a tavern. What shall we do, Matty? Have a cup of tea at home and a game of cards?'

'It is inquest business,' I said. 'I must gather evidence.'

'A likely story, but go on with you.'

On warm midsummer Saturday nights such as this the people of Accrington, New and Old, made a custom of gathering on the bridge and in the open space in front of the Black Bull to drink, gossip and argue, and some to dance to Billy Whist's incessant succession of crude jigs and reels.

Crossing the bridge, I looked carefully left and right. The parapets were lined with men and women sitting and smoking and drinking ale, while their children dropped seeds or bread-crumbs into the water for the ducks and fishes. Other children chased in and out of the shadows with shrieks that excited the dogs to yap and yelp in competition. I did not see the Stirk brothers or Harry Hawk.

With almost all its customers enjoying the open air, the close rooms of the inn were sparsely occupied. We separated at the entrance and navigated different paths through the inn's complicated interior, looking for Hawk and the Stirks. By the time I reached Mistress Malkin's serving hatch – where she was in conversation with Susan Bacon, the woman who had behaved threateningly to me and Elizabeth on our first night in Accrington – I had not found our quarries.

'I'm very vexed with you, Mr Cragg,' said the innkeeper when she saw me. 'You never brought me back the pots I gave you to take that food up to Hatchfly Hall. And when I sent the boy this morning for them, he had his ears boxed and came back in no fit state to work.'

My apology was received by a not very graceful sniff from Jane Malkin, while her companion spat on the floor. The innkeep-er's manner changed, however, when Luke Fidelis appeared.

'Ah, Doctor!' she exclaimed. 'May I get you some supper? I jugged a hare only this morning, and right good it is.'

Fidelis assured her he had his supper at the Dower House – news that Mistress Malkin received by directing another unfriendly glance at me. I took Fidelis aside.

'Any sign of Hawk?'

'No, nor the Stirk brothers. But a fellow back there told me all three of them'd be in before closing. We must wait.'

At half past ten the Stirks swaggered in, each carrying a laden sack, with their lanky dog in attendance. Simon's sack was stained here and there with seeping blood. He passed it without a word through the hatch to the innkeeper. Charlie's burden was different – fuller and with a hole in its side, through which I could see what it contained: string netting tightly rolled. If this was what they call a long net, the source of Mistress Malkin's jugged hare was clear.

Three tankards of ale were ordered, indicating the Stirk brothers had a companion. Leaving the room, I cast back through the inn until, in a parlour at the back of the building, I found what I was looking for – a man with a wide-brimmed hat pulled down over his head and a scarf wound around the lower part of his face, just as highwaymen do to conceal their faces. He was sitting on a bench alone, with a roughly tied bundle beside him. The sack that contained the bundle was bloodstained, just as Simon Stirk's was.

'Are you Harry Hawk?'

He looked up sharply but made no reply.

'I am Titus Cragg, the County Coroner. I was at your house this morning.'

His eyes, which were the only visible part of his face, narrowed.

'I wanted to speak with you about what happened to Anne Gargrave on Sunday last.'

With his face concealed, I could not accurately judge Hawk's mood. But from his movements, he seemed to be agitated and uncertain, shaking his head and drumming upon his thigh with the fingers of his left hand.

'Your wife told me you were present at the stang ride that was inflicted on both the Gargraves. I wanted to know what you saw as I am to conduct an inquest into her death.'

Suddenly, in a sharp change of manner, Hawk rose from the bench, picked up his pack, and made for the door. This took me quite by surprise and I was so slow to follow him that a minute had passed before I realized he had left the inn altogether. Then I went out after him.

He had a good forty yards start on me, a dark shape working its way up the track that rose gradually above the inn, towards the black line of the trees. Increasing my pace, I was soon panting with effort, but I kept on. The sky was clear and the moon, which was two days past the full, shone out of a clear sky, so that Hawk was clear in view until he reached the wood. But when he crossed the shadow line of the trees, he disappeared from sight.

By the time I reached the same place, I was quite out of breath and could go no further without resting. The air was still and very quiet except for the bleating of sheep and the soft churr of a nightjar perching somewhere overhead.

I peered into the darkness, along the rising path that cut through the trees towards the high moor above, and listened. I heard the call of an owl somewhere amongst the trees, but nothing else. It occurred to me that my quarry might be lurking somewhere close by, perhaps concealed behind a bush with a cudgel in his hands. The man had, after all, been a soldier and was no doubt accustomed to violence. I felt the urge to hide myself in the shadows, but after a moment thought better of the impulse. It is a poor coroner that plays the coward, I thought. So I backed out into the moonlight until I stood several yards from the treeline, and called out 'Harry Hawk! Are you there? Come out so I can see you.'

A little way to my right, on the very edge of the wood, a spark flashed and a small blue flame appeared. It illuminated a pipe and, with each of the smoker's puffs, the glow flickered over the lower part of a hideously torn face.

TEN

Harry Hawk was sitting a few yards to the right of the path on a beech trunk that had conveniently fallen just outside the wood, along the line of the trees. In daylight it would have given a fine place to sit and contemplate the view.

'Please believe me, Mr Hawk, I mean you no harm,' I said, approaching him up the slope.

His head was lowered as if making a count of his waistcoat buttons. I now stood ten yards from him.

'In the affairs of others – unless in the service of justice – I am neutral,' I went on. 'May I join you in a pipe? I have my own tobacco.'

He raised his head and grunted. Then, in what I took to be a significant conciliatory gesture, he made room by shifting a little along the log. I sat down and we kept silence for a while as I stuffed my pipe. Out of the darkness below us, the squeaky violin music and the accompanying whoops and cries faintly reached our ears. They came, it seemed, from a different plane of existence.

'I ask you to remember that I am a stranger here,' I said, 'and I find myself at some disadvantage. There are never many incomers in a country place like this, so people are short of trust for them that do turn up. It's natural, but human life and enterprise do not flourish without trust, don't you agree? I think you yourself have suffered a similar failure of trust since your return.'

He gave a grunt, rather than an answer. I pressed on.

'To come back from a war so much changed – I expect folk found that hard to accept. May I trouble you to light me a match?'

Still without a word he snapped open his tinderbox, struck a spark, and lit a new match. He handed it to me as it flared, illuminating his face under the slouch hat so that I now saw close-to the full hideousness of his damaged mouth, chin and cheeks. The skin looked like melted and scorched cheese. It had been not just pierced but jaggedly holed, and the teeth and perhaps some of the bone beneath blasted away.

As I drew the fire into the pipe, he spoke for the first time.

'And I find it hard to take likewise, Mr Coroner. They don't see my face, they see my wound.'

His speech was impeded like that of an idiot, the consonants slipping and sliding around in his ruined mouth, but I understood him well and soon realized the man was anything but idiotic.

'How did you suffer it, if you don't mind my asking? I've heard it was last summer, at Dettingen.'

'Yes. French grapeshot is the devil. We were attacking them along the side of the river, but the French guns were on the far bank. Flanking fire. A vast number of men were cut to pieces worse than me.'

'Yet the nation rejoiced at the King's ultimate triumph.'

'It's easy for them to rejoice. They weren't there. The truth is we were lucky. The French were even more fools than us.'

'I wonder if you saw his Majesty at all during the engagement. It is common knowledge that he took over the generalship just before the engagement. Did he give a speech before battle, as a general in the field is supposed to do?'

It was strange to hear this morose wounded man suddenly laugh – or that is how I interpreted the tongued-congested huffing sound that came out of him.

'He did attempt such a thing, but was carted away by his horse as soon as he opened his mouth. It turned and bolted back through our ranks. We heard the King screeching at it in German, at the top of his voice, but he couldn't pull it up, so they careered all the way to the kitchens in the rear, where it threw him off. He came walking back to the front in his laced regimentals, cursing and stamping the ground like a four-year-old child.'

'But the battle went bravely, did it not?'

'Bravely? You don't act bravely in the ranks. You shit yourself. You see things no one should witness. Guts spilled, men choking to death in their own blood, eyes hanging out on strings.'

I looked down into the velvet darkness, where a few points of light sparkled faintly, like distant stars. Accrington's concerns were far from the bloody clash of armies and the horrors of mangled limbs and murderous cannonades. Yet even here, only a week ago a woman had been cruelly and bloodily bundled to her death.

'What made you join the army? You had a wife here, and you rented a farm. Were you not well set?'

I heard again that snuffling, choking laugh.

'The farm, as you call it, isn't good for much. It has no land worth the name, and there was never enough money coming in. So we got a loom to work at home, but had to borrow the price from a usurer in Manchester.'

'I have seen the loom. It is a formidable machine and must have been expensive.'

'At first we couldn't earn enough from it to pay the money back, because you have to get the trick of working it. Besides which, my wife was pregnant. So my going into the infantry was a way to cover the repayments, until revenue from the cloth started to come in.'

'From my observations, I would say your wife has learned the use of the machine admirably. And now you are returned and can earn money yourself.'

'For paltry wages. I can't work like I used to. And what I look like stops many hiring me, 'specially in Accrington – which is why I often have to go over the hill for work. Of course Mr Turvey was different. He gave me work with his bees. He was a good man till he sent me packing.'

He fetched a deep sigh.

'It would've been better for everyone if I really had been killed in the battle.'

'Come, come, man, don't say that!'

But I looked at him. He had reason for self-pity. He even found difficulty in smoking, having to draw in the smoke while using a hand to stop the hole in his cheek.

'If I *were* killed, she would not have to feed me or sustain my miserable life.'

'But she would grieve for you.'

'She does so now. On rent day, 'specially. She gives me hard words of grief then.'

'Is that why you don't keep her company much, at home? As last Sunday, when you were in Accrington I understand?'

He removed the pipe from his mouth and gave me a knowing sideways look.

'Is that your way of leading me on to talk about the stang ride?'

I smiled.

'The Stirk brothers are saying you put them up to it.'

Again his bungled laugh.

'They don't need much putting up. They like a bit of sport, do Charlie and Simon.'

'Then you deny that the punishment of Anne Gargrave was your idea?'

'You will have a hard time proving it was.'

'Well, at any rate, your participation in it cost you your position as beekeeper with Mr Turvey.'

'Yes. But it couldn't be helped. Mr Turvey did the right thing by his own ideas.'

'I think his own ideas *are* right; and if you don't mind my saying so, yours are all wrong. You assisted in persecuting John Gargrave but he was also your benefactor – he rented your house to you. Why did you grudge at him?'

'He didn't do it as a benefactor – only a factor. He saw an opportunity to get some people into the house. It was on the way to being a ruin and needed a tenant.'

'Is the rent not fair?'

'It's fair enough. Any road, the fact is I don't hold anything against Gargrave. His missis was another matter. She was the first of those that went around saying I was not Harry Hawk after I'd returned but called me an impostor – herself and that Bacon witch.'

'So it would not be surprising if you did grudge at her. Anyone gossiped about like that would, I think.'

'Bearing a grudge is one thing – and I won't say I didn't – but no one liked Anne Gargrave in Accrington. Not even Susan Bacon, who made out she was her friend. Now, that's a spiteful one. She went along with the stang ride as heartily as anyone, from beginning to end. It's her you should talk to if you want to find out how it all blew up, and how it ended too. There's no business going in these parts that she doesn't know about.'

My pipe was done. I knocked it out and rose to my feet.

'I have met Mistress Bacon briefly. She's a woman who doesn't mince her words. But we should be getting home to our wives, you and I. I'm glad we talked. The inquest is on Monday, at New Manor. I hope you'll be there.'

'If I have no work.'

'Please make sure of it. I hope you know I have the authority to compel you.'

He uttered that laugh once more.

'Good luck with that. This is not your charter town. Authority works differently here.'

I left him and started back down the hill towards the Black Bull Inn, where the sounds of merry-making had died away at last. How much of what Hawk told me was true? His memories of the disgust and fear of battle seemed quite real. His anger at being rejected by some in the village likewise. But perhaps they were only ways of gaining my sympathy, and of disguising the leading part he'd played in the stang ride.

I'd said some high-minded things about trust, yet I didn't trust him. I nevertheless told myself that my enquiries should turn in the direction Harry Hawk had suggested. He'd told me Susan Bacon had been a friend of Anne Gargrave but turned against her at the last. Why? I knew Susan Bacon was a forthright woman, but was she capable of causing real harm? I resolved to hear what tale would come out of that particular old wife's mouth.

Frances Nightingale told me where Mrs Bacon's cottage was. It was one of half a dozen in New Accrington that faced the churchyard and was in good repair, with tidy thatch and with a neat garden on either side of the short path to the door. A strong working party of Squire Turvey's bees were foraging among the climbing roses and hollyhocks, humming the one note of their song.

As I turned in at the gate, at about nine o'clock in the morning, Susan Bacon was at her open door spinning a mop to shake the water out of it. The wind gusted and drops of water spattered my face. She did not apologize.

'Housework?' I said, cleaning the drops away with my handkerchief. 'On a Sunday, Mrs Bacon?'

'Just a spill of milk,' she said. 'I have a naughty cat that knocks over the can to get himself a drink. But what brings you to my door, Mr Coroner? Dirtier work than what I'm doing, I'd say. It should be *me* telling you not to do business on the Sabbath.'

I ignored this and explained myself, while she stood propped against her mop handle, her face impassive.

'It is regrettable, but I must make enquiries. Tomorrow I shall be holding the inquest into the death of Anne Gargrave that occurred here in Accrington a week ago. I have had little enough time to prepare, but I prefer these proceedings to come no more than seven days after a death, if possible. Now, I think you were present at the stang ride, were you not?'

'With many of the village.'

'I ask because I have been told you were friendly with the unfortunate Mrs Gargrave.'

'I was.'

'So why were you present at her punishment as a shrew?'

'She wasn't a shrew with me, was she? So I liked her.'

I was finding this hard to comprehend.

'So why—'

'Use your noddle, Mr Cragg. You may like a hunchback while hating the hump. There was nowt Anne could do about being a shrew. It was in her nature. She called a spade a spade, but she often used it like a fork.'

'The fact remains you took an active part in making her and her husband ride the stang.'

'Not active. I followed it up and down. I watched.'

'But I've heard you egged the young men on.'

'Who told you that?'

'I was told by one that was there himself – Harry Hawk.'

She uttered a scoffing bark of laughter.

'That man's a liar and a deceiver. Don't believe anything he says. I know what game he's playing.'

'You mean, you think he is an impostor. Yet his wife must surely know her own man?'

'Any man that calls himself Harry Hawk will do for her. She's his confederate – must be.'

'In what, Mrs Bacon?'

'The double-dealing. The pretence. He's got his hooks in her. So if they say it was me that egged them on to the stang ride, the real truth is it were him did that. He hated Anne because she threatened to give out the proof.'

'What proof?'

She gave me a cunning, knowing look.

'Her husband and that man were having an argument over the rent and he – the supposed Harry Hawk, I mean – was asking for it to be reduced because his money coming in was less. He showed Gargrave his discharge papers, like, so he'd know there was nowt coming in from the regiment. And the first thing Gargrave saw was that it had the wrong name. It wasn't the discharge papers of a Harry Hawk.'

'Whose was it, then?'

'Someone going by the name of Martin Ware.'

'Why did Lord Petre's factor not challenge him about this?'

'He asked him all right, and the fellow had some cock-and-bull story that he'd not wanted to sign the army papers as Harry Hawk, so he signed on with a false name. Ask me why ever he would do that, and I can't think of a reason.'

'But you maintain that not only is Harry Hawk not Harry Hawk, but that the impostor instigated the stang ride to punish Anne Gargrave for saying so?'

'Like as not.'

'Can you explain why this man Martin Ware would masquerade as Harry Hawk in the first place?'

'For gain, isn't that why folk do fraud?'

'Gain of what, Mrs Bacon?'

'Of the farm. Of the wife. Of prospects.'

I thanked her for her time and, after asking if she would be kind enough to give evidence at Monday's inquest, I left feeling that we parted on better terms than before. This I thought was

because she felt gratified by my attention, and looked forward
to holding the centre of the stage on Monday.

I went immediately to Frances Nightingale's house and rapped
urgently on her door.

'I may have the key to what happened here last Sunday.
It's Harry Hawk. Or the fellow who's calling himself that.
We must have him at the inquest tomorrow. He seems to have
had a very good reason to want Anne Gargrave out of the
way. Or at the very least to put her in fear of her life. Will
you draw the summons?'

She fetched pen, ink and paper and I sat down at her table
to write.

'Shall I fetch the boy to take it to Gubb?' she asked.

'No. I'll take it myself. I want to impress on the man the
importance of this.'

On my return to the Dower House, I found Elizabeth and
Luke Fidelis breaking their fast. They had been to Altham,
where a Catholic priest lived who provided discreet Sunday
services for adherents of that faith, which included both my
wife and Fidelis. Having walked there and back, they had
returned hungry.

'He's a jovial fellow, that priest, but he's hurt his eyesight
by reading,' said Elizabeth, biting into a piece of bread and
dripping.

'And he has an excellent library,' said Fidelis. 'It was the
room where he said the . . . you know, where we prayed. I
had a look. There were numerous theological tomes in Latin,
but also modern literature in English and French.'

'If he has a library, he must be agreeable,' I said.

Elizabeth swallowed her toast and took a drink of small
beer.

'I'm sure you would like him. His name is Henry Vaux. I
said you are a great reader and book collector – and he
immediately desired to meet you, as he says the locality is
quite destitute of men of that kind. He has invited us to visit
him this afternoon to take tea. We must go. Perhaps he will
lend you books.'

'I should mention something else of interest,' said Fidelis. 'John Gargrave was amongst our small congregation today, and the Mass was a requiem for the soul of Anne.'

'Of course! I had forgot the Gargraves were of your faith. We shall certainly go over to Altham after our rabbit-pie dinner. Mr Vaux may have useful things to tell us and, besides, I have to see Constable Gubb.'

ELEVEN

We invited Fidelis to join us on our visit to the priest but he excused himself, having correspondence to complete for the next day's postman to Preston. So Elizabeth and I left Matty to watch over Hector and walked briskly by the northward road through Old Accrington. After passing the gates of Hatchfly Hall, the road climbed up the fell to the north that is known as Henfield Moor.

'Did you happen to see Michel de Montaigne's essays among your priest's books?' I asked.

'I did not, but I never looked very closely.'

'I'm hoping he has them. There is a passage somewhere that bears on imposture – which is what Susan Bacon has been telling me about today.'

I mentioned that I had learned that, supposedly, the Harry Hawk who went to war was different when he came back.

'He certainly *was* different,' said Elizabeth. 'He was very much disfigured by his injuries.'

'I mean, what some are saying is that it was an impostor, and not Hawk at all. Mrs Gargrave was the one that started the rumour. She spread it all over the village.'

'I can hardly believe it. His wife would recognize her own husband.'

'I don't know. French cannon fire did alter his appearance and his voice. But it is a puzzling thing all right, which is why I want to get hold of a volume of Montaigne's essays. I am sure he mentions a similar case in France in his own day.'

'Perhaps Mrs Hawk is not particular as to the man's true identity, Titus. To be a widow in a lonely spot is a hard prospect. Maybe she connives in the deception.'

I sighed.

'That's something like what Susan Bacon says.'

At the top of the fell, desolate and windswept under the glaring sun, was a crossroads. Here we turned right and after a couple of miles descended steeply into Altham, a settlement more than twice the size of Accrington. At the village centre an ancient bridge crossed the River Calder, a more substantial river than Accrington's stream.

Constable John Gubb lived in one of a row of cottages close to the bridge. A tiny woman came to answer my knock. When I told her who I was, she immediately reddened and executed an inexpert curtsey.

'Is John Gubb at home?'

'Excuse him, Your Honour, but he's not. He'll be back shortly, or I can send our boy for him.'

'Oh no, don't trouble. Are you Mrs Gubb?'

'Yes, Your Honour.'

'Would you give him this commission and say I shall call again in a couple of hours, if he will be kind enough to wait in for me?'

I handed her the sealed paper, which she held as if it were a holy relic. Leaving her and crossing the bridge, we continued along the street and a quarter mile after the point where the houses petered out we reached the junction with a narrow lane.

'He lives down here,' said Elizabeth.

The lane was grassy and, as I remarked, evidently little used.

'Mr Vaux keeps as far as possible out of view. The families that come here for his Sunday Mass are few.'

'Is that all he does – say Mass?'

'I'm sure he instructs the children and does baptisms, confessions and marriages. But there cannot be many of those.'

The way was soon enclosed by a grove of oaks, on the other side of which lay a scattering of homes around a duckpond. All but one of these were hovels, walled in the material they call 'clat and clay', with roofs of an inferior thatch of wheat stalks and crooked doors roughly assembled from split logs and a carpenter's offcuts. The people were as unkempt as their homes – the children had no shoes, just as the windows had no glass. I thought to myself what marvellous civilizing inventions are shoe leather and window glass, for those that can afford them.

Vaux's house was the exception to this general dilapidation, being larger, glazed upstairs and down, and more solidly built.

We found him dozing by his door in a basket chair, with a book and pair of spectacles on his lap. He was a short man in his fifties, with a straggling white beard and straw hat. His dress was respectable but threadbare: nothing about him suggested the priest.

Starting out of his sleep at the sound of our steps, he greeted us with every sign of pleasure.

'Come inside! Come in, dear Mr and Mrs Cragg! I am glad to welcome you. My mother will bring tea and cakes to the library.'

He ushered us through a hall and into a sizeable room lined with bookshelves from floor to ceiling. There were no signs of the religious uses the room had been put to earlier in the day.

'Oh! You have put everything out of sight,' exclaimed Elizabeth.

'Discretion, Mrs Cragg. It would be unwise of me to display the sacred vessels or have the room look in any way like a chapel. I must keep my head below the battlements, you know, and besides I need this room on weekdays for my library.'

The elderly Mrs Vaux came in with the tea tray. She set it on the table and invited us to sit round. Apart from her apparel and lack of beard, the mother looked very much like the son, and seemed to have a similarly benign temperament. She poured from the pot and distributed the cakes, which were oaten rounds sweetened with honey. The tea was weak.

'So tell me, dear people, what brings you to this corner of the world?' she asked. 'I can only think you were obliged to come, else why would you favour this wilderness over the town?'

'Mother, Mr Cragg is our County Coroner,' said Henry Vaux. 'He is enquiring into the terrible events at Accrington last Sunday.'

'Oh, but that is not why we came here in the first place,' said Elizabeth.

She explained about the outbreak of disease in Preston and our fears for our baby son.

'So your arrival just after the death of Anne Gargrave (God rest her soul) was a matter of chance?' said the priest. 'That

doesn't much surprise me. Folk round here wouldn't be calling
in the likes of a coroner, unless they had no choice. They
prefer to settle all matters of life and death amongst themselves,
not least in a case like this.'

At this juncture old Mrs Vaux sensed we were broaching
matter unseemly to be discussed over tea, and turned to politer
subjects – the weather, the high price of Flanders lace, the
doings of the Court. I was nonplussed by the last topic, as she
kept referring to events in Italy, until I understood she was
speaking of the court of the Pretender, in Rome, though
'Pretender' was not the title she gave to James Edward Stuart.

After half an hour of tea and conversation, she offered to
show Elizabeth her herb garden, leaving Vaux to give me a
tour of the library.

'What I love most in life is an old, rare edition and I have
quite a number here,' he told me with pride.

First he showed me some volumes of his father's and
grandfather's. Vaux's grandfather had been a great playgoer
once, and a lover of the works of William Shakespeare, of
which the priest's library had some unusual editions. He
showed me with reverence one entitled *All Is True*.

'You may know it under its other title, *King Henry the
Eighth*. The printer expected that he would sell vastly more
copies if his customers thought there was nothing invented in
it. He was disappointed, however, as the book is exceedingly
hard to find.'

'I wonder if you have a volume of Michel de Montaigne's
essays? There is a particular one I should like to consult.'

'Sadly not in their original French. I fear they are listed in
Rome's General Index of forbidden books, Montaigne being
a far from godly writer. I do allow myself a little equivocation
in the matter by keeping a copy of them done into English by
John Florio. Allow me to lend them to you.'

He quickly found three volumes and, bringing some string
from his pocket, began to tie them up. After assuring myself
that the women were not yet rejoining us, I reminded Vaux
of what he had been saying earlier at the tea table, before his
mother's intervention.

'Mr Vaux, you mentioned that around here the people like

to deal with a dubious death without calling in any outside agency. That should not continue. It does not do for people to mete out rough justice.'

'They do have magistrates to call on, though it is a pity good Mr Turvey as a Roman Catholic cannot be one. Although he is one of my flock, he does not visit here in the regular way. Poor Thomasina is rather confined to the house, so I have to go to New Manor to give the sacraments.'

'Do you know anything of the circumstances of Mrs Gargrave's death? There is a smell of guilt throughout the village – I sense it everywhere, though no one speaks out. That greatly hinders my enquiry.'

'They may not be guilty so much as ashamed, Cragg. Guilt makes us into cheats and liars but shame wants only to hide itself from sight. Perhaps the people are ashamed for the hatred they have in their hearts.'

'Hatred for what?'

'For us Catholics, of course. We may no longer be liable to be hunted down and arrested, then given a farcical trial and tortured to death. But the laws are still in place and there are those around here who would cheerfully string me up, and many more who would look the other way while they did it. So I suggest the fate of poor Anne Gargrave is merely an instance of the same emotion – which, by the way, no one knows better than Mr Turvey, whose family held to the old religion throughout the worst persecution.'

'Yet anti-popery is not part of the story that's going around,' I said. 'The men I'm led to suspect of instigating the outrage don't appear to be religious men. Two are poachers and the third is an ex-soldier.'

'Forgive me, but that is beside the point. I am saying they believed their actions would escape censure by the majority because the Gargraves are Catholics. Here anti-Catholic feeling is all around us. It is in the air we breathe. So, even if they had non-religious reason to persecute that couple, they could expect to be protected by that sentiment.'

'It is very different in Preston,' I said. 'The Catholics are left alone. There are many of them.'

'Including your delightful wife, and your friend the doctor.'

'Exactly. Preston is a town that prides itself in a certain tolerance in religious affairs.'

Vaux sighed.

'I wish that were the case here. Instead it is all whispering, suspicion and festering hatred. Well, here you are Cragg! Your books securely tied.'

As I took the books and tucked them under my arm the women returned, Elizabeth carrying a large pot of parsley, a gift from the Vaux's garden. It was time to go, and as we said our farewells Vaux pointed to the books he had lent me.

'I am rather inclined to believe the judgement of Rome upon Monsieur de Montaigne. He could not accept the mercy of God.'

'He does not accept much of anything,' I said. 'That is the cast of his mind. It is a mind full of doubt.'

'Ah! Doubt. I am afraid in my profession I am not allowed it.'

'Did you like Mrs Vaux?' I asked as Elizabeth and I made our way back towards Altham.

'Extremely. She is old-fashioned but does not sacrifice her common sense. She has promised, by the way, to bring her son to dinner on Wednesday.'

I must have looked doubtful, for she reproved me with a poke in the arm.

'It will be Midsummer's Eve, Titus. It will be good to have company.'

After crossing the bridge at Altham, we knocked once more at the house of Constable Gubb. A wizened tufty-haired old man with bandy legs and a trembling head came to the door.

'I seek Constable Gubb,' I said. 'Would you be kind enough to fetch your son to me?'

The old fellow let go of the door, tottered sideways, and bounced off the door cheek. He shook his head.

'My son, Sir?' he asked in a reedy voice. 'I have no son, not on this earth, any road. No, it is me you are wanting.'

'Are you the constable?'

Gubb's head continued to shake.

'You are not . . .?'

'Have been for the past twenty-six year.'

I realized it was not only his head that shook but his entire body. The man was palsied. With rapidly weakening faith in his powers, I made my formal request that he summon Hawk to the inquest.

'Don't fret, Mr Cragg,' piped Gubb, showing a bare set of gums. 'I'll have Harry down there in irons if I have to.'

It had become my habit to rise in the middle of the night when Elizabeth got up to see to little Hector, and to read to her while she fed him.

'Tonight we shall have a rest from Dean Swift's ironies and try a passage from Montaigne's essays, which I got from Mr Vaux and are very sincere.'

I had regarded this author as a sure guide to sensible thought ever since Mr Sweeting, my bookseller, had sold me a volume of his essays a couple of years before. I was particularly anxious to try out on my clear-headed wife the passage I had already mentioned where the author discusses an imposture not unlike the one alleged in the case of Harry Hawk. To give it in his own words, it was one whereby 'two men presented themselves one for another', and one of them was hanged, which Montaigne thought unjust.

'Is that what Susan Bacon told you has happened in this case?' asked Elizabeth, lifting our son to her shoulder and patting his back so that he gave a lusty burp. 'Did Hawk and another man exchange places?'

'Not exactly. Supposing her story is to be believed – and I say "supposing" because who is to say if it is true? – we do not know what happened to the old Harry Hawk. The first intelligence was that he had been killed in the battle, and perhaps he was.'

'Then it is different from what your Monsieur is writing about, for he says two men exchanged places.'

'It's close enough. Anyway, Montaigne's point is to question whether the impostor should have been hanged; on the grounds that the full truth of the case remained unknown, or at least misunderstood. And that bears strongly on my own duty, don't you agree? To find the cause is not always to find the truth, or at least it risks only finding a narrow truth and missing the larger and more important one. That is exactly what Henry Vaux was trying to tell me, also.'

'In what way?'

'He's got me thinking I am pursuing the wrong wolf.'

'Is this a wolf hunt?'

'Anne Gargrave died savagely enough. But you see I've been hoping the inquest will find the particular wolf or wolves responsible for it.'

'But we know who they are – the Stirk boys, who obtained the piece of wood.'

'That's very important, yes. And there is also the question of how far Harry Hawk, so-called, was behind them. But these men only started things off. Vaux reminded me that the fatal ride was attended by almost the whole village. So it wasn't a lone wolf, but a wolf pack.'

'More like a herd of cows.'

In spite of myself, I laughed.

'Very well, but that presents the same difficulty. Even if we could identify which cow's trampling hooves struck the fatal blow, we could not with justice simply prosecute that cow. We would have to indict them all.'

TWELVE

In theory, a coroner conducting an inquest has the responsibilities of the author of a novel – or that's how I see it. He alone sees every person's face and notes everything that happens, while the people he observes – audience, jury and witnesses – are all turned towards him. Like the author's characters, they see what he permits them to see, and know what he thinks it proper for them to know. But, I say 'in theory'. In practice, it does not always come out like that. An author can exercise complete control over the proceedings in hand, but a coroner is at the mercy of time and chance, and human whimsy. And the chances of his losing control much increase when the witnesses and jury are strangers to him, and he to them.

I looked around the Chamber Major. The villagers were arrayed before me in their stuff gowns, spit boots and patched buffin coats. Their mouths hung open in bovine fascination, most showing toothless and diseased gums and yellowish mottled tongues, and I felt a sudden surge of disgust. What had they to do with me or I with them? We belonged to different worlds that could never truly connect, however much we called across the void that separated us. To my urban ears their speech sounded like the grunting of pigs, and I sometimes thought the things I had to say to them might as well have been spoken in Hebrew.

Well, the inquest was in progress now. I had already taken the jury across to the church and unsheeted the body for their viewing. Most of these men, though they were from Altham way, had known Anne Gargrave, and probably to a greater or lesser extent disliked her. In front of her mortal remains – which were about to be displayed to them naked, as custom prescribed – these feelings were a little softened, though this did not loosen their rigid views on death and destiny.

'I'll not say I'm glad, but nor do I weep,' said Cyril

Washbrook, adopting a gloomy tone. He was a butcher and the jurors' foreman, elected perhaps because of his familiarity with blood and guts. He was noted for watery eyes, beneath which the skin had formed lugubrious swags or pouches.

'Aye,' said another by the name of Higgs. 'This was ordained so, and so it happened.'

His remark was affirmed by a low chorus of 'Ayes' from several mouths.

'Not ordained but preordained, brother Higgs,' growled James Greaves, a man in the plainest of garb that stood beside him. 'Our sister must take what she gets in the hereafter. She was a papist. It is not our part to pronounce on her, for she is pronounced on already.'

There was a further outbreak of 'Ayes' and 'Well saids'.

'One thing I can pronounce, though,' put in a sandy-haired juror, John Statham. 'In the face, she don't look very like she did alive. She used to look like a vixen, and now she's more like a rabbit.'

'That's right, Johnny. She don't look so sharp-faced,' said another, Thomas Wharton, with a snorting laugh that he quickly suppressed.

'Please pay attention,' I said, raising my hand. 'You are not here to rule on the woman's character, only on how she died and on whether it was natural or unnatural. Now, let us look.'

I drew away the sheet and revealed the body. Once the men had recovered from shock at the evidence of Fidelis's surgical investigations – a roughly sewn-up gash from her breastbone to her navel – I pointed out the injuries she had received.

'We can see numerous bruises about the body – here, here and here, then here and here. And, as Mr Statham has accurately pointed out, there are several more about the face which are quite disfiguring. Note them well.'

I was using a wooden rule to measure the worst of Anne Gargrave's bruises and cuts, while Mrs Nightingale noted down the details.

'There are bumps and scrapes on top of the skull, but nothing so serious as might kill her.'

'How did she die, then?' asked Statham.

'That's what we're here to discover, boy,' the butcher told him sternly.

Statham turned to me.

'However shall us, though, Mr Cragg, if she was not killed by the wounds that appear?'

'We shall hear evidence from the doctor and that will help us judge.'

I covered the body with the sheet.

'Shall we go then?'

The audience had grown restive during the half hour we were away, but having settled the court, I was able to call the first witness, the Gargraves' servant, Gerald Piper, whom I had identified as first finder. He told how he had stayed indoors during the disturbance, being afraid, but when it was all over had come out and helped John Gargrave into the house. He had then gone back to fetch his mistress.

'She were lying in the wet ground. I tried to get her to rise, but she were senseless.'

'Was she alive?'

'I couldn't tell straight away, Sir. I called the boy and we carried her inside and to bed. Not that her bed could do her any good, like, because it was then we found she were dead as a stone.'

'In other words, she had died before you put her to bed?'

'Yes, Sir.'

Piper had nothing to add, so I called for Susan Bacon. I wanted the court to hear the view of the village as a whole, which I believed she represented. The witness scurried forward in her haste to become the centre of attention, but as soon as she sat in the chair and felt every eye upon her she became abashed. So the first of my questions about how the stang ride began, and what happened as it progressed, elicited no more than monosyllabic answers.

'Did you witness the stang ride meted out on Mr and Mrs Gargrave?'

'Oh aye, I saw it. Everybody did.'

'But not everybody was active in it. Were you?'

'If you mean did I follow the stang, then yes, I did. A crowd of us did.'

'Several times up and down the village street?'

'Yes.'

'And some people were banging pots and others were throwing missiles of various kinds at the unhappy couple?'

'Yes.'

'Did you yourself throw things?'

'I may have. I don't remember.'

'Do you know who were the instigators of this? The ringleaders?'

'I don't know.'

'Were Simon and Charles Stirk among them?'

'I couldn't say.'

'What about Harry Hawk?'

'Happen.'

'That is not what you told me yesterday, is it? You said you thought he was in on it from the very start.'

'I am saying what I meant yesterday, if only you'd been listening, was he *might* have been and he might *not*.'

'Do you not think the guilt for this crime is spread wider than two – or three – men? That there is a common guilt in all those who took part in the stang ride?'

'I do not speak of guilt, Sir.'

'Well shame, then. Do not folk feel any shame for what happened to Anne Gargrave?'

'It may look different to someone like yourself – not knowing country ways – but the stang wasn't meant to do her harm, only good. It was to remind her not to spoil her life, and everyone else's, by being a shrew. It were to tell her to be ruled by her husband like a proper wife, and not the other way around.'

'And what about John Gargrave? Why was he made to ride?'

'He were stanged because he wouldn't put his wife in her place. He let her rule his roost, as you might say, contrary to the commandment of God which is in the Book of Genesis.'

'Are there not less cruel ways of teaching such a lesson?'

'There's more than one sort of cruelty, Mr Cragg. There is that which means to be cruel, and that which means to be kind. The stang is the second sort. If Anne Gargrave hadn't learned to behave herself by the age of forty, she would not learn by being told. She had to suffer or else never learn.'

'Were there some there with other reasons for wanting Mrs Gargrave to suffer? Not such worthy reasons?'

'How do you mean?'

'You were telling me yesterday about Harry Hawk, who she called a fake.'

'I don't know what you are talking about.'

I repeated the question in a different form, but I could not get Mrs Bacon to repeat what she had told me the previous day about Hawk.

There was a small disturbance at the back of the room. The big doors creaked open and the boy that I had last seen at Clayton's Quarry appeared. Behind him, his hand clamped on the boy's shoulder, Billy Whist shuffled into the room.

'Ah, Billy Whist!' I said. 'The court is right glad to see you. May we also hear from you? Would you please bring him up to the chair? You may get down, Mrs Bacon.'

The boy brought the blind man to the front, stood him in front of the chair, and then pressed the top of his head so that he sat down. Frances Nightingale passed over the Bible and Billy swore the oath, using a light, ironic voice.

'Mr Whist,' I said, 'you were present at the ordeal of Mrs Gargrave on the tenth day of this month?'

'Aye.'

'Did you understand why you and many other villagers were there?'

'Aye. To deal with a shrew wife.'

'And make her ride the stang.'

'Aye.'

'Is this an old custom?'

'As old as Methuselah.'

'But it had not been practised around here in living memory, I have been told. Was it you that told the young people how it is done?'

'No.'

'You did not instruct them in the conduct of a stang ride?'

'I did not.'

'That is contrary to what you told me at your house the other day.'

'It may happen you didn't follow my meaning.'

'You were speaking in English were you not?'

His face twisted into a leer.

'Aye, but the English of here is not the same as your Preston English.'

'Did you have a conversation of any sort with the Stirk brothers or Harry Hawk in the days before the tenth of June?'

'I might have.'

'Where?'

'In the Black Bull, like as not.'

'And what did you tell them?'

'I told them nowt. They were telling me.'

'Telling you what?'

'I was needed with my fiddle. They wanted some rough music next Sunday.'

'Rough music?'

'Pots and pans and clappers. Bull bells. Anything to make an infernal noise. When there's call for it I untune my strings, see?'

He sniggered.

'It sounds horrible. Musical torture.'

'Did they say why they wanted this rough music?'

'They said I'd see on the day. I near pissed myself laughing at that. I couldn't see a bloody thing to save my life.'

There seemed little point in continuing with this flim-flam. I gave it up for a bad job and let Billy Whist go, calling instead for Peter Castleford.

He stumped to the witness chair and occupied it with confident ease, crossing his wooden leg with his good one and swinging it.

'You are the village carpenter?'

'I am.'

'I understand you were not present when Mr and Mrs Gargrave were subjected to the stang?'

'I wasn't.'

'Most people were there – why were you not?'

'I wanted no part of it, so I went over to my sister's in Altham for a visit.'

'So you knew in advance there was something like that in the air?'

'Two men came to my workshop on the Saturday morning, asking for the loan of a spar of wood, see? I asked what for and they said it was for trying out as a gatepost, and they'd pay me for it later if it served, or bring it back if not. But then I heard a whisper up in the village of some action against Mrs Gargrave being planned for Sunday, so I guessed what that spar was really for.'

'Was your spar returned?'

'Aye. I found it on Monday morning in my yard.'

'What state was it in – was there blood on it?'

'No. It was clean. Happen it'd been scrubbed. There were nail holes in it, I noticed, that hadn't been there before. That's all.'

'And who were the two men who came to your shop?'

'They were Simon and Charles Stirk.'

'Thank you, Mr Castleford. You may get down.'

I ran my eye around the room.

'I would like to call one of the Stirk brothers, but I do not see them. Simon or Charles – either would do. Can anyone say where they are?'

Heads turned this way and that, and lips moved in a flurry of whispers, but there was no word on either Stirk brother.

'Then Harry Hawk. Is he present?'

The susurrations and head-turning intensified, but to no greater purpose. Gubb, for all his promises, had failed to deliver Hawk. Like the Stirks, he had chosen to keep away. Having seen the constable's age and decrepitude, I was exasperated but not surprised at his failure, and turned to the next witness on my list. This one would have the most difficult of all my questions to answer.

'Would John Gargrave come forward, please?'

However painful it would be for him, I had little choice but to call Gargrave. He had been next to his wife when she died, and had suffered much the same torment as her. I could only hope that his evidence would steer the jury in my preferred direction, and that he would not break down in giving it. I took a deep breath and began.

'Mr Gargrave, were you contentedly married?'

He cut a pale figure in the chair and his voice trembled when he spoke.

'No more so, nor less so, than most that have lived in one house twelve years together.'

'Were you aware of what your neighbours thought of how you two were together?'

'Aye, I've heard some hard words against us.'

'What sort of words?'

'That I didn't rule her as I should, like Susan Bacon was saying just now.'

'Was that true?'

'It might have been better if she were a good obedient wife, but then that wouldn't have been her, d'you see? It wasn't in her.'

'How did this show itself?'

'She was always ready with a strong opinion. She would not be corrected. Many's the time we've disagreed and she would never give me the last word.'

His eyes were growing watery as he remembered.

'So you're saying that, in common parlance, she was a shrewish woman?'

'That's not my word but it's one way of saying it, yes. It was just her nature to be forward.'

'But in many people's eyes she did deserve the traditional punishment that she got last Sunday?'

Gargrave had been staring down at his interlaced fingers. Now he glanced up, his eyes flicking this way and that for a few seconds, before he looked down again.

'I suppose she might have.'

'And what about you? Did *you* deserve it?'

This time there was no nervous glance up, but only an inaudible murmur.

'Speak up, please, Mr Gargrave.'

'I reckon I might have an' all.'

There could hardly be any clearer indication of Gargrave's

distressed, even broken, state than this public admission. I had respect and sympathy for the man, but thought he would have done better to deny his tormentors the satisfaction of hearing such an answer.

'May we turn to the men said to have started it off? Deplorably the Stirk brothers are not here to speak for themselves, but it has been said that they disliked you.'

'I don't know. They had no cause.'

'How did they treat you on that Sunday?'

'They took the lead in everything. Their eyes were crazy.'

'What about Harry Hawk?'

The witness lifted his head at last. 'What about him?'

'I have been told that your wife was telling tales about him – that he was an impostor, come back from the war in place of the real Harry Hawk – and that's why he might have encouraged people to persecute you.'

'She thought she had cause for her suspicion. He was arguing with me about his rent one day and he shook his army discharge papers in front of my eyes. It was only for a moment but I could see there was a different name on them.'

'What name?'

'I believe it was Martin Ware, or some such.'

'Did you question him on that point?'

'Yes. He said he had signed on under an assumed name.'

'And did you believe him?'

'I was prepared to at first. My wife, when I told her, was suspicious.'

'Why were you prepared to take him at his word, contrary to your wife's opinion?'

'I thought there might be an innocent explanation. But Anne, she said we'd heard in the first place that Harry Hawk had been killed, and happen it was a true report, and this fellow had taken our tenant's place, see? His hair and eyes were the right colour, but with his face all disfigured he was impossible to recognize for certain.'

'Mrs Hawk, his wife, had accepted him, however.'

'Even so, my wife told me we couldn't be sure. She made me think about it again by telling me that if he were an impostor it would make the tenancy at Gunwright's Heath invalid in law.'

This, of course, might have been true. It would depend on how the lease was written.

'And do you consider this suspicion of hers caused the man to wish harm on your wife?'

'It's possible.'

I told Gargrave he could leave the chair and called Luke Fidelis, asking him first to describe the injuries he'd seen when examining the deceased.

'And in your medical opinion,' I said, when he had finished, 'did any of these injuries cause Mrs Gargrave to die?'

'They did not, or not directly. Mrs Gargrave drowned.'

This caused a new outbreak of whispering among the audience.

'Please explain, Doctor.'

'She was found lying in a rut filled with water. I think she fell into it face down in a faint and so began to drown. Awakening, but weakened and without thought, she inhaled thick mud from the rut's bottom. It stopped her nose and mouth. She could not breathe, and so succumbed.'

'If not for the ordeal she had just undergone, would she still have died?'

'I think a healthy person would have got up out of the water, coughed, and gone on her way. But judging from her wounds, Mrs Gargrave had suffered much. She was weakened, and by the end her wits may have been astray.'

'Thank you, Doctor. You may leave the witness chair.'

Now it was time for me to give my summary of evidence. When I had done so, I concluded as usual with some instruction about possible verdicts.

'Gentlemen, you have, as I have told you, only to decide the manner and cause of Mrs Gargrave's death, nothing more, nothing less. I think we can rule out self-slaughter, so I shall lay before you five possible findings. First, you may decide that she gave up the ghost by some natural cause, such as the failure of her heart. Second, you may think her death was an act of God – in other words, an accident without any human agency.'

Up to this point they had been listening to me intently. Now

I noticed the Puritan Greaves whisper something to Higgs, his neighbour. Higgs did not reply, but Tom Wharton, on Greaves's other side, plucked his sleeve and shushed him. They two exchanged scowling looks.

'Your third possibility,' I went on, 'is that she was murdered deliberately by a felon with malice aforethought. And your fourth is that she died by chance medley. In case you have not heard that phrase before, I should explain that "chance medley" refers to a death caused by another's actions that, even if they were violent, were never intended to kill. Last of all, if you cannot agree on any of the positive verdicts I have already mentioned – and I very strongly urge that you do agree on one of them – you may return a finding of death by causes unknown. However, I must tell you that I would consider such a verdict lazy, unsatisfactory, and not in the best interests of anyone. It must be a last resort.'

It only remained for the jurors to discuss all this among themselves. I brought them to a huddle around my table, reminding them to try for civility and unanimity, and then stepped back.

I was at the side of the room speaking with Frances Nightingale when we heard the first raised voices from amongst them.

'Cause of death? There's nobbut one cause of death, brother Wharton, and that is God's will.'

This was the voice of James Greaves. Tom Wharton's reply was equally vehement.

'And does God will a man to be murdered? Answer me that.'

'Aye, it's all one.'

'That cannot be. That's a mortal sin, man! Is tha saying God's a mortal sinner?'

Another juror laughed.

'I've lived a long time and I never heard that!'

'Tha'll not live much longer if tha make mock of the Almighty.'

'Don't tell me how long I shall live. I'll see more years than tha'll.'

A fist was shaken across the table.

'By God's hooks, I'll black those eyes of thine and tha'll see none of 'em.'

'Shall tha try? Or are tha shy?'

A moment before, the jurors had been standing around the table engaged in a common task. Now all of a sudden two of them were sprawled on it, kicking and punching at each other while the others took sides, cursing into each other's faces, tweaking their noses and yanking their hair.

I had picked up my bell and papers when I left the table. Now I began furiously to ring the bell and to shout for order. There was no response. Indeed, there were more bodies wrestling and punching each other, on and around the table, which was bouncing under their weight. One of these was sent reeling towards me, and in my surprise I pushed him away with full force. He staggered backwards, lost his balance, and fell on to the table. With a loud crack the boards split and the table legs collapsed, leaving the entangled men rolling in the ruins. This shock did not stop the fighting, but seemed to intensify it. I could hear the audience, who were thoroughly enjoying the brawl, cheering in encouragement. One enormously fat young fellow in the front row stepped forward to join in, kicking one body in the ribs and kneeling on another's chest while roaring abuse into his face. I retreated to the wall, picked up two of the fire buckets from their stations, and gave one to Frances. Then I caught Luke Fidelis's eye in the middle of the room and nodded at a third bucket standing within his reach. He understood me instantly, seized the bucket, and came to my side. As one, we hurled our water, mine and Frances's into the writhing heap of jurors and his over the head of the violent young giant.

Instantaneously the brawl was stilled. Some of the combatants started up, howling in surprise, their mouths locked open. The fat one gasped and could not have looked more stunned had Fidelis walloped his head with a broomstick. Another fellow seemed to freeze in the act of biting another man's arm. And yet another stopped on one leg, just as he was swinging back his foot for a kick, and straight away fell over. Then, all at once, the tableau subsided into embarrassment and rueful laughter, and the battle of the Chamber Major was over.

THIRTEEN

I supervised the bruised and, some of them, bleeding jurors as they cleared the broken bits of table to one side. Then I ordered the non-jurors back to their seats, while forming the jury itself into two head-hanging ranks, like a sorry platoon of the militia.

'Is this seemly?' I barked. 'Is it reasonable? Is this how theological questions are settled in the Lancashire countryside? By the evidence of my own eyes I am forced to believe it. But howsoever that may be, this inquest does not turn on Scripture, which is the law of God. Here, we are only concerned with earthly law. I know that earthly law is imperfect and sometimes disappoints, but it serves a necessary purpose. Do not disrespect it.'

For the most part, they now looked as crestfallen as defeated fighting cocks – though not Greaves, who was standing with his back upright and his jaw jutting. When I said I expected a verdict on which they could all agree, Washbrook stepped forward and took me to one side.

'It's not on, Mr Cragg,' he said in a low voice. 'We'll never all agree. Greaves for one will not give up his opinion that it was an act of God and cannot be questioned.'

I glanced at the Puritan for whom 'act of God' covered everything from a tray of burned cakes to a European war.

I sighed.

'Very well, I will accept the verdict of the other eleven, without Mr Greaves.'

'I'll try, Sir.'

They conferred together in a huddle for five minutes, after which Washbrook returned to me.

'It doesn't end with Greaves, Mr Cragg. Some of us think she had a disease and would have died anyway, others that it was an accident, and others that she was murdered. As to the who and the why of it, I have as many opinions as I have jurors.'

I thought I had given them firm directions in my summary of evidence. Now, I began to wonder if these had been firm enough.

'You must try harder to agree, Washbrook. Impress on them what we heard from the doctor – that Mrs Gargrave drowned. Then you ask yourself what caused this to happen. Go on!'

They went into a huddle again and I watched over them from a distance, attentively. The group remained very agitated and, while physically the fight had gone out of them, the moral argument continued. I began to suspect that their 'grunting of pigs' was no such thing, but a language that, however strange to the educated ear, was quite capable of expressing serious thought, as well as having all the arts of evasion, duplicity and equivocation. The more fool me, I thought, for underestimating these men.

After another few minutes, Washbrook came to me again.

'Excepting Greaves, they'll agree on "cause of death unknown" – nothing more, since every man has a different explanation for it, and won't be shifted.'

I sighed.

'Very well, man, so be it.'

So it would be an indefinite verdict, and not even a unanimous one. I felt ashamed that the Gargraves would get no justice, but there was little more I could do. The proper procedure had been followed, and at least John Gargrave could now bury his wife and have the priest recite her requiem.

Mr Turvey had asked Elizabeth and me, as well as Fidelis and Mrs Nightingale, to stay after the end of the inquest and dine with him. Fidelis refused, saying he had to leave for Preston at once, but my wife and I accepted and were soon sitting together over slices of potato-and-ham pie, with pickles, in the Chamber Minor. I said how unhappy I felt at the chaos into which the inquest had degenerated and its unsatisfactory outcome.

'You must not be downhearted, Titus,' said Elizabeth tenderly. 'You could not have foreseen such discord amongst the jury.'

'Does the fellow Greaves really believe what he says, though? Or is it mischief?' I said.

'Oh, he believes it,' said Frances Nightingale. 'He is a complete determinist. I hate such beliefs.'

'So do I,' said Elizabeth. 'We are the only beings with the faculty of reason – must we deny that? In Mr Greaves's view we cannot love justice or love each other. In Mr Greaves's world, we cannot even think.'

Our host had been eating silently, and seemed little interested in the discussion. But now he eagerly seized on Elizabeth's remark to pull the conversation in a direction more to his taste.

'But *are* we the only thinking beings, Mrs Cragg? There are many who reckon the beehive possesses something like rationality, you know. No bee can reason by itself, of course, but when you put them all together as a hive they together constitute something like a thinking brain.'

'What do they think about, do you suppose?'

'The bees range into our gardens and homes, so we may suppose the hive is actively interested in the affairs of men and women – indeed, some say they take an interest in order to have an influence over us.'

'How can the bees have influence over humans?' I said. 'They belong to a sphere apart – the insect world.'

'It is not so strange, Mr Cragg,' said Turvey. 'After all, we are intensely interested in their affairs, so why should they not be equally so in ours? Also, it has long been thought that they have the power to turn away evil and bring good. That's why it's been recommended – since bible times, if not before – to converse with the bees and confide in 'em.'

This was hard to take seriously.

'You mean to say you solemnly go to the beehives and talk to them?'

'Oh yes. I talk to them as I work with them, and Thomasina too speaks to them regularly.'

'Do you, Thomasina?'

'Oh yes, Mr Cragg, once a week at least,' she said.

'And what do you talk to them about, Thomasina?'

'I inform them of everything that passes in Accrington,' Thomasina said. 'I read to them from my journal, which I write every day. They are avid for all kinds of news, you know – births and deaths especially, but also the coming of strangers.'

'Do you go around all the hives, then, even those far from the house?'

'There's no need. It's enough to give the news to a few bees in the garden here. They are such gossips that soon every hive in the neighbourhood has heard everything. I make sure my father's hives are the best informed anywhere in the North Country.'

'So you must have told them of our arrival here?'

'Of course I did. They were very interested.'

'So did you also tell them – for instance – of the doubtful return of Harry Hawk?'

'I told them everything I know about him. That he is sadly maimed about the face so as to be unrecognizable and that he may be an impostor, although his wife has accepted him, which is a pretty strong mark in his favour. I expect the bees sent scouts up to Gunwright's Heath to have a look at him.'

'And what did they report back?'

She looked at me with mock pity for my ignorance.

'They don't tell *me*, Mr Cragg! They tell their Queen, I expect.'

When we had eaten, Turvey proposed that I come with him to look at some of the hives he had installed to the west of New Accrington, in Clover Field, a meadow he owned that was particularly abundant in clover.

'I expect a rich harvest of honey this year, especially from the clover,' he said. 'The climate has been highly favourable. A week of gentle rain until a fortnight ago, and since then uninterrupted sunshine making the bees full of energy and enterprise.'

We set off, walking through the part of New Accrington known as the Higher Fold. Here a dozen cottages were concentrated around a stream, the Woodnook Brook, that ran in from the west to meet the Hyndburn just south of New Manor. The water in this stream was low and sluggish but there were enough pools to entertain some naked Higher Fold children. We saw them splashing and shrieking in the water as we crossed the broad stepping stones and turned off the southerly road to follow the rising path beside the beck. Soon after this we heard, mingled with their cries, the pounding of hooves and turned to see a rider on an imposing bay horse galloping down at speed from the Accrington side. The rider's hat was pulled low over his head.

'Coming through!' he shouted in a rasping voice. 'Out of the way, damn you, out of the way!'

The children leapt out of his path as he took the stream in one great leap.

'That is Grevel Horntree,' I said. 'Where's he going in such a hurry?'

As Horntree's mount thundered away along the southerly road we clearly heard his whip coming down on the horse's rump.

'Happen Manchester,' was all Turvey would say on the subject.

Calling at one of the cottages, we collected Seb Cook, who Turvey had engaged and had been training up as his new helper in the apiaries, in succession to the dismissed Harry Hawk. We chatted with Cook's mother while the youth, a lad of twelve or thirteen, clobbered himself up in beekeeper's gear, and then we set off again up the rising path beside the Woodnook. We passed a few more clat-and-clay cottages, interspersed with fields where cattle and goats grazed. The smell of flowering grass was heady and soothing, and the vexations of the morning slowly dissolved like ice in the sun as we climbed.

After fifteen minutes, we took a rest. Behind us lay a distant view down on to the roof of New Manor and the church tower, though the bulk of the village was hidden by trees. Turvey, his theme as usual being apiculture, was talking about the poet Vergil, though it was not the epic poem of how Aeneas escaped from burning Troy and founded Rome that beguiled him.

'The greatest five hundred lines of verse ever written are to be found in the fourth book of Vergil's *Georgicks*. You know it, of course.'

'I believe I read it as a schoolboy.'

'Almost entirely devoted to bees, you see. How to keep them, how to humour them, how to capture a swarm, and so on. To call a swarm down to a new hive he advises clashing cymbals together, or was it tinkling brass? When a colony swarms, folk still do give them noise – or "rough music," as we call it – to get them down. Wooden spoons on pots and pans, and the like.'

'I've heard the phrase,' I said. 'Billy Whist construed it for me.'

'Ah! Billy knows more than most about rough music.'

We crossed the stream by a plank bridge and started up a twisty rising lane towards a narrow wood about half a mile further on. Soon the path rejoined the brookside and followed it through the whole length of the wood, after which we climbed another four hundred yards to a fine viewing place, where we paused again to catch our breath.

Turvey gestured to a prominent hill that lay far away across the valley in the south-east.

'See over there? That's Boggart Hill. At its foot there's a well that folk not very politely call Lady May's Hole.'

'Who was Lady May?'

He shrugged.

'Who knows? Some old witch from long ago, I expect. In two day's time it'll be Midsummer's Day, and all the people hereabouts will be out there for the Lady May's Hole game. The people not taking part climb the hill to watch the game's end. Have you heard about it?'

'No. What is it?'

'It's an old raggermash of a game between Old Accrington and New,' said Turvey. 'They've done it every year for centuries. We've tried to stop it, but they pay us no mind.'

I had heard of these country sports – football, cricket, wrestling – that happened seasonally and always ended in broken bones.

'I expect it is violent.'

'Oh yes. They call it a ball game, but don't be fooled. It's a battle.'

We set off again, and now the ground levelled off. The fields on either side were enclosed by dry-stone walls and inhabited successively by sheep and goats and, in the last field, by a bull.

'Farmer Oldroyd's bull, is that,' said Turvey. 'He's famously sociable. Loves people.'

'Mr Oldroyd?'

He laughed.

'No, not Fred. He's genial enough. His bull's the one I mean. The animal's like a dog for loving human company. He likes cow company too, of course. He services most of the cattle around here.'

We now came to the gate of the sloping, undulating Clover Field. It contained six beehives standing in an arc in one corner, protected on one side by a well-made fence of wooden poles and on the other by the bulk of a small stone building, some kind of old barn or byre. The bees were placed here in the field's corner so that, as Turvey explained, the barn and corner hedgerows would shelter them from the cold of the prevailing wind – 'Exactly as Mr Vergil recommends,' he added. Not that there was any cold wind today.

Access to the apiary was gained by a wicket gate, through which Turvey now ushered me. He went into the barn and fetched a pair of leather gloves. One or two of the straw-made hives – or skeps, as Turvey called them – showed signs of leaning, and he went around instructing Seb in how to gently straighten them. I was struck by how the skeps hummed from within, and vibrated warmly to the touch like an animal body. Each was provided with its own small doorway, and below it a short length of flat wood to make a doorstep where the forager bees could land and take flight. Meanwhile, others walked around about the entrance – on guard duty, so Turvey told me.

'It is like a row of houses,' I said. 'Or a hamlet.'

'Ah yes, and bees are admirable hamlet-dwellers. They cooperate with their fellows all day and night.'

He pointed at one of the skeps.

'Look there! Watch how they deal with a foolhardy wasp.'

The wasp had landed on one of the doorsteps and seemed intent on going inside.

'It's attracted by the honey smell,' said Turvey. 'But attempted robbery isn't a very clever idea.'

At first just a single bee landed on the wasp and the two insects tangled, as in a wrestling match. The wasp seemed to be getting the better of the bout, but now other bees joined in, one after another, until the interloper was entirely overwhelmed, lost in a writhing, stinging knot of indignant bees. After about a minute, just as they had joined the fight, the defenders began to leave off – until just two remained by the now supine and feebly twitching wasp. This pair seemed to confer for a moment, gesticulating with their antennae, then moved into position and rolled the robber off the ledge to lie and rot in the grass. It had all been done with a perfect economy of effort.

'There's a lesson there,' said Turvey with a certain pride. 'The wasp is stronger than the bee, and it may be that its sting is deadlier. Yet by ganging together the bees prevail.'

He returned to the barn to deposit his gloves, and I glanced through the door. The musty cobwebbed interior contained a collection of tools pertaining to apiary and agriculture, two or three spare skeps, some fencing posts and a bale or two of straw. Turvey closed the door and we left the enclosure to walk around the large undulating field. I noticed that a long bed of dug earth had been worked along the dry-stone wall behind the barn.

'I have sown flowers there: stocks and foxgloves, cranesbill and roses, all kinds. They will provide my bees with plenty of good nectar when the clover ends.'

We walked down the steeply sloping field to its farthest declension, beside a wooded copse. I remarked that the clover was still very dense underfoot.

'Oh, yes, we'll have a good honey crop this year, a very good one,' Turvey chirped happily. Never have I seen a man more at one with his surroundings than Tom Turvey was in that place, on that day.

We completed the tour of the field and set off on our way back down the track. Less than an hour later I reached the front door of the Dower House, and to my surprise found Luke Fidelis's saddle horse tethered beside the front door. He was sitting inside at the table, dressed for riding but with writing materials and a sheet of paper in front of him. He had only written a few words. There were several botched attempts crumpled on the floor at his feet.

'I thought you would be halfway to Preston by now,' I said. 'What's kept you?'

'A quandary, Titus,' he said. 'Read this.'

He handed me a sheet of paper covered in a small well-formed conventional script. What that script conveyed was far from conventional.

Dear Sir,

I send this to you secretly by the hand of my trusted servant Peggy Stirk. I can only write to you secretly as any letter that I send with my husband's knowledge is first read through by him. If he does not approve it, he immediately tears it up. He would certainly tear this up, as I am writing to tell you of his cruelty towards me and to appeal to you for help.

When you saw me at Peggy's house swooning, I could not speak. I did not even know you were there. But Peggy has given me an account of the whole of the circumstance. She says you are an honest gentleman who is very kindly disposed towards me and would wish to help me in any way possible.

My husband is a violent man in word and action. In drink his violence becomes extreme. He often curses and rails at his enemies, both those that are real and others he imagines, but even more often he is content to abuse me.

All this I could perhaps bear but it is the confinement of my life in this house that tortures me most. My present predicament is well expressed in a dream I have had more than once. I find myself enclosed in a hole in the wall, just like a cupboard with a locked door over it preventing my escape. The cupboard is dark and stifling and it seems that my imprisonment there is for ever. But sometimes the dream lets me know that there is one who will come and release me from this hell.

I have the temerity to hope that you may be the one. Please write to me only through Peggy Stirk at Lodge Cottage.

Flora Horntree

'Great God, Luke!' I exclaimed when I had read the letter through twice. 'She has latched on to you indeed. How are you going to get out of this?'

'I don't mean to get out of it. My difficulty lies in how best to help her.'

'I don't see how you can. I mean, not safely. Horntree is a jealous husband and, as she says herself, a violent one. He may murder you, and if he does the law will take his side.'

Fidelis began writing again.

'I agree that intervening is not without risk. But I must do something.'

He added only two more lines to the letter, then blotted and folded it.

'I've written that I cannot avoid going away to Preston today,' he said as he warmed the sealing wax, 'but will return as soon as I can, and that she'll hear from me again then.'

He dripped the wax and stamped it, then tucked it into his coat pocket.

'I must be on my way. I'll leave this with Peggy Stirk as I pass the gate of the Hall.'

He strode to the door, then turned as if for an afterthought.

'Oh! I should add that I've taken the liberty of mentioning your name, as someone she might appeal to in case of need while I am away.'

Before I could reply, he had gone.

Three hours later, after darkness had fallen, as I was reading Montaigne by candlelight while Elizabeth and Matty played a game of cards at the table, there came a rap on the front door. Rather than disturb the women's game, I picked up the candle and went to open it myself. A woman stood there with a valise beside her and wearing a traveling cloak, its hood concealing her head and much of her face. In the flickering candlelight, I saw strands of fair hair within the hood and features that seemed regular and pleasing.

'I am Flora Horntree,' she said in a clear and, so it seemed to me, defiant tone, 'and I have come to throw myself upon your protection.'

FOURTEEN

'Does your husband know of this, Mrs Horntree?' I said.

I had ushered her in and she was sitting with us drinking tea. Despite having announced her seemingly urgent need for protection, our unexpected visitor had been in no hurry to explain herself. Instead, spotting Hector on Elizabeth's knee, she had cast off her cloak, knelt by their side, and begun chucking him under the chin while exclaiming over his charm and chubbiness. Her facial swellings had disappeared and she exhibited none of the lassitude that had perturbed Fidelis at the Hatchfly Lodge. When tea was brought, she rose from her knees and, just as if this were an ordinary social call, took her place at the table.

'He does not,' she said.

'I ask about your husband, Madam, because I am wondering if we should prepare for the arrival of Mr Horntree himself, looking for you.'

She shook her head, drawing attention to the dangling pearl earrings she wore, which matched the rope of small pearls gracing her neck.

'No one knows I have come here. Grevel is in Manchester. Even when he returns, he won't know I am absent.'

'And you have recovered from your ailment?'

'Oh yes, it was nothing.'

'I trust your husband is pleased.'

This was a calculated remark. I wasn't in the slightest interested in whether Grevel Horntree was pleased, but I did want to know more about his attitude to his wife's ill-health.

'My husband hasn't noticed. He is absorbed in some project he is subscribing to, which constantly takes him to Manchester. I have locked my bedroom door, as I have done in the past, and left a note to say I wished not to see him. He will ignore me, as always, expecting me to come out in due course and

take my punishment. But this time, of course, I won't come
out as I am not there! The stratagem will afford me at least
another day before he starts to look for me, I am sure.'

'But to what purpose?'

'That is simple. I have quit my marriage.'

Her words were plain enough, spoken as a matter of fact.

'Oh, goodness!' exclaimed Elizabeth. 'You have left your
home and mean never to return?'

'Not ever. I would rather die.'

This alternative was not one I liked the sound of.

'Please do not speak of dying, Madam. We are very sorry
for you, of course, though we would like to know the reason for
your distress and why you need our help.'

'I ask for shelter only until your doctor friend returns. He
wrote to me assurances of his protection. I rely on him. I trust
he will convey me to safety.'

'Are you quite certain you have understood him right?'
Elizabeth said. 'Nobody is more scrupulous than Dr Fidelis
when he engages himself professionally. But this is hardly a
professional matter, and I wonder if he means you to abandon
your home.'

'I am sure he will approve of it.'

'But Fidelis would only come between a man and his wife
in dire circumstances.'

'These circumstances are the direst.'

Tears glazed her eyes.

'Mine was not a home but a prison. Oh, Mrs Cragg, I know
it will be hard for you to believe, yourself having a husband
who is kind. Mine spends much time away from me, and is
unkind whenever he sees me.'

She glanced at me, and her eyelids fluttered to stop the tears
falling. I will admit this was a sight so pretty that the iciest
heart would have melted as she went on.

'I am that most defenceless of creatures, Mr Cragg, a woman
driven from her home in fear for her own life, with not a
penny piece. Most of the world does not sympathize, I know
that. Women who suffer abuse within doors are told by other
women they can stop it by mending their naughty behaviour.
Men, of course, rally to their own sex. If they are bad husbands

themselves, they will defend another bad one. If they are
not, they are blind to the cruelty of those who are. If all is
well in the kingdom of marriage, it must ever be so.'

'You say you were abused, Madam,' I said. 'In what way
was that? Will you be specific?'

'He kept me like a prisoner. I could do nothing and go
nowhere except he expressly approved it. And if I defied him,
he was not above raising his hand to me and – yes, Mr Cragg!
– even striking me.'

She mopped her eyes with a handkerchief and raised her
face, giving a decisive sniff and a wan smile.

'But let us speak of happier things. What a pet your little
boy is! How soon will he walk? When will he speak?'

The rest of the evening was passed in the discussion of
comparatively trivial matters, such as the welfare of babies,
domestic life, the latest modes of dress in Preston, and the
best shops in London as they used to be when Mrs Horntree
lived there. In the conveniencies of the latter she seemed
particularly knowledgeable.

Later, with Flora Horntree lodged in the second servant's
room, and Hector settled to sleep in his cot, Elizabeth crept
into bed and into my arms.

'How long will it be,' she whispered, 'before her husband
catches up with her?'

'He has gone to Manchester. She came out alone, hooded,
and after dark. She told no one she would come here. She has
calculated that it will be some time before he is even aware
she has taken this step.'

'But what will he do when he does find out? I hope she
does not stay long. She brings trouble, Titus.'

'We cannot refuse to help her, not only by the rules of
Christian hospitality but because we are Luke's friends and
we know he has offered to help her.'

'If he has, he did so as a doctor. She, on the other hand,
thinks he is Sir Lancelot du Lac.'

'Well, there *are* elements of the knight errant in our friend.'

'But in this case, may she not be reading him wrong? The
letter he wrote to her had but two sentences in it, yet she
purports to read into them that he will go to all lengths to help

her flee from Hatchfly Hall and become her protector – and who knows what else?'

'She has put her whole future in hazard by running away. It cannot have been for nothing.'

Elizabeth turned until her mouth was close to my ear and said in the softest, slyest whisper, 'I think she's a schemer, Titus, as well as a flibbertigibbet. I think Flora Horntree is tired of marriage to a boorish fellow in a dull place and is looking for a way out.'

'That is a very suspicious thought, my love,' I said. 'Is it not a little unworthy?'

'I was prepared to think that until I took her up to her room just now. She brazenly asked me for money.'

'She did?'

'Ten guineas was the sum she specified.'

'What did you say?'

'I said we had no such cash to spare.'

'That is certainly true. But if she needs cash, she can pawn those pearls of hers.'

'They're fakes, Titus. They'll be worth a few shillings at the pawn shop, at best.'

'She must need money. I doubt Horntree ever let her have any. You may be misprizing her.'

'Am I? Be careful. I suspect she is nothing but a common mooch, Titus, playing the truant.'

Her mouth touched my ear and I turned and looked at her. In the dim candlelight her lips looked so ripe for a kiss that I did not resist.

The new day was bright and fresh, and after breakfast I took myself into the garden at the rear of the Dower House to enjoy a pipe, surrounded by the scents and colours of geranium, foxglove, lavender and flowering honeysuckle. Flora Horntree had not come down, but after my talk with Elizabeth she was very much on my mind.

This was a pretty woman, certainly, and despite her ability to prattle forever about fashions in costumes and fans, she was not quite a fool. When she said that the world was prejudiced against wives that leave their husbands, she was speaking the truth; and her distinction between the views of men and women on the subject was an acute one. When a man hears of a neighbour's wife running away, he fears for the safety of his own domesticity. But his wife may scorn the runaway neighbour as a faint-heart who cannot bear the rigours of marriage; or conversely, as a hussy who thinks only of herself. And here the question of money obtruded. A wife has only the ready money that her husband allows her, and from what I knew of Horntree there would have been little or nothing of that in Flora's case. Yes, I thought, the combined forces against an absconding wife were formidable.

My thoughts were interrupted by Matty, bringing the news that two visitors were at the door asking to see me.

'Two of them, Matty?'

'Yes, two.'

'You had better show them out here, then.'

I braced myself. With no idea who the other fellow would be – a lawyer, perhaps – I fully expected to be dealing with the fury of Grevel Horntree, bent on retrieving his errant Flora. In the event, neither of these arrivals was Horntree, and both were strangers.

They were contrasting types, one short and the other tall. The first was the farmer Frederick Oldroyd who worked a fair parcel of land above the Woodnook Brook, to the west of Old Accrington. Beyond Clover Field, where I had been with Turvey yesterday. He was stout, ruddy-faced and curly-topped; and wore coat and breeches of good quality, with a clean stock at his neck. The second – thin, pale and straight-haired – was Jasper Johnson, operator of the mill on the New Accrington side of the bridge. Mr Johnson was as prosperously dressed as his companion.

I seated them on a garden bench where, declining my offer of a pot of beer, they came straight to the point.

'I represent New Accrington in this matter,' said Johnson. 'And my friend Oldroyd here speaks for Old Accrington.'

'In what sense do you speak?'

'In the sense that we lead the teams in the game between the two that is played every Midsummer's Day.'

'Yes indeed! Mr Turvey was telling me about it. What is it called? The Lady May's Hole game.'

'That's it, Mr Cragg,' said Oldroyd. 'It's been played between Old and New Accrington since before memory. I have the honour of assembling the team of men from Old Accrington.'

'And I am convener for the team of New Accrington,' said the miller.

'My congratulations to you both. But what can I do for you?'

'It's like this,' said Oldroyd. 'Each year we invite a person that does not take sides – a neutral – to officiate in the game. It must be a person of repute.'

'We've had the master of Burnley's grammar school do it before now,' said Johnson, 'and Major Walmsley, who lost his arm at Malplacket. But we've never had such as the County Coroner.'

'So we're asking will you do us the honour, Mr Cragg?' said Oldroyd.

'As a referee, is it?'

'That is it exactly.'

'I see. Well, why not? As long as it doesn't require any athletic ability on my part.'

The two men thought this a great joke, nudging each other and laughing.

'Oh no, Sir,' said Oldroyd. 'All you have to do is launch the ball off from the bridge in whatsoever direction you think fit – up, down or sideways, as you prefer. And then give judgement over any disputes, and finally pronounce the winner.'

'But I don't know the rules of the game. I will have to have them explained to me.'

'That's easy. There's only two rules that matter. No man's to attempt to kill another player, or that man's disqualified. And the first team to put the ball into May's Hole wins.'

'That does not sound too difficult, then. And this is on Midsummer's Day, yes? This coming Thursday?'

'That's right. Thursday morning, nine o'clock. It will start on Accrington bridge, after which you must go to May's Hole. You must be there if, or when, the goal is achieved.'

'That's more than three miles away. How long does it take to play the game?'

'Oh, you will have plenty of time to get there. The play lasts for most of the day and sometimes until dark.'

'And if it's not won by then?'

'It's called as a draw.'

They rose, as one, to take their leave. We shook hands and I brought them back through the house and showed them out of the front door. Just as I closed it behind them, Flora Horntree descended the stairs. It was a near thing. If Oldroyd and Johnson had seen her, her flight from Hatchfly Hall would have been around the village by dinner time.

I asked if she had spent a restful night.

'I lay awake for some time, Mr Cragg, dwelling sadly on the turns that my life has taken. There are songs that claim melancholy is sweet: I do not find it so.'

Elizabeth appeared. She had heard our guest's remark.

'Come and have some breakfast,' she said. 'Demons that visit us during the night are happily dissolved, I find, by the rising sun and a cup of chocolate.'

'You take chocolate at breakfast?' said Mrs Horntree.

'Oh yes, on special occasions – as when we have a guest staying.'

'How very pleasant. My husband would not permit it. Can you be surprised, then, that I have left him?'

Later I followed Elizabeth when she went out to fetch onions from the store.

'How very cruel Horntree is,' she said. Her mischievous smile flashed in the gloom of the outhouse. 'He will not allow her chocolate! What did those two men want?'

I explained about the Lady May's Hole game and my proposed role in it. Elizabeth saw it as a positive sign.

'It shows that we are more accepted here, I think. But you shall be safe, I hope, and not embroiled in the contest.'

'I shall be removed above the struggle, my dear. I am presiding over and adjudging it, like a god who looks down from the heavens at mortal affairs below.'

'Then make sure to stay perched on your cloud, Titus Cragg. These football games that they play in country places are nothing but violent brawls, so I've heard, and your youthful brawling days are behind you, I fear.'

'Don't disturb yourself on that account. I am presently at greater risk from Horntree than from any football game.'

I told Elizabeth how Flora Horntree had barely escaped being seen by Oldroyd and Johnson.

'A fortunate escape,' she said. 'I hope Luke returns very soon to take her off our hands. If Horntree comes here, we will be lucky to escape a rumpus – and he will certainly visit before very long, as someone is sure to spot her staying in this house. Also, tomorrow we are expecting Mr Vaux and his mother for dinner. It will be awkward if this guest is still with us.'

I laid my finger on her lips.

'I have a stratagem,' I said. 'Your part is to keep our guest indoors, or in the back garden. Don't let her show her face in the village. I'm going to have a word with Mrs Nightingale and then with Mr Turvey. If all goes well, she will lay her head somewhere else tonight.'

I found Frances Nightingale at home.

'Have you heard about Mrs Horntree?' I asked as she showed me in.

'What about her, Mr Cragg? I've heard nothing.'

'I am glad to hear it, as I suppose you are a tolerably well-informed person in the affairs of Accrington.'

'If a word's on the wind, I catch it.'

'Good. We can live in hope that no one saw her.'

'Saw her doing what, if I may ask?'

I told her of the events of the previous evening, and that I took Flora Horntree's tale of her husband's brutality to be the plain truth. I was discreet about Elizabeth's misgivings.

'I must ask you to keep this secret, Mrs Nightingale. Mrs Horntree came to us in the dark, and I would like to keep it dark for the time being.'

I went directly to New Manor and told Mr Turvey, to his astonishment, of the unexpected arrival of Flora Horntree.

'Well, well, well!' was all he said.

'But what do you make of it, Turvey? I assume Horntree is a cruel husband who beats her.'

'Nothing would surprise me about that man, whose name

I will not utter. As for his wife, I have never met her. I doubt anyone in the village knows her at all, except perhaps Mrs Stirk in the lodge cottage, who cooks and cleans at the house. The wife does not go abroad.'

'She has done so now.'

A discreet smile appeared on Turvey's face.

'I will not say I am sorry for the husband. I do believe he is a dangerous fellow. So let me consider. No, the Dower House will not serve. She must come to New Manor, which has high walls and a gatehouse, and—'

'You mean you would take her in?'

'I had that in mind, yes.'

This was wonderful. Turvey had adopted my plan without even a hint from me.

'That man rejoiced in the flight of my bees on to his land – for which, if your clerk is right, I cannot even punish him. So this is a . . . what d'you call it? A quid pro quo, yes? When will you bring her? I will tell Sukey to prepare a room. We shall defend her, if need be, as a matter of honour. How long will she need to be put up?'

'That I cannot tell until I know Dr Fidelis's intentions. He promised to come back soon, but did not name the day.'

Turvey rubbed his hands together, relishing the prospect.

'When he does, we shall plot our course. Or rather, we shall plot her course.'

Back at the Dower House, I found the women sitting around the table playing cards. Matty was in a state of some excitement.

'We are playing Ombre, but Mrs Horntree has promised to teach us Quadrille. It is all the fashion with ladies and gentlemen in London. They stake money on the cards, which makes it much more exciting, but we are using peas.'

I picked up a pea from Elizabeth's store.

'I have heard that in London they use ivory tokens of various sizes, depending on the value put on them. How much is a dried pea worth?'

'They are not convertible, Titus,' laughed Elizabeth, 'and that is a very good thing, as Mrs Horntree is rather an expert player, I think.'

I joined them and under Mrs Horntree's instruction we played Quadrille until dinner time. While we ate, I tried to elicit some of our guest's life story.

'You are not from the North Country, I believe? Your manner of speaking is that of the south.'

'I come from a small village in the county of Surrey. A place of little significance where life is utterly quiet and dull. I was glad enough to leave for London – only to fetch up in a place at the other end of the country that isn't so different.' She laughed. 'Such is life. But this is an excellent juicy brisket, Mrs Cragg.'

'Joseph Reed is a reliable trader, I find. Have you not found him so yourself?'

'I take it Joseph Reed keeps the butcher's shop here,' Mrs Horntree said.

'Surely you know that there is no butcher's shop in Accrington?' said Elizabeth. 'Reed has the meat van that comes through the village every Saturday from the Clitheroe market. Do you not buy your meat from him?'

'Buy? I know nothing of buying meat.'

'Did you have no good butcher shop in your village in Surrey, I wonder?' I put in.

My question was ignored, as were all my other questions about her past – ignored or deflected – so that by the end of the meal her origin in an unnamed Surrey village was all the information I had gleaned of her early life.

In the afternoon I went to Frances Nightingale's cottage to work with her on the inquest paperwork. On my return, I found that Quadrille – or was it Ombre? – had recommenced, and there was no further chance to probe our guest. In the meantime, a note had come from Turvey to say he was expecting Mrs X (he would not write her name) to be brought after dark.

The card game had petered out and we sat nervously through the twilight until it was dark enough for the errant wife to be shrouded in her cloak and hood and led briskly, with myself and Elizabeth on either side of her, to New Manor. The moon was up and still not past the half, so it gave a degree of light. But the street was completely deserted as, rather than burn a candle, Accrington people go to bed with the sun. I did not think anyone had seen us.

Turvey greeted us warmly and offered Mrs Horntree a glass of wine. But she said she was tired and would like to go straight to her chamber. We said goodnight too, and Danny accompanied us to the gate. We heard him lock it securely behind us.

FIFTEEN

Later that evening we were all sitting at the dining table around the oil lamp. Elizabeth nursed Hector, while Matty – still bubbling from her day spent playing Ombre and Quadrille – mended some stockings. Having decided to leave off Montaigne, I picked up *Gulliver's Travels* to read aloud from Book III. It was partly in deference to Matty that I had put aside my philosophical Frenchman, who I thought might be a trifle abstruse to hold her interest. On the other hand, one of the many admirable qualities of Jonathan Swift is that he wrote in the plainest language for all classes – masters and servants alike.

We had reached the point of Gulliver's arrival at the peculiar empire of Balnibarbi, whose governors float above the oppressed land on their flying island of Laputa. These rulers keep their womenfolk confined to this island in the air – rather as the Turks do in their seraglios – and, resenting their captivity, the women lose no opportunity to be naughty and disrespectful. Swift tells the tale of the Prime Minister's wife, a beautiful and pampered lady, and how she escaped perilously from the island in order to live with a penniless and hunchbacked old footman on the ground below, even though he regularly beat and abused her.

'Well, I wouldn't do that, not me!' exclaimed Matty. 'A life of luxury she lived. She'd no business running away to stay with a low brute of a huckleback. It's a sin.'

'Others commit the same sin,' I said. 'Didn't we take in one such only last night?'

'But you said Mr Horntree mistreated her,' objected Matty. 'It's not like that in the story. The Prime Minister's rich and kind, and will even forgive his wife, but she's an ungrateful hussy.'

'I doubt anyone imprisoned is grateful to their captor, not if they have spirit. All they must want is to abscond.'

Matty pouted.

'Well, I wouldn't – what d'you call it? – abscond, not if they kept me in luxury.'

'If you'd asked me at the start,' Elizabeth said, shifting the baby off her breast, 'I'd have said Flora was a little like that Prime Minister's wife. She was bored with her country marriage, so she flit. But her aim is different: what she's after is a comfortable life. Just a few minutes of her conversation and you're in no doubt of that.'

She tenderly wiped Hector's chin, then draping him over her shoulder patted his back while jiggling him up and down.

'She is certainly very interested in shopping and fine clothes,' I said. 'It's one of the few things we know about her.'

'She married Horntree expecting to be doing nothing but spend his money. She has more to say about braited shoes and costly sack dresses in silks and satins than I would have thought possible. At the same time, she knows nothing at all about housekeeping. Her education seems to have been all in the *mode*.'

'So if he wanted to be cruel to her, he didn't have to beat her but only keep her starved of cash.'

Hector burped and, I fancied, looked proud of his achievement.

'But on the other hand, did you not see some injuries to her face, Titus?' said Elizabeth.

'Yes, they were not explained.'

Matty refused to abandon her earlier position.

'It's still not the same as in the story of the flying island,' she said flatly. 'The Prime Minister gave his wife jewels and everything. It was the ugly old footman in his hovel that beat her black and blue, and she was such a fool to go to him.'

'She chose the old footman freely, however,' I said. 'Human affairs are undoubtedly very puzzling!'

'In the end I think there is one big difference between the two cases,' said Elizabeth. 'The wife in Dean Swift's book chooses freedom over comfort. Flora Horntree sees the two as being the same. I think perhaps both women are fools, but Flora is the bigger fool.'

I shut the book.

'Well, that is enough of the Dean for one night. Our author certainly likes to swim in paradoxical waters.'

Early on Wednesday morning I wrote to Fidelis at his house in Preston.

> *Dear Fidelis,*
>   *There has been a remarkable development. Just a few hours after you left us, Mrs Horntree came to our door without warning to say she has left Horntree and Hatchfly Hall forever. She took the chance of his being away at Manchester on business. She asked for shelter, which of course we gave, and now she's waiting for your assistance before making any further move. You must return and deal with this matter, which is of your doing and none of mine. Our uninvited guest has removed now to New Manor, where she can be better protected. Horntree has not shown his face – we presume he has not yet returned home from Manchester. When he does, we expect to see him rampaging through the village to find her. Hasten back!*
>   *Yrs etc Titus Cragg.*

I read it through, then added a postscript:

> *P.S. We both agree with you that Mrs H. is exceedingly handsome, but Elizabeth says she has a very different character from that which you imagine.*

I sealed the letter and took it to Jane Malkin at the Black Bull. Then I strolled back towards Gargrave's. I had not visited him since the inquest. I now meant to see how he was and make the verdict clear for him, if he needed it. Gerald Piper opened the door and I asked after his master.

'He's back working today, Mr Cragg, which is a hopeful sign. I feared for him when he would do nothing but mope in the parlour.'

'Yes, it may be that he has rounded the corner. I am glad. Can you direct me to him?'

'He's haymaking. You'll find him in Drift Meadow, two miles above the village on the far slope of the valley.'

I heard the church clock striking nine as, following Piper's instructions, I crossed the bridge and made my way along the eastern bank of the river. There were no houses lining the path between myself and the Hyndburn, and I had a good view of the clear amber water as it rilled and gurgled along and of the dwellings along the far side. The last and largest of these was New Manor, which I was now seeing from a new angle. The whole perimeter of the house and courtyard was enclosed by a high wall except here, though the river had exactly the same protective effect as a wall, with the difference that one could see across it from ground level. So I enjoyed a clear view of the New Manor garden lying between the house and the Hyndburn, and could see to my considerable alarm that a woman in a deep-red dress was walking there: Flora Horntree. She noticed me and waved.

'I hope you passed a peaceful night,' I called out.

She walked to the edge of the stream. There was less than twenty yards between us.

'Oh yes, I think I have never slept so well, Mr Cragg, thanks to you and Mr Turvey.'

'I have written to Dr Fidelis. He will receive the letter this afternoon, after which I expect him to return.'

'I am counting on him.'

'But in the meantime, please have a care, Mrs Horntree. It is not at all wise for you to be alone in the garden and so visible to the world.'

'Well, I need air and sunshine from time to time. I cannot stay all day indoors. But fear not. The main gate is securely locked. It's the only way in.'

'Has there been any sign of your husband?'

'No. He must still be in Manchester.'

'Well, once again, take every care.'

I continued along the river until the path began to bend away up the slope of the valley. Forty-five minutes later I arrived at Drift Meadow.

A line of men with scythes was slowly advancing through the knee-high grass, leaving behind them a swathe of sweet-smelling hay. Women and children, following in a second line, raked the hay into small heaps and forked these on to the haycart drawn by two horses that moved up and down the line behind them. Gargrave was on the back of the cart, receiving the pitched hay and packing it tight under a secure rope netting. He was working like fury, not being one of those overseers who prefers to sit at ease on his horse and watch his men sweat. He was an active practical farmer, not a slave driver, and I respected him the more for it.

A pause for drink was called as I approached, and the scythes, rakes and pitchforks were abandoned while the workers gathered round the cart. Two fresh breakers full of beer were tapped, and pewter mugs repeatedly filled and passed among the hands. Among them, I noticed both of the Stirk brothers.

I beckoned to Gargrave and we walked out of the workers' earshot.

'Have you held Mrs Gargrave's funeral?' I said.

'Aye. I took her up yesterday to Altham. Mr Vaux read the service. We have a small graveyard there.'

'I wondered if I might clarify Monday's verdict. I fear it may not entirely have satisfied you.'

'Nothing would do that, Mr Cragg.'

'Yet I think a finding of "murder" was what you wished for, so that the guilty parties could be punished. But the jury were an unfortunate mixture, you see.'

Gargrave held up his hand, as if not wanting to hear me, but I persisted. During my walk from Accrington I had developed a metaphor for the jury's behaviour on Monday morning, with which I was pleased and I did not want it to go to waste.

'Some of the jurors were saltpetre, some were sulphur, and some were charcoal – all very peaceful when each group is on its own, but mixed together they make gunpowder and are liable to explode. Do you see?'

'Aye, and that they did. It wasn't pretty,' agreed Gargrave.

'The result was a verdict that fell a little short of perfect, though it was quite understandable. They simply couldn't concur on the cause of Anne's death. It means I cannot name any individual in my report as being responsible, which I deeply regret. Unfortunately it means there is little likelihood of any prosecution to console you. I am sorry.'

Gargrave patted me on the shoulder, as if it was I who needed consolation.

'I have no expectation of justice,' he said. 'I am reconciled. I pray for her soul and my own, which is all I can do.'

'Of course. And differences in the manner of praying are perhaps at the bottom of this. Mr Vaux says so. I have spoken of it with him and he holds that you and your wife were the victims of anti-popery.'

John Gargrave shook his head.

'Mr Vaux may think that, but I heard no such talk during the . . . during those events. Like all Catholics, I've been called many things in my time – traitor to the King, Jacobite, idolater, Pope's lackey, whore of Babylon. I heard nothing of the kind on that day.'

'Yet many in these parts are strongly against Rome, are they not? While those that follow your religion are rather few. Anyone with a mind to persecute you might think they would have general approval and so escape the law.'

'They will face divine judgement. I must be content with that.'

I looked over towards the haycart. Two of the young men were wrestling in the half-humorous way that young men have. One of these was Charlie Stirk.

'I see you have the Stirk brothers working the hay, Gargrave. That is remarkably cool of you, if I may say so, considering their role in the events of last Sunday week.'

'I need hands to cut the crop.'

'You do no harm by it,' I said. 'All flesh is grass, and those that are guilty will face the scythe of the Lord when they must.'

My mind was a fountain of metaphors today.

'Very true, Mr Cragg, very true. Now, I must get these young blades back to work before any bones are broken.'

In the corner of my eye, a young farm lad of almost gigantic size was watching us from thirty feet away. As Gargrave parted from me, the fellow began lumbering towards me, the expression on the lad's face signalling that he wouldn't mind a word.

I waited for him, and quickly realized he was the member of the inquest audience that had pitched into the battle of the jury with such force and fervour.

'Is it right you're to see over the game, mister?' he said.

He was perhaps twenty years of age, and weighed as many stone.

'The football game, you mean, between Old and New Accrington?' I asked.

'Aye, the game. Is that right?'

'Yes, it is. I've agreed to be umpire. But why do you ask?'

'You've to play fair. That schoolmaster they brought in were rubbish last year. He weren't straight. He found for Old in everything.'

In addition to his size, he was disadvantaged by a savage squint and it was disconcerting to converse with one whose right eye stared into my face while his left looked at some spot in the distance over my right shoulder.

'And you, I take it, are shouting for New Accrington?'

'I'm not shouting, I'm playing. I'm New and proud of it. We've not won the past three year, but this time we shall hammer them – if you play fair.'

'I always play fair.'

He showed me his fist.

'You'd better.'

He paused, as if thinking of how best to phrase his next remark.

'The schoolmaster last year regretted it, after finding for Old Accie in everything.'

'Did he? In what way did he regret it?'

'Got his windows broke next day when a few lads from New Accie went over to his house.'

'I see. There will be no need for that in my case as I shall certainly play fair. That means I shall not be partial to your side just because you haven't won for three years.'

He hawked and spat, then bobbed his head and retreated, leaving me with the uncomfortable feeling that I had just been threatened by a man twice my size.

Leaving the haymakers as they returned reluctantly to their task, I dismissed the idea. The lad only wanted to make himself known, being curious about my identity. Then as I followed the track back down towards the village, I recalled my conversation with Gargrave and thought how tough the human spirit is. Only ten days earlier the factor had suffered terribly at the hands of the villagers. When I saw him in his parlour, he had been deeply morose and sorry for himself; now he seemed to have risen from the pit of despair and returned to the philosophical surface. Or was it only a performance? A few days earlier I had heard Harry Hawk laughing over the clumsy antics of the King on the battlefield – the very same field where his comrades were about to be slain and he terribly mutilated. His ironic laughter concealed his anger about the battle, but cannot have soothed it. His levity had been nothing but the expression of sorrow turned inside out.

Who, I wondered, was the more hurt by what they had suffered through the violence of others: Gargrave, Hawk or Flora Horntree? Which of them deserved sympathy the more? And which of them was the better actor?

These reflections and many others occupied me as far as the stretch of river bank that stood opposite New Manor. There was now no sign of Flora Horntree in the garden.

SIXTEEN

It was after one o'clock, dinner time, by the time I reached the Dower House. I found, to my surprise, Henry Vaux and his mother sitting comfortably at the table. I had completely forgotten we had invited them.

Elizabeth having evidently just finished telling the Vauxes the whole story of Mrs Horntree's sudden appearance at our door on Monday night and how we had successfully transferred her to New Manor, I found old Mrs Vaux tut-tutting while her son tugged his beard in thought.

'What do you think lies at the bottom of this terrible adventure, Mr Cragg?' demanded Mrs Vaux shrilly.

'Well, Mrs Vaux, I think Elizabeth's view has much to commend it. Mrs Horntree is an impetuous person who resisted her husband's rule.'

The priest was more measured than his mother.

'It is not something to be encouraged, the leaving of one's husband. But when it is done, it is not done lightly. The poor woman must have been in distress. I will remember her in my prayers at Mass tomorrow.'

'I have seen marks and swellings on her face,' I said. 'She may have fallen, of course, or met with some other accident. But it is quite possible that Horntree resorted to violence.'

After that we sat down to our meat: a rich stew of lamb kidneys. I told Vaux of my visit to Gargrave in the hayfield, and the remarkable forgiving spirit he seemed to show in employing the Stirk brothers as haymakers.

'John Gargrave and his wife have more than once sat around a dinner table with my mother and me, just as we are doing now,' said Vaux. 'Aside from the confessional – of which, of course, I cannot speak – I judge him to be quite simply a good man. A holy man, if you don't mind the word. But also, while he possesses intelligence and is very dependable, he has hardly any passion about him

– very few strong feelings, you know – and at the same time very little self-regard.'

'You have described the qualities necessary in a good servant,' I said.

'So I have!' said Vaux. 'And Gargrave is indeed a servant – to Lord Petre. The fact that his master lives hundreds of miles away in the south calls for even higher excellence in the serving man, and he rises to it. I have it on Lord Petre's own authority—'

'You know Lord Petre personally?'

'Yes, I have stayed as his guest at his home in Essex, his Lordship being of our religion. His estates, he told me, are very scattered and he perforce employs many local land managers or factors to work them. We discussed Gargrave. He regards him as one of his most trustworthy.'

Elizabeth and Matty had now cleared the dirty plates away and were clattering around in the scullery.

'Mrs Gargrave, on the other hand, had a poor reputation,' I said.

'I doubt Lord Petre knew anything about Mrs Gargrave.'

'I mean here, in Accrington.'

'She was a faithful attender at Mass,' said Vaux, 'and scrupulously observed the practices of our religion. And of course there are many who would attack her on that count alone. But let us say, as charitably as we can, that Anne Gargrave was not known for her smooth tongue. I will offer in her defence that she did not always know when she gave offence.'

'Did she not see the result, though? That nobody in this village loved her.'

'Ah, well, I would not know about that.'

Matty now came back bearing a great pudding of summer fruits in batter and put it before us. At the sight of it, Henry Vaux rubbed his hands together.

'But speaking of love, I must say I do love a batter pudding.'

'Are we speaking of love?' said Elizabeth, following our girl in with a jug of cream, which she placed before our guests. 'If you want my opinion, there was not much of it latterly between John and Anne Gargrave. She was inflexible and he was too yielding.'

Vaux swallowed his first large mouthful of pudding.

'Gargrave did defer to his wife over many matters,' he said. 'That is not a sin.'

'The village lads think it was. It is why they inflicted the stang ride on them.'

'As I said on Sunday, I believe they were really acting on anti-Catholic feelings.'

'But what if that is just one of a large tangle of motives in this case? Another, for example, might be Harry Hawk's feelings against the woman. Anne Gargrave made him the subject of gossip and suspicion all over these hills and valleys, and he was bitter about that.'

'Maybe he was only *pretending* to be bitter,' said Vaux with a laugh, 'which would be only natural if he is really an impostor, as Anne believed. And if the man *is* playing a role, does it matter? All the world's a stage, is it not?'

'The law does not agree, Vaux,' I said. 'It takes the view that imposture is a parasite on the laws of property, which are the very foundations of society.'

'Forgive me, Cragg, but do you really believe that? I see it from another angle. The foundation of society is society – under God of course, but God is good enough to leave the arrangements to us – and society is more important than property because it is the crucible of love, which is the most valuable thing of all. And what is even more, society, like love, outlasts our earthly life and like love it comes with us to paradise. Property we leave behind. They cast lots for his coat, remember?'

'Vaux,' I said, 'you would make an admirable man of law. I bow to you.'

Vaux sighed and shook his head.

'It really would be much better if the world could reach balanced judgements and not run to extremes.'

'That is very much what Monsieur de Montaigne says on the matter. I must give you the book back, by the way.'

We had finished eating. I rose to fetch the volumes and handed them to him. He in turn fished in a large linen bag and fetched out a volume which he placed in my hands.

'And I have something for you. It is excellent light reading, Cragg. There is no theology of any kind in it.'

I opened it at the title page. It was volume one of the *Works of Shakespeare*.

'It is from the late edition of Mr Lewis Theobald,' he said, 'which is vastly superior to that of Alexander Pope.'

'It is very handsome,' I said.

'This is the first volume, which contains *A Midsummer Night's Dream*. I thought, as it is midsummer, you know.'

I thanked him sincerely and carried the book to the window and flipped it open. My eyes met the lines:

> *Lovers and madmen have such seething brains*
> *Such shaping fantasies that apprehend*
> *More than cool reason ever comprehends*

I got no further, as a shadow fell across the page and I saw that outside the window a head loomed. Then a knuckle was rapping on the frame.

'Titus!' Luke Fidelis called through the glass. 'I rode as fast as I could. What in God's name has happened?'

As I let him in, Elizabeth sent Matty to the larder to fetch left-over food and some ale. Vaux and his mother, who had seen Fidelis in the Sunday congregation, gave him a warm greeting, then sat quietly while I related all the things that had happened since his departure.

As I brought my tale up to the present moment, Fidelis sat looking down in thought at the floor, his elbows on his knees. One of the knees was jiggling.

'Had she any further signs of abuse?'

'Nothing.'

'And she came directly from Hatchfly Hall?'

'So she said. It had been her habit when her husband vexed her beyond endurance to lock herself in her room and stay there two or even three days. She told us that after Grevel Horntree rode away to Manchester, she did the same – but this time with the stratagem in her head of stealing away in the night. Which is what she did, without money or a very clear notion where she would go in the end.'

Fidelis leapt to his feet.

'I must see her.'

But now Matty landed a platter on the table.

'You'll eat this first, Doctor.'

A few minutes later, the Vauxes left us to walk home.

'I'll see you on Sunday,' said Elizabeth, waving to them from the doorstep and then watching their progress down the street. She was still at the door when Luke returned to the Dower House from the other direction.

'That was a short visit,' she said. 'And why the puzzled look?'

'Mrs Horntree declines to see me. I'm damned if I know why.'

Coming inside, he sank into a chair.

'Does she not say, or give a clue?'

'She lies up in her room saying she is indisposed, according to Sukey.'

'That may be because she really is indisposed,' I said.

'And not see me? I am a doctor, Titus.'

'There is indisposed and there is *indisposed*, if you follow me, Luke,' said Elizabeth. 'If she is ill, that is one thing. If she is not disposed to see you, it is another. Either way, she may say she is indisposed.'

'And either way, she should see me. According to you, Titus, she was only too anxious to be in my company the day before yesterday.'

'I'm sure she is unwell, but in some unimportant way,' I said. 'A small headache, or something like.'

'It cannot be serious, I think, because the household is in no way alarmed. Thomasina plays jigs on the spinet, and Turvey whistles cheerfully and laughs. I would not be surprised if he'd been drinking that vile honey concoction of his.'

'Then perhaps you will see Mrs Horntree tomorrow.'

Fidelis sighed. 'All activity is suspended tomorrow, all except the May's Hole game – the match between Old and New Accrington. I, fool that I am, have engaged to run in it.'

'Are you serious? You are taking part?'

'Yes, in the interest of Old. I engaged a room at the inn on my way here, and it was then that the challenge was thrown down. Of course, I picked it up. Indeed, I should go back there now. There is to be a meeting of all our men this evening to discuss tactics.'

So he left us and we passed a quiet evening at the Dower House, during which I read some more from *Gulliver's Travels*. We had come to the part in Book IV where Gulliver finds himself explaining to the rational horses in Houyhnhnm Land the basis of British law and the work of my own profession. His account is not at all flattering. The Dean mocks lawyers as practising the art of proving that black is white or white is black 'according as they are paid'. They are not interested in justice any more than in reason, and they are addicted to speaking in a 'particular cant or jargon' that no one else can understand.

I laughed about all this with Elizabeth but then, sitting down to write my journal at the end of the evening, I thought about my own practice in the law. How well did it stand in relation to Swift's jibes? My journal frequently records my pious determination to serve justice and oppose wrongdoing. But the audit of my performance here in Accrington had shown little success in bringing justice in the matter of the assault on the Gargraves and Anne's death. Moreover, that very day I'd told Vaux that law exists mainly for the regulation of property. Did I really believe that? Vaux had asked. Did I? Perhaps I was so soused in a lawyer's way of thinking that I was willing to argue white into black if it suited the case. Vaux had seen through it, anyway. He'd challenged me because he thought I was talking from mere form, and not from the heart.

I opened the volume of Shakespeare that the priest had brought to me, and read again those lines from *A Midsummer Night's Dream*. Do lovers and madmen know more than reason can tell them? Fidelis was a man adamant for reason and yet often fell in love quite unreasonably, as he appeared to have done with Mrs Horntree, a woman he hardly knew. So even my cool friend was subject to frequent Shakespearean humours. As for me, while I regarded my long love for Elizabeth and my more recent love for Hector as being perfectly rational, there was in truth much heart in it. Much heart and soul.

Later, in bed, I lay waiting for sleep. The wind was rising. Over the course of the day and evening heavy cloud had stolen

into the sky, and the heat had grown thicker and more oppres-
sive. But now this wind had come and then, just as I closed
my eyes, there was a tree-splitting flash of lightning and a
cannonade of thunder, followed quickly by a steady pissing
sound outside the window. The weather had broken.

SEVENTEEN

In the early morning iron-grey cloud bulged under the heavens, delivering bursts of drenching rain from time to time and thunderous rumblings. The storm, however, was passing by breakfast time, when there was again weak sunshine on the gleaming soaked ground.

I was passing through the hall as there came a knock on the door, and I opened. Jasper Johnson and Frederick Oldroyd stood there expectantly.

'Well, Mr Cragg?' said Oldroyd. 'Ready for the fray are you?'

I had not expected them so early.

'Come in, gentlemen, and sit yourselves down. Give me five minutes and I'll be ready.'

In that time I changed into an old pair of breeches and riding boots, and so went out with them.

We found a crowd of people around the bridge, and at the heart of them, closest to the bridge itself, were a mob of young men in shirtsleeves and strong nailed boots. I noticed that these men had some sort of scarf tied around their forehead or upper arms, coloured either red or blue. The red scarves were predominant on the Old Accrington side and the blue on the New side.

We pushed through the crowd until we reached a triangular podium fenced by shepherd's hurdles and placed exactly on the shallow summit of the bridge. This we mounted as the players and their supporters milled around, laughing, pushing each other, eating a last slice of pie or draining a mug of ale, then bending and stretching in readiness for the fray. Johnson put his fingers to his mouth and emitted a piercing whistle.

Only now did the teams' supporters withdraw to the edges of the mob, and the men that would play lined up in ranks with their arms around each other's shoulders, waiting for the off. There must have been thirty or forty men on each side.

Then Oldroyd handed me the ball, a rough globe about a foot across, consisting of an air-filled bladder in a casing of roughly tanned but firmly sewn patches of cowhide.

'What do I do?' I asked.

'You say a few words,' said Johnson, 'then wait while the two sides mingle together to give them equal chances at the throw-up. Then simply do it – throw the ball up as high as you can and set the game afoot.'

Again Johnson whistled and the restive crowd fell silent. I looked around, seeing a number of faces that I recognized, including the Stirk brothers, who were wearing the red of Old Accrington. I cleared my throat and spoke to them as loudly as I could.

'I have been told there are two rules,' I said. 'Nobody must attempt murder, and the game is won by the team whose man puts the ball into Lady May's Hole.'

There were a few ribald cries and cackles of laughter. I went on.

'I suppose this game has been played since time began, so the lady must be quite used to the indignity by now.'

This drew a raucous cheer from the players. I signalled to Oldroyd, who whistled a third time, and the players broke ranks and mixed together on both sides of the bridge, generally forming groups of three or four that would run together. While this was happening, I looked over the heads of the crowd towards the inn door and Luke Fidelis emerged wearing the clothing of a competitor and tying a blue scarf around his arm. He caught my eye and shrugged in an exaggerated way, as if to say there was no going back now.

I hefted the ball, which probably weighed about three pounds, and then on the sound of a fourth whistle from Oldroyd I summoned all my strength to launch it upwards as another collective roar went up with it. The ball began its trajectory vertically but a gust of wind blew it to one side, over the bridge's parapet and then in an arc down to the water. It landed with a splash and immediately began to float under the arch of the bridge.

In anticipation of this, many players had posted themselves on the river bank. These plunged straight into the water, while others fought each other to get across or round the bridge's parapet and join the fray. The fury of splashing and plunging continued for some time until some hand smuggled the ball into the open, where it reached the bank and suddenly a man sporting a red scarf was running with it tucked under his arm along the Whalley road pursued by the rest of the pack. I caught sight of Fidelis haring along with the rest.

'Aren't they going the wrong way?' I said. 'Lady May's Hole is towards that big hill, isn't it? It's in the opposite direction.'

'That's Boggart's Hill, is that,' said Johnson. 'But you'll see what's going to happen in a minute. Look at the chasers. Some of them are already breaking off the road by every gate to get into the fields. They know that the runner with the ball will aim to get himself across the wall and into the fields, probably before he reaches the gates of Hatchfly Hall. Then he'll go up the slope and wheel back in this direction, either through the fields or into the woods, or even through the woods on to the moor if he can get there. Mark my words, the first serious battle this year will be up there among the trees.'

'Meantime, we must make our way to the goal, Mr Cragg,' said Johnson. 'It's essential you're at your post in case someone makes a breakaway run and makes it as far as Boggart's Hill without getting caught. I've known the game to be over in an hour when that happens.'

Our horses awaited us in the inn yard and we rode smartly out of New Accrington by way of the Manchester road. After a mile or so, we crossed the Hyndburn by a plank bridge and followed a track up towards the craggy Boggart's Hill, below which the game would climax – at Lady May's Hole itself.

This stretch of land, on the lower slopes of Boggart's Hill, was neither exactly a moor nor a pasture, but something in between. It had patches of tussocky grass, gorse, bracken and heather, as well as screes and rock faces higher up the slope where stone or slate had once been quarried. Sheep wandered around eating whatever they could find. Higher up the hill, a goat was shredding the leaves off a bush;

closer at hand, there were the exits and entrances of a well-populated rabbit warren.

The Hole itself was neither more nor less than a well that collected spring water gushing from the side of the hill. At some time many years ago the hole into which the spring poured had been enlarged and deepened so as to contain a volume of water, though why this had been done was uncertain as there was no sign of any farm or dwelling nearby to make use of it. At the same time someone had gone to the trouble of erecting a protective iron rail around it, of a kind known to blacksmiths as a 'brandreth'. Leaning over this brandreth and looking into the well's depths, I noticed the glint of metal at the bottom and wondered how long people had been coming up here with their coins in hope of bribing the fates.

We sat on a boulder that rose immediately above the well. This would afford an excellent view at the game's end, though as yet there was nothing to enjoy but moorland birdcalls high in the blustery air. Johnson produced a bottle with three silver cups from his saddlebag.

'I had some Nantz bottled up for us at the inn to keep up our spirits. It may be a long vigil.'

After we'd clinked our cups together we settled down to wait, passing the time in conversation about village affairs. The stormy late inquest came up and Johnson told me about the prevalence of nonconformism in this part of the country, not least the kind of Calvinism exemplified by the juror Greaves.

'You will never convince those people that anything happens without the Lord wills it – from a flea bite or a stub of your toe to a man rogering his neighbour's wife. For them there's no law, no morality, just God pulling strings. You'll have another drink, Mr Cragg?'

'I feel the pull of that string,' I said.

We drank another round and the talk moved on to other things. Hours went by. Later we ate the bread and cheese that Oldroyd had brought with him. Every so often one of us would scan the countryside around for signs of the approaching game. To my eyes, the landscape presented much contrast. First, apart from the hybrid land in the immediate vicinity, there were swathes of green fields divided by stone walling, running down to the hedgy bottom of the valley and then extending in the same way up the opposite slope. Then there was the belt of mature woodland that formed a wide border between pasture and the wilderness of the high purple moors that reached up to the horizon. All around us was birdlife – crows and hawks, wagtails and larks, curlews and cuckoos, their cries and songs mingling with the monotonous bleating of sheep.

We were not alone with nature for long, however, as gradually the villagers joined us – men, women and children, who formed up on the hillside above the well to see the climax of the game. They were in a holiday mood, chattering and laughing, eating and drinking. As the excitement mounted, the children played chase and the younger adults danced and sang to the accompaniment of Billy Whist's fiddle. Elizabeth had been escorted to the place by Frances Nightingale, who came to cheer on New Accrington.

'Is Tom Turvey not with you?'

'He has apiary work to do, so he says. I think the truth is he abhors the violence of all this and prefers to stay away.'

No one would have imputed the same motive to Grevel Horntree, although he too was absent.

Elizabeth moved about in the crowd speaking with various women of the village, many of whose husbands or beaux were out there in pursuit of the bladder ball. At length, above the crowd's excited chatter we heard shouts, and picked out some dots at the distance of a mile moving on the fells above the trees. Oldroyd was one of several spectators who produced a spyglass, claiming he could see the men with the ball, though when he offered me the glass I couldn't make anything out at all.

The dots disappeared again, no doubt because the game had descended into the woods once more. It did not come back into view for another hour, though now much nearer, and I could see that there was a running fight going on between the reds and the blues. Probably no more than forty of them were still in the running, and they were mortally tired as you could tell by the frequency with which the ball changed hands. Every now and then a man would break free of the pack and

make several stumbling yards of progress in our direction
before being caught up with and everything would stop again
in a confusion of bodies.

The striving pack went out of sight for some time, masked
by a dip in the ground, but appeared at last about two hundred
yards below us. The spectators cheered madly and waved blue
and red colours in the air, and I took my place on top of the
boulder from which I could look down directly into Lady
May's Hole in readiness to adjudicate the result. But now,
because of the upward slope of the land and the exhaustion
of the players, progress towards the goal stalled.

For half an hour or more, some forty yards down the slope
from us, men grunted and yelled, sometimes in triumph, more
often in pain, in a heaving ruck of human bodies, deep inside
which was the object of the exercise, a bladder filled with air.
My thoughts were divided between a sense of the utter foolishness and absurdity of this war-to-no-purpose and concern
for Fidelis. I knew he would have thrown himself into the
game with all his heart – that was his nature – but the more
he did so the more he might be injured. My eyes searched the
contending players but could not see him, which wasn't a
surprise as the men were now so covered in mud that you
couldn't tell them apart. You couldn't even make out whether
they were wearing red or blue colours.

The ruck of men continued to writhe and groan, like a
monstrous, shapeless sea creature trying to give birth. Then
a man rolled out of this body and into the open. He had a
great swollen belly – or so it seemed until he produced the
ball from under his shirt and began to flounder up the hill
towards us, encouraged by the cheers of the spectators gathered on the hillside above the well. Below him the ruck
continued to heave and roar, still unaware that the object of
their struggle had escaped them and had almost reached its
ultimate destination.

Before he could complete his triumph, however, the player
with the ball had to scramble up a steep scree below the well,
its surface covered by loose rocks and crumbling earth. Another
player, who may or may not have been from the opposite
team, was the only one in pursuit. He got within reaching

distance and grasped the would-be goal scorer by his ankle.
He pulled hard and the upper man rolled back down the
slope, landing on top of the other and letting go of the ball.
The two men started fighting in the weary, ineffectual way of
prizefighters after about thirty rounds of punching. Meanwhile,
the dropped ball rolled several yards back down the hill.

Two players from the outer part of the main scrimmage
saw what was happening, peeled off, and headed for the
ball. One was a big man, very large of girth. The other was
not so tall and much slimmer and nimbler, and it was he
that reached the ball first, picking it up and racing on up
the hill towards the well. But now the two men who had
been fighting at the foot of the small scree settled their
differences and stood together shoulder to shoulder to block
the advancing threat.

To my considerable dismay, I suddenly saw why the man
running with the ball looked familiar. His face and hair were
entirely caked and smeared with mud, as was his clothing,
but his general build and his way of moving told me he was
Luke Fidelis. He tried to dodge the waiting pair, but tripped
on a rock as he did so and went down, hugging the ball for
as long as he could. The big man, wobbling with fat, now
lumbered up, hurled the other two players aside and threw
himself on top of Fidelis, to a great roar from the crowd. This
caught the attention of a few more members of the larger
scrimmage, and they began to detach themselves and make
their way towards us, forcing their limbs onwards against
mortal weariness to try to win the accolade.

None of them got there in time. I now realized that the big
man kneeling astride Fidelis's body was the same wall-eyed
bruiser who had threatened me at Drift Meadow and who had
previously joined the affray at the inquest. All his attention
at this moment was given to pummelling my friend into
submission. His great fists landed again and again – and again,
finally dislodging the ball from Fidelis's arms, so that it rolled
free. However, absorbed in the pleasure of inflicting violence,
the fat man paid no mind to the ball. So the other two players
picked it up between them, and once more began climbing
towards the well. With half an eye on the brutal punishment

being meted out to Fidelis by the giant, I beckoned urgently, trying to hurry them.

At last the two players reached the wellhead, both breathing hard. They jointly held the soaked and smeared ball over the iron brandreth, but were in no hurry to conclude the business.

'Drop the ball!' I shouted. 'End the game for God's sake! Do it now!'

The two men waited and waited, and I became increasingly frustrated. Fidelis's attacker had now shifted his attentions to the doctor's face and head.

'Drop the ball!' I shouted again. 'For Christ's sake! Drop it, at once!'

EIGHTEEN

They preferred to savour their moment of triumph a little longer. Looking down on the rest of the players, who had at last untangled themselves and were coming up in almost a single mass, the pair were satisfied in the knowledge that these efforts would be too late. All they had to do was release the ball and finish the May's Hole game for another year. There were perhaps forty men trudging up the shifting scree below the well – half the original field – with the foremost of them within a few steps of the well's parapet. Their faces were a conspectus of extreme human expressions, not unlike the examples published by a French physiognomist in the last century. Anger, hope, despair and the lust for violence were all present, but in much evidence also was the vacancy of pure exhaustion.

One fellow lunged forward to pluck the elbow of one of the two ball holders, in a last effort to stop the goal being scored. This was in vain because they now, finally, let the ball go. Soaked as it was with mud and ditchwater, it was much heavier than when I had thrown it up from the Accrington bridge and it hit the well water with a considerable splash. The crowd of spectators raised a cheer of confirmation, and the game was over.

I gestured to Frederick Oldroyd to signal with one of his whistles, at which the players immediately stopped labouring up the slope and stood with fists on hips. Fidelis's fat assailant left off his exertions and rose to his feet. Fidelis, however, lay where he was.

'Who's won?' This was Johnson speaking in my ear. 'You must pronounce, Mr Cragg. We're all waiting.'

I looked down at the two men who had jointly dropped the ball into May's Hole. They were too filthy to show any colour except mud brown. I slid down the side of my rock and landed on the ground beside the wellhead, where they stood, smiling and laughing and brandishing their arms in the air. I asked one for his scarf. He untied it from his arm and, unfolding it, I discovered it was red. I then turned to the other and received his scarf also. I shook it out: this one was blue.

I showed the scarves to the two men. They looked at them and then at each other, nonplussed.

'I thought he were blue, same as me,' said one of them.

'And I thought *he* were red,' said the other.

There were shouts of 'Who won? Who won?' I waved my hand to silence them.

'It has been a long day,' I said, addressing the muddy mass of players below me. 'Some of you have come here by a very arduous route, and I congratulate you on your courage and zeal. But the goal was scored by a member of each of your teams simultaneously and I find it impossible to adjudicate between them. I therefore declare that the result is a tie.'

There were collective groans, some laughter, and a scattering of applause. A tie in a game is not immediately satisfactory to either side, since both want to see their opponent crushed. But a little reflection may reveal that *they* could have been the ones that were crushed. So, although it may not be considered a complete success, a tie or draw was not necessarily a resounding failure.

I hurried down to Luke Fidelis. His eyes were closed and his face was bloody and bruised, but he was alive. Groans were coming out of him, and he raised one of his arms and waved it.

'You are such an ass,' I said.

Elizabeth came over, full of concern.

'Is he badly hurt?'

'I don't know,' I said. 'He's the doctor, but if you ask him he'll only give you a stupid answer.'

She knelt and spoke into Fidelis's ear. His lips moved in reply.

'What does he say?'

'That he wants a rematch with the fat one.'

'You see? He is ungovernable. Can you walk, Luke?'

This time he didn't reply. I said, 'We'll need a litter.'

I looked around. Shortly after Oldroyd, Johnson and myself

got to May's Hole, a cart had arrived loaded with litters. The idea was that, when the game was over, able-bodied men would retrace the game's path, carrying these litters, and take up any players found along the way that were wounded and unable to walk. I called for one of the litters immediately and Fidelis was loaded on to it.

'I cannot understand it,' I said to Elizabeth. 'That he would put his life at risk in this ridiculous fashion.'

'You know his adventurous nature.'

'To die for one's country or one's faith, that I can understand. But to die for Old Accrington! He's not even *from* Old Accrington, or anywhere nearby. It is beyond all comprehension.'

'Well, he hasn't died, Titus, so we should not complain but thank God.'

There being no further ceremonial duties for me to do, we set off back to the Dower House with two of the appointed bearers carrying Luke. I looked down at him and noticed his lips moving. I bent down.

'What did you say, Luke?'

His voice was a hoarse whisper.

'Who won?'

'Neither side. It was a draw.'

He answered with a groan.

'I am glad it was a tie,' Elizabeth declared. 'After all those fellows went through, it would have been cruel for anyone to lose.'

'But, you know, for someone to lose is the very purpose of these sports.'

'You men! You see the whole of life as a matter of winning and losing.'

'Don't women compete? And love to win?'

'We do, but in our hearts we know it is better to cooperate.'

We were walking past fields in which the hay had been cut, gathered, stacked in ricks and covered in sailcloth.

'See?' she said. 'All this was done not by fighting but by men and women working together. The ladies bring out the gentleman in you. Without us you would all be savages.'

I laughed.

'There is much to be said for savages, you know. Michel

de Montaigne argues almost conclusively that we should see
them as our equals.'

This brought an answering peal of laughter from Elizabeth.

'Your beloved Michael Mountain! According to you, he's
like Scripture and has the solution to everything.'

We came at last to the village street of New Accrington,
after crossing the Woodnook. The first thing we saw was Old
Sukey and Danny, the servant boy, standing at the gate of New
Manor.

'Oh, Mr Cragg!' called Sukey. 'I'm right glad to see you.
Have you seen our guest? Squire's out with his bees and I
don't know who to ask.'

'Is she not inside?' I asked.

Sukey shook her head.

'Not here. She's disappeared. No sign of her. Gone.'

'She must be in the house. I warned her to stay indoors and
not show herself openly.'

'She's not. We've looked in her room and called out. And she's
not out in the garden neither. I'm thinking she might've gone
off to look at the game with her shawl over her head to stop
being noticed.'

'And she hasn't returned?'

'We've not seen her since first thing.'

'Are you sure she's not in her room?' said Elizabeth. 'She
has a habit of shutting herself in, so we are told, and refusing
to come out.'

'Oh, we've looked all over. In the room. In the house. In
the garden. Madam is gone.'

Glancing up at the windows of the house, I saw the white
disc of a face behind one of them. Thomasina Turvey was
watching.

'Perhaps I should come in and have a word with Miss
Thomasina? She may be anxious.'

We went inside and found the child in the Chamber
Major, where she had wheeled herself to greet us. She had
no more idea than had Sukey of what had become of Flora
Horntree.

'I told Sukey to look everywhere in the house and garden,
but there was no sign. We think she must have either gone

out through the gate, or else – as we fear – she went into the river and drowned.'

'Oh, that is not at all likely,' I said. 'Someone would have seen her if she fell into the water.'

'Not if she weighted herself with stones. Then she would have sunk to the bottom.'

'You fear self-murder? Had she shown any signs of wanting to do that? I know she kept to her room yesterday.'

'Not for long, Sir. Otherwise she's been ever so cheerful. Might she have got across to the other side and climbed out up the bank? Maybe she went home to Hatchfly and regretted ever leaving.'

'That's possible, but I doubt it. She was quite determined to leave the place. Has your father returned yet? Does he know anything of what's happened?'

'No, Mr Cragg. He left this morning to go to his bees. He'll return for his supper. That is his usual way.'

'Well, with your permission I will go over the house once again.'

Elizabeth touched my arm.

'You must install our wounded hero at his inn first, Titus. I have to go back to the Dower House as Hector will be hungry, and Matty at the end of her wits by now, I shouldn't wonder. And when you get back here, perhaps Mrs Horntree will have returned.'

'Very well. I'll get the casualty to safety and then come back.'

I caught up with Fidelis and his bearers before they reached the Black Bull, where, on seeing the sore, aching and much bruised doctor taken from his litter and brought hobbling inside, Jane Malkin exclaimed and clapped her hands to her cheeks. No sooner had we got him up to his room and on to his bed than she bustled in with two maidservants, one with a hip bath and the other bearing two buckets of hot water.

'You'll have a hot soak, Doctor,' she said, leaving no possibility of dissent. Fidelis groaned at the effort this would cost him but the servants fetched more water until the tub was full.

'There'll be broth and a bottle of Nantz to cheer you when you've done,' Mrs Malkin said, and she and the maids left the room. I dismissed the litter carriers and, having no manservant to hand, myself assisted Fidelis to get undressed and into the bath, as best I could. Once it was cleaned his body showed much bruising, especially about the ribs, kidneys, breast, shoulders and arms. Sinking back into the hot water, he groaned again but now with relief.

While Elizabeth and I were speaking to Sukey and Thomasina, Fidelis's carriers had continued on past the gate of New Manor and consequently he knew nothing about Mrs Horntree being missing. In his present state I thought it best to spare him the news, as he could do little about it, though he would be bound to try and thereby probably do himself more grief. Instead, I asked him if he felt he'd taken any serious harm other than cuts and bruises.

'I have no broken bones,' he said, his voice hoarse and rising little above a whisper, 'and no deep pains inside. I think I've been lucky, because that big brute was after me with some sort of intent all day. I caught him looking at me more than once, with such malevolence in his eye that I was sure he was trying to kill me – contrary to the rules of the game.'

'Why on earth would he?'

'Because I was the one that soaked him with water the other day, when he joined in the fighting at the inquest. The perfect time to attack me, of course, would've been when we were scattered through the woods – but he couldn't catch me. By the time he did, it was in full sight of yourself and he could hardly actually kill me then because you would have disqualified his team. Ha! Ha!'

His attempt at a laugh ended in a cough and more groans.

He soaked for fifteen minutes more and got out of the tub feeling better. Presently Mrs Malkin came in with bread, onion soup and the promised drink, still as solicitous as ever. I'd seen it before, this effect he had on women of all ages and classes. Except in choice of courtesies, I hope I behave more or less the same to a woman as I do to another man. Fidelis did not. He was often combative, assertive, impatient and insistently rational with his fellow men, whereas he made a point of listening to women, laughing with them, and enjoying light bantering exchanges, and as a result they adored him. From time to time he adored one of them, but that was different.

I therefore left him in good hands when I said good night, having drunk a glass of Mrs Malkin's brandy.

The inn was only half a mile from the gates of Hatchfly Hall – and if Flora Horntree had, as Thomasina suggested, found her way back to the home she had rejected a few days earlier, it would be as well to know sooner, not later. I resolved to go there at once. I was also, naturally, interested in whether I would encounter her husband. On my way down the lane, I stopped everyone I saw and asked after him.

'Have you heard whether Mr Horntree's at home? Has anyone seen him ride through from Manchester this morning?'

But no one had, and at Hatchfly there was only Peggy Stirk, who was kneading bread in the kitchen.

'Mrs Horntree is in her room, Sir,' she told me. 'She's locked herself in there these last three days and nights and won't come out. Starving herself she is, and I'm at the end of my wits worrying. I'm baking bread in the hope the smell will bring her out. It's not the first time she's done it, but never as long as this. I found a note she'd pushed out under the door – see?'

From a shelf in the kitchen dresser Mrs Stirk took a folded piece of paper, which she handed to me.

I opened it and read: *Peggy: I am not to be disturbed. I do not want to see or speak to anyone.*

'Is this her hand?'

'Yes, Sir.'

'And you say it's not the first time she's locked herself in her room?'

'Nor is it. The master's always simply let her be – let her *rot*, as he's said before now. She always comes out in the end, and then she has to ask for his forgiveness. Which, as I always tell her, is only making matters worse.'

'And has your master returned? Does he know of this? I believe he went to Manchester.'

'I haven't seen Mr Horntree since he went away. I was

thinking I'd write to him if only I knew where to write. Very hard and cold towards her he is. It's that which causes these scapper-boiling pets she gets into.'

'Mrs Stirk, I must tell you, this time her pet was something of a ruse. Your mistress left this house on Monday night and came to me saying she was leaving Mr Horntree for ever. But now she's nowhere to be found, so I wondered if she'd changed her mind and come home. Could she have stolen back this morning, without a servant seeing her? I expect you were all at the game, were you not?'

Mrs Stirk shrugged.

'Happen,' she said.

'Then will you take me to your mistress's room so that we can look?'

Peggy led me up the back stairs and out on to the landing that led to the bedrooms. It was a shadowy, unfurnished corridor without pictures or hangings of any kind. We stopped at a door, on which Peggy rapped with her knuckles.

'Mrs Horntree! Mrs Horntree!'

There was no answer, but we heard a faint noise.

'There's someone inside,' I said. 'She must have come back unnoticed after all.'

I turned and rattled the knob but the door was locked. I squinted through the keyhole and saw light: the key was not in place on the inside.

'Mrs Horntree!' I called again. I was answered with a sound that might have been a stifled screech of pain.

'She is there!' I exclaimed.

Mrs Stirk gave a laugh.

'Eh, no. It's her cat wanting feeding, is that.'

I felt a momentary twitch of anger at her mocking my gullibility, and spoke a little roughly.

'Then we must get the door open, Mrs Stirk. Surely there is another key?'

'Not that I know of. Master might have one.'

'Then, as he is not here, we'd better get one of the outside men up here with a tool to force the door.'

Peggy put her hands to her cheeks in dismay.

'Oh, Sir! What will master say?'

'Fortune wastes while the cat is hungry, as they say, Mrs Stirk. And in the meantime, how many other servants are there indoors?'

'Just Agnes, Sir, the housemaid.'

'Will you fetch Agnes to me?'

'I will, but you'll not get more than a farthing's worth out of her. She's a good girl but gormless.'

Agnes soon appeared holding a feather duster. She had a lopsided face and one opaque eye, and was plainly terrified of me. No, she had not seen the mistress this day, she told me in a quaking voice. She had not seen her since Sunday, when mistress had shouted at her for not looking sharp about doing something or other.

A stableman came up carrying an iron crow bar, which he applied to the lock with splintering results. As soon as we pushed the door open, the cat hurtled out and we went in. The room was empty, the bed unslept in, and the chamberpot clean. On the dressing table lay a sealed paper, which I snatched up. It was addressed to Grevel Horntree.

'There's nothing to keep me here, Mrs Stirk,' I said. 'I shall be on my way.'

'What shall I tell the master when he comes back? Shall I tell him . . . what you told me?'

'About his wife leaving him? There's no need to.'

I handed her the letter.

'Just give him this. I fancy it tells him what he should know.'

Emerging from that coldness, I felt glad to return to what had now become a distinctly warm afternoon.

NINETEEN

A t New Manor, I found Tom Turvey at home at last. But in an uncomfortable, fidgeting state. He was walking back and forth in the yard, wringing his hands from agitation and seeming at a dead loss in face of this development.

'Oh! Cragg! What's to be done? I was seeing to the hives all day. I had no idea. No idea at all.'

'You must walk me over the whole of New Manor,' I said. 'Mrs Horntree may have become ill somewhere, as she did once before at Hatchfly Hall. She fell into a swoon and could not be immediately revived.'

He took me through the whole of the ground floor and then into all the bedrooms on the upper floors, and even asked Danny to find a lantern to light the cellars. But although he took us everywhere, I cannot say Turvey helped very much. His manner continued highly nervous, as if he was afraid a ghost might jump out of the wainscoting or flit from a wardrobe. Evidently, the disappearance of the lady had much affected him.

I inspected every recess and cranny. Then we visited every one of the rooms, outhouses and stables around the courtyard, and every part of the garden along the bank of the river. No trace of Flora Horntree could be found.

'I should like to look at the belongings that were in her bedroom,' I said to Turvey. 'They might yield some sort of clue to her fate.'

'Oh!' exclaimed Turvey in agitation. 'Did you say "fate", Cragg? You do not conclude she is dead, I hope? That some fatal chance has overtaken her?'

'I make no conclusion,' I said, 'but something has happened to Mrs Horntree, either by her own will or against it.'

Her bedchamber was a curious little corner room with a round oriel window in the corner itself. Her hooded cloak lay across the bed beside her valise, which I opened, taking out a few handfuls of female clothing and placing them carefully to one side. I reached deeper inside, and to my surprise the first thing I felt was heavy and hard. It proved to be a silver candlestick in a cloth bag.

'Good heavens!' said Turvey. 'That's one of mine!'

The Squire appeared to have regained some of his self-possession. He pulled the bag towards himself and rummaged inside, producing several smaller things: the necklace of true pearls (if Elizabeth was right), two bracelets, various earrings and brooches, and a tiny silver-stopped perfume flask.

'This was my wife's,' he said. 'And this. And this. All from her jewel box on the dressing table.'

He felt around inside to see if he had missed anything.

'Look here!'

He withdrew what looked like a small rounded pillbox made of silver.

'This too, I suppose,' he said, studying it. 'It has a monogram with an *H*, who I presume was my late mother-in-law. Her name was Henrietta.'

He held the item up and pointed to the entwined initials engraved on the lid: *H* and *F*.

'You are surprised at our finding these,' I said. 'I take it you did not give the valuables to her, Turvey.'

'Of course not! They were my wife's. The only possible explanation is that . . . that the lady is a thief, Cragg.'

'Were none of these goods her own? There may be things she brought with her from Hatchfly Hall.'

'A few items I don't recognize,' said Turvey, his voice again beginning to tremble with emotion. 'But I am mightily offended by the woman's deceit of me. Mightily. She has grievously abused my hospitality.'

'Well, there is enough stolen value here to hang her many times over, if she should be prosecuted,' I said, glancing at him. There was moisture in his eyes.

To give him time to recover from his unwelcome discovery, I began replacing the items taken from the valise.

'I should make an inventory of everything we have found in her baggage. It may prove essential to have such a list. So

I'll take the bag into my own keeping, with your permission, Turvey. You shall have your wife's things back in due course.'

He sniffed and fetched a great sigh.

'As you wish, Cragg.'

Back at the Dower House, I found a letter had been delivered by the hand of the potboy from the inn, having arrived earlier by the post. It was in Furzey's finest hand.

> *Dear Mr Cragg,*
>
> *Item the first, we have had notice of a death needing Coroner's attention at Manchester. I think you are near enough to attend and I have written to say they can expect you. Go to the inn called the Swan Inn and the matter will be explained. The deceased is one Greenwood.*
>
> *Item the second, with further reference to the case of the stray examen of bees, insofar as the bees have settled on a neighbour's land, and irrespective of whether they have remained in sight, the law says the neighbour has control over them and the first owner cannot recover the said bees except by agreement. If he goes and takes them, he is liable for theft and trespass. The neighbour is free to do with the bees as he sees fit. I trust this is to the purpose.*
>
> *I am, Sir, etc., Robert Furzey, Clerk at Law.*
>
> *P.S. Mr Oldswick wishes to sue Jerome Snelgrove over a pair of shoes.*
> *P.P.S. The dog Suez is well, but he is unkind to my mother and likes to keep her pinned in corners. I have had to rescue her more than once.*

'Oh dear!' said Elizabeth when I had read the letter to her. 'Shall you go to Manchester?'

'I suppose I must. Tomorrow, I think. It's strange – I come to one of the least frequented parts of the commonwealth and I've never been busier. But first things first. I must draw up this inventory.'

I fetched pen, ink and paper and spent half an hour at the

dining table, listing the contents of Mrs Horntree's valise, with its cargo of ill-gotten gains.

'So, you did not after all misprize that woman,' I said to Elizabeth as I worked. 'It seems she was indeed a criminal – a thief, in fact. Turvey was extremely distressed at the discovery. But what can have happened today? Has she fallen ill somewhere? Or killed herself through guilt? Or did she merely go out to see the May's Hole game and is safe but not yet returned?'

'There cannot be much safety for her now, even if she *is* alive,' Elizabeth said. 'As soon as she reappears, she will be arraigned as a felon. My fear is that she's in the hands of her husband, he having come back from Manchester. Why else would she have left her valise behind?'

'But how could Horntree have abducted his wife from New Manor in broad daylight without them being seen? And besides, she is not at Hatchfly Hall. Is it not more likely she has harmed herself?'

'She was not the kind. And I don't think she was abducted, Titus. I think she left New Manor by herself, maybe to go to May's Hole, and was found by Horntree, somehow. The village was almost deserted and, with everybody at the game, this might easily have been unobserved. And he could have taken her somewhere other than Hatchfly.'

'Why on earth didn't she stay where she was? To leave her sanctuary was the act of a madwoman. And why did she refuse to see Luke Fidelis yesterday, when she is supposedly relying on him to help get her away?'

I drummed with my fingers on the table impatiently. The questions were going round in my head like a screw that turns in bad wood and will not take a grip.

'I wish we knew a little more of her history. What we do know is puzzling. If her thoughts are so much centred on herself, why would she ever willingly become subject to a man like Horntree? Can we believe that it was as simple as falling in love with him?'

'Do you think love is simple?'

'It is for me.'

'But you have an unusual soul, my dearest. I suppose she

may have loved him at some point, but I doubt it. There was much of calculation in that young woman's mind. So what brought her to the North Country, so far from her home?'

I looked again at the things laid out on the dining table, alongside the schedule I had drawn up.

'The fact that she left all this surely means she intends to come back today. Something must have happened to prevent her.'

One by one I re-examined each object and ticked it off on the list. There was nothing remarkable about the clothing, except perhaps that there was not very much of it – a skirt, blouse, two camisoles, some silk stockings and the hooded cloak. The candlestick had punchmarks that told they were made in the previous reign – that is, at least twenty years before.

The more personal possessions comprised a silver thimble, comb, brushes and mirror, and a cosmetic bag containing white hair powder, face powders and lip paint in various colours. There was also a selection of face patches.

'What do these things tell us?' I asked Elizabeth.

'She has more cosmetics than I would expect in a country wife. She puts a high value on her appearance.'

'What else?'

'Apart from the thimble, there are no sewing materials. And no books or writing materials. She was not a reader or much of a writer. She was definitely more interested in adorning her body than in improving her mind.'

I began to separate the pile of jewellery with my fingers: a bracelet made of bone, a pair of enamel-headed hatpins, and then the little monogrammed pillbox. I picked it up. It was an oval, an inch and a half long, of tarnished silver, having plainly not had a rub of vinegar for many weeks.

'Look,' I said, showing Elizabeth the two engraved inter-wreathed letters.

Elizabeth examined the monogram.

'*F* and *H*. It must be for Flora Horntree.'

'No. Mr Turvey told us it belonged to his wife's mother as a girl. Her name was Henrietta.'

'Oh, well! A coincidence that would have appealed to Flora when she helped herself to it. What is that on it?'

Elizabeth took the box from me and put her finger on a tiny ring soldered into place at the top of the box.

'To hang it on a chain around the neck as a locket?'

'There is no chain now. Is there anything inside?'

She inserted a fingernail behind the tiny flange that allowed the locket to be opened. It did not yield immediately, but when she applied more pressure it snapped open and she picked out a lock of wispy hair and a folded scrap of paper.

There was no knowing how long the paper had lain in the pillbox. It might have been a year or two, it might have been decades. The paper itself was clean but not of any particular quality, and appeared to have been torn from an octavo-sized piece of paper from a book perhaps. But as the page had been torn in half lengthwise and this was the right-hand portion, only the second half of each poetical line was visible:

> . . . *lovely styled,*
> . . . *what nature mild,*
> . . . *ect, all are filed*
> . . . *is one child*
> . . . *ming of the soul,*
> . . . *we keep this roll.*

'These are rhymes,' I said. 'But from what book?'

'A puzzle which you will enjoy resolving, dearest,' said Elizabeth. 'And when you do, we may yet know this locket's secret.'

TWENTY

When I left him, Fidelis had seemed to be mending. Yet arriving again the next morning, I learned he had been very poorly in the night, and it was a job to persuade Mrs Malkin to let me see him. In the end I was allowed, but found my friend in a shallow fitful sleep.

'He looks bad, yet the fever is less than it was at midnight,' the landlady said.

'Perhaps he is over the worst, then.'

'Should we call the doctor from Haslingden to him?'

'I would advise against it, if there is no sudden turn for the worse. Unless he is *in extremis*, Dr Fidelis has a sharp tongue and disagrees with other doctors on principle. If he can speak, he will certainly say something offensive to your doctor from Haslingden.'

A look of compassionate admiration lit Mrs Malkin's fleshy face.

'He is a clever one, I'll say that. You leave him with me, Mr Cragg. I'll do all I can to nurse him back to his feet.'

I looked down on Fidelis. His face was covered with a sheen of sweat.

'If he comes to himself, you must tell him I have left for Manchester, where there's been a death I am needed to enquire into. If, however, he should take a turn for the worst, please send for Mr Vaux the, er, Catholic priest, as he is of that faith.'

Frances Nightingale was sitting with Elizabeth, while Matty clattered around the range preparing a pike fish for the oven. When I asked Frances, she agreed straight away to come with me to Manchester. She told me she had visited the town, and I asked her opinion of it.

'It has all the extent and appearance of a borough,' she said, 'but in reality it is only a village grown to a prodigious size. There's none of your aldermen, councillors and mayors that you've got in Preston, but only the parish council and constable to manage its affairs, directed by the gentry that own most of the town, one of which is Sir Oswald Mosley. It is a very serious place, is Manchester, with little by way of diversions going on there. The people keep their noses to the grind and regard the sparks that come off as money flying into their pockets.'

'I have been directed to the Swan Inn. Do you know it?'

'When I was there with my late husband, we stayed at the Sun & Stars.'

'We shall ride there this afternoon, to make more time to investigate this matter.'

'But I don't keep a horse.'

'But you do ride? Mrs Malkin will provide a mount. We shall be able to recover the expense, I'm sure, as Manchester is a prosperous enough place and will pay our costs.'

After we had eaten the great roasted fish for dinner (or eaten what we could, for it was much too large to be finished at one sitting), I suggested that before my departure Elizabeth walk with me in the air a little.

We took the path alongside the Woodnook Brook that led up towards Turvey's Clover Field. We passed the cottages and as we climbed towards the brookside wood we passed through a small meadow, stubbly after the haymaking and with half a dozen ricks, each covered with a square of sailcloth. The hot air was spiced with the scent of hay. Then we entered the wood itself, whose shade refreshed our senses on a day on which the summer's heat had returned.

'Are you anxious about Luke?' she asked.

'A little, but he is young and strong.'

'I will go to him later and see how he progresses.'

'He does not know that Mrs Horntree is missing. You must inform him, if you judge he is strong enough to take the news. You may then bring him the list of the contents of her valise. Luke will need some convincing that the lady he admires so much is a thief, but I think that should do it.'

'He will be sorely disappointed.'

'I shall be particularly interested in his opinion of the locket

and the fragment of poetry. Turvey says it belonged to his
mother-in-law, but Flora might have put the paper in herself
during the short time she had it. In either case, it is intriguing
to wonder what secret significance the poetry has.'

'There are all sorts of secrets women keep, Titus. Oh! Look
there, forest strawberries!'

She was pointing to a patch of the fruit growing around the
foot of a tree near the edge of the water. She immediately
whipped off her straw hat and put it on the ground.

'Have you a clean handkerchief? It is fearfully bad luck to
come upon wild strawberries in fruit and not pick some.'

She unfolded the handkerchief that I gave her and used it
to line the crown of the hat. For five minutes we stripped the
little crimson fruits from their stalks and piled them into it.

It would take at least four hours to ride the twenty-five miles
to Manchester. Leaving Accrington in the mid-afternoon, I
calculated that we would be at our inn before supper time
when, it being midsummer, there would still be a couple of
hours of daylight. We rode through Haslingden and reached
Bury by six. The going was rough on occasion, but mostly
dry and firm. We met several herds of cattle crowding the road
on their way to milking, and overtook three or four trains of
mules laden with bales of cloth made up in the Lancashire
valleys and now on their way to the Manchester market. We
also met three or four other pack-trains laden with raw cotton
and wool going in the other direction.

What is required in a riding companion on the road is the
ability to be amusing or instructive on any subject when
the horses are walking, not to lose the thread during stretches
where the road is good enough to go at a trot or canter, and
to pick up the conversation as the surface worsens and the
horses must walk again. By these criteria, Frances Nightingale
was excellent company. She gave me a lively commentary
on the villages we passed through, made jokes, and laughed
at mine.

The Swan Inn stood in Market Street Lane, an address
lined with opulent houses, rather better appointed than the
best Preston could offer. I put this down to the industry of

the town, with its single-minded devotion to money-making through the cloth trade. I engaged rooms for us, and as soon as we were settled in asked for the landlord. His name was John Blow.

'I am Titus Cragg, County Coroner,' I told him, 'and I've come to Manchester to enquire into the death of a person called Greenwood.'

'Oh yes, a very mad accident was that, Mr Cragg.'

'Who was this Greenwood?'

'Mr Quentin Greenwood, from I know not where. Possibly Macclesfield. But I do know he was shot in the butts.'

'The butts?' I said, with some incredulity.

'Oh yes, archery is greatly practised here.'

'Ah, I see. The butts. So how did it happen?'

'He took an arrow in the neck. It went in behind one of his ears.'

'Mr Greenwood was an archer?'

'Oh, no. He was a silk merchant, or so we think.'

'When did this happen?'

'On Tuesday last.'

'And who fired the shot?'

'A young lad of fifteen. A very lively boy and well known for his antics.'

'Hmm. If this is "antics", I wonder what counts as evil-doing in Manchester? Did you witness it?'

'No. Greenwood was brought here because this is the nearest inn to the butts. They're just the other side of that wall there, next to the pinfold.'

'So you are keeping his body here?'

'Aye, in a shed I use for storing tools and such.'

'Who brought him?'

'Mr Bower ordered it.'

'Who is Mr Bower?'

Blow looked shocked at my question.

'You don't know the name of Jeremiah Bower? He is our headman – our bailey or, if you prefer, our reeve. He was sent for when it happened.'

'I had better have a look at the body. Please take me to it.'

Blow shook his head.

'That I cannot, not without Mr Bower's warrant. He told me to lock the body up and let no one near. He said he must write to Preston to fetch the Coroner.'

'But, as I told you, I *am* the Coroner.'

'That's as may be. But you are not Mr Bower, and he has the final say.'

'Then direct me to his house, if you please.'

To give the headman of Manchester his formal title, Jeremiah Bower was Boroughreeve. As Frances had told me, the town has no Mayor and no Corporation but is ruled by the Court Leet of the lords of the manor, who have been members of the Mosley family since ancient times. The Mosleys were (and are) largely content to leave daily town business to this court and to the Boroughreeve, its president. Accordingly, it was this official who wielded most of the power in this 'village' of 10,000 inhabitants.

His house was a substantial residence in an elegant and recently built street off the long and straight thoroughfare called Dean's Gate. Having left Frances Nightingale to rest after the journey, I walked over there in ten minutes. A maid admitted me into Bower's hall.

Like many entrance halls, it was an ill-lit shadowy space and this left me quite unprepared for a succession of rapid clicks at the level of the floor and a rushing, sliding noise, followed by the sudden impact of a head against my midriff. A dog, I realized, had propelled itself out of the gloom and butted me in the stomach. The creature had rebounded but immediately renewed its attentions, panting wetly, licking my hand and pawing me as it bounced up and down on its hind legs. Unable to see it clearly, I patted its head.

'Don't mind the dog, Sir,' said the maid. 'It's a very lively one but loves people, as you can see. It's come with a visitor who you'll find in here with Mr Bower.'

She took the dog by the collar to prevent it erupting into the room as she opened the door to announce me. Going in, I found it was evidently Bower's business room, as it contained shelves loaded with legal books, more than one document cabinet and a broad writing desk. There was also a large fireplace (unlit on this hot day), beside which sat a large man wearing a finely tailored coat and an expensive wig – obviously the Boroughreeve himself.

Opposite him, to my utter astonishment, sat Robert Furzey.

'Furzey! By the heavens, man! You have come here for this inquest?'

'Yes, Sir. Not knowing your time of arrival, I took the opportunity of making myself known to Mr Bower.'

'And tell me, Furzey. It's a little dark in Mr Bower's lobby, but that dog – that dog who was all over me just now – is it who I'm thinking it is?'

'I cannot know what you're thinking, Mr Cragg,' said Furzey, as literal-minded as ever. 'But I've brought you Suez, right enough. My mother's at her wit's end with him and the cat's run away. We can have him no more, and that's a fact.'

Looking a little bemused at our exchange, Bower levered his considerable bulk into a standing position and we shook hands.

'I won't speak of your dog, but you yourself are welcome to Manchester, Mr Cragg,' he said in a sonorous voice. 'Take a seat, take a seat. Your reputation, you know, precedes you. Indeed, Manchester has heard of your many exploits as Coroner, and Manchester has long been hoping to have a death sufficient to require your attendance. So it is very satisfying to have you here at last. Ha! Ha!'

He clapped his hands together, and presented the very picture of delight.

'I doubt that Mrs, Miss and Master Greenwood, if there are such persons, would concur with your satisfaction, Mr Bower,' said Furzey.

Bower took the point without argument, and assumed a graver face as he drew up a chair for me.

'Ah yes! The unfortunate Mr Greenwood. Well, *mors nihil vita omnia est*. Isn't it so? "Life trumps death", or words to that effect. But to business.'

A bailiff quoting Latin tags: Manchester was indeed an unusual place.

'Yes, indeed, to business,' I said. 'I understand that the corpse is at the Swan Inn. What do we know about Greenwood? John

Blow mentioned that he was a silk merchant, possibly from Macclesfield.'

'The silk trade is very extensive in a few places round here – as it is in Macclesfield, for example. But there is also silk weaving in London, is there not? Manchester doesn't have much truck with silken stuff, mind. Plain woollens and the finest cottons are Manchester's cloths of choice. So I cannot tell you what Mr Greenwood's precise business was here.'

'Did you know him yourself?'

'I did not, but it seems he was a fairly frequent visitor here on business.'

'Were there any witnesses to his death?'

Instead of answering me, Bower now rose, opened one of the document cabinets, and took out a sheaf of papers, which he handed across with a flourish.

'You will not find Manchester unmethodical, Cragg. These documents are the depositions of several who were present, after examination by myself. You will see when you read them that the death was a perfect accident.'

'Well! To have my witness statements all prepared and packaged up is . . . very gratifying. I shall also need a room for the hearing.'

'We have put the court room at the Exchange at your disposal. It will not be put to other use tomorrow. The inquest is scheduled to start at ten sharp in the morning. I have also summoned a jury – here are the names.'

He took another sheet of paper from his desk and handed it across, in the same manner as before.

'They will all be there or they'll answer to me. So now you have everything you need, I think, to complete this unfortunate business in short order. As I said, there is no doubt about what the verdict will be.'

TWENTY-ONE

A s we walked out into Dean's Gate, Suez leaped and capered around us. Furzey too was cock-a-hoop and himself almost capering.

'It's wonderful, Mr Cragg. When I came here to meet you, I expected I would be doing – as ever – all the hard work on this inquest. What do I find? The drudgery is done for me. No copying, no shorthand notes, no finding of premises or chasing after truant jurors. Nothing. It's all arranged beforehand. Oh aye. This is a very wonderful place indeed for efficacy.'

I, on the other hand, felt uneasy.

'I am not so sure, Furzey. All this—' I touched the bundle of witness statements that I held under my arm – 'it's all too neat, too tidy and parcelled up. Do you not sense we are being hurried along? I would prefer to look into this matter for myself, and I wish Doctor Fidelis were here to examine the body.'

'Did we not manage before the doctor came to Preston? You can do just as well without him, and you have myself to help you.'

'Ah, yes, on that question – of your help, I mean – I should tell you something . . .'

I cleared my throat. This was probably going to be awkward.

'You should know that, when I reached Accrington, I straight away found, to my surprise, that there was coroner's business waiting for me. In fact, I had to hold an inquest very quickly and, rather than have you summarily abandon the Preston office, I engaged a temporary clerk who is a clever and knowledgeable person. This person I have brought with me here to Manchester – never imagining, of course, that I would find you waiting.'

Without warning, Furzey seized my arm and made me stop and face him.

'I am supplanted, then, am I?' he said in a tone at once fierce and wounded.

'No, of course not. As you *are* here, I want no one else but
you to clerk the inquest.'

'Ha! But shall you then bring your new helper back to
Preston? Shall I be replaced when all's said and done? Shall
I be trussed and sent to market? Put up on the auction block?
Plucked and beheaded?'

'No, Furzey! Enough! Don't stir up mischief, and mind
you are civil to my friend.'

'Civil? Aye, I've to keep my true feelings on a leash, like
the dog. As, unfortunately, I depend on you for my livelihood,
I'll be civil to him.'

I did not correct his pronoun's gender.

'Yes, Furzey, if you wish to please me, be civil. Do not
prejudge. Besides, I am sure you will soon like each other.
Now, let us go on to the inn. I must find a messenger able
to take a letter at speed to the Doctor in Accrington. I left him
there lying unwell in his bed, but if he is recovered I want
him here as soon as possible.'

'The inquest'll be over before ever he'll arrive. It's at ten
o'clock in the morning, the Boroughreeve says, and the
conclusion is a foregone one.'

'It's I that am Coroner, Furzey, and I say the case is not
foregone, never mind what the Boroughreeve says.'

'He only wants to get it over, I expect. The death of this
merchant is an embarrassment that may harm business. It
cannot be left to fester.'

'I care nothing for business. My responsibility is to justice,
if I can find it.'

Furzey made as if to interrupt me, but I stopped him.

'I won't dance to Bower's tune. You may call that tune
time-saving, he may call it methodical. I call it officious and
am beginning to suspect it to be interference. Now, let us go
on to the inn.'

The light had begun to fade and the servants were busy lighting
candles at the Swan Inn. I realized that I had failed to ask
Boroughreeve Bower to send John Blow an order to unlock
the corpse for my inspection. Well, it would do no good
now. The light had gone and there was no possibility that

Fidelis could arrive in time to make an examination before
our proceedings opened in the morning. I would get my first
view of Greenwood's body in company with the jury, as
coroners do in the normal course of things.

The Swan Inn was a house with a single large parlour
furnished with many tables, at which patrons sat having their
tea or their liquor. As we entered the room, I saw Frances
Nightingale at one of these tables in earnest conversation with
a clergyman.

'There is your *locum tenens*, Furzey,' I said as we
approached them.

'A *parson*, Sir?' He was hissing to avoid being heard by
the gentleman in question. 'You have given my job to a
parson! And what would he know about writing in the legal
hand, may I ask?'

'No, not the parson, Furzey,' I murmured.

We reached the table.

'May I introduce Mrs Frances Nightingale, who has been
kind enough to act as my clerk *pro tem* in one or two matters?
Frances, this is Robert Furzey, my regular clerk in Preston.
He has come all this way to deliver a dog to me.'

Furzey looked for a moment like a man presented to the
Basilisk, or to a bearded lady. But he collected himself and
made a formal bow.

'To be more accurate, Madam, I come to act as Mr Cragg's
clerk in the inquest into the death of Mr Quentin Greenwood,
of which we had notification at the office in Preston.'

Frances Nightingale was not at all put out to meet a rival
for her clerkship.

'How do, Mr Furzey?' said Frances. 'I am right pleased to
meet you. May I in turn present the Reverend Septimus Postumus?'

The clergyman was in middle life: a cherubic figure, plump,
pink and smiling.

'A very good day to you, Mr Cragg, Mr Furzey. It has been
such an unforeseen joy to meet my old friend Mrs Nightingale
here. We have been talking with such pleasure of old times.'

'Mr Postumus's living is at Clitheroe,' said Frances
Nightingale. 'He was often our guest when my husband was
alive. He has come to Manchester by special invitation to give

a sermon in honour of the feast of St John the Baptist. He is a famed preacher.'

'Come, come, Madam,' said the cleric, growing still pinker. 'I cannot lay claim to fame. Some modest esteem, perhaps.'

'And what text shall you preach on, Mr Postumus?' I asked.

'One from the Gospel of Matthew: "Oh ye generation of vipers, who hath warned you to flee from the wrath to come?" I shall not err too far in the direction of enthusiasm, I hope, but I can scarcely avoid considerable reference to the fires of hell and condign punishment. I hope I will have the pleasure of your attendance. The service begins at eleven.'

He stood.

'Well, I should go to my room. My sermon is still in the making and I must work on it. Goodnight, Mrs Nightingale, and goodnight all.'

Furzey and I pulled out chairs as he left us. Suez strained to get near Mrs Nightingale, eager as ever to make a new acquaintance.

'What is your dog's name, Mr Furzey?' Frances said, patting its head.

'It is no dog of mine, Madam. It is Mr Cragg's dog – and a very naughty dog that has been lodging with me by an arrangement which I now bring to an end at the wish of my mother, who I live with.'

She tilted her face enquiringly towards me.

'Mr Cragg?'

'His name is Suez,' I said. 'He developed the habit of herding Mrs Furzey and pinning her in corners. But he is otherwise extremely friendly and will accept a kick or a sharp word from all that love him. Now, I shall leave you for a while, as I must write my note to Dr Fidelis and find a messenger to take it. I will rejoin you later for a little supper.'

Having found the reading and writing room, I wrote a few lines to Fidelis in which I told him of Bower's mysterious desire to hasten the inquest. If my astute friend had recovered his health and spirits, he would be reading my letter over breakfast and on absorbing this suggestion of intrigue would surely be calling for his horse.

I also wrote a short note to Elizabeth.

Dearest wife,

*We made a good journey. This is a very busy, pros-
perous town. The gaffer of the place, who calls himself
the Boroughreeve, has presented me with the paperwork
of this inquest already copied and bound, and a hall
has already been appointed for a hearing first thing
tomorrow (Saturday). Until I know why he wants to
proceed with such dispatch, I intend going slow in the
business and may not return until Tuesday. I will write
again before then.*

Yr loving T.C.

*P.S. A surprise: Furzey was here at the inn to greet me,
and Mrs Nightingale will come home sooner than me if
I can find someone to ride with her. Furzey brought Suez
and says Mrs F. was penned up once too often in her
own home.*

*P.P.S. Have you asked Mr Turvey about the torn page of
poetry in the silver box?*

*P.P.P.S. Give our son a tender kiss for me. I hate to
be parted from him, just as much as I do – always –
from you.*

I sealed the letters and gave them to John Blow, who promised
to find me a fast rider who would depart at first light and cover
the distance to Accrington in less than four hours. I paid the
charge, not without a sigh. These were Manchester prices, and
I fully intended Manchester to pay them back – though if
anything about civic administration is certain, it is that there
never was a town that willingly paid a coroner.

Returning to the parlour, I felt some apprehension as to how
my two clerks and the dog would be rubbing along. I need
not have been troubled. They had ordered what looked like a
veal pie and, having eaten their fill, were talking with a young
man of striking good looks though dressed in plain black
clothing and an unorthodox foreign-looking wig. Suez had
taken a liking to him and was sitting with his muzzle resting
on the stranger's knee.

I took my seat and the stranger bowed in my direction.

'I am Charles Burnet at your disposal, Sir.'

He pronounced his name 'Burnay' and in general used a curiously accented, though fluent, English. In truth, his tongue at this moment was superfluent – by which I mean slurred, as he appeared to be in the early stages of becoming the worse for drink.

'Where are you from Mr Burnet?' I asked, helping myself to a portion of the pie.

'I am from the Spital Fields in London. My family is engaged in the silk trade.'

'Ah!' I said. 'You are one of our good Huguenot cousins.'

'Yes, Sir. I was born in London, in the year of Our Lord 1720, but my father was a Frenchman born. As you say, a Protestant, not a papist – and most zealous for the theology of Monsieur Calvin.'

What, I asked, brought him to the north of England?

'I have come to learn about the methods of silk manufacturing they use in the nearby town of Macclesfield. In certain ways these differ from our own ways in London. I am presently a guest of Mr Mosley at his great house, Ancoats Hall, but today I have been visiting the centre of town in order to peruse the London newspapers. The best selection I have found is here at the Swan Inn.'

'As you are attached to the silk trade, you must know of the sad event that occurred this week to one of your merchant fraternity here in Manchester.'

Burnet looked blank.

'You may have known Mr Quentin Greenwood.'

Burnet's expression did not change.

'Greenwood? No, I have not heard that name.'

'We believe he was a silk merchant. The same business as you are in yourself.'

'Well, of course, you understand I have been in the north only a short time and have not met everyone.'

My conversation with Burnet went no further, as he began to attend to what Furzey and Frances were saying.

'I don't foresee them Jacobites attacking Lancashire county,' Furzey opined. 'In 'fifteen they were slaughtered at Preston, and the place is fatal luck to them.'

'No doubt you are right, Mr Furzey.'

'It's my belief they'll be trying their luck invading Yorkshire first.'

'Or Ireland. There's plenty to encourage them over there.'

'Ireland, Mrs Nightingale? Whoever puts Ireland first? They're savages in Ireland. No, it'll be Yorkshire where they'll land, mark my words.'

'Why not Scotland?' Burnet suddenly put in. 'I have read in the newspaper that the Pretender has strong support among the clans.'

'The same reason as rules out Lancaster,' said Furzey, who was becoming increasingly opinionated as wine loosened his tongue. 'They came to Scotland last time and no good it did them. If they do come, they'll do something different – that's a solid fact.'

The discussion moved on, while the young silk merchant continued to drink steadily. In due course, with a scrape of his chair, Burnet stood unsteadily up.

'I must go. Be on my way. I bid you g'night.'

He turned abruptly, and for a moment teetered sideways then forward. It seemed he would recover his balance since he straightened up, but in reality he was only on his way backwards. He went down with a clatter and lay sprawling, though not hurt, with a contented smile playing across his lips.

I knelt and rolled him over, then hooked my hands into his armpits. He was not a heavy young man and I easily raised him to the vertical, while Frances retrieved his wig and planted it on his head.

'We must get him to Ancoats Hall.'

'I'll see him there,' I said. 'Suez needs a run, anyway. Come on, Mr Burnet, put your best foot forward.'

Out in the street, Mr Burnet required a degree of support, as his legs were unruly, continually bending and staggering under him. So we lurched a few hundred yards through the dark streets while Burnet sang something in French. When I asked, he told me it was a Huguenot hymn. To me it sounded jollier than any hymn I had ever heard, but I made no remark.

Finally we arrived at the house in question, a fine old-fashioned wooden-framed mansion with mullioned windows and three gables, the whole surmounted overall by a square tower. A many-ribboned maid came to the door and, seeing Mr Burnet's inebriation, solicitously helped him into the house.

Furzey and Frances were still engaged in earnest talk when Suez and I returned.

'The iron tongue of midnight hath told twelve,' I told them. 'Lovers to bed! I fear we shall outsleep the coming morn.'

While Frances said good night and went upstairs, Furzey stubbornly sat on to finish his glass. He flashed me a sly look.

'Lovers, did you call us? Lovers? Your wits are a-wandering, Mr Cragg. That is a good decent woman, but she's at least ten years older than me.'

'It isn't my wits we need to worry about, but yours,' I said severely. 'You will need them about you tomorrow or you'll outsleep the inquest as well as the morn.'

The Exchange at Manchester, still less than twenty years old, was a temple-like edifice designed to hold the cloth market below and the court above. Aside from St Paul's Cathedral, the columns supporting the great triangular pediment over its entrance were the hugest in width that I had ever seen.

At a few minutes before ten in the morning, I passed between these columns and on to the trading floor. The whole area was covered with rank upon rank of trestle tables creaking under the weight of bolts of finished cloth. Merchants in their tricorn hats and gold-embroidered waist-coats walked up and down inspecting the cloth, rubbing it between fingers and thumb. Business was now at its height, but you would hardly have known it, so quiet was the air. There is an absolute ban on shouting while one trades in the Exchange, with the result that business is done wholly in murmurs and whispers. It is a sound I can only compare to that of the tide on a shingle beach – a rustling and whis-pering as bargains were snapped up and deals were done all over the hall.

I was directed by a uniformed beadle up the stone staircase that ascended to the upper room. This chamber above the market was where the Court Leet normally conducted itself and, as I took my seat on a raised throne-like seat from which to look down on lesser mortals, I thought it was the most imposing room in which I'd ever held an inquest.

From my exalted position, I swore the jury in and then explained to them why we were all there.

'We have gathered to determine why and how a man, Quentin Greenwood, died. We go first to view the body, and then we will hear evidence. Yours is the final say, but I ask you to listen carefully and impartially to the witnesses and come to no premature conclusions. And, however you disagree with me or each other, please keep the peace at all times.'

That last request seemed hardly necessary in this case. My jury at Accrington had been incurably at war with itself, whereas this group of men seemed eager to do exactly as I requested. I took them down the Exchange stairs and along to the Swan Inn to get our first sight of the late Greenwood. Once assembled in John Blow's shed, they stood around the shrouded body as placidly as a herd of cows looking into a lily pond.

In case any of the jurors were afraid of death or the dead, I said a few more stiffening words before giving Furzey the word to remove the sheet from the body. When the time came, Furzey did it with as much ceremony as he could, drawing the sheet upwards from the feet. The shoes, we saw, were expensive. The stockings were silken and the breeches and shirt were of the best stuff imaginable, though the latter was soiled with dust and partly blood-soaked. When the neck came into view, there was a gasp – for the arrow was still buried in it, the feather-end protruding on one side and the tip on the other. Then, with a final flourish, Furzey removed the sheet completely and revealed the face, frozen in a rictus of absolute surprise.

My own face must have mirrored it, as a sudden gasp issued from my mouth. For only I knew – and therefore only I could be astonished – that the face we were looking at was not that of Quentin Greenwood. I had never met Quentin Greenwood, but this face I knew immediately. It was the face of Grevel Horntree of Old Accrington.

TWENTY-TWO

t took a moment for my head to clear. What did this mean? Was Greenwood really Horntree? Or, conversely, was Horntree really Greenwood? And either way, what would that reveal not only about this shooting but about the events in Accrington over the past couple of weeks, too? I may have managed to disguise my confusion from the others – but not from Furzey, who fixed me with one of his most quizzical looks. I frowned a warning at him as I tried to think what to do. I needed more time, that was it. The answer came to me a moment later: correct procedure. I could slow everything down by insisting on following all the established rules to the letter, not to mention a few others that I might get away with inventing.

'Have any of you been a juryman in a death inquest before?' I asked the assembled company.

One of the jurors raised a timid finger.

'Ah! And your name is?'

'John Matthews, Your Honour.'

'Well, Mr Matthews, do you remember the body that time?'

'I do. It were Michael Murthwaite.'

'What state was the body in when you saw it?'

'He were dead, Your Honour.'

Nobody so much as smiled.

'Of course he was, Mr Matthews. However, was there anything else about Murthwaite that you noticed?'

'No, Your Honour.'

'His clothing, perhaps?'

'Oh no, Your Honour.'

'Why not his clothing?'

'Because he were stripped naked.'

'Just so. Thank you, Mr Matthews. Now, gentlemen, I don't know the case of Michael Murthwaite, but I do know that his body had to be stripped for the jury, because it is laid down that inquest juries must view the naked body of the victim

before hearing evidence. Now let's consider this body here
– has it been stripped?'

They all shook their heads together.

'Which means we cannot view it,' I said.

Another juryman raised his hand.

'Shall us strip it now, Your Honour? We can get it done in
a minute.'

'No, no! That is not the proper way to go about things.
There are women whose task this is, and they have failed to
do it. So follow me please. We shall return to the court room,
having locked the door of this place behind us.'

Back in my throned eminence, I scanned the public benches
and saw that Bower had just arrived and was sitting expectantly amongst a group of other middle-aged men, some as
well-dressed as himself. This was, no doubt, the ruling
oligarchy of Manchester. I rang my handbell to subdue the
chatter of the court.

'I regret to say that we have been unable to view the body
in the manner laid down by law and tradition,' I said. 'It is
necessary for the said body to be prepared by being entirely
stripped bare for the jury's examination, which has not been
done. I therefore direct that those usually appointed to such
duties be ordered to properly prepare the corpse in time for a
full and correct viewing on Monday morning. And as we can
do no more business until that viewing is accomplished, I
adjourn this inquest for resumption on Monday at ten.'

I glanced across to Bower. He was looking in perplexity
to the fellow on his right and then to the fellow on his left.
As I descended from my perch, he hurried up to me and stood
directly in my path. He largely stifled his frustration but was
nonetheless fuming.

'This is a quibble, Cragg! We can have the damned body
stripped in five minutes. I'll order it to be done now and you
can go and ogle it to your heart's content. Then we can all
come back here and get a verdict.'

'I cannot, Mr Bower, not now. The procedure is quite clear
and well-known. I have prorogued until Monday and this
inquest can only resume on that day.'

Bower clicked his tongue, and perhaps bit it, before turning away. I crooked my finger at Furzey, who bent his ear to my mouth.

'There's something very peculiar going on,' I said in a low voice. 'Bring all the court documents to the Swan. I had a superficial look at the statements bundle at breakfast this morning, but I now think I must read them through more carefully.'

There were four witness statements in all. The first that I unfolded, written in legal hand, was the one that during my earlier perusal I had marked 'First Finder'.

> *I, Joanna Prescott, aged 28 and laundress of Manchester, do declare that on the morning of Tuesday last, being the 19th day of June, I was carrying a basket of laundry in Pratt's Court and going past the archers' butts that stand next to the pinfold, when a gentleman that was walking in front of me went down all of a heap. I ran up to him and found he was bleeding very much from the neck. His body was twitching and he grunted but was unable to speak in reply to my questions. I then saw that an arrow had pierced him in the neck and was stuck there. I did not see the arrow flying at him but it must have been from the butts, which I could see the targets of through a gap in the buildings from where I was standing. Daniel Sayer from the tailor's shop across the way came out and we turned him over. Mr Sayer asked if I knew him and I said not. Mr Sayer then took a letter from the man's coat pocket and said it was addressed to Mr Greenwood. We had not been beside him long when the gentleman gave over his noises and movements and lay still. A surgeon came and he pronounced the gentleman dead.*

A cross had been put in place of a signature, certified by Jeremiah Bower as being Joanna Prescott's mark.

I now turned to the second statement, that of Isaac Clooney, surgeon, who stated that he had been called at ten o'clock or thenabouts from his rooms on Market Street Lane to an incident in Pratt's Court. There he found a man lying on the ground, having been grievously wounded by an arrow. From the quantity of blood that had spurted and spilt on the ground, it was clear he had bled so profusely that there was no saving him. Indeed, by the time Mr Clooney reached the place the man was already quite dead. Clooney stated that he was shown a letter found in the dead man's pocket, addressed to a Mr Greenwood in Cold Harbour Lane. A scrawl that must have been Clooney's signature appeared at the bottom of the statement.

The third statement was headed *EXAMINATION OF MASTER ASHTON LEVER* and was in the form of questions (those of Jeremiah Bower) and answers (those of Ashton Lever).

> *Q. How old are you Master Lever?*
> *A. Fifteen.*
> *Q. Where do you live and what do you do?*
> *A. I live in Market Street Lane at my mother's house and attend the Grammar School.*
> *Q. And your father?*
> *A. He was Sir Darcy Lever. He died two years ago.*
> *Q. And how long have you been practising archery for your own amusement?*
> *A. Toxophilia, you mean. That is the proper term for what you call the amusement of archery.*
> *Q. Very well, how long have you been engaged in toxophilia?*
> *A. Three or four months. I have lessons from Mr Moorcroft, who keeps the butts.*
> *Q. When was the last time you shot an arrow?*
> *A. On Tuesday morning last.*
> *Q. What happened?*
> *A. I was about to shoot at the target when I caught sight of a sparrowhawk, and I tried to shoot at it as I hate the bird.*
> *Q. Did you hit the sparrowhawk?*
> *A. No.*
> *Q. Do you know what became of the arrow you shot?*

> A. *It flew up and came down outside the butts, between two houses I think.*
> Q. *Two houses in Pratt's Court?*
> A. *Yes.*
> Q. *It was a foolish thing to do, was it not, to try and shoot the sparrowhawk?*
> A. *(No reply.)*
> Q. *How soon did you know that your arrow had hit someone?*
> A. *We heard a cry and ran over to the place and found a man lying there, wounded in the neck.*
> Q. *And was it your arrow in the gentleman's neck?*
> A. *I couldn't say, as all arrows look the same.*

That is the complete interview. At the bottom was written: *The foregoing is a true copy of my answers to the questions of Mr Bower, signed Ashton Lever.*

Next came a brief statement by Abel Moorcroft, saying that after his pupil shot at the sparrowhawk they heard a cry from the direction of Pratt's Court and ran there. He could confirm what they found. The arrow in the dead man's neck was identical to the one Ashton Lever had shot in the air and, in Moorcroft's opinion, was indeed that same arrow. Young Ashton was in general a fairly good bowman and had been making particular improvements recently. He had been warned never to shoot at anything but the target and Moorcroft could not account for Ashton Lever's sudden breaking of that injunction, especially as he professed to be very fond of birds. Finally, Abel Moorcroft estimated the value of the arrow at 6d and the bow from which it had been discharged at 4s 6d.

The final statement was that of Jeremiah Bower himself.

> *On Tuesday last I was at my business room in the Exchange when I was summoned to an incident in Pratt's Court. It was not long after ten o'clock in the morning. I found a crowd of people gathered round the dead body of a man, evidently (from his clothes) a gentleman, who had been struck in the neck and killed by an arrow. I did not recognize him. I asked if any present knew his name.*

One or two said they had seen him in our town but could not name him. Mr Clooney, however, had mentioned that a letter was found in his coat pocket addressed to Quentin Greenwood Esq. at No. 17 Cold Harbour Lane. I inspected the letter and found it was to do with the silk trade. I went to the house named in the address and was told Mr Greenwood was from out of Manchester and had taken rooms there on a lease some three years ago, but was an infrequent visitor. I have written to leading citizens of Macclesfield, Stockport and other towns where the silk manufacture takes place with enquiries as to Mr Greenwood, but with no positive reply to date.

I laid Bower's statement down and sifted through the evidence bundle. The letter found in Horntree's pocket should have been there, but it was not. The only other paper was a receipt for delivery of the corpse, signed by John Blow of the Swan Inn.

Ten minutes later I was on my way alone to Cold Harbour Lane, a twenty-minute walk away. The house to which, according to Bower, the letter had been addressed was one of a terrace built in the reign of Queen Anne in what had been the periphery of Manchester, though the town had extended itself greatly since. All of these particular properties were inhabited and in a good state of repair. The windows of number seventeen, however, were shuttered and there was no response when I knocked on the door.

I now called at number fifteen, where a cautious intensely blushing servant boy with a stammering tongue said he was alone in the house and could not think of anything to tell me about next door. At number nineteen it was a different story: the lady of the house, a Mrs Quinto, immediately agreed to see me.

Her maid invited me to wait in a comfortable room with softly upholstered chairs and Turkey carpets. The pictures were in the French style and showed richly dressed ladies and gentlemen enjoying outdoor pleasures such as picnics and open-air concerts. From upstairs, I heard murmuring and a trill of female laughter. Shortly after that, came the sound of a tread upon the stairs and the lady swept into the room.

She was a dark-haired, scented, gaily dressed woman of middle age who spoke with a foreign accent (she told me she had been born in Lisbon). I asked if she expected her husband to come home soon, at which she laughed.

'My husband? If he did, I would certainly not let him in. Shall we sit?'

She opened her fan as she did so and hid half her face, but widened her eyes as they looked across at me.

'So what can I do for you, Mr Titus Cragg? You have not visited us here before. I suggest you are quite frank with me and that will make it all the easier.'

I could not think what she meant by this, but I told her I was making inquiries about her neighbour, the gentleman who lived at number seventeen. Immediately her manner changed, becoming brisker.

'Oh! And I was thinking you were here to have your fortune told. I have the gift, you know, in a highly developed form.'

I merely bowed and waited for her to speak about the tenant.

'Our neighbour, you say? He is some kind of merchant, I believe. I do not see him very often. His name is Greenwood.'

'What servants are there in that household?'

She mused, shaking her head.

'I really don't know anything about them. I can ask my own servants if you like.'

'And in the last few days, have you seen Greenwood himself at all?'

'No, I haven't seen him. But wait! I think he was in residence at the beginning of the week. Monday, perhaps. Let me ask my maid.'

She reached for a handbell on the low table beside her, but I raised my hand to stop her.

'Thank you, perhaps later. How well do you yourself know Mr Greenwood? Have you had occasion to tell his fortune?'

Again she laughed. Hers was a different laugh, huskier than the one I had heard in the room above us.

'La, no! He is such a very serious gentleman. I know that much, though very little else about him.'

I waited. Sometimes a silence can elicit more information than a question. But Mrs Quinto knew exactly how to sustain a silence. She fanned herself and looked in a reflective, serene way at the lion depicted in the carpet at our feet.

Finally, I said, 'I am sorry to have to tell you that a man was killed on Tuesday last in the centre of town. An accident, it seems. He carried a letter addressed to Mr Greenwood.'

In a manner that seemed both contrived and at the same time perfectly appropriate, she shut her fan with a snap and dropped it into her lap. Her hands went to her cheeks.

'Oh my goodness! How terrible! Is it Mr Greenwood himself?'

'It is not certain who he is.'

'And how did this happen?'

'I am the Coroner, Madam, and am charged with finding out. My inquest will be held at the Exchange on Monday. We may need someone to identify him – perhaps one of the servants at his house?'

'Ah, yes. I will ask my maid.'

Mrs Quinto stood and moved towards the door that gave into the hall, but stopped with her hand on the knob, fingertips to brow.

'Oh, but I quite forgot. The one that let you in is an idiot, so I wouldn't bother with her. The other girl, who is more intelligent, is on her day off. I'm sorry.'

She went out into the hall and opened the front door. A gust of warm air mixed with street dust wafted in.

'If necessary, may I come back tomorrow and speak to her?' I asked.

'If you wish. I shall expect you in the afternoon. Good day, Mr Cragg.'

Thus bustled out of Mrs Quinto's house, I was as a snail that feels a few drops of rain on its shell. My tentacles were extending with curiosity. A fortune-teller? She looked the part, but if she really were a professional clairvoyant she must also have private means. No gypsy at a travelling fair could earn enough to live like that.

It was still only just after midday. I decided to call on Ashton Lever.

Furzey, who knew much about the leading County families of Lancashire, had told me that the Levers were the denizens of Alkrington Hall in Cheshire but also owned a number of tenements and other properties in and around Manchester. Their town house was in Market Street Lane, and it appeared one of the best of what was in general an opulent part of Manchester. Here it was that young Master Lever lived, presumably so that he could benefit from an education at Manchester's well-known grammar school.

Having been shown inside by a servant, I waited in an anteroom for at least ten minutes before a youth with a heavily pock-marked face and carrying a small wicker birdcage appeared. This was Master Ashton Lever.

'I am sorry to detain you,' he said carelessly. 'I was checking my bird traps. Look what I've just nabbed for my aviary. It's a goldfinch – the first one I've ever caught. Isn't he a handsome fellow?'

The bird was about the size of a sparrow, with yellow on its wings, a black-and-white head, and a scarlet face. Every now and then it sang out in notes somewhere between a musical tune and a flow of squeaks. I agreed that it was a fine specimen.

'Are you the Coroner?' he asked.

'Yes.'

'I suppose you've come about the thing at the butts.'

'I have.'

He placed the cage on the mantelshelf.

'I trotted along to the inquest this morning, like a good boy, and all for nothing. Just because of that, I missed seeing a clutch of song-thrush eggs hatching out. I've been watching the nest for the last three days.'

He pouted moodily.

'Is your mother at home?' I said.

'Mother is at Alkrington. She knows nothing about this little accident.'

'I would describe it as quite a big accident, young man. May I suggest you send for her? She might be interested that her son has killed a man.'

He put the birdcage on a table and gestured for me to sit,

which I did. The boy then began pacing around with his hands behind his back as he talked.

'Ah! You say I killed that fellow. I dispute that. It was not my agency that killed him. I was merely shooting at a bird. The wind is no doubt to blame for deflecting my arrow from its mark and towards a new one. Therefore I argue that the wind has killed this man, Sir, just as surely as if it had blown a roof tile on to his head. At all events, it was not me.'

'You say you were shooting at a bird. But you are fond of birds, are you not?'

'Fond! That is not the word. Birds are my life. My absolute *life*.'

'So why were you shooting at one?'

'It was a sparrowhawk! Do you not know the feeding habits of the sparrowhawk? It is shocking. They slaughter small birds without mercy. I hate them.'

'So this sudden impulse to change your aim from the target at the butts to a sparrowhawk that came flying across was out of a desire to preserve the lives of smaller birds?'

'Yes. Not just sparrows, but finches, warblers, wagtails, wrens, even blackbirds. The female will even sometimes take a pigeon. It is bigger than the male, you see.'

'Unfortunately your desire to preserve birdlife has resulted in the loss of a human life.'

'But logically there is no connection, Sir. As I just told you, it was an act of the wind.'

'Why did you not listen to the orders of Abel Moorcroft, that you must shoot only at the stuffed targets on the ground?'

'I thought I had told you that. I saw a sparrowhawk.'

If Mrs Lever's maternal instincts towards her son had indeed been blunted, it was no wonder. With a sigh, I thanked him for his time. It was the dinner hour and I was hungry.

TWENTY-THREE

The dish was a loin of boiled pork with dumplings. I had reserved a closed room in which Furzey, Frances Nightingale and myself could sit down together and eat in privacy. I had so far told no one what I had discovered in the morning during the viewing of the body and I had been longing to unburden myself of it. Now I did so.

'You see what this means, don't you?' I asked when I had broken the news that the dead man was Grevel Horntree. On hearing this, my two companions quite stopped eating, which in Furzey's case rarely happened unless he was powerfully distracted. 'Bower mistakenly thought that the letter in the dead man's pocket had been received by the dead man, which led him to call the man Greenwood. But we know he was Horntree.'

'Mr Horntree must have written the letter and was on his way to send it,' said Mrs Nightingale.

After a moment of reflection, Furzey asked, 'What is in the letter?'

'Bower states that it was about silk business. But I haven't seen it. It is missing from the evidence bundle, which greatly concerns me.'

'But mind what this tells us about a different matter, which is also of concern,' said Frances. 'I mean the disappearance of Mr Horntree's wife. Horntree couldn't possibly have been doing things to his wife in Accrington on Wednesday when he'd died in Manchester on Tuesday.'

'Someone might have acted on his behalf,' said Furzey. 'A hidden assassin, a dastardly household steward who had not yet heard of his master's fate.'

I shut my eyes for a moment. The way Furzey was painting this, it began to look like the plot of an Italian opera.

'I think that when we know the facts we may better understand what's been going on at Hatchfly Hall,' I said. 'We will surely hear more at the inquest on Monday – the dead man's business with this Quentin Greenwood, for instance. After our conversation last night with the genial Mr Burnet, I wonder if it had anything to do with silk at all. He told us he had never heard of a Greenwood in the silk trade, which made me suspect Burnet of not being all that he said he was. But, on the other hand, if Greenwood were posing as a silk merchant, there is no reason for Burnet to have ever heard of him. It seems even Greenwood's next-door neighbours in Manchester knew little about him.'

I described my visit to Cold Harbour Lane and the encounter with Mrs Quinto, but had some difficulty conveying her singular quality.

'The woman has an amplitude about her.'

'Fat, is she?' asked Furzey.

'No, no! Well, she is not slim, but there is something larger than life, something of the actress, about her. I can well imagine that she is a great success in entertaining her guests by reading their palms or laying out the cards.'

Frances Nightingale had resumed her meal but was listening closely.

'What if she laid out the cards for Greenwood?' she said. 'She may have seen through him if he was a fraud.'

'Does a man with a secret consult a clairvoyant? And she says she hardly knew the man.'

'While living next door to him,' said Frances. 'It's hard to believe.'

'It would be in Accrington, and even in Clitheroe. But Manchester is different, isn't it? A great place of business, a hive of industry, in which many strangers come and go, and neighbours grow used to being foreigners to each other. Ten thousand people – imagine it!'

We carried on in this speculative vein until the end of our meal. I then went to the post office to ask if there were letters from Accrington, this being the day on which the rider came into Manchester from that direction. The man had not yet come.

Not wanting to lose the details of what had been said, I spent an hour dictating to Furzey memoranda of my interviews with Mrs Quinto and young Lever – 'the bird boy', as Furzey kept calling him. Afterwards, Mrs Nightingale said she would like to see the celebrated Exchange. I agreed to go with her and we set out with Suez. The tables were now all folded away, the merchants gone, and all that was left was a game of football between some local boys.

We watched the game for a few minutes.

'Not very like the Lady May's Hole game,' I commented. 'It is a superior version of the sport that they play here in Manchester. Look at that! That was well done.'

I heard a voice behind me. 'Yes indeed, Mr Cragg. These boys employ skill, not muscle. We would not permit them to practise in the Exchange if it were nothing but fighting and main force.'

I turned to find the voice belonged to Boroughreeve Bower. He spread his arms to indicate the noble structure in which we stood.

'This is above all a civilized place, and built on civilized classical principles.'

'It is impressive, Mr Bower.'

'I very much hope there will be no further delay in your proceedings on Monday, Cragg. Manchester is counting on you to deliver a verdict before the morning ends.' Before I could stop him, Suez, who had been becoming increasingly excited by the sight of the football, slipped his collar and bounded joyfully towards the players. The beadle gave a cry of warning and tried to grab him but, intent on getting to the ball, Suez swerved and plunged into the middle of the game. Delighted by the spaniel's frantic effort to join in, the players kicked the ball this way and that as he yelped and scrambled after it. I stepped forward with collar and leash but the boys were having such an enjoyable time with Suez that it took a minute or more to get the dog back under control. When we returned at last to Mrs Nightingale, who had looked on with much amusement, I did not find the Boroughreeve. He had gone.

'Did you note Bower's manner, Frances?' I said on our way back to the Swan. 'I am suspicious of that man. He wants to get this inquest out of the way – though I still don't know why.'

'I confess I am in a maze, Mr Cragg. What with Mr Horntree dead and Mr Greenwood nowhere to be found, I don't know who's who or what's what in this case.'

'If it's any comfort, you are not alone there, Frances.'

There was still no word at the inn from Accrington and I began to hope that, instead of writing, Fidelis was on the way himself and might arrive at any moment. I passed the evening in this expectation, playing a few hands of piquet and conversing with other guests at the inn until eleven o'clock. But Fidelis did not appear.

I abandoned hope of seeing my friend that night and decided on bed. But first I had to give Suez his late-night walk. We set out into a town that was still much engaged in Saturday-night drinking, singing and dancing – some of it in the open air, as the nights had continued warm. I led the dog away from these populous streets until we found a large open space called Parsonage Croft, and here I let Suez run.

He bounded off into the dark, and a few moments later bounded back to me. Then he bounded off in another direction and similarly returned. But the third time he left me, I heard barks and growls and a human cry of pain. I ran towards the sound and saw that Suez had a poorly dressed fellow by the wrist, and had pulled him down to the ground. There was another fellow there, who was dressed as a gentleman, and he was now kicking the fallen man in the ribs, with grunts and a volley of curses in a mixture of English and French. I called Suez off with a few curses of my own, and asked the kicker also to desist. As soon as he did so, the man on the ground rolled, got up, and ran away into the dark.

'Don't scold the dog, Sir,' said the gentleman. 'He is a lifesaver and a true friend. That rogue was trying to rob me.'

The half moon gave enough light for me to recognize him now.

'Mr Burnet, Sir!'

We shook hands warmly.

'Mr Cragg!' he said. 'I am grateful to you, and to your faithful pet. Suez, is it not?'

'You felt in danger of being murdered, Sir?'

Burnet shook his head and caught hold of the flap of his coat, pulling it aside with a certain flourish. I saw the silver glint of a dagger's pommel in the moonlight.

'No, your hound has done the valuable service of saving me, not from being *killed* but from having to *kill*.'

We walked back across the grass towards the houses edging Parsonage Croft. I asked Burnet what had brought him so late at night into this part of the town – right the other side of it from Ancoats.

'Oh, visiting people, you know. Collecting information about the cloth trade and so on.'

'You must be careful in future. Manchester may not be as dangerous as London, but it is lively enough. Always hire a pair of linkmen to light you home in the dark. Or get a dog like this one.'

Burnet reached down and caressed Suez's ears.

'He is a spaniel? Then I shall. We have had many of the breed in my own family also.'

We parted at the north end of Dean's Gate.

'I have found it pays to remember the faces of people who have done one a service,' said Burnet. 'You have done me two, on consecutive nights. Thank you, Sir. I shall certainly remember you, and of course I'll remember the admirable Suez.'

He spoke with a degree of earnestness that I could not quite account for. It was as if Burnet was making me a promise – but what for, and how it might ever be fulfilled, I could not suppose.

The next morning, as Frances and I breakfasted together, she said she would be attending the service at the parish church, in order to hear Mr Postumus's sermon. I too wanted to hear this noted preacher and we walked there together. Arriving with twenty minutes to spare, we found the church almost full, many extra worshippers drawn in to hear the noted preacher.

The sermon did not disappoint. Postumus spoke lightly and fluently, with great sincerity, and for no more than two hours. His account of the meeting between the Saviour and St John by the River Jordan, with which he began his address, was

suitably moving; and his explanation of baptism – 'the simple
but bountiful act with which all Christian lives begin' – was
lucid, interesting and learned. Then as he turned to the theme
of his text ('Oh ye vipers . . .'), he varied his voice to one of
gentle anger, underscored by the ever-present incipience of
hellish retribution, as he exhorted us to defy the devil and all
his works with the courage of St George. I am not very often
impressed by a sermon. Biblical law is such a blunt instrument
compared with our own subtler legal traditions, common law
and rational statutes. But in speaking of retribution, Postumus
found words in Scripture that seemed far more reasonable than
the bludgeoning prescriptions of Leviticus and Deuteronomy
which are more often heard.

'No one shall be judged in haste,' he told us in a cool, low
voice. 'There must always be a trial and there must be testimony from more than one voice, as it says in the Book of
Numbers where the crime of murder is discussed . . .'

And now he gradually raised his voice again, as the sonorous
words of the English Bible rolled from his tongue.

'"Whoso shall kill another shall be put to death . . ." Oh,
yes, it does say that – but note how it goes on. Note that this
death must be only "by the mouth of witnesses, but *one* witness
shall not testify against any person to cause him to die."
Therefore let all of us remember these words from the Book
of Numbers, so that no man or woman, however provoked,
shall take the law into their own hands. There is recourse
enough in the Church and in the state by which to ensure that
divine law is observed on earth.'

Having sounded these notes, he brought the tone of his
voice right down almost to a whisper.

'I have spoken of the wages of sin, now I must speak of
the fruits of sin, and in particular the fruits of those most
execrable and most damnable sins – I mean those of fornica-
tors. And I must speak in particular, on this feast day of the
Baptist, of the children born to those fallen women, shameless
Salomes of our own sinful times. While these infants are
abandoned by their strumpet mothers, who only wish to
continue to wallow in the stinking mire of their sin, we must
in the words of our Saviour "suffer the little children, and

forbid them not, to come to me" – that is, these lost children, these foundlings. All righteous Christians have a duty, I say, to come together to ensure the holy baptism and religious education of these benighted children. And more! I say we must ensure their education also in useful trades to make of them both good Christians and productive subjects.'

The parishioners, as they gathered to talk in the church precincts after the service, were clearly stimulated by Mr Postumus's rousing call to action on foundling children. As I passed among them, I heard phrases he had used being quoted and discussed. Mrs Nightingale was enraptured.

'Oh, Mr Cragg! If only we had such a preacher at Accrington. I have heard nothing better since Mr Wesley, when he visited Burnley, though that was very different in content and circumstance. Mr Wesley preaches in the open air.'

'And do not the Methodist preachers draw intemperate howls and hysterics from their listeners, with many falling down and writhing on the ground overcome with emotion? There have been no such demonstrations here, unless I missed them.'

She laughed.

'Yes, the Methodists and Moravians are absurd at times, but I confess to finding my spirit refreshed when I hear them.'

'You fall down and writhe?'

She laughed again.

'No, I do not, for as you know I am a churchwarden and it would not be seemly.'

We hoped to get the chance to congratulate the eminent preacher, but he was standing at the church door so mobbed by well-wishers eager to touch his hand that after twenty minutes we gave up and began to make our way back to the Swan Inn. I was about to enquire there after any letters that might have come, when none other than Dr Fidelis walked – or rather limped – in after us.

'Good heavens, Luke! Where did you spring from?'

His face was still discoloured and swollen here and there, and he could manage only a crooked smile.

'I've followed you back from the churchyard. I'd seen Mr Furzey here at the inn and he told me where I would find you, but the crowd was so large that I lost you.'

'Well, I am right glad to see you,' I said clapping him on the shoulder. 'What news from Accrington?'

'I know now of Mrs Horntree's disappearance and her associated misdeeds at New Manor, Titus, and I cannot say I am happy. She has not turned up, by the way. Turvey is very disturbed. Well, we cannot be sure what it all amounts to until we find her, but it seems we were all grossly deceived in her.'

I did not mention that Elizabeth had never been deceived.

We went into the coffee room while Fidelis fetched from his room a sealed package, addressed to me in my wife's hand, and handed it to me.

'And I have other news too, I—' But first of all I wanted to be alone with Elizabeth's letter, so I stopped him.

'And so have we. But first I shall attend to this, and in the meantime Frances will tell you what a wonderful discovery we have made here.'

I left them alone and took the package into the newspaper room, finding inside four pastry tarts of wild strawberries, and with them a letter.

> *Sunday morning, early* (Elizabeth wrote). *Dearest Husband, I am glad you have found interesting employment in Manchester and a new farmyard tyrant – your cock of the walk – to defeat. However, I miss you, and so does Hector. There is no sign or word of the disappeared Mrs Horntree, and none either of her husband. Perhaps they have run away together. Dr Fidelis, as you will have collected by seeing him, is somewhat better and is determined to ride to Manchester. He will carry this, with all my love. Enjoy the strawberry tarts.*
> *Written in great haste. Elizabeth.*
>
> *P.S. Yes, I asked Mr Turvey about the contents of the little silver box. He knew nothing of it. Luke will tell you his feelings about the matter.*

Often, as here, Elizabeth's letters are on subjects of no great historical interest, but they are as lifeblood to me. I take special pleasure in her handwriting, which is as clear as print yet as flowing as conversation. Just to see it tugs at my heart.

I tucked the letter into my coat pocket and went to find the others. They were preparing to order dinner in the great parlour, but I insisted that we again have the private dining room in order to be able to talk freely amongst ourselves.

I placed the strawberry tarts in the middle of the table, and we sat down to sample them with beer and trivial talk while the pantryman carved some slices of roast meat. When these were distributed, I said, 'I understand from what Elizabeth has written that no trace of Mrs Horntree has been found in Accrington, alive or dead. But what do you think of Grevel Horntree being discovered here in Manchester, and in such extraordinary circumstances?'

'I can't say I am sorry,' Fidelis said as he began a circum-spect examination of the food on his plate. 'Horntree perhaps had enemies here. We knew he was a regular visitor, but never what business he did.'

'I expect to find out more tomorrow when I open the inquest.'

'Give me the whole story again as far as you know it, Titus.'

Fidelis was what country people call a 'chisely' eater: so quaint and fastidious in his knife-and-fork work that for him feeding and talking were incompatible with each other. On the other hand, he could listen while he ate, making it better that I give him my news before he gave me his. I told him all the details of how Horntree had been found shot with an arrow, then of my visits to the constable, Mrs Quinto and the Lever boy. When I had finished, my friend sat back before his empty plate.

'I am deeply disappointed by the death of Horntree, Titus.'

'Why so?'

'Because we have no murder, only an accident.'

'Don't say that, Doctor!' said Frances Nightingale, in reproof. 'Don't go looking for murders, if you please.'

I laughed.

'I'm afraid Dr Fidelis is invigorated by nothing so much as a murder, Mrs Nightingale. As for me, I am equally interested in accidents.'

Fidelis looked incredulous.

'How can you equate a mere accidental death with murder? What bores me about an accident is that it proceeds from simplicity.'

'Accidents are not always so simple. Consider "chance medley." There is a death caused by another, but is it culpable? That can be a knotty problem indeed.'

'I prefer to expose the secrets and mysteries of a black-hearted villain than some inept bungler.'

'Isn't Horntree villain enough for you, though? And as for secrets, we have the disappearance of Mrs Horntree to consider.'

Fidelis's face acquired a faintly self-conceited look.

'Ah-ha! I might have found something in that connection.'

The curling mischievous smile across Fidelis's mouth suggested he had recovered remarkably from the discovery that the woman whom he'd fancied so much appeared to be a liar and thief. He reached for his wine glass and took a mouthful.

'Go on, Doctor,' said Furzey, impatiently. 'Tell us what it is.'

Fidelis swallowed and said, 'I cannot at the moment connect what I have found in Accrington with Mrs Horntree's disappearance, never mind the doings of Horntree here in Manchester. But when I do, I believe it may be germane to the secrets of both the Horntrees.'

'So tell us,' I said.

TWENTY-FOUR

L uke Fidelis began by taking us back to the previous Friday evening, when Elizabeth had visited him during a lull in his fever and told him the news of Flora Horntree. All that night he could not rid his mind of Flora, with thoughts wildly speculative. Her stealing a horse and riding furiously away . . . A secret lover coming to her rescue, or a vengeful father, or even a previous husband . . . Who, after all, was this woman? A sorceress? A runaway? Where had she come from? And how had she ever fallen under the sway of the domestic tyrant Grevel Horntree?

At last Luke returned by stages to his right mind and, as Elizabeth's latest information sank in, cold reason began to assert itself.

'I applied the rational physician's method to the puzzle,' he explained, 'just as I would to a disease. Once you have heard the sufferer's complaint, there is no other way but to look with care at the patient's body – any unusual physical signs such as twitches, swellings, tenderness, sweats, an irregular heartbeat . . . Things that are not the disease itself but the *effects* of it.'

By the effects in the puzzle of Flora Horntree's disappearance, he meant the things she had been found in possession of – that is her baggage. So Fidelis ran over – as I had done on my dining table at the Dower House – the inventory of what had been found in the valise at New Manor, mentally searching for anything unusual or indicative. Much of it was not rightly Flora's but had been deliberately taken by her for its money value from the Turveys, but what else had the bag contained that was precious to Flora in a different way? What was there that might act as a key to unlock her true nature? Fidelis still found it hard to believe that she was nothing but a common thief and that all she cared about was money.

He reviewed each object and dismissed it until at last, as

he told us, 'I came to the little silver box. You remember it, Titus? It was in the form of a pillbox, though a very thin one.'

I told him I did, and he went on. 'The pillbox had been adapted by means of soldering a tiny ring on to it, so that it could hang from a silver chain. But hang where? Why, from a lady's neck, of course. To be used, in other words, as a locket.'

'Yes, I drew the same inference. There were even a few wisps of hair inside, as well as a paper with a fragment of verse.'

'Then consider this. There is nothing in the whole armoury of personal adornment that hints at secrets so well as a locket. I was wondering what secret this one contained when quite suddenly the image of another pendant – one I had also seen very recently – hit my mind's eye. It was very like the one found in Mrs Horntree's valise – very like indeed.'

Sitting over the remains of our dinner, we were listening intently now.

'Go on,' I said.

'You will think I am veering away from the subject,' he continued. 'But I must tell you a little more about the Lady May's Hole game, because if I had not taken part in it I would not have received that hit. The day went as follows. After much to-and-fro around the bridge at Accrington, some lads got the ball and took it away in a run up the fields of the Hatchfly estate. From there they entered the woods, hoping to throw off the pursuit. I was with a chasing group who climbed up above the woods with the idea of cutting the ball-runners off should they break cover on the side of the high moor. The shouts of the hunters could be heard deep in the woods, so that we easily kept pace with them until we came within sight of Gunwright's Heath a little above us. It is the only dwelling on that slope of the moor. We were thirsty now, so we raced up to the farmyard where the young farm wife – who, as you know, is Mrs Hawk – came out with pewter cups so that we could refresh ourselves from the well. Before leaving, I went over to her and giving her thanks I noticed a chain around her neck. As you know, she is a very pretty woman with a long and shapely neck, so my eyes were naturally drawn to it as we spoke.'

'Oh, quite naturally!' I repeated.

That teasing smile flickered again across his lips and he took another leisurely mouthful of wine. In his impatience Furzey rapped the table.

'Go on, Doctor,' he said. 'Never mind Mr Cragg. Tell us.'

Fidelis put down his glass and took a taper to relight his pipe. He puffed the smoke towards the ceiling.

'Whatever hung from that chain was hidden under her clothing until Rosemary Hawk saw a feather that adhered to the bottom of her dress, and bent to remove it. As she did so, a pendant slipped out from her bodice and swung clear of her for a moment, so that I had a good sight of it. The thing had no significance for me at the time so, of course, I said goodbye and we went on with the pursuit. I forgot it. But, when on Saturday I was well enough to go to your house and inspect the contents of Mrs Horntree's valise, including the pillbox or makeshift locket that she had in her baggage, the one that I had seen adorning Mrs Hawk's graceful neck struck me as being virtually identical.'

We fell silent, each of us pondering the possible significance of this, without being quite able to say how the two lockets connected.

'What is your conclusion, Luke?'

'That the peculiar coincidence of a pair of almost identical yet unusual pieces of neckwear, in possession of two women who had both lived at Hatchfly Hall, cannot be accidental.'

I considered this point.

'But Flora had stolen hers from Mrs Turvey's jewellery box. She didn't have it while at Hatchfly.'

'I would not be too sure about that, Titus. The monogram—'

'Was *H.F.* The initials of Turvey's wife, and she got it from her mother. We know that.'

'Ah, yes, I had forgot. Yet the coincidence remains.'

'But can you explain it?'

He shrugged.

'I can't. One thing I am sure of, however, is that Flora had nothing much by way of cash or valuables of her own. I visited Peggy Stirk at Hatchfly Lodge. She told me she had known full well that Flora wanted to flee her marriage, even though she was not privy to her departure last Monday night. She also said that Flora had no money and always meant to beg some from you, Titus, or from me. Mrs Stirk said she was that desperate to get away.'

'Did Mrs Stirk know anything about a locket?'

'Nothing.'

Towards four in the afternoon, taking Furzey (and Suez) with me, I set off to keep my appointment at Mrs Quinto's to interview her servant. I had already instructed John Blow to provide Dr Fidelis with the key to the outhouse in which Grevel Horntree lay, to enable him to examine the body in my absence.

Turning into Cold Harbour Lane, we found number seventeen unchanged in appearance. I nevertheless thought it worth trying the door, so I mounted the steps and rapped the knocker. There was still no response. Number nineteen, which had shown every sign of habitation twenty-four hours earlier, now had every one of its windows shuttered and there was no answer to my knock. I repeated it twice at half-minute intervals before giving up and retreating to the pavement, where Furzey was in conversation with a passer-by, a ragged man who carried a knobbly sack that clinked. Even on a Sunday, it seemed, the itinerant bottle-picker's work carried on.

'Aye, there's always a big lot of empties from here,' he was saying. 'Specially Sunday morning. But there's been nowt this morning. Closed for business it is.'

'Business?' said Furzey. 'There's a lot of empty bottles put out, you say. Why is that? Does the lady of the house have company on Saturday nights?'

The bottle-picker began to wink and tap his nose in an exaggerated way.

'Company. Oh, aye. You could say company. Gentlemen company and lots of it, do you follow me? Not just Saturdays. Every night it is – but Saturdays, oh, that's their big night, which is why I am surprised there are no bottles this day.'

Furzey and I exchanged a glance. His insinuation was not difficult to read. We thanked the fellow and moved off. Furzey was full of disgust.

'Your friend is not only a palm-reader. She's nothing but a stinking brothel-keeper. We must call her Mother Quinto.'

I thought back to my talk with the woman on the previous day, and in particular her initial manner towards me. She had seemed to treat me as a nervous new customer who needed to be put at ease but, seeing I was no such thing, smoothly turned herself into a mere fortune-teller. It was a cool, intelligent performance. 'Gentleman company', the bottle-picker had talked about. I thought, with a degree of admiration, that Mrs Quinto would be equal to the company of any gentleman.

'You have not met her,' I said mildly. 'Yet, if number nineteen is a whorehouse, it is a superior one. As for Mrs Q, she is certainly an unusual person. She comes from Portugal, I believe, but I can assure you she does not stink.'

'I am surprised,' said Furzey, 'at you defending the commerce in fornication, as it is one of the most abominable of trades.'

'Well, you are at one with Mr Postumus in that, Furzey. However, it helps us no nearer to discovering Horntree's business in Manchester, apart from the fact that a man he was in correspondence with, Quentin Greenwood, happened to live next door to a brothel.'

Back at the Swan Inn, we found the shed locked and Fidelis in his bedroom, cleaning his instruments.

'Well? You have examined the corpse?'

'I have. Nothing very unusual about it. The man was in pretty good health – in his prime, even.'

'The cause of death?'

'Exactly as we have heard. The arrow entered his neck at a downwards angle. It cut into a large blood vessel in his neck, the carotid artery. When that happens, there is a fountain of blood. It would have taken him only a minute or so to die.'

At supper Mrs Nightingale told me that, if her services were not needed for the resumed inquest, she would prefer to go home to Accrington in the morning. I spoke to John Blow, who said he could arrange for her to go in company with the Preston post-rider, leaving town at six. His stops at inns along the way delivering and picking up the mail would make the journey slightly longer than our ride into Manchester had been on Friday, but his presence (and his pistols) would make

Frances safer on the road. She could hope, at all events, to be sitting once again in her own parlour by midday.

I went into the writing and reading room and wrote a note for her to convey to Elizabeth. The London papers had just come in and, finishing my letter, I looked over them. They were full of news of Anson's return in his flagship *Centurion* from a voyage round the world, having lost the rest of his fleet along the way. I was oppressed by the thought of those sailors: so miserably drowned, starved after shipwreck, succumbed to scurvy, dead in battle or from squabbling amongst themselves, or the victims of any other such dangers one meets with far from home. I broke the seal of my letter and added a postscript:

> *I read in today's papers that Commodore Anson is back after four years, with less than 10 per cent of the men he started out with. He has been all the way round the world and is feted and rich beyond dreams. They call the exploit glorious, but think of it: five ships lost and a thousand and a half questionable deaths – enough to keep a coroner busy for years. There's nothing glorious in it as far as I can see.*

With Furzey and Frances Nightingale gone to bed, Fidelis attended me and Suez on our nightly late stroll.

'Is the outcome of tomorrow in any doubt?' he asked as we began a circular walk around Parsonage Croft.

'No. Unless the jury goes mad, there can be no verdict other than manslaughter by chance medley. Young Lever never intended to kill anyone except the sparrowhawk, but he is not without responsibility in the death of Horntree.'

Fidelis picked a stick from the ground, showed it to the dog, and hurled it into the darkness of the middle of the field. Suez hurled himself after it.

'Then the remaining question is,' he said, 'who is Greenwood?'

'We want to find that out. We want to know if there is any connection to what has happened to Mrs Horntree.'

'Ah! Mrs Horntree!'

I could not have stated for sure that Fidelis found himself

in love with Flora Horntree, but that 'Ah!' was expressive
enough to be love, though perhaps mixed proportionately with
disappointment. According to Elizabeth, disappointment was
a necessary element in all Luke Fidelis's affairs of the heart.

'He is one of those unfortunate young men,' she told me
once, 'who can only fully enjoy a girl when his heart is not
engaged.'

Whatever the truth of that, I made no comment now. I had
learned my lesson three years before, after one of Luke's
impossible amours had caused a painful rift between us, and
I now never interfered in his entanglements. So, after ordering
Suez to drop the stick at my feet and throwing it once more,
I spoke to Fidelis not of love but of duty.

'As far as we know, Mrs Horntree is still missing. She was
discovered to be so while under our protection, and it remains
our task to find her.'

'If we can.'

'If we uncover Grevel Horntree's secrets, I think we might.'

TWENTY-FIVE

A s soon as I had pulled the sheet away from Horntree's body, now correctly stripped to the buff, one of the jurors uttered a retching sound, staggered back, and vomited in the corner of the shed. Even allowing for the likelihood that he had spent Sunday in an alehouse and was suffering from the ale-passion (drooping eyelids, thick head and queasy stomach), it was a terrible sight – not the hole in the man's neck (the arrow shaft had been removed by Dr Fidelis) but the more ghastly wound, gouged from neck to navel, suffered during the doctor's examination with knife and shears.

'I'll be damned if he didn't die of having his chest and belly slashed,' said one. 'A terrible deep wound, is that.'

I explained that this was not the case as I had authorized Dr Fidelis to look into the dead body to see if there was any illness or injury that might have played a part in the death.

'But why, Your Honour? Everybody knows he died from being shot by that arrow.'

'That is so. But it is good to gather as much information as possible. When Dr Fidelis gives his evidence, we shall hear if anything significant was found. In the meantime, who will help me turn the body? We must see both sides of the subject before we are done.'

Perhaps it was the influence of those with sore heads; perhaps there was a more general resentment at having been made to return to duty forty-eight hours after they'd first assembled. For whatever reason, the jurors were a less pliable bunch today and, as we walked back to the Exchange, I could hear a few of them muttering about wasted time and damned doctors.

Jeremiah Bower was sitting, surrounded by his cronies, in the same prominent section of the public seats. The other witnesses in the case were also present. Young Ashton Lever was a fidgeting figure, beside a finely dressed middle-aged lady that I took to be his mother. Joanna Prescott, Clooney the surgeon from Market Street Lane, Abel Moorcroft and John Blow were there and, of course, Luke Fidelis, who sat a little apart as he glanced through a paper that I guessed contained his written report of the post-mortem examination. Also in this buzzing audience, to my great surprise, was Mrs Maria Quinto. Indeed it would have been hard to miss her as she was the most colourful figure in the room.

We began with Joanna Prescott, who told how she saw the gentleman struck down in Pratt's Lane and went to his assistance. And then we heard from the surgeon, who confirmed that the man had bled to death where he lay. Dr Clooney also described how a fellow standing by had handed him a letter addressed to Quentin Greenwood, which had been found in the victim's pocket, and that he later gave this to Mr Bower.

'Did you read the letter?' I asked him.

'No, Sir. Only glanced. I saw the name and direction on the cover, and noted that the word silk appeared in it more than once. That is all.'

'Did you see the signature?'

'No, Sir.'

Now it was young Lever's turn. He came sulkily to the witness chair and I had to work at coaxing the evidence out of him.

'You say you have not practised archery long?'

'Toxophilia.'

'Very well. How long have you been doing it?'

'Not very long, yet long enough.'

'And are you good at it?'

'Very good. If you doubt that, ask Mr Moorcroft.'

The examination followed much the same course as my earlier conversation with this self-pleased young man, with his flat denial that the death had been anything but an accident. I dismissed him and called for Abel Moorcroft, who qualified young Ashton's opinion of his own talents by describing him as a fairly promising archer for his age. Asked what precautions he took in the matter of public safety, he insisted that all his students were told to aim only at the target and never to shoot negligently.

After the archery teacher came John Blow, who related the corpse's passage from Pratt's Lane to its temporary resting place at his inn.

'You are an innkeeper and know a large number of people in the town. Did you recognize this man?'

'Happen I'd seen him round and about. I didn't know owt about him.'

'But a letter had been found in his pocket which gave a name and where he lived.'

'It was Mr Bower had that.'

'Did you know the name Greenwood when you heard it?'

'No.'

'And Mr Bower hadn't recognized the dead man?'

'He didn't say that he did.'

I now called Bower himself to explore this point further.

'When you saw the dead man's face, could you put a name to it?'

'No, I could not.'

'Why did you assume that the name and direction on the letter were those of the dead man?'

'It was a reasonable guess.'

'I must tell you, then, that it was also a wrong guess. As it happens, I have recently been living in the small village of Accrington, some miles to the north of here, and to my astonishment I recognized the corpse under inquest as soon as I saw it. This, Sir, is not Quentin Greenwood, but a gentleman named Grevel Horntree, of Hatchfly Hall, which lies in that part of the village known as Old Accrington.'

Bower's mouth opened. There was no doubt he was properly surprised, but it was difficult to tell if this was primarily because the body was Horntree, or because it wasn't Greenwood.

'Did you know Grevel Horntree?' I went on.

'I did not.'

'I turn to the letter found in the dead man's pocket. You took possession of it?'

'Yes.'

'Was it signed?'

'Letters usually are.'

'By whom, then?'

'I cannot recall the name.'

'That is a pity. You see, I did not find the letter among the case papers you so kindly put together for me in advance of this inquest. I would like you to provide it for me now, if you please.'

'I'm afraid that is not possible.'

'Why?'

'I no longer have the letter. I have concluded that a servant swept it away when tidying my office. It had perhaps fallen to the floor and was put out with the refuse.'

'Is there no hope of its recovery?'

'No. It would have been burnt.'

It seemed that Bower was not quite the paragon of efficiency he had previously claimed to be, and at this point I might have vented my disappointment at missing an important piece of evidence. But instead, keeping my powder dry, I chose to allow Bower to stand down and made an appeal to the public.

'I would like to know more about the victim's business here in Manchester, and in particular whom he met and where he stayed. Did anyone present in this court have dealings of any kind with Grevel Horntree?'

I looked around. No hand was raised.

'Or with Quentin Greenwood?'

Again, I saw no hands.

'Very well. Dr Fidelis, may we hear your evidence please?'

The rest of the session ran a predictable course. Fidelis told of his examination of the body, in which he found that the only cause of death was the wound of the arrow. He explained how the arrow had penetrated the neck artery known as the external carotid artery, and how this led to a copious spurting of blood and death within a short time. The public listened to these physiological details intently and in perfect silence: all coroners are aware of the insatiable curiosity that there is about death and the bewildering variety of its ways.

There being no more witnesses after Fidelis, I gave the court a summary of the evidence and invited the jury to come to a verdict. What it would be was not much in doubt, and after a few minutes of discussion they found that 'the said Grevel Horntree of Accrington was grievously wounded by an arrow shot in his neck from the bow of Ashton Lever and did die by chance medley, and not otherwise.'

'Why in God's name did you not call *her* as a witness, Titus?'

I had closed the inquest and we were making our way back to the inn, with Mrs Quinto and her companion walking – or, more accurately, hurrying – ahead of us in the same direction.

'What would I have questioned her about, exactly?'

Fidelis was in an excitable state, as he would often be when an idea or hypothesis possessed him.

'About her next-door neighbour, naturally.'

'Greenwood? I have already done so. She knows almost nothing about him. She has nothing to say.'

'Her house has been shut up since he was mentioned as the dead man. Why, do you think?'

'A precaution. She was afraid her line of business would be exposed in the inquest and might be closed permanently.'

'She knows more about Greenwood than she is saying. I am certain of it. You would have got more out of her if you'd questioned her under oath.'

'It was not called for. The corpse is not Quentin Greenwood, but Grevel Horntree. The doings of Quentin Greenwood were finally of little importance to this inquest.'

'But Greenwood is the key to what Horntree was doing here in Manchester.'

'Is he? Horntree was probably doing nothing more than making an investment in silk manufacture, which is no concern of mine as Coroner.'

'Well, my concern is to find out what has happened to Flora Horntree – and to that end I want to know everything I can about her husband, including his connection with Greenwood. Mrs Quinto may know something about this and, as you have not done so, I am determined to put her to the question myself.'

'Why should she have more to say to you than she has said already to me? Greenwood's rooms are not in her house but the adjacent one.'

'You miss my point, Titus. I suggest you put yourself in his place. You are Quentin Greenwood, a man of means, in full health, and with no strong religious scruples.'

'How do you know that Greenwood is any of those things?'

'Indulge me. You stay at Manchester from time to time, on affairs of business let us say, but alone and some distance from home. You discover that the rooms you have taken are immediately next door to a whorehouse – so, naturally, wouldn't you pay it a visit at some point? As you consequently rather enjoy yourself, you go there again the next time you are in Manchester, and in time it becomes a habit.'

'This is a tissue of guesswork.'

'It may be. But I will try it on Mrs Q, anyway.'

I looked up the street and saw that the two hurrying women had disappeared from sight.

'They are in a fret to get home.'

'No doubt to open up the shop and be ready for business. An establishment like that can ill afford to stay closed for a run of three days. I shall go there directly. Are you coming?'

The pain of Fidelis's bruises still impeded him and it was twenty minutes before we reached Cold Harbour Lane. Number nineteen was even more desolate than before. A note stuck to the door read: *Gone away. All correspondence is directed to the sign of the Magpie.*

'Why would she go to an inn, Luke?'

'Because she's leaving town, by God! The Magpie is the stage for coaches to Chester and Yorkshire.'

'Then we must hurry or we'll miss her.'

But when we got to the Magpie we found that the York coach had left more than half an hour before, and we'd missed the Chester departure by fifteen minutes. To our even greater frustration, the coaching clerk had gone home for his dinner and the landlady had been busy in the laundry and never saw the coaches depart. No reliable intelligence as to the passengers in either direction could be found anywhere at the inn; and finally, the landlady assured us she had been given no sending-on address for anyone by the name of Quinto.

We stood together at the side of the street outside the Magpie.

'We must get the horses,' I said. 'We shall easily ride down both coaches, starting with the one for Chester. And if she's not on that, we ride after the other.'

'No. First I want to see the ticket clerk, who I am told lives a few minutes' walk from here. You go to the Swan for the horses and I'll meet you there.'

Fidelis strode into the Swan's yard a little more than half an hour later. Our saddle horses had already been brought out by the ostlers and we mounted immediately.

'The clerk denies selling tickets to any such woman, either for York or Chester,' he said. 'The note on the door was a ruse. She wanted it thought she was gone either to the west or to the east, while actually meaning to go south on the London coach. It departs from the Sun & Stars inn, but the fellow told me she would easily have had time to board it. We'll catch them halfway to Stockport if we ride now. And by the way, Titus, I've changed my opinion of Greenwood. We have been considering him as a customer of Mother Quinto's. I now think he stood in a quite different relation to her.'

Without further explanation, he kicked his horse on and clattered ahead of me out of the yard.

The town of Stockport, the next stop down the southern road from Manchester, was seven miles distant – but the coach had not even travelled three when, after some hard riding, we came up to it at a standstill on the road. A cart up ahead had turned over and spilled its load of heavy timber building spars, blocking any progress. Having unharnessed his horses, the carter was laboriously dragging the great spars one by one out of the way, cursing furiously. The coachman and guard and a few passengers had disembarked, not to help but to watch him at work, no doubt making sarcastic comments, which cannot have improved the carter's temper.

As we neared the coach, the heads of two inside occupants appeared, one at each window, having heard our horses' hooves. They were Mrs Quinto and the younger woman we had seen with her earlier. They looked alarmed.

'Do you remember me, Madam?' I called out.

'Oh! Mr Cragg, is it you? Our distinguished Coroner. I am glad to see a face I know. Oh, la! We are mortally afraid of highwaymen.'

Fidelis and I dismounted and hitched our horses to the rear transom of the coach.

'May I present my friend, Dr Fidelis?' I said.

'Dr Fidelis! *Enchantée!* I found your testimony this morning quite enthralling.'

'Are you alone?' I said.

'Just one gentleman has been riding inside with us,' said Mrs Quinto. 'He has got down to watch the fun up ahead – though I don't know why I said fun, as I think we have a long wait in store.'

'May we join you inside for a few moments?'

'Of course.'

Pulling the coach door open, Fidelis swung himself up, using the mounting step, and went in. I followed and we sat side by side on the bench opposite the two lady passengers.

'You must remember my visit to you last Saturday, Mrs Quinto,' I began. 'I was enquiring about a certain gentleman. Dr Fidelis and I are still enquiring about this gentleman and that is why we have followed the coach this afternoon. I wonder if he—'

The appearance of a head at the window on Fidelis's side of the coach interrupted me. It was that of a man of about twenty-five years, genteelly dressed and wearing his natural hair with side curls beneath a stylish hat. He had already mounted the step to come in but now hesitated to open the coach's door, evidently taken aback by finding two men in the shadowy interior. For a moment he gawped through the aperture, then jumped backwards, spun around, and took to his heels. We saw him leap the ditch by the roadside and set off helter-skelter across a turnip field. He was heading for the thick wood several hundred yards beyond.

'By God!' exclaimed Fidelis. 'I should have foreseen this. Never mind, I'll have him yet.'

Before I could say a word of caution he was out of the coach. With a speed and agility incredible in one so lately mauled at Lady May's Hole, he mounted and urged his horse to leap the ditch. Once across, he set course at a gallop in pursuit of the disappearing fugitive.

TWENTY-SIX

While Luke Fidelis was galloping over the turnips and into the wood, I stayed in the coach with the two women. I told Mrs Quinto that, although my inquest had led me in another direction, I was still interested in the affairs of Quentin Greenwood and wondered if her companion might be able to assist by providing some information.

'This is Louisa, Mr Cragg,' said Mrs Quinto, 'and she won't mind your questions.'

Louisa was dark-haired, with intense green eyes, a small nose and full lips. I am sure she was naturally lovely, but powder and paint overlaid nature with too much artifice for my taste. I guessed her age at more or less twenty-five.

'If you mean Mr Greenwood from next door,' said Louisa, 'I don't really know him, I'm sure.'

'I think you do know him,' I said. 'Or have known him – I mean in the sense that is used in the Bible.'

Louisa looked surprised at my question but was far from blushing. She glanced enquiringly at Mrs Quinto, who said, 'You may tell him, my dear. He has seen through us and well understands what business we carried on in Manchester. It matters little now.'

Louisa turned back to me. 'When I said I didn't know Mr Greenwood, I meant it in the ordinary meaning of the word.'

'But he did visit your house?'

'Oh yes.'

'How often would that have been?'

'He'd come in two or three times in a week, and then we'd not see him for a month or two. But he always came back.'

'Did he visit just to see you?'

'No. There were three of us girls in the house. He'd pick according to his fancy at the time. I had my share of him, of course.'

'But you say you never got to *know* him.'

'We generally don't get to know the gentlemen. They come and they go. Sometimes they like to talk – though it's never about anything to remember – and sometimes they don't talk hardly at all. Mr Greenwood was one that didn't. He was very brusque in his ways.'

'What sort of things did he do – apart from the obvious thing?'

Louisa looked at her mistress, who patted the girl's hand.

'Mr Cragg,' Mrs Quinto said, 'I had better tell you that Mr Greenwood was more than just a customer of ours. He was also a partner in the business, and an inspiration too.'

'Oh? In what way?'

'He showed us how we could provide special services for our gentleman guests. For example, by providing them with female attire. Many gentlemen find their pleasures increase if they dress as ladies, you know. Mr Greenwood would pay for this clothing. It has to be specially made because it must be in large sizes.'

'And it is silk clothing, I expect,' I said.

'Oh yes, silk or satin. That is essential.'

I turned back to Louisa.

'Now this is very important, my dear,' I said. 'Was there anything distinctive about Mr Greenwood physically? Did he have any marks or scars on his body?'

'Oh! Nothing that would alarm a girl, if that's what you mean. It's the first thing we look out for.'

'He would have been ejected from the house if he had anything like that,' put in Mrs Quinto.

'No,' I went on, 'I don't mean signs of disease. Just anything that would distinguish him.'

Louisa considered the question.

'There was a mole. It was in the middle of one of his arse cheeks.'

'A very noticeable one?'

'Yes.'

'Which, er, cheek was it on?'

She shut her eyes, as one does when making a mental picture.

'His right, because I'd feel it with my left hand when we were . . . you know.'

'Anything else?'

'Not that I can think of. He had the necessary equipment for the job, I can say that.'

I turned back to Mrs Quinto.

'Where are the other two girls in your household?'

'I sent them on ahead with the servant. They left yesterday.'

'So you are leaving Manchester entirely?'

'The lease will soon expire. The renewal would have been too costly, so I have given it up. We return to London and will set up again there. London is where we came from at first.'

'I am curious to know why you and Louisa stayed on this morning to attend the inquest.'

She opened a fan and began to waft it vigorously.

'You are full of curiosity, Mr Cragg. We stayed only to close up the house. Going to your court was a matter of passing the time before the departure of our coach.'

At that moment we heard cries from outside, though still at some distance. We looked out and saw Luke Fidelis on his way towards us. He led the horse, on whose back sat his quarry, complaining noisily of how he had been treated.

'I hope that poor gentleman can continue his journey with us,' said Mrs Quinto. 'Louisa and I have found him very gallant. We have quite taken to him.'

I got down and stood by the side of the road, waiting for Fidelis and his prisoner.

It was a shrill, outraged, rather bedraggled fugitive that Luke Fidelis led back towards the roadside ditch. Astride Fidelis's horse, with the reins binding his wrists, he never stopped calling for his immediate release.

'He pulled a knife on me,' Fidelis called out when they were still thirty yards away. 'I had to take it off him and tie his hands.'

He held up a knife with a silver pommel and a deadly sliver of a blade.

'He's also been telling me a fairy story that he's not Quentin Greenwood and doesn't know anyone of that name. Pretends he's called Fuckerson or some such nonsense.'

They arrived at the edge of the turnip field and, having

pulled the luckless captive from the saddle, he untied his
wrists and thrust him roughly into the ditch between us. I
looked down at the figure, who was a little shocked at standing
ankle-deep in ditchwater. I greeted him.

'Good day, Mr Burnet.'

He squinted up at me with no sign of recognition. The sun
blazed just behind me, its dazzle obscuring my face.

'Why do you call me that?' he said, shading his eyes with
his hand. 'My name is William Farquarson.'

He was no longer dressed like Burnet but it was certainly
Burnet's voice, with those faintly foreign notes.

'Do you not recognize me, Sir? I know you by the name
of Charles Burnet.'

'Oh, by my life! Mr Cragg from the inn!'

'The same.'

I reached and grasped Burnet's hand to help him up to the
road. Reaching my level, he continued to expostulate.

'Your associate has formed the conceit that I am someone
else. Has he lost his wits?'

'He sometimes gives that impression,' I said, 'but in this
case he has something of a point. Who are you in truth, if I
may ask? Burnet or Farquarson? Or perhaps, as Dr Fidelis
believes, Greenwood?'

'I would be grateful if you would call me William Farquarson.'

He gave a courtly bow, which was rather spirited of him
considering the circumstance.

'You called yourself Charles Burnet when we met in
Manchester,' I pointed out.

'Because I *am* Burnet.'

'Then why say you're Fuckerson?' said Fidelis. He had
brought his horse across to the road and was tethering it to
the back end of the coach. 'I don't believe you are called
Burnet, or Fuckerson. I say you are Quentin Greenwood, in
the act of fleeing Manchester before you are exposed.'

'I'm *not* this accursed Greenwood,' said the young man,
stamping his foot.

'He speaks the truth, Luke,' I said. 'I don't know if he is
really Burnet or Farquarson. I am certain, however, that he
is not Greenwood.'

But Fidelis was far from ready to abandon his position.

'Why would he run away then? He saw us here with Mrs Quinto. She had told him that we wanted to speak to him. There can only be one construction on his flight: he didn't want to speak to us about his connection with number nineteen Cold Harbour Lane.'

Fidelis turned angrily to the man calling himself Farquarson and shook his finger. 'You own the business, don't you?' he blustered. 'You finance it. You reap the profits. You are a brothel-keeper, Sir!'

'I am nothing of the sort. I merely mistook you gentlemen, can't you see? I mistook you for bailiffs. Unfortunately, I have debts in Manchester which I find impossible to pay. I am therefore now quitting the town incognito. What was I to think but that, having tracked me down, you meant to arrest me on behalf of my creditors? My fear of the consequence of arrest – a very long imprisonment in store, I think – was only confirmed when I retreated and you gave chase on your horse.'

'Retreated?' said Luke. 'You ran like a rabbit.'

'Your language is offensive, Sir. If the circumstance were different, I would call you out.'

'If it's a fight you want, you shall have one by God,' said my friend, his truculence rising.

'Luke,' I said. 'Stop this. I have been speaking to Mrs Quinto and her young lady companion, and from what they have told me it is certain that this man, whatever his real name, cannot be Quentin Greenwood. We must therefore allow him to go on his way without further hindrance.'

Less than half an hour had passed, and Fidelis and I were riding back to Manchester. The spilled timber having at last been removed from the road, the coachman, guard and outside passengers had come back to the coach and taken their places, inside and out. Charles Burnet, who had recovered much of his natural geniality – towards me if not Fidelis – thanked me through the coach window just before their departure.

'God bless you, Mr Cragg. I owe you my thanks once more. Farewell, and I hope we shall meet again in circumstances where I may do you some good in return.'

As the coach pulled off towards Stockport, the faces of the ladies appeared beside him. They waved their handkerchiefs.

I found that Fidelis remained far from reconciled to the idea that the man was not Greenwood.

'You seem to have met the villain before, Titus.'

'Twice, as it happens, and not in the character of a villain. We spent a pleasant evening together at the inn on Friday last, when he became unfortunately intoxicated and had to be helped home. He'd introduced himself as Charles Burnet from a family of Huguenot descent engaged in the silk trade in London. The next night, Suez and I met him again, quite by chance, as he was crossing Parsonage Croft.'

'The silk trade! That is supposed to be Greenwood's calling, too. It is another telling point of identity.'

'It is not particularly telling. This part of England swarms with clothiers of one kind and another. But I have reason to believe that it was not the manufacture of silk that Greenwood was engaged in, but its making up.'

'I still say the name and occupation are a blind, just as his masquerade as Fuckerson is a blind.'

'I see no reason why the man cannot be what he has just told us – a debtor fleeing from his creditors. I can prove to you that Greenwood was someone else.'

'Give me the proof, then.'

'Very well. First of all, you will remember that we've already considered Mr Greenwood – the man from number seventeen Cold Harbour Lane – as a patron of Mrs Quinto's establishment.'

'Yes, but when I first gave my reasons for that,' said Fidelis, 'I would have said he was a patron in the sense of being a customer. Now I think he was another kind of patron. I think he was the whoremaster himself.'

'Mrs Quinto says he was more of a partner. However, while you were gadding around in the mud, I had a talk about Greenwood with Mrs Quinto and the younger woman, Louisa. And on their evidence he was also a customer, and rather a frequent one. He bedded any of the girls according to his fancy, Louisa being one of them. What she then told me makes it certain he is not the man on that coach.'

'You can't take the word of a whore, least of all on the subject of her customers.'

'Yet she told me something the significance of which she could not have known.'

'Tell me.'

'She said that Greenwood had a large mole on his buttock.'

I said no more, and Fidelis too fell silent. We rode in silence for two or even three minutes and, looking sideways, I saw that Fidelis's eyes, separated by a deep frown, were fixed straight ahead and his mouth sulked. A bend in the road came into sight, where it turned around a wayside alehouse, and all at once he came to life.

'Ya!' he shouted, kicking his horse hard with his heels.

The horse sprang forward and Fidelis galloped away ahead of me. I watched as he reached the alehouse and went out of sight. When I too turned the corner, I found Fidelis sitting on the bench by the street door while the landlord put two pots of beer on an upturned barrel before him. I dismounted and sat alongside.

'The right buttock, was it?' Fidelis said.

'It was.'

'In the same place as the large mole on the arse of Grevel Horntree, which I noted during my examination of his body?'

'Exactly the same.'

He raised his mug.

'Then goodbye and good luck to Mr Charles Burnet, alias Fuckerson. Who cares who he really is? Our interest now is in the late Grevel Horntree, alias Quentin Greenwood. It seems we are stopped at every turn by deception, fraud and impersonation.'

'You are right,' I said. 'It is the plague of our times, is it not? As surely as truth makes headway against superstition, so the perversion of truth comes along in its wake. It is too easy to pretend to be what one is not.

'And not to be what one is,' said Fidelis.

In Manchester, I had arrangements to make before we departed next day. On occasion it falls to the coroner to arrange a funeral, and this was one such occasion. I therefore visited a joiner's shop and ordered a coffin for immediate delivery to the inn, as I had decided I would return with the body of Grevel Horntree to Accrington and see him buried in his own parish. Luke Fidelis did not think much of the idea, saying the fellow was not worthy of charity and should be thrown into any old pauper's grave in the place where he died. He came around to my opinion, however, when I suggested that news of Horntree's death and burial might flush out his missing wife from her hiding place, if she did happen to be hiding. I then asked John Blow to find me a jagger willing to convey the corpse.

The sun had blazed all the time I was in Manchester, but on the day I left it skulked behind leaden clouds, though the warmth continued to stifle the air. Having said goodbye to Furzey, who was to return directly to Preston, we had meant to accompany the coffin all the way. But the slow pace of the cart and the fact that Suez would not cease tormenting the jagger's mastiff (a gigantic drooling beast called Buller) led to a change of plan. Suez continually danced around Buller while issuing volleys of yaps – probably invitations to play, which Buller proved disinclined to accept, and I was concerned that he might soon have Suez not for his playfellow but his lunch. Meanwhile, Fidelis was itching to ride on in order to pursue the search for his missing inamorata, and I was impatient to see my wife and son after our four days' separation.

It was therefore agreed that we two would press ahead, leaving the carter to go at his own rate. So Fidelis and I kicked our horses on and made another ten miles in decent time, though not fast enough for Fidelis, who was frustrated by having to limit himself to a pace that Suez could maintain. Then we came upon another impediment, in the form of a clergyman on a fat and stately mare, ambling in the same direction as ourselves. I saw, on coming level with him, that it was Mr Septimus Postumus, making his way back to his parish at Clitheroe. He wore spectacles and was reading from a book as he rode, which – when I came alongside – I saw was a volume of hymns.

'Ah, Mr Cragg, is it?' he said peering at me through the

lenses of his spectacles. 'How very pleasant to meet on the road. Do you go to Accrington? I travel that way myself. Shall we keep company? I have been reduced to singing psalms and hymns, but I would much rather converse.'

'An excellent plan,' said Fidelis before I could reply. 'Titus, why don't you and the dog accompany the reverend gentleman while I hurry on ahead? This horse is a beautiful galloper and I should reach there an hour before you. I'll warn Elizabeth to prepare for your coming. She will provide a splendid dinner I am sure.'

'An adventitious dinner!' said Mr Postumus before I could get a word in. 'I am fortunate indeed. I was certainly wondering where and how – and even if – I might dine on my way home. Inns are so rowdy, I find.'

I could hardly refuse the eminent preacher without the risk of impoliteness. Besides, I was curious to know him better.

So Fidelis rode off, a liberated man, and I adjusted my own mount's pace to that of Mr Postumus. I congratulated him upon his sermon and in particular on his care for the orphans and foundlings. He proved to be very garrulous on the subject.

'In the large cities, it is a great and growing scandal. There is so much of gross immorality there that hundreds of children are born with none to care for them. Our capital is the worst of our cities, do you not agree?'

'Oh, undoubtedly.'

'Naturally, it is not as bad as on the Continent, where iniquity is on a scale not dreamed of even in London. In Paris you will find bastardy so great that there is a hospital with a hatch in the wall for loose women to deposit their newborn brats at night. I shudder to think what the French do with these bantlings. Send them to be galley slaves or Jesuits probably – would you not say?'

'Oh, yes. Galley slaves and Jesuits, undoubtedly.'

'There is now in London a similar hospital but governed strictly on Protestant lines. Its wall is equipped with no such hatchlike contrivance, as the fallen women are required to present themselves with their bastards in a good Protestant way, face to face. It was begun by an association of very worthy Christian merchants, with the boys to be schooled up as seamen or apprentices in various trades and the girls as servants and seamstresses.'

I mentioned something I had been reading in *Gulliver's Travels* – that among the Lilliputians all parents were forcibly deprived of their infants, who were raised in residential nurseries. They considered parents the worst possible educators of their offspring since their thoughts during the act of conception were not on serious matters, but only on fleeting and frivolous pleasure. Postumus laughed.

'That is a godless book for a clergyman to have written, Mr Cragg, though I admit a diverting one. I myself do not denigrate the natural pleasures of congress between husband and wife. It is fornication and sodomy without marriage that I bear down on and deplore.'

Fornication and sodomy were so much his favourite subjects that he continued to discourse on them for several miles.

TWENTY-SEVEN

We arrived at the Dower House near two in the afternoon. Suez and Matty greeted each other boisterously, Elizabeth embraced me tenderly, and our reverend guest used his finger and thumb solemnly to shake Hector's pudgy fist. Then we sat down to the dinner of mutton pudding that Elizabeth had stayed until our arrival. Postumus ate up his portion with grateful gusto and returned his plate for more, while discoursing on matters that interested him – though, allowing for the presence of a mother and child, he referred only in oblique terms to fornication and sodomy.

We rose from the table after an hour and, excusing myself, I went to Mrs Nightingale's cottage to alert her to the coming burial. She immediately raised objections to Horntree's rapid interment in St James's Church graveyard.

'Mr Rishton will never be persuaded to come at less than a week's notice. He has no regard for Accrington, and he would not put himself out for Grevel Horntree. They detested each other.'

'But we must get him into the ground, Frances. Tomorrow, if possible. He begins to stink. Besides, I have an idea that should the news of his death and burial spread it might draw out his errant wife.'

'To bury him tomorrow, we need a clergyman tomorrow. Find me one of those and the thing might be arranged.'

'Is that all you need? As it happens, I brought one with me. His name is Septimus Postumus.'

'Oh! Mr Postumus, is it? Here in Accrington?'

'We travelled together. He is at this moment sitting in the Dower House digesting his dinner.'

'What good fortune indeed! I shall have to ask Mr Rishton to allow the Reverend Postumus to priest the funeral, but I have no doubt he will defer to such a good and famous clergyman. I'll write to him now and young Roger Eales shall carry the message.'

She sat down to write her letter, and I was about to leave
her to it when she stopped me.

'There is another thing. How are we ever going to dig a
grave? Since our last rain, the ground's baked hard as
rock again.'

At the same moment a distant discharge of thunder grum-
bled in the west and I said, 'There's your answer, Frances.
More rain is coming. With luck, by morning the ground will
take a spade as a jelly takes a spoon. I suggest you make the
arrangements with the sexton.'

All day there had been these thunderous murmurs behind
the pall of swollen cloud that countrymen call 'groiling'. Now,
as I headed back to the Dower House, the clouds burst and
I came inside dripping from the downpour. Our guest was
asleep in the fireside chair and I stood behind him and
coughed, which failed to rouse him. I was drawing breath for
a louder cough when a great clap of thunder forestalled me,
seeming to explode in the sky directly overhead. Mr Postumus
leaped in terror from his chair.

'Oh, my word! What was that? I was dreaming so pleasantly.
What a fearsome shock to be awoken by that hellish detona-
tion. Is it a very great storm, Cragg?'

The intrepid defier of Satan and his works was shaking
furiously at the sound of thunder.

'It is a big storm, certainly.'

'Oh, I cannot go out in it. I ought to be on my way to
Clitheroe but I really cannot go through the violence of a
thunderstorm, I cannot. May I crave your shelter until the
greatest shocks are over?'

I reassured him that he was invited to stay all night under
the safety of my roof, adding that I would ask just one favour
of him in return.

'I am the resurrection and the life, saith the Lord.'

The clock had just struck ten when the opening words of
the burial service rang out in Mr Postumus's resonant voice.
He was standing in the porch, spectacles on nose and book in
hand, to welcome the coffin. Borne by six men from the
Hatchfly estate, two being Charlie and Simon Stirk, this

crawled like a huge many-legged insect up the church path towards him.

After a night of heavy rain the sun was blazing once again from a flawless sky, yet no one had gone to the fields this Wednesday morning. The death of a prominent local employer might have suggested that the future for many of them was uncertain. But as the villagers assembled, it became clear that foreboding was not their humour. Inside the church the benches were crammed with cheerful souls, fidgeting and whispering, nudging and sniggering, enjoying the day off. Few it seemed had come to mourn.

But Septimus Postumus was not just a masterly preacher, he was a virtuoso in the performance of church rites. He processed down the aisle before the simple workaday coffin (the same that I'd transported the body in from Manchester, but now concealed under a black cloth), intoning that he knew his Redeemer liveth and though worms destroy the body yet the flesh shall see God, and without effort took command of the congregation. By force of character and good acting, he gathered them in until they hung on his every gesture, his every prayer and incantation.

'*We brought nothing into this world, and it is certain we can carry nothing out.*'

Reaching the altar steps, the celebrant spun around with some of the grace of a dancer.

'*The Lord giveth and the Lord taketh away.*'

'Amen!' cried a lone but fervent voice from the congregation. I looked around and saw that it had been Susan Bacon giving this enthusiastic response.

Well-worn though they are, the words of the ceremony – now laden with doom, now uplifting with the hope of resurrection – received all the power of expression and subtle variations in tone and loudness for which Postumus's sermons were famous. By the time he came to the grand climax of the Epistle to the Corinthians – *O Death where is thy sting? O grave where is thy victory?* – the entire church was spellbound.

I stood in the heart of the congregation beside Elizabeth, who in spite of her Catholicism would come to the English church out of loyalty to me. Looking carefully around, we agreed that Flora Horntree had not appeared. Later we became so absorbed in Mr Postumus's performance that we did not review the benches, or the crowd of latecomers standing at the back, until the service inside the church reached the homily. In the hiatus during which Mr Postumus ascended the pulpit, I looked around once more but still saw no Mrs Horntree.

The celebrant had the unusual task of orating on the life of a complete stranger. Vicars know their parishioners and fellow villagers all too well, but Postumus was not the minister in Accrington and it would have been easy for him mistakenly to expatiate on virtues in Horntree that everyone knew the dead man didn't have, such as patience, sweetness of nature and a strong vein of humour.

But Septimus Postumus was no fool and he had been in Accrington just long enough to understand that the man in the coffin had never been much liked. He did not, of course, mention this directly – but having spoken for a mere twenty minutes on the general rudiments of a good Christian life, he closed his address by asking an interesting rhetorical question with a bearing on Horntree's local reputation.

'The Bible orders us not to slander the living, but does this command extend as far as the dead? Should Christian kindness also reach those no longer among us? *De mortuis nil nisi bonum* – speak not ill of the dead – is a pagan maxim. Scripture does not bind us to it. And yet . . .'

He raked the crowded church with his gaze.

'Have not the dead gone forever out of our jurisdiction? Nothing we say can affect them. Our words may, however, do terrible harm to us, the living. I leave you to think about the Old Testament proverb which says "*The tale bearer revealeth secrets, but he that is of a faithful spirit concealeth the matter.*" Or, in the more succinct words of the Saviour, "*Judge not, and ye shall not be judged; condemn not and ye shall not be condemned.*" So I say let the criminal, the liar and – yes! – the fornicator be punished according to his deserts, not by man but by Almighty God who holds such evil-doers in contempt.'

Holding himself still as stone, he let the resonance of 'contempt' die in the roof beams. Then he picked up his book and descended the pulpit for the final prayers and procession. But before he could begin these, a sound – something like a sob – broke the silence and all turned to discover who it had come from, and we saw for the first time that Tom Turvey was in the church.

He was standing among the latecomers at the back, and was behaving so oddly that I wondered at first if he had an ague. His face was damp with sweat and pale as paper. His eyes were closed, not in churchy prayer but with the lids tightly squeezed together as if he feared to open them. Also his limbs and his lips were trembling violently. Unlikely though it was, he looked transported by grief – at this funeral of a man whose hated name he had for years refused to utter. Elizabeth noted this too, and gave my elbow a nudge.

We filed outside to witness the lowering of Grevel Horntree into his grave. This is the moment when, in all funerals, I most clearly picture the human remains shrouded and alone in the dark, formerly full of life and now quite drained of it. The body would come to ground at a depth of six feet; dirt would be piled and packed in, entirely smothering it; and there it would lie until nothing remained but a litter of mould and bones carpeting the bottom of the coffin. Death where is thy sting? In the air above any open grave and in the minds of all those standing around it, that is my answer. It was hard enough to contemplate such a state for myself, but almost unbearable when I pictured the burial of Elizabeth or Matty. Even Hector would sooner or later come to this. Is there life beyond, as St Paul promises? We can only hope.

To distract myself from such thoughts, I stepped back and looked around. The previous gaiety of the people had long since been dampened, both by the force of Mr Postumus's words and the sober reality of the occasion. I noted for the first time the presence of John Gargrave who, as a papist, would not enter the church but was willing to pay his respects in the churchyard. I saw no sign of the widow Horntree, grieving or otherwise. And I could no longer see the apparently grieving Tom Turvey.

The handfuls of dirt were cast. The final Amen was pronounced. The crowd dissolved as the people went home or to their work, or coalesced in groups to murmur together.

Elizabeth had just gone up to Septimus Postumus to congratulate him on the conduct of the ceremony when I caught sight
of Fidelis, alone, in contemplation of a pair of tombstones,
one of them quite new, standing a little apart from the rest of
the graves. I joined him.

'You should have been in church, Luke. You missed a service
most consummately performed. Mr Postumus's delivery of the
prayers was powerful indeed.'

But my friend was not listening to my words. He had on
his face an expression I had seen many times before: his eyes
narrowed and the tip of his tongue protruded very slightly
between his lips, which curved fractionally upwards in the
faintest of smiles. It was the look he often acquired when he
had made a discovery or was on to a scent.

He nodded at the stones.

'What do you make of these graves, Titus?' he said.

I noted their inscriptions.

'They are the graves of women of the Turvey family,' I said.
'Tom Turvey's wife and his mother-in-law, side by side.'

'Is that all you see?'

'I believe so. Can you see more?'

'What I see exposes and corrects a foolish mistake.'

'How do you make that out?'

'Read the words on the mother-in-law's stone again.'

I spoke them aloud: '*Here resteth Hannah Entwhistle,
daughter of Ben Bristow, who lived blamelessly in this life
until she departed it on 2 April 1744 and now reposeth eter-
nally with the Lord.*'

I looked at Fidelis and back at the stone. Nothing occurred
to me.

'Are you saying the poor woman was not blameless?'

'No. I refer to the fact that you told me the locket found in
Mrs Horntree's valise had belonged to Mrs Entwhistle as a
girl. But look, she was born Hannah Bristow.'

'And?'

'Come, Titus! Even if the monogram on the locket in Mrs
Horntree's valise is read as *H.F.*, it cannot refer to Mrs
Entwhistle's maiden name, as Tom Turvey stated, since we
see here that she was born Hannah Bristow. Nor was it anything

to do with the supposed theft at New Manor. The monogram is, of course, *F.H.* and, as I suspected all along, the locket was Mrs Horntree's own property.'

'But why would Turvey say it was his mother-in-law's?'

'Ignorance, carelessness. It doesn't much matter. He is not an observant man, except when it comes to bees, and he was (as you told me) very distracted at the time. He misread the monogram and simply assumed the thing belonged with the rest of the loot.'

We joined Elizabeth and walked back to the Dower House, passing small knots of Accrington people as they stood about in the sunshine, discussing the funeral. A few called out to me in friendly greeting.

'That is a change,' I said. 'They begin to like me after all. Or some of them do.'

'It is just as I said on our first day, remember?' said Elizabeth.

'And yet today the people look serious,' said Fidelis. 'I think the thought of who will run the Hatchfly estate has begun to bite, and whether there will be work for them on it.'

During our absence Matty had filled the Dower House with cooking smells, and she was now rocking Hector and singing to him. She planted the baby in his mother's arms and handed me a piece of paper, folded but not sealed.

'What's this?' I said, following Matty as she went back to her cooking pots.

'The boy from New Manor brought it,' she said, stirring one of the pots, 'Danny, that keeps giving me cow-eyed looks. I take no mind of him.'

I unfolded the paper and found a note written in a careful literate hand.

Dear Mr Cragg,
  Please come, and bring Dr Fidelis, as soon as you may, to see my father. He has been very peculiar, and gave himself up to outbursts of weeping and lamenting throughout the night so that we could do nothing with him. We are at our wits' end as he will not explain. Sukey says he has gone mad. Please come.
  Thomasina Turvey.

TWENTY-EIGHT

'**W**hat time was this delivered, Matty?'

'Not long after you went to church.'

I showed Elizabeth the note.

'You had better go to him,' she said after reading it. 'Poor Mr Turvey. He's been a good friend to us. We must help him, if we can.'

'You will not come?'

'Later. I must see to Hector first.'

So Fidelis and I went ahead to New Manor, where we found Thomasina in the Chamber Major. Her bath chair had been wheeled into position in front of one of the tall windows, and from here she gazed out across the garden.

I sat close to her on the window seat and asked after her father.

'We have not seen him since he went out, earlier this morning.'

'He was at Horntree's funeral and seemed very affected.'

'He did not come back here afterwards.'

'Do you know the reason for this apparent grief?'

'I can't see that it *was* grief. My father is not a man to rejoice over a death, but this one would not have made him very unhappy, I think.'

Fidelis, who had been idly inspecting the array of family portraits, now joined us at the window.

'What was the origin of the quarrel between your father and Mr Horntree?' he asked.

'It was a very old grudge, Dr Fidelis, which I'm sure started when that man first bought Hatchfly Hall. I was quite small then. I cannot explain why they quarrelled, as my father made a vow never to mention the man and so could not tell me.'

Sukey entered the room.

'Oh, Sukey,' said Thomasina. 'Is the kettle boiling? Will you make these gentlemen some coffee?'

'Ha!' cried Sukey with a light ironical laugh. 'Do you think we have money for the likes of coffee?'

'Then what have we?'

Sukey came to the child's side and stroked her hair.

'We have mead, small beer and tea, Missy.'

'Then we'll have tea.'

Thomasina's eyes were bright. She had momentarily forgotten her father's woes as she played the hostess. Sukey went out and Luke joined me on the window seat.

'This may seem a strange question, Miss Turvey,' he said, 'but believe me it is to the point. Are you, I wonder, familiar with what is in your mother's jewellery casket?'

'Oh yes, very. As a little girl I played with it endlessly. I would make Sukey bring it to me and I would take everything out and try to wear it all at once. But what has it to do with all this?'

'Your father told us that Flora Horntree had stolen, or tried to steal, some of this jewellery. Did he not tell you of it?'

'Good heavens! Did she? He said not a word.'

'I am interested in the origin of some of the pieces in the box. For instance, was any of it passed on to your mother by her own mother?'

'By Grandmother Entwhistle? Oh no, I don't think so. Grandmother had her own jewel box and, as you know, she was still alive when my mother passed away. So it came directly to me on her death. I have it still.'

'And is it intact? Has anything been taken from it?'

'It is. I often look at it.'

'Very well. And is or was there something like an engraved silver pillbox there, made to hang around the neck as a locket?'

'A locket? No, Doctor, Grandmother Entwhistle had no locket. And no pillbox that I've seen.'

'What of your mother? Did her jewellery box contain such a locket?'

'No, there is nothing of the kind and never has been.'

'It is exactly as I thought, Titus,' said Fidelis.

Thomasina looked bewilderedly at Fidelis, and then at me.

'What is the meaning of all this? Why are you asking about lockets?'

'There was a silver one among the things in Mrs Horntree's valise. It was engraved *F.H.*, of which the obvious interpretation is that it was hers and that she brought it with her to New Manor. But your father said different. He made out that Mrs Horntree had pilfered it from this house.'

'Pilfered from here? That can't be right. The letters are wrong to be my mother's, or grandmama's. So where did it come from?'

'At the moment I cannot say,' said Fidelis. 'I hope we will know more soon.'

Sukey came in with a tray bearing teapot and cups, so our conversation was interrupted by the pouring and distribution of tea. Thomasina momentarily forgot her father as she played the hostess, and we sipped from our cups and complimented the old servant on her tea.

'Sukey,' I said, 'you know your master better than anyone. Can you apprehend the reason for his recent behaviour?'

The servant's face took on a wary expression.

'Apprehend, Sir? No, I reckon it is not for me to apprehend. I leave apprehending to my betters.'

'You may go, Sukey,' Thomasina broke in. 'You have things to do, I am sure.'

She waited until the servant had withdrawn.

'It was just a few days ago,' she said. 'I only noticed it after you had left for Manchester with Mrs Nightingale. My father was distracted and very quiet. Then I thought I saw his eyes with tears in them.'

'Is it unusual for Mr Turvey to weep?'

'I have never seen him in tears, Mr Cragg, except one time when he discovered foul brood in one of the hives. That is a deadly disease of bees, you know. Of course, this time we thought – Sukey and I – that he was worrying over the disappearance of that woman who came to live here. She agitated my father even before she went so suddenly away, and now he is very much worse.'

'And did he not tell you why?'

'No. He was very silent and melancholy. I asked him what the matter was, but he did not reply except to shake his head. I asked if it was the woman's disappearance and he shrugged his shoulders in a most helpless way. I believe this meant he did not understand his feelings himself.'

'Do you know where he might have gone after the funeral?'

'Perhaps to Clover Field. Before he went out first thing this morning, I asked him where he was going. He just said "Clover Field", and nothing about going to Mr Horntree's funeral.'

'Clover Field, where he has one of his bee colonies.'

'Yes, one of his favourites. I suppose he meant to look at the hives, and maybe remove some honey.'

'Dr Fidelis and I shall go up there at once. We don't want him to come to any harm.'

I should not have said that. Thomasina's face showed sudden alarm. She clapped her hands to her cheeks.

'Harm? Oh, I hope not, Mr Cragg. I hope not indeed!'

Fidelis and I climbed the path beside the Woodnook Brook at a steady pace. After we'd emerged from the brookside copse where Elizabeth and I picked wild strawberries, and passed the place where she and I had admired the view over the valley, my nose picked up an unmistakeable smell on the still air.

'Something's burning.'

We continued along the footpath, which went up and down beside a field, then crossed a stile and skirted another pasture. By now a haze of smoke could be seen ahead, though its source was in hidden ground.

After crossing two more fields, we reached the stone hut and the site of the beehives – or what remained of them, for the source of the smoke was now revealed. Where each skep had stood, there was a circle of blackened, smouldering ashes mixed with molten wax. Dead and dying bees lay scattered everywhere. The caramel scent of scorched honey mingled with the smoke and thickened the air.

'It's like a scene from war,' said Fidelis. 'After the King of France's men have come to call.'

I remembered the comparison I had made on first seeing this apiary in company with its owner.

'The hamlet has been sacked and burnt,' I said. 'Its inhabitants have been raped and killed. If Turvey was up here and saw this, how much more distressed he must be now, with his beehives burnt. Who could have done it? Who held such a grudge against him?'

I scanned the field and then turned, searching the horizon. There was no sign of anyone, but in the next instant both of us heard a sound from inside the stone shed.

'Who's there?' I called.

As Fidelis and I advanced towards the hut door, it swung open and a man in labourer's clothing came out. His lower face was concealed by a red kerchief, pulled over the bridge of his nose and knotted at the nape of his neck. Harry Hawk. He touched his forehead.

'How do, Mr Cragg. Doctor.'

'Hawk! You must explain yourself. What are you doing here?'

'On my way home. Been working over yonder, at Mr Oldroyd's.'

His voice was the same hollow baffle-tongued sound, all sliding vowels and indistinct consonants, that I remembered from our chat in the dark above the Black Bull. He pointed to the south-west. Oldroyd's Farm was barely a mile away, though hidden in a fold of the land. I gestured at the incinerated skeps.

'Are you responsible for all this?' I said. 'Was it you that burned these hives?'

He shook his head with a certain weariness.

'Not I. I saw the smoke and came to see what was up, as I used to look after Squire Turvey's bees for him. There's no saving them, though. The colonies are burned beyond recovery.'

'So what were you doing in the shed?'

'I went inside in case who did this was there. There was no one. Then I heard voices coming. I was waiting to find out who you were before I showed myself.'

That did not seem unreasonable.

'We are looking for Mr Turvey,' said Luke. 'We believe he may have come up here. Have you seen him?'

'No, Sir.'

Hawk and I looked down at the blackened ashes and the strewn bodies of the bees as Fidelis walked towards the barn. He opened the door and glanced inside.

'You must come back with us to New Manor,' I said.

'Happen Squire Turvey's come home by now. He will want an explanation for what has occurred here.'

Hawk shrugged.

'It's my way home.'

Fidelis had gone out of sight behind the rough building. A few moments later he returned to us from the other side.

'You two go on,' he said. 'I shall stay here.'

'To do what?'

Fidelis beckoned me back to the barn and pushed me inside, ahead of him.

'What do you see, Titus?'

The only difference compared to the last time I had been in there was that one of the straw bales was broken into. Looking closer, I saw that a bed of straw had been laid on the ground and partly covered by sacking.

'It looks like someone's made a bed here.'

'It does.'

'So who was living here?'

Fidelis stooped, removed the sacking, and inspected the straw. He picked something out of it.

'Hold out your hand Titus.'

He dropped into it a delicate silver chain of the kind a woman uses to hang a pendant around her neck. The clasp had been broken.

'Oh! This could be Flora's, Luke!'

'Precisely.'

Fidelis took off his coat, hung it on a protruding nail, and began sorting through a stack of wooden-handled tools. He pulled out a long spade.

'Now, go quickly down to the village. It's more urgent than ever that we find Turvey. As soon as you get there, send Danny up to me. I shall need his help.'

Thomasina's eyes filled with disappointment on learning we had not discovered the Squire.

'Oh, poor father! What can have become of him?'

'Don't despair,' I said. 'He may turn up yet, though I do fear for him. We found all the Clover Field beehives burnt and destroyed.'

'His precious clover hives gone? That will sorely grieve him. Happen he's off looking for the one that did it.'

'Happen.'

Hawk having declined to enter the house, I had left him sitting on a stone seat in the courtyard. But now, going out again, I found the seat deserted.

Gone home to his dinner, I thought, and I didn't blame him. I'd eaten nothing since breakfast myself and I suddenly felt a sharp hunger. So after finding Danny and instructing him to hurry off to the stone shed, I hurried back to the Dower House.

'We haven't waited dinner for you, Titus,' said Elizabeth when I walked in.

I must have pulled a disappointed face, for she took me gently by the ears and kissed my mouth.

'I had to feed Mr Postumus before he left us, but there's a plate of mutton and potatoes for you and pickles with sage cheese. Matty found a farm that makes it and it's very good. Sit yourself down. You won't go hungry.'

I gratefully obeyed.

'I would like to have thanked Postumus for conducting the burial, and am sorry I missed him,' I said.

Elizabeth went to the fireplace and took something down from the mantelshelf, which she put into my hand. It was a pair of spectacles.

'Well, he's left these behind, so you can say your piece in a letter when you send them back.'

'So I shall, but let me tell you about my morning first. It's been a very interesting one indeed.'

I told her how Tom Turvey was missing after the funeral and how, going to look for him, we had found the remains of his skeps at Clover Field but no sign of Turvey.

'How horrible, Titus! It must have been someone with a violent grudge who did that.'

'Killing Mr Turvey's bees was perfectly calculated to make the Squire suffer. Who could have done it?'

'We found Harry Hawk there. Rather skulking inside the shed, he was. He claimed to have been merely passing by and noticed the smoke and went to see what caused it.'

'A likely story! Remember that Mr Turvey used to employ Harry Hawk but he was dismissed for joining with the Stirk brothers in the frightful death of Mrs Gargrave. Hawk is very poor. He must have resented the Squire and bemoaned his lost job.'

'Yes, and he was assistant in the beekeeping, which makes the destruction of the hives, if he did indeed do it, very apt. But a more urgent question is what has happened to Turvey himself.'

I told how we had noticed straw laid inside the shed, like bedding, and found the chain amongst the straw.

'There is the possibility that someone has been living there.'

'Oh! Could it have been her, Titus?'

'Luke's up there now, and being very mysterious. I mean to go straight back myself.'

'We can go out together. I shall go to Thomasina. The poor child must be suffering terribly.'

As soon as I rose from the table, Elizabeth went to fetch her hat and came back with Suez jumping around her heels and Hector wrapped for going out.

'I am bringing the baby and the dog. They will help amuse or at least distract the child.'

Before we left, I returned Mr Postumus's eyeglasses to the mantelshelf. And promptly forgot all about them.

TWENTY-NINE

A t New Manor, we enquired of Sukey and learned that Turvey had not returned. So I left Elizabeth, Hector and Suez at the door and strode away to cross the Woodnook Brook and climb the path to Clover Field. Coming to the stone barn, I heard grunts of effort from behind the building and, peering around it, saw Luke Fidelis and Danny excavating a rectangular hole in part of the bed that had been dug for the cultivation of nectar-rich flowers. As a digger Fidelis had more gusto than skill, wielding his spade like a bayonet, and then an axe, to spear, hack and hurl aside the earth. The youth, Danny, however, knew well how to dig. His spadework was elegant, spitting just as much earth as he could lift and then in one easy movement slinging it out of the hole and bringing the spade back to earth in an elliptical curve.

'Stop!' said Fidelis. 'That's enough with the spades.'

He drew his sleeve across his brow to catch the sweat.

'I fancy we must go more carefully from here.'

He hurled his spade out of the hole, picked up a trowel, and dropped to his knees. His face was flushed, and to a degree hectic: he was at the same time exhilarated and appalled, which told me he was looking for a body. Precisely why he thought it was there, I could not tell. As so often, he had run ahead of me. I watched as he plied his trowel, more gentle now than with the spade, using it experimentally to lift up the earth and peer into it and then moving the trowel a few inches aside to repeat the procedure.

'Here! There's something here!'

He planted the trowel to one side and, using his fingers, clawed the earth aside.

'It's clothing. Here, Danny, a hand please.'

I watched, appalled, as little by little they scraped and brushed the dirt away, delicately forming out of the earth the appearance of a human being – a woman in a begrimed shift who seemed to rise like an apparition from the very deep. Her face was undoubtedly ghostly: grey and indistinct, the eyes open and horribly sightless. The body was displayed as if in moulded relief and I was almost ashamed to look at it. But when I did, there was no need to ask who she was.

It was Danny's idea to fetch a carrying platform from inside the barn, used for transporting skeps from place to place. Meanwhile, Fidelis carefully lifted the woman out of the earth and into the air. The dirt-stained body hung limp in his arms as he stepped from the grave and carried her to the makeshift litter, on which he laid her. Then he went back to the hole and brought out a ball of clothing that had been buried alongside her. He shook it out, scattering clods of dirt from the folds, and laid it out on the ground. There was a red gown like the one Flora Horntree had been wearing in the New Manor garden, when I'd last seen her from the river bank. There was also a full set of bee armour – padded breeches and jerkin, hat and net, boots and leather gloves.

We took turns carrying the litter down to Accrington.

'How did you know she was there?' I asked Fidelis as we progressed laboriously downhill.

'I didn't. But I couldn't miss an area where someone had been digging very recently, and not just gardening.'

'Hawk knew the place, and he was in the barn when we were up there earlier. Suspicion must fall on him in this.'

'We must resolve some other questions about the body before we name a culprit.'

'And they are?'

'What took her up to Clover Field? How did she die? Why was she buried? And why was the bee armour in the grave with her? I will know more when I've examined her body.'

Fidelis's emotions may have been filled with vagaries and irrational impulses, but when working he was always ruled by method. I watched his face as, an hour later, he stood in the aisle of the church with Frances and me, peeling the sodden muddy shift from the body on the table where two weeks before Anne Gargrave's body had lain for a similar examination. With his lips pushed outwards, his eyes wide to miss nothing, Fidelis was a study in purposeful attention.

Flora Horntree's naked body, which had been most beautiful in life, had lost all its grace and bloom – although its size and proportions had not changed, which goes to show that beauty is not a question of eternal mathematical symmetries, as some Vitruvians and collectors of ancient marbles believe. I have looked at a hundred bare corpses and never found one to be beautiful. Beauty I have concluded belongs only to life.

'Look at her face!' Frances Nightingale said. 'It's like someone seeing horrors.'

'If we want to know what happened to her,' murmured Fidelis as he lifted one of the dead woman's hands, 'we will find the expression on her face useless. What is under her fingernails, on the other hand, may tell us something.'

This comment would have baffled previous generations of coroners. My own father, as Coroner in Preston, always tried to read a corpse's face, as he was certain it conveyed information about how the death occurred. He would not, on the other hand, have wasted time minutely examining the hands and fingers as Fidelis did now – scrutinizing first the palm as if engaged in palmistry as practised by Mrs Quinto, then the back of the hand, and finally the tips of the fingers.

'So what do these fingernails reveal?' I asked.

'That she was not above biting them.'

He opened his medical bag and selected a canvas roll containing his cutting tools. I signalled to Frances with a jerk of the head that this was my usual cue to leave him. We went out together and sat on the bench in the porch of the church.

'Who killed her, Mr Cragg?'

'It was not her husband, we know that.'

'One acting as his agent, then?'

'No. He didn't commission her death. He himself was dead before he could have known that she had deserted him. For some reason she left her sanctuary in New Manor, and then for some reason – which may not have been the same reason – she met her death.'

'She was buried in her shift. Her dress had been removed.'

'I noticed.'

'So perhaps someone took advantage of . . . of her defence-lessness.'

'That is often the case with defenceless people.'

We sat in prolonged silence until we began to hear a commotion in the village street. Shouts and hoots broke the late-afternoon air to the accompaniment of loud blurts, metallic bangs, wooden clacks, and a wheedling violin. Rough music, it seemed, had returned to Accrington.

We hurried out of the churchyard to discover that Billy Whist was out again with his guiding boy. He was dancing and playing at the head of a rout of people that advanced up the village. Between him and the bulk of the crowd a man was being pushed along in the custody of two other men; he had his wrists tied together and wore a flour sack over his head. His custodians were two villagers that I knew well: Charlie and Simon Stirk.

The cacophonic music that led the procession was a signal that the villagers had not come to celebrate, but had a harsher purpose. Looks were hard, and voices harder, as I heard shouts of 'Murdering bastard!' and 'Make him pay!' being chanted.

'What is this?' I asked an elderly villager who stood at his door on the street. 'Who is it they've arrested?'

'The murderer of the Squire's wife,' said the old worthy.

Frances and I exchanged an incredulous glance. The woman's corpse had been brought back barely two hours before. This mob had formed and moved into action with terrifying speed.

'Who is it they're accusing, Frances? And what do they mean to do with him?'

'Oh, they've got the idea to hang him, I fancy – whoever he is.'

'Then we must stop them.'

We shadowed the rout until it reached the oak tree at the beginning of Lower Fold, where it stopped – a thick crowd, perhaps fifty strong, with their blood up. Now began a shouted debate about where to find a rope, since no one had one on their person. Throughout the discussion, hoarse inarticulate cries issued from inside the flour sack as the prisoner at the centre of attention tried to make himself heard.

Then someone appeared with a coil of rope. He jumped on to the wooden bench that encircled the oak tree's bole and slung it up and over one of the tree's high horizontal boughs. A burly fellow in the garb of a Puritan got up alongside the rope-thrower and whispered to him. At once, the latter began to fashion one of the rope ends into a noose, while the big Puritan, his eyes gleaming with fervour, addressed the crowd in the following uncompromising terms.

'You all know that we're here for a Godly reason. A murderer shall not be suffered to live and therefore shall he be put to death. That is Almighty God's law.'

They answered him with cries of 'Yea!' and the Puritan pointed at the hooded prisoner, adopting the pose of an actor on the stage.

'Are we all agreed, then, that this man has done a murder most foul?'

There were shouts of approval.

'And doubtless a loathsome rape an' all?'

There were further shouts.

'Hang him! Hang him!'

'Well said,' shouted the burly man. 'We should cleave to the law of God and hang him to death without further delay.'

The other fellow flourished the noose he had made, above his head, and received a roar of approval from the audience. I knew that there was little time left in which to act. With a silent prayer, I began to shoulder and shove my way to the front of the crowd.

By the time I got there I was hearing volleys of abuse from the mouths of the people around me, and receiving enraged pushes and jostles. My hat was knocked flying from my head. I thought that if they killed me I would get little glory afterwards for my sacrifice, but it was too late to worry about that now.

'I am Titus Cragg, the County Coroner,' I said when at last I reached the front, 'and I must be allowed to speak.'

'Nay, Coroner,' said the Puritan leaning close to my face, 'for we know what tha'lt say. Tha'lt try to turn us from our purpose, and we cannot be turned. This man must die. Look on him and tha'lt see how the devil has marked his face.'

The hapless victim was still held in the grip of the Stirk brothers who, at the Puritan's signal, heaved him up on to the bench and turned him to face the crowd. There was a collective gasp as the Puritan plucked the flour sack away and the torn, twisted face of Harry Hawk was exposed to the view of one and all. At once, his neck was encircled by the newly-fashioned noose and its maker began to draw it tight.

I stepped up on to the bench beside him and turned to face the crowd.

'I challenge you to let me speak!' I shouted. 'If your cause is just, God will let it prosper, whatever I say. If it is not, then you will, I know, desist.'

At this, there were shouts and whistles of dissent until a bellow was heard from the very back.

'Let him speak!'

They all turned to see who this was. I shaded my eyes and saw Jasper Johnson, the miller.

'Titus Cragg should have a hearing,' Johnson went on. 'We have no justices left in this village, so he is the nearest. I say hear him and then – if we must – we may do what we came here to do.'

Some muttering persisted, but the rattles and pan-beating fell away. For all their fervour, the crowd was suddenly interested in what manner of piece I might say. It was clear to me that these people would not be turned from their purpose by the arguments I was used to making in court – points of logic, and of common law or the statutes (least of all the statutes). Country people are moved more than anything by scriptural law as they see it – a black eye for a black eye, a cake for a stolen cake, a life for a life that's been taken. What could I possibly say against that old talionic bargain that they all believed in so passionately? Quote Jesus's 'turn the other cheek'? I doubted it would work.

It was Frances Nightingale who came to my rescue. She had wriggled and writhed her way after me to the front, and now grabbed my coat and tugged it until I paid attention.

'Think, Mr Cragg, think! Mr Postumus's sermon in Manchester. The wages of sin, remember? He quoted the Book of Numbers. You must do the same! You must tell them!'

As further muttering and mithering broke out amongst the crowd, I tried to remember precisely what the Reverend Postumus had said on the matter. I pictured him standing in the pulpit, his words ringing through the church in Manchester. He had repeated the simple nostrum on retribution: *Whoso shall kill another shall be put to death.* And then a solemn limitation had immediately followed: that there must be a trial in which corroborated evidence is heard. The actual scriptural words he quoted suddenly came back to me in full. I held up my hand.

'By the mouth of witnesses!' I shouted. 'Listen to the true word of God on this matter: *Whoso shall kill another shall be put to death by the mouth of witnesses.* It is the Book of Numbers. That is God's true law – there must be a trial of witnesses! And mark! Not just one witness, but *witnesses.* So, come forward, come forward now, anyone who saw this man commit murder and rape. We need at least two people. Let them tell us how it was. And if they say they saw Harry Hawk commit rape and murder, then let him be hanged. But let no one give false witness – we all know what follows from that.'

I glanced at the Puritan by my side. He was uncomfortable and a little chap-fallen. I cupped my ears and spoke again to the crowd, pressing home my advantage.

'I hear no voice. Does no one speak? Charlie Stirk? Simon? You called this man your friend and now you would put him to death. Shame on you, if you have no witnesses. "Judge not, that ye be not judged" – we heard those words quoted only this morning. But let this man go and I give you my oath that I shall hold an inquest into the woman's death. And if this man be found guilty of it, I will myself deliver him to the courts, where he shall be judged by proper authority and hang just as you wish to see him hanged.'

The Puritan was now clearly troubled. The light of inspiration that I had seen in his eyes had guttered out.

'Cragg is right. These proceedings are not according to God's law. We must stop.'

He unlooped the noose and untied Hawk's wrists with his own hands. I felt giddy and light-headed at the success of my oratory. The people, though they did not disperse, no longer pressed together in a single mass. They broke up into smaller groups, discussing and arguing among themselves over what I had said. The Puritan grasped my arm at the elbow.

'I believe you have done us a service, Mr Cragg. You have prevented an ungodly occurrence. I had forgot the Book of Numbers. I thank you.'

I nodded at Frances Nightingale and we each took a gentle hold of one of Harry Hawk's arms to get him away. We steered him towards the Dower House, where Elizabeth was standing at the door to receive us, her face white with fear. Without a word, I brought the exhausted Hawk inside and sat him down. When later I went out in search of my hat, I could not find it anywhere.

Matty made tea and added some sugar into Hawk's cup, for he was trembling as if mortally cold. She watched him sip, which his damaged jaw made awkward for him. Satisfied he could nevertheless drink without help, she sat down to listen to Frances's relation of all that had happened in the street.

Elizabeth caught my eye and jerked her head towards the stairs. She wanted a word alone with me. 'What you have just done was a very foolish, thoughtless thing, Titus Cragg,' she said in our bedroom as I took off my coat and threw myself down on the bed. 'I grant you it was brave, but its foolishness outweighs its bravery by ten to one. They might have hanged you too or – I don't know – stoned you. They are capable of it. And we would have been left abandoned and destitute. How could you risk that?'

I did not allow her reproof to affect me. I was still a little euphoric.

'I had to do something. I just charged in. Luckily, Frances reminded me of the exact form of words I needed. Ha! If she had not, they would have strung the poor man up in minutes.'

'It is nothing to laugh at. I might have seen the matter differently before Hector came along. Now, I hope never to see you risk your life like that again. You have our baby to think of, as well as me and Matty.'

I heard a new voice downstairs: Luke Fidelis had arrived.

'And so I do,' I said. 'But today I did not have time to think.

Now, that's Luke come in. He's been examining Mrs Horntree. I must go down and hear what he's found, if anything.'

I rolled off the bed and she reached out to touch my cheek.

'It seems to me that the dangers here are worse than any we may face in Preston, in spite of the Paralysing Ague.'

'You mean—'

'I mean, Titus, I would like us to spend the rest of our summer together at home – our true home. You see, I have come to the conclusion that we two are town mice at heart and not country mice, after all.'

Luke Fidelis occupied the chair vacated by Harry Hawk who, I was told, had five minutes earlier wrapped up his face and taken himself off.

'So what happened to her, Luke?' I said. 'I rather hope you are not going to say killed by Harry Hawk.'

'Why not? You were quick enough to suspect him earlier.'

'That was before this afternoon – when I saved Mr Hawk from a summary hanging, at no small danger to myself. I must feel the effort was worth my trouble.'

'Who was going to hang him?'

'Most of the village. It was like the Gargraves but with a noose instead of the stang. A crowd came down the street parading the poor fellow as a prisoner – led, of course, by Billy Whist. The word had spread all over that Hawk had been caught lurking at the place where we dug up Flora Horntree. They drew their own conclusions and were intent on stretching him at a rope's end from the big oak tree. You must have heard the uproar.'

'I was busy with my examination. You put a stop to it?'

'Yes.'

'That's good.'

He did not ask how, but merely got up and stretched.

'I am going back to my room at the Black Bull. I need to eat and then sleep, after which I will write you a full report. It has been a long day.'

THIRTY

We rose at six in the morning to find it had rained again in the night, a gentle rain this time, which broke the heatwave and produced a refreshing new day. There was no sign yet of Fidelis – a notorious slugabed – but Frances Nightingale appeared by my request at the Dower House shortly after seven. Our business was the need for a new inquest and, as we sat down to confer over the details, Elizabeth appeared in her hat to say she would go to New Manor and see if Mr Turvey had come home.

'What are they saying of this in the village, Frances?' she asked.

'There's still much hostility towards Harry Hawk. Some are saying he's not just killed Mrs Horntree but Squire Turvey an' all. And the story that Hawk's an impostor and a fraud and his real name is Ware – that's going around again, too.'

'It is very misleading to put unconnected notions like those together,' I said, 'though people love to congratulate themselves on the conclusions they draw when they do. Now we must think about this inquest. I am determined to hold it tomorrow.'

'Where shall we have it, Mr Cragg?' said Frances.

'The Chamber Major served very well last time.'

'Oh, but the Turveys have much to think about without this.'

'There is no better room in the village. The Black Bull is only a warren of little parlours. It will have to be the Chamber Major.'

'Very well. I'll send to Gubb at Altham to call another jury.'

'Must it be Gubb?'

'There's no one else.'

'Then tell him in your note for God's sake to make it a more harmonious group than he sent us the last time. So, let's move on to witnesses. We begin as ever with the first finder of the body, who was Dr Fidelis – which is convenient as we can hear the details of his corporal examination at the same time. The second witness ought to state formally who the dead woman is. We have no close relative, so who shall it be?'

'Perhaps the servant at Hatchfly Hall, Peggy Stirk?'

Mrs Stirk's name was added to the list, and that of Sukey, the servant at New Manor, who seemed preferable to Thomasina as a witness to the last day at New Manor on which Flora had been seen. Finally, there was the delicate question of Harry Hawk. He had been found near to the buried corpse when it was discovered, and should be examined. But Frances said, 'You remember how Gubb failed to produce him when we summoned his testimony on Susan Gargrave? I doubt we shall do better now. Hawk must be less willing than ever to come to Accrington after what happened yesterday. He will know that just by calling him we'll inflame all the suspicions against him.'

'But his evidence might damp them down. I'll go up to Gunwright's Heath and persuade him that these suspicions are a boil ripe to be lanced. Voluntary is better than by force. I'll go this morning.'

I could hear the loom clacking as I stood at the door. It was opened by Hawk, holding the carbine I had seen on the wall during my first visit. His face below the eyes was covered as usual with his red kerchief, but those eyes glowered at me.

'Good day, Hawk,' I said, trying to stay calm in face of his gun. 'I hope we can have a few words. May I come in?'

He neither spoke nor moved. I repeated my request, and after a few more seconds the sound of weaving ceased. Rosemary came to his side.

'It is only Mr Cragg, dearest,' she said to Hawk. 'We ought to let him in. Don't you remember what he did for you yesterday?'

Holding his arm gently, she drew him out of the way and I let myself into the farmhouse. The child was crawling around on the floor after a black-and-white kitten. The smell of pottage hung in the air. Rosemary Hawk gestured to a chair and I sat down.

'Hawk isn't one for the courtesies, Mr Cragg, 'specially

after what happened in Accrington. Even the Stirks turned on him, who had called him their friend. But he is grateful for your speaking out. I never knew about it till he came home last night. They seized him from the Black Bull, you know. I reckon they wouldn't have done what they threatened, though. It was only a drunken mob having some fun. But your support was very welcome.'

I did not contradict her with the truth – that her husband had been minutes from death. She had only what her husband had told her to go on, and I was content to leave it at that. I began by speaking directly to Hawk, who had sat down opposite me, with the gun resting on his knee and his narrowed eyes resting on mine.

'Now, Hawk, I was wanting a word. As you know, shortly after we met at the Clover Field the body of Mrs Horntree was found there, buried behind the barn where Dr Fidelis and I came upon you yesterday. It's because you were there that the village was so fired up against you, so I am here to offer you a chance to give your side of the story. Come to the inquest I shall hold tomorrow and you can explain everything.'

He did not reply, but sat looking at me. Uncertainly, I looked up at Rosemary, who, standing behind his chair, was resting her hands on her husband's shoulders.

'Mrs Hawk?' I said. 'It will be good for both of you if your husband says his piece. His silence, on the other hand, will do nothing but prolong people's suspicions indefinitely. He needs to tell the truth.'

She shook her head and smiled.

'You make it sound so simple, Sir. Yet on any subject there may be more than one truth, I think.'

I took a deep breath. This seemed a surprising remark to hear from a cottage weaver, until I remembered she was the daughter of a priest.

'Not if one limits the range of the enquiry, which is what the coroner's inquest seeks to do. We are concerned only with what happened to Flora Horntree: and about that matter, while there may be many lies, there is only one truth. Our object is to cut away those lies in order to reveal the truth. It is like clearing ivy off the trunk of a tree.'

I don't think I could have made the position clearer, and
Rosemary seemed to take the point. Still standing behind her
husband, she smoothed his hair with the palm of her hand.

'People say Harry is guilty of a terrible crime – assaulting
and killing Mrs Horntree, then burying her body. That is a
great lie and, yes, it must be challenged.'

Her eyes were filling with tears, and I saw the depth of
her fear of village prejudice and village violence. She brushed
the tears away with the back of her hand and darted across the
room to pick up her child, who had just been scratched by the
kitten and was bawling. I spoke again to Harry.

'Don't you see how afraid your wife is, man?'

He flashed me a look that suggested defiance, if not raw
anger.

'I don't trust you, Cragg. I don't trust anyone now.'

'I am not of Accrington, Mr Hawk. Did I not just save you
from being murdered by Accrington? I do not take sides and
I shall make sure the truth is found.'

'It's easier to be saying that than doing it.'

'Perhaps, but it *can* be done. And in the end only you can
exonerate yourself. You will never have a better opportunity.
Come to the inquest, Hawk. Speak honestly, and the truth – as
it says in the Gospel – shall make you free.'

Hawk's eyes narrowed.

'Gospel's never done much for me.'

We regarded each other steadily while ten seconds passed,
then I rose from my chair.

'I must be on my way,' I said, moving towards the door.
'I'll expect to see you at New Manor at ten o'clock, Hawk. I
shall not ask Constable Gubb to serve you with a summons,
as that would clearly be a waste of time. But please, don't
disappoint me. And whatever you do say in private, I would
caution you not on any account to disparage Scripture from
the witness chair.'

As I crossed the yard, Mrs Hawk, with her child on her
hip, came running out of the house and caught up with me
at the gate.

'I know he is not saying much,' she said, 'yet he *is*
grateful. I'll get him to the inquest, if I can.'

I thanked her and set off up the track. I was thinking about what Rosemary Hawk had said about truth. Despite my contradiction of her, I knew that on many subjects there are numerous truths indeed, and was wondering if Hawk's taciturnity had been a mark of his confusion between one truth and another. Hawk was a challenge to truth in his own person. His role in the death of Anne Gargrave had been equivocal. His very identity was a matter of debate. What was his real relation to the truth?

When I reached the path's intersection with the lane that led down towards Accrington, I noticed a figure coming on foot towards me from the high moor to my right. It was Henry Vaux.

'I have been visiting a poor soul over the moor who is likely to die soon,' he said. 'Now I am on my way to visit New Manor. I have had word from Miss Thomasina that her father has not come home. She must be frightened and in need of comfort.'

We walked together off the moor and down through the woodland, where a light breeze freshened the treetops and muffled the cries of the rooks in the sky above. At the point where the woods ended, Mr Vaux felt a touch breathless and proposed that we sit down to rest, indicating the same fallen tree trunk at the edge of the trees that I had once shared in the dark with Harry Hawk.

The prospect below us now was quite different from the velvet vale lit by moonshine that Hawk and I had looked over. In this sunshine, greens and yellows predominated. The River Hyndburn glittered as it snaked its way between sheep pasture and recently cut fields studded with mow stacks. From the houses of Accrington, there rose chimney smoke and the cries and echoes of human activity: sawing, rattling, hammering, dogs barking, and mothers shrieking after their children. A buzzard wheeled above, adding its cat-like cries to those of the humans and the sheep.

'A scene worthy of poetry,' I said. 'A pastoral sonnet, at the very least.'

'So it is,' agreed Vaux. 'And that reminds me.'

He suddenly dipped into his pocket and brought out two folded sheets of paper.

'Last Sunday, after Mass, Elizabeth gave me this.'

He handed me the first sheet and I saw that it was Elizabeth's transcript of the verse fragment she had found inside the locket, supposedly belonging to Turvey's mother-in-law:

> . . . *lovely styled,*
> . . . *what nature mild,*
> . . . *ect, all are filed*
> . . . *is one child*
> . . . *ming of the soul,*
> . . . *we keep this roll.*

'She had an idea that I might know it. Well, at first I had no idea, but Mother and I much enjoy riddles and rebuses, and all those sorts of thing, so we set our minds to the task. What kind of verse is this? we wondered. Not a love lyric, Mother thought, and not a sonnet, as the rhyme scheme is wrong. It appears to be praising some person – "what nature mild" – and I thought it might be part of an elegy. Those last four words speak of a record or a register; and so does the word "filed", taken in the sense of "made into a record." And the words "one child" might mean that a child is being recorded. May this be not a few lines from a longer poem but a six-line dedication? Or even better, an epitaph for a memorial stone?'

'That sounds plausible.'

'But where to look for such a thing? Perhaps the orthography could tell us. The language appears not very archaic, but the *v* is set as a *u* and "styled" has the old *f*-like *s*, which I think places the printing in the earlier part of the last century. I searched books by some likely poets of the time – Donne, Herrick, Waller, Lady Pembroke – and at first had no luck. Then I thought I would look into Ben Jonson – a ruffian but a fine lyricist (though now remembered as a play-writer). And would you believe it, Mr Cragg? I struck lucky. Look at this.'

He handed me the second paper, on which he had transcribed the following lines in a meticulous hand:

What beauty would be lovely styled,
What manners sweet, what nature mild,
What wonder perfect, all are filed
Upon record in this one child
And, till the coming of the soul,
To fetch the flesh we keep this roll.

'I am astonished, Mr Vaux,' I said. 'You have found it. Well done indeed!'

'It was chance more than anything.'

I read the lines through again.

'The sentiments are finely expressed,' I said. 'And you were right, it is surely an epitaph to be carved on a gravestone.'

'I can confirm it. The lines appear under the title *Epitaph for Elizabeth Chute*. Perhaps that name is to the purpose.'

'I think not. Jonson died more than a hundred years ago. The poem is put to a new use here, but how? Did the locket's owner mourn a deceased child? And if so, why keep only half the poem? Where is the other half?'

We speculated fruitlessly on the question for several minutes more before the priest said he was feeling rested and ready to go down to the village. It was when we reached the bridge that more news reached us – news of a sensational nature. Squire Turvey had been found in Clover Field. He had been horribly stabbed and was dead.

The discovery was made by Farmer Oldroyd's goatherd, whose name was Jim Strensall. He had come panting down the Brooknook path, his face alternately aghast at his discovery and flushed by excitement at being for once in his life the centre of the whole village's attention. His dog had made the find, he said. In deep grass at the extreme corner of the Clover Field from the barn. Jim could tell that it was Turvey and was sure that he was dead.

Fidelis and I reached the place, with a small crew of village men, half an hour later. We found Turvey practically concealed in long grass. We turned him over. The eyes stared in death, the hands were clenched, and the belly had a gaping wound crusted with dried blood and flies.

I sent two men up to the shed, having remembered it contained a second litter like the one we had used to transport Flora Horntree.

'How long has he been lying here?' I wondered.

Fidelis looked around. The field sloped steeply down from the shed, which from this point of view lay behind the field's horizon. Turvey's body had been found on the edge of a patch of sodden ground, where evidently a spring arose. Beyond this, the field was bordered by a line of trees and a tumbledown fence.

'This part of the field is hidden from on top. If only we had quartered the whole field when we came up yesterday, I think we would have found him.'

'What sort of weapon was it, would you say?' I asked.

'I couldn't, at this juncture.'

Fidelis rose and started walking in a widening circle around the body while searching the grass with his eyes. Having found nothing within fifteen yards, he left off and walked into the soggy lowest part of the field, which was bounded at the far side by a fence and the elongated copse.

By the time he rejoined me the men had arrived with the improvised bier, and the body was loaded on to it. With four burly villagers on hand, it made lighter carrying compared to the previous day.

'I was thinking earlier that Harry Hawk might come safely out of this,' I said as we began to make our way back to Accrington. 'But Turvey's death up there makes it look bad once more for him, does it not?'

We were following far enough behind to prevent the bearers from hearing us.

'He had a grievance against Turvey,' I went on, 'and he was at the scene of the crime.'

Fidelis said nothing.

'His time as a soldier makes me think he must have been inured to fighting. He must have been accustomed to settling arguments violently.'

We caught up with the corpse as it was being manhandled over a style.

'Furthermore,' I said as we continued on our way, 'we

cannot consider Hawk a saint. His participation in the death of Anne Gargrave shows he was rather the other way.'

I had still prised not a word out of my companion.

'And another point which must interest you in particular, both Anne Gargrave and Tom Turvey were papists. Do I weary you with my conversation, Luke?'

But, lost in thought, he was more oblivious than tired of my voice. We continued in silence as far as the village, where I directed the men to take Turvey straight to the church and lay him alongside Flora Horntree.

'I shall inquest both cases one after the other tomorrow,' I told Fidelis. 'Will you look over Turvey and come to the Dower House later? Happen we can have that conversation then.'

With a heavy heart, I went to tell Thomasina Turvey about the body in Clover Field. The child was sitting with Henry Vaux, who had already let her know of Jim Strensall's discovery. I now confirmed that the body was indeed her father's. She cried, but not with a child's abandoned grief. These were the restrained tears of an adult, as perhaps she felt she now was. I explained that the inquest into the Squire's death would follow Flora Horntree's, and requested the use of the Chamber Major for the purpose. Her tears had for the moment dried, and with a tight smile and heartbreaking courtesy she granted it.

By evening we were almost ready for the next day's business. Gubb had empanelled a jury, Frances had summoned witnesses, and I was smoking in the Dower House garden with Luke Fidelis. He had come to tell me his conclusions.

'I admit that I was misled by that woman,' he said. 'I could not until yesterday see her as she really was.'

'But you knew by then that she was a thief.'

'That was on Tom Turvey's account. I wanted to appraise her for myself.'

'And what conclusions did you come to? How, for instance, did she die?'

'She suffocated.'

'You don't mean . . .?'

'No, she was not buried alive.'

'Thank God!'

'Your imagination is lurid.'

'In the village, they are saying she was raped. Is that lurid?'

'No. Nor would it be surprising. After all, she was found wearing only her shift, with her dress buried in the ground beside her.'

'Is there anything to confirm rape?'

'Her face had swellings. She might have been struck in some way. And I did find what is probably semen.'

'Where?'

'In the appropriate place.'

'So she *was* raped.'

'Perhaps.'

He puffed again.

'There is something else.'

'What?'

'She had given birth.'

'Good God! Recently?'

'Probably years ago.'

'What else did you find?'

'Something very remarkable. This.'

He drew from his pocket a folded paper and handed it to me.

'Open it carefully.'

I put the paper on my knee, unfolded it, and found the crushed body of an insect.

'A bee,' I said. 'Why is that remarkable? There were thousands of bees up there.'

'But this one was in her throat.'

At this moment, Elizabeth showed a somewhat dejected Henry Vaux into the garden and we rose to greet him.

'I am making my way home to Mother,' said the priest. 'The Turvey household is terribly sad. Thank the good Lord for Sukey. The poor child is inconsolable by anyone but her.'

As we sat Mr Vaux down and Elizabeth went in to fetch him a glass of wine, Fidelis drew me aside.

'I must go. I have enquiries to make in the morning which will mean a walk into the country. So I must start early and would therefore like to go to bed early.'

This was extraordinary. Fidelis never retired or rose early except under compulsion.

'You haven't finished giving me your report. You've told me nothing about Turvey.'

'At this stage there's nothing I can tell you that you don't know yourself. But I hope to have the truth in time for the inquest. And I may have a surprise witness for you.'

'What about the bee in Mrs Horntree's throat? What is the significance of that?'

'Ah! That will be revealed in good time. I must first be sure myself.'

I was used to Fidelis's fondness for tantalizing, and indeed rather liked it. I let him go and returned to take a sip of wine in the garden with Mr Vaux.

THIRTY-ONE

Next morning, with an hour until the opening of the inquest, I was pacing about the Dower House wondering where Luke Fidelis was. I had gone up to New Manor and satisfied myself that the Chamber Major was ready. I had been to the church, where I met Peggy Stirk from Hatchfly Lodge and showed her the body of Flora Horntree so that she could give her evidence. Now, I was anxious to get the proceedings started on time, but could hardly do so without Fidelis.

I opened Mrs Horntree's valise and once again laid out on the dining table the candlestick and every item of jewellery that she had, apparently, stolen from the jewel box of Turvey's late wife. Turvey himself would not be testifying on the subject, and I was wondering whether I should question Thomasina on it instead. I was just looking the collection over, wondering what might be its exchange value in cash, when a knock came at the door. I opened it on Septimus Postumus, who stood on the threshold blinking and apologizing profusely for any disturbance.

'I was just on my way to Blackburn,' he explained, 'to visit my clerical friend Mr Taylor. But I have deviated into Accrington in the hope that I may have left my spectacles here. I have missed them since I was with you, and I find it very hard to get along without them.'

Calling for Matty to pour our visitor a pot of ale, I sat him down at the table and went to the mantelshelf. The eyeglasses were still there and I brought them to him.

'I have been meaning to send them,' I said, 'and at the same time to thank you for doing the burial of Grevel Horntree. It was good of you.'

'Oh, it was nothing but a pleasure, you know. Hatches, matches and dispatches: without them, what would we priests do?'

He donned the spectacles, looked around him, and beamed. 'Ah! Everything is suddenly clearer. How wonderful is the optical science. Upon my word! What do we have here? Your wife's treasures?'

'No, they are not Elizabeth's,' I said. 'They are to be produced at an inquest I am holding this very morning. I am trying unsuccessfully to extract from them something to the point.'

The item nearest at hand was the silver locket. He picked it up and, behind the glasses, I saw his eyes suddenly shed their appearance of idle curiosity.

'Well, I don't know if it is to the point, but this particular piece is certainly interesting.'

'It is the one that puzzles me the most, also,' I said.

'It does not puzzle me, Mr Cragg. I have seen many like it.'

He was now prising open the lid of the makeshift locket and peering inside. He took out the hair and piece of paper and smoothed the latter open on the table in front of him. I moved to his side and bent to look once more at the half page of poetry.

'Ah yes!' said the famous preacher, putting his finger on the paper. 'It is cut in half, as it should be. And where a verse is used for the purpose, this is one of their favourites. By Ben Jonson, I believe.'

I straightened my back.

'Mr Postumus, do not tell me you recognize what this is!'

'But I do, Cragg. Would you care to hear about it?'

Mr Postumus then told me a story so astonishing and so to the point that I asked him if he would be kind enough to delay his departure to Blackburn and repeat it all for the benefit of the inquest jury. He replied that it would, of course, be nothing but a pleasure.

For the second time that week, Accrington had not gone to work in the morning. As I swore in the jurors, every chair and bench in the Chamber Major, and every square inch of standing space, was occupied. The only significant absences from the room, as far as I could see, were the Hawks and – to my considerable anxiety – Luke Fidelis. But when the jury and I returned from St James's Church after viewing both bodies

– a procedure that had affected the jurymen variously, with expressions of pity over Tom Turvey and of horror and queasiness at the sight of Flora Horntree – we found the doctor sitting at his ease in the witness chair, waiting for us. I immediately began my questioning.

'Would you please tell us your name?'

'I am Luke Fidelis, M.D.'

'And were you the first finder of the dead body presumed to be that of Mrs Flora Horntree?'

'I was.'

With the formalities completed, I asked him to tell us what had prompted him to dig for the body in a corner of Clover Field.

'When I first visited the place with you on Tuesday last, we found Squire Turvey's beehives had been destroyed and burned. And when I looked inside the stone barn just by, I noticed a bale of straw had been pulled apart and laid on the ground in such a way as might have made a bed. Mrs Horntree had been missing for quite a few days, and this made me wonder if she had been secretly living there. I later saw that an area of ground behind the barn had been dug over to make planting beds, some of it more recently than the rest. I began to think she may have been the victim of someone who'd discovered her alone up there, so I started digging.'

'So when you found her in the ground, this suspicion was proved right?'

'Yes. And confirmed when, at your request, I made a medical examination of her body.'

'How was that?'

'There were visible signs that she had had carnal relations shortly before her death.'

This caused a small sensation in the room, though it quietened almost as soon as it arose. No one wanted to miss a word.

'And what do you mean by that, Dr Fidelis?'

'There was what I believe to be male seed inside her. It would have been absorbed and disappeared had she not died soon afterwards.'

'What did your examination tell you of the cause of her death?'

'That she had suffocated.'

'Was she, then, attacked and strangled in some way?'

'No, I don't think so. The signs were that she died by being deprived of air, but not as a result of human attack.'

'She suffocated, but not as a result of being attacked?'

'Oh, she was attacked, certainly, but not by a person. She was attacked by a bee. This bee.'

He took from his pocket the folded paper that I had already seen. He unfolded it and passed it to me.

'Where did you find this?'

'It was in her throat.'

I passed the paper to the foreman of the jury, who gingerly lowered his nose into the paper to see the bee at close quarters. Before passing it on to the next juror, who in turn passed it on, and so on down the line.

'The bee got into her mouth,' Fidelis went on. 'It was drawn into her throat by her breath, and there it stung her. I have seen like cases. Everybody knows that a bee sting normally causes a small swelling in the adjacent flesh. But for some people that swelling is very great and very sudden, and if this happens in the throat the result may be a total closure of the windpipe. Death from smothering follows very rapidly.'

'And is it your opinion that Mrs Horntree was one of those unfortunate people?'

'Yes, it is. I saw her very ill once before, at Hatchfly Hall. At the time I mistook the cause, but I now think it, too, was a bee sting.'

'Yes, I remember the occasion. That will be all for the moment, Doctor. We will hear from you later, but may we have Mrs Peggy Stirk to the chair now?'

After Peggy Stirk's tearful confirmation that the body dug up in Clover Field was that of Mrs Horntree, I had a few supplementary questions.

'When did you last see Mrs Horntree alive?'

'On Monday, not the last but the one before.'

'What had she earlier confided in you?'

'She told me she was shutting herself in her room. She must have stayed there all day and stolen out of the house after dark.'

'Why did she steal away?'

'Because she meant to leave the Squire on account of his
cruel treatment, that's what I think. He was away from home
at the time, as he often was, so she took her chance. But having
no money, I believe she meant to go to the Dower House and
hoped to get some money from you, Sir. As soon as she had
money, she'd have got right away from here, I'm sure.'

I thanked her, let her go, and called Susannah Widdop.
Sukey came modestly to the chair and gave her answers in a
straightforward manner. Mrs Horntree, having been taken
under Mr Turvey's protection on Tuesday, was last seen at
the house on the Wednesday morning. Sukey had been busy
about her tasks at the time. She had seen Mrs Horntree through
a window, walking on the lawn. She had seen her in the
Chamber Minor speaking with Mr Turvey, though she did not
know what they were talking about. Their guest had not
crossed her path again and must have left the house some
time after Mr Turvey himself had gone off to see to one of
his apiaries, which he did most mornings. Sukey said she had
nothing more to add, and I thanked her and let her go. I then
spoke directly to the jury.

'You may feel you do not yet have enough information
to satisfy this inquest with a sure verdict. Who was Flora
Horntree? Why did she flee her marriage? I now call a witness
to help answer these questions. I call the Reverend Septimus
Postumus.'

Expressions of surprise buzzed around the room. Most of
the people present had attended Postumus's burial service for
Grevel Horntree. But no one could imagine what he might
have to contribute to the present proceedings.

'Mr Postumus,' I said, when he had sworn on the Bible, 'we
have heard that Mrs Horntree had left her home, Hatchfly
Hall, and did not mean to go back. Now, found in her valise
was a small silver box like a pillbox. It could be fixed on to
a chain and so act as a locket. Here it is.'

I held it up for all to see, and handed it to Postumus. Having
looked at it, he passed it to the jury.

'As you can see, it has a monogram engraved on it, which
we have read as *F.H.*, considering it to be the initials of its

owner. Inside there was a lock of hair and half a page from a book of poetry, of which no one has been able to construe the significance. Now, however, I understand you can enlighten us to some extent.'

'That I can, Sir. It is a matter in which I take a specialized interest.'

He straightened his back and cleared his throat, as one preparing to sing.

'The lock of hair is that of a child given up by its mother,' he stated.

There were gasps from the audience and a few murmured comments. Alive, Flora Horntree had been a hidden and mysterious presence in Accrington. What secrets would she yield up in death? To those of a prurient nature, the auguries were looking promising.

'How do you know that?'

'Because I recognize the monogram engraved on the lid. It is not, as you may suppose, a personal name. *F.H.* stands for the Foundling Hospital.'

'And what is the Foundling Hospital?'

'It is an enlightened charitable institution in London, begun by the efforts of Mr Thomas Coram. It takes in babies and infants and gives them a home.'

'And where do these children come from?'

'They are the product of a great evil of our age, Sir. I refer to fornication. They are the bastards of women whose morals are sunk so low that they are got with child out of wedlock. Such women and girls are sometimes members of the servant classes that have lost their employment. Sometimes they are daughters of good homes fallen into destitution. They are forced, as they see it, to sell themselves in the stews and whorehouses of London, or in the streets, and such women have neither the means nor the inclination to care for their bastards. The Foundling Hospital exists to provide a Christian upbringing for these unfortunate souls.'

'Can you tell us the significance of this locket's contents? Such neckwear is usually used for keepsakes, is it not?'

'Yes, and so is this one. These lockets are manufactured and sold in London for the use of the depositing mothers. The

snippet of hair is presumably from the head of the child in
question and is retained by the mother as a remembrance. The
paper is different. It is a keepsake with a particular purpose.'

The locket was being passed around the jury. It had by now
been opened. I signed to the foreman.

'Mr Duckworth, would you extract the paper and hold it up
for all to see?'

Duckworth did so.

'Mr Postumus, please explain this "special purpose."'

'Every child accepted by the hospital is given a new name
on entry. The mother's name is, however, recorded in a file and
this is kept with one half of a token or keepsake. The other
half is kept by the mother.'

'For what purpose?'

'Against the possibility that a woman might mend her life.
She can come back to the hospital and by showing her half
of the token lay claim to her child and take it back.'

'I see. So the matching half of this page of poetry is to be
found in the records of the Foundling Hospital?'

'Quite so. The poems are produced by certain enterprising
printers and sold with the silver keepsake boxes, which are
often paid for by the women's seducers.'

'In summary, then, Flora Horntree's possession of this locket
means that she was one such mother.'

'It is more than likely.'

Did I need to go any deeper into this? I had wished – only
this morning – to know Flora's true nature. How unexpectedly
can such a wish have ever been supplied? Mrs Horntree was
revealed to have once been a girl who lost her virtue and
turned to whoredom, then was got with child and gave it up
to charity. Looking back to the moment when she stood
brazenly on the Dower House threshold and announced that
she was throwing herself on our protection, remembering
Flora's vanity in her appearance, her knowledge of London
shops and her extremely changeable nature, and recalling
Elizabeth's doubts about her truthfulness, it all seemed to
cohere with what Mr Postumus was saying. But had she
mended her ways at last, I wondered, or lived and died here
in Accrington still a harlot at heart? Fidelis's evidence was

that there was seed inside her, but that told us only that she had been with a man. It said nothing of the circumstances.

Well, she was dead and it did not matter, or so I now thought. I was content to bring evidence about Flora Horntree to an end, and so thanked Mr Postumus and invited him to leave the witness chair.

I now proceeded straight to my summary of evidence.

'We have heard that Mrs Horntree left her home with no money and sought refuge at the Dower House and then here at New Manor. Meanwhile, her husband, unknown to her, had suffered a fatal accident in Manchester. At some point on the morning of her death, while the May's Hole game was in progress, she left this house; and several days later her body was found in Clover Field. It is probable that she had encountered a man and they copulated in the stone shed – something this court might have very readily disbelieved had we not already heard from Mr Postumus that Mrs Horntree probably lost her virtue, in London, some years before her marriage. The suspicion is, therefore, that in her need for money to finance her flight from Grevel Horntree she was prepared to sell her favours here in Accrington. But in the throes of her passion she inhaled a bee, and died in the manner we have heard described by Dr Fidelis. We must suppose that to cover up his sin the unknown man buried her body nearby, where the ground was already dug over, and made himself scarce.

'Under normal circumstances,' I went on, turning to the jury, 'I would now be inviting you to consider a verdict. However, we must now go on to consider a second death, which probably occurred in the same Clover Field where Mrs Horntree was buried. We need to consider whether the two deaths are connected, so I wish to hear all the evidence in this second case before proceeding to both verdicts. Is that clear?'

It was.

'Then I adjourn for one hour's dinner break. You are each allowed tuppence for some bread and ale at the Black Bull, if you wish.'

THIRTY-TWO

Elizabeth had brought boiled eggs, bread and pickles to the upper room of the Gate House, since there would be no time for dinner. However, I had three highly piquant conversations during this hour, the first and the third of these being with Luke Fidelis.

'Why didn't you tell me before we started about the cause of her death?' I said, cutting a slice of bread. 'It changes everything. Instead of a rape and murder, we have . . . what? A bounce in the hay and a bee in the throat.'

'That is exactly what we have, Titus.'

'Who did she bounce with, then? And why in the old barn?'

'I should have thought it was obvious. But Titus, you yourself exploded quite a large bomb-chest with that information about the Foundling Hospital. I was much taken aback. I had already lost my illusions about that woman, but I never until now pictured her as a brazen harlot. Also, this must force us to think again about how Turvey died.'

'Have you drawn any conclusions about that?'

He pulled a folded paper from his coat pocket.

'Here's my report. It is concise but tells you what you need to know.'

There was mischief in his eyes. Was he paying me back in kind for having surprised him with my 'bomb-chest'?

I took the paper over to the window and was about to unfold it when Rosemary Hawk marched into the room.

'Harry is here, Mr Cragg,' she said. 'He is ready to give you your evidence.'

I hastily pocketed Luke's report. There was a gleam of pure determination in her eye.

'I am right glad, Mrs Hawk,' I said.

'I have been arguing with him all morning, trying to persuade him to come down and give his side of the story. I wore him out at last and he agreed. But walking through the village, we've had to listen to some hard words. And on top of that, they now tell us we are too late for the inquest.'

'Ah! Well, you are not. We've heard evidence on the death of Mrs Horntree, but this afternoon we turn to the matter of Mr Turvey. I have not yet called for a verdict on the lady and might allow more evidence if necessary. You know my friend Dr Fidelis, I believe.'

Fidelis bowed and she favoured him with a tight smile before turning back to me.

'So will you call Harry to speak? He has been so cried against and slurred, and near killed, as rapist and murderer of Flora Horntree, that this is certainly his best chance to tell the truth.'

'By all means, Mrs Hawk. But we are now sure that no man killed Flora Horntree.'

'Then who?'

'A bee. She died by a bee sting.'

Rosemary clapped her hands.

'Oh! An accident! How wonderful!'

She realized what she had said.

'I'm sorry, I didn't mean . . .'

'You should know that there was something else we learned this morning,' I said. 'It is about this.'

The pillbox locket lay wrapped in a cloth on the table. I removed the cloth and revealed the object to their eyes, with the monogram *F.H.* uppermost.

'Thanks to the Reverend Septimus Postumus, we know what it is. He takes a special interest in the Foundling Hospital.'

The instant she set eyes on the pendant Rosemary began trembling and was, I thought, about to cry.

'I think you know what it is, too, Mrs Hawk, do you not?' said Fidelis.

It was the first time he had spoken. After a moment, she seemed to come to a decision. She put her hands to the silver chain around her neck and slipped it over her head, and we now saw the pendant that had been hidden under her bodice. She placed it on the table beside the other. It too was a locket, and it bore an identical monogram.

'Flora and I were friends in London,' she said softly. 'We

met when we were waiting to bring our babies to the Hospital. We had no money to keep them.'

She picked up her locket, opened it, and took out and unfolded a piece of paper. She laid it on the table and I saw at once that it was the same poem, torn through in a similar way to the one found in Flora's locket.

'The lockets are sold by peddlers at the hospital gate to such girls as can afford to buy them. The poem has been chosen with deliberation, as the words are so fitting.'

'Tell me the procedure.'

'What they do at the hospital, if they accept your baby, is give it a completely new name and enter it in a register. You leave half of some token, such as this poem, to be kept in the hospital file and you keep the other half. In this way I could match the torn halves of the poem and prove I am the child's mother, if I should ever happen to come back for it.'

'If you had no money, how did you pay for the locket?' I asked.

'A gentleman befriended us outside the hospital. There are people that produce these lockets for the mothers, and he bought ones for both me and Flora. After that he brought us to live in a house in London; and from there brought us to Manchester, where we lived with a woman in a house next door to his.'

'And that gentleman, of course, was Grevel Horntree,' said Fidelis.

'It was.'

It was like the click of a beautifully made lock. Or the final balancing figure in a mathematical equation. All at once I saw not only the forces that had driven these Accrington people – the Horntrees, the Turveys and the Hawks – into their troubles, but also the way in which these forces could come to bear on the inquest. The answer to the death of Thomas Turvey was also, I thought, crystal clear.

'I have the whole picture,' I said to Fidelis after the tearful Rosemary had left us to find her seat in the Chamber Major. 'I am pretty sure what happened and I fear Harry Hawk's neck is once again at risk – though not now for the rape and murder of Flora Horntree.'

'You will enlighten me, I hope.'

I let the ironical tone go by.

'Hawk arranged to meet Flora at the barn in Clover Field on the day she died. He knew the place well, having worked for Mr Turvey until he was dismissed, and knew it was an excellent place for an assignation. So he met or took her there and – knowing all about her past as a whore from his wife – knew she might be agreeable to the idea, especially if he offered her money, which we know she needed. So he took her into the barn and lay down with her. And in the moment of greatest passion her mouth gaped open, and a bee happened to fly into it and stung her in the throat.'

Fidelis had nodded his head judiciously throughout. Now he patted my arm.

'This is excellent, Titus. "Moment of greatest passion" – no one in the court will be in any doubt what you mean by that. So Hawk buried her to conceal his part in it, you think?'

'Yes. And a few days later as he was on his way back from his work for Farmer Oldroyd – who I've seen in the audience and shall call to confirm the time Hawk left – he burned Mr Turvey's beehives as condign revenge for losing his employment as beekeeper. But Turvey himself arrived and caught him at it, and tried to put the fires out. They fought, but Hawk was much the stronger. He seized one of those sharpened fencing posts, of which there are a few inside the barn, and stabbed Turvey with great force in the stomach. Then he took him down the field and tossed him into the long grass. What do you think of that, Luke?'

'I think it is marvellous. It is a little arsy-versy, but marvellous all the same. I am glad you intend calling Oldroyd. I've been making his acquaintance and you will find him full of information, especially on the question mentioned in my report. Should we not go down to the Chamber Major now?'

As we went down, I told him that Elizabeth and I were of a mind to return to Preston as soon as possible.

'But you have been there most recently,' I said. 'Will it be safe for Hector?'

'In respect of the Paralysing Fever, yes, I think so. The

disease has not come to Preston and I have not heard of any new cases anywhere round about.'

Waiting for the room to settle, I looked around the walls, with their crossed swords, mounted armour and stiffly-posed portraits. The last in the male line of Turveys was gone now. The sacred rites would be performed by Henry Vaux in due course, but it fell to me to do the secular obsequies. I would have liked to conclude them pleasantly but knew it could not be so. The truth was going to be spilled like blood this afternoon, and would surely leave another blemish on a village already stained with blood.

'We heard this morning of one body that lay in Clover Field,' I began. 'That one was under the ground; but there was another body subsequently discovered there, which was *on* the ground a hundred and fifty yards away. It is this second body that will concern us this afternoon. May we hear from the first finder please?'

Strensall made his way to the front of the room in a confident bobbing walk. I directed him to the chair, and while he settled into it I looked around for Fidelis. He was standing with his arms folded near the back of the room with a conceited smile on his face. Beside him was the substantial curly-headed figure of Strensall's employer, Frederick Oldroyd.

The goatherd made the most of his chance to shine. He told how he was on his way back, having moved his goats from one field to another, and as he was passing the trees that bordered the bottom of Clover Field his dog ran through the trees and into the field itself.

'He's only lately been a pup, so's not yet trained to the best, like. Well, I called him but he was busy smelling summat, so I ran through the trees and up to him. And bugger me, he'd found a body! A dead man.'

'How was it lying?'

'It was in the long grass just at the side of this boggy patch in the lower field. It was sort of bent and lying on its side with its face in a molehill.'

'Did you touch it?'

'Not me!'

'And did you know who it was?'

'No. Like I said, his face were in the mud.'

'And what did you do then?'

'I knew he were dead. So I ran down here to the village. I told what I'd found. I said—'

'Thank you, Strensall, we have the essence and that will be all. You may leave the chair.'

He bobbed back to his place smiling triumphantly, like one who has scored a goal at football. I said, 'Will Susannah Widdop come to the chair, please?'

Sukey came forward for her second visit to the witness chair and stated that the body she had seen at the church was indeed Thomas Turvey. Thinking this discharged her duty, she began to rise.

'Just one moment, Mrs Widdop. The peace of Mr Turvey's mind had been disturbed of late, had it not?'

'Yes, Sir, ever since Mrs Horntree came to stay with us he was acting nervously. When she disappeared he got worse, and he seemed to break down altogether when they brought Squire Horntree back from Manchester.'

'Can you explain this?'

'No, but I'd seen him looking at Squire Horntree's wife while she was with us. I've not said this to anyone. But he looked at her like a man looks at a woman that he wants to . . . Well, a woman he's taken a fancy to.'

Could this be true? I had not thought of Turvey in such a light. It was surprising to hear a supposedly loyal retainer drop such a hint, but there is no judge of a man so clear-eyed as an old servant.

'And when was Squire Turvey last seen at New Manor?'

'The morning of the burial of Mr Horntree.'

'Was that before or after the burial?'

'Oh, before, Sir. He went out some time before it was due to start and never returned home.'

I thanked her and let her go, then called Seb Cook.

'You were Mr Turvey's beekeeping assistant?'

'Yes. Training, like.'

'Do you know that the beehives at Clover Field have been burned?'

'I went and 'ad a look this morning. I couldn't believe what I was seein'.'

'Can you think of any reason why anyone would do such a thing?'

'No, Sir, 'cept as revenge.'

'For what?'

He shrugged.

'Don't know. There's not many people didn't like Mr Turvey.'

'We've heard that Mr Turvey had been very upset the last week or so. Are you sure it couldn't have been done by Mr Turvey himself?'

'Oh no, Sir. He loved his bees, him. Like I say, it must have been done by someone that either hated him or hated the bees.'

'Thank you, Seb. You may get down.'

I was feeling excited now. I felt like a hunter stalking closer and closer to the truth. I called Harry Hawk and he came, almost furtively, to the chair. His face was covered in the usual way by a kerchief.

'Mr Hawk, you are a former soldier?'

'Aye.'

'Previously you lived in the household of Grevel Horntree?'

'I did.'

'How did you come there?'

'I am an orphan, a foundling. I don't know my true parents. Grevel Horntree was given me or found me – I don't know the truth – and took me in. He treated me more or less as his son.'

'But you quarrelled?'

'We did.'

Gradually, punctuated by scandalous comments coming at intervals from the body of the hall, I teased the story from him. There was a servant girl, Rosemary, who Horntree had brought to Old Accrington from Manchester, though she was originally from the south. Young Hawk and the girl fell in love and the pair absconded. After marrying they returned to Accrington and, being told by Grevel Horntree never to darken his doorstep again, were housed by John Gargrave at Gunwright's Heath. Shortly after that, Horntree brought Flora

– another young woman from Manchester, whom he told the world was his wife – to Hatchfly.

Much of the rest of Hawk's story was well known. All communications with Grevel Horntree were cut off, and the newly-weds were extremely poor. Harry went away to the war in the hope of bringing back enough cash to set them up in the weaving trade. Which he did, at the cost of the painful and unsightly wound to his face.

'There were rumours,' I said, 'that it was not Harry Hawk that returned from Dettingen. That the real Harry had been killed there, and that you are another man posing as Harry. What do you say to that?'

'It's a damnable lie. I may be hard to recognize, yet it is me, Harry Hawk, you are speaking to.'

'But word did come back that Harry Hawk had been killed?'

'There are many misreports after a battle.'

'So how did the story that you are an impostor come about?'

'I'd signed on under what they call a *nom de guerre*. When Mrs Gargrave heard about my paybook having a different name from my own, the witch jumped to the wrong conclusion. She could have talked to me about it, but instead she spread the rumour. That was worse than foolish, it was malice.'

His voice under its normal muffly tone was beginning to sound hard, as the tide of his anger edged higher. I noted this warning sign as I turned back to the events that now concerned us.

'Tell me why you were at Clover Field on the day before yesterday.'

'I had been working at Oldroyd's Farm. I passed by the barn, and the beehives where I used to work. I found them burned and was curious.'

'What time was that?'

'I knocked off my work at noon.'

'Do you have any idea who had done this burning?'

'No.'

'Was there any sign of Mr Turvey there?'

'No. The only ones I saw there were you and the doctor. While I was looking inside the barn, I heard you coming.'

'And at first you didn't show yourself. Why not?'

'I am shy, meeting people. The state of my face makes me so.'

So far I had not been hard on him. The time had come to take a tougher line.

'Mr Hawk, would you say you are a violent man?'

'I've seen much violence done. I have had to do some myself, like any soldier.'

'But you were dismissed from the position of Turvey's assistant apiarist because of your part in the very rough treatment of Mrs Gargrave, were you not?'

'So Turvey said.'

'And you much resented it, no doubt. You are subject to bouts of great anger, are you not?'

'I get angry, yes, like anybody.'

'"Like anybody." Is that really so? So what did you think of Flora Horntree?'

'Didn't know her.'

'I am not sure that is the truth, Mr Hawk. I think you did know her, and indeed liked her. So much so that you made an assignation with her at the Clover Field barn. I think *that* is the truth.'

The witness jumped to his feet in a passion. The kerchief across his lower face dropped away and the audience gasped in dismay at the revelation of his twisted and punctured face, contorted even more now by this sudden storm of rage.

'The truth?' he roared. 'You villain! You wouldn't know the truth from a cow's arse. You whore son! You trapped me! You made me think I came here to clear myself, and all you want to do is bring out these pig-dirty accusations. I'm done here. I'm done, and so is my wife. Rose! We're leaving. We're going home.'

He left the chair, sending it tumbling backwards, and pushed his way through the people packing the side aisles of the room. Rosemary, whose face was white with alarm, reached for his hand as he passed and he pulled her after him. After more struggling past the throng, they got out of the room.

THIRTY-THREE

The audience was in uproar. Many people were calling out obscenities and stabbing their fingers in the direction that the Hawks had fled. Others were jabbering to each other; some laughing, others apparently enraged.

'We shall continue the evidence, if you please,' I called out as the tumult at last subsided and I could make myself heard. 'Dr Luke Fidelis, will you come to the chair?'

Fidelis came forward in a businesslike manner and the room settled down to hear him.

'How did Thomas Turvey die, in your opinion?'

'By a deep lacerating wound in the abdomen, which penetrated upwards as far as the heart. He must have died very quickly.'

'Was it from a knife?'

'No, a thicker object.'

'A sharpened wooden stake, then?'

He smiled at me archly.

'That is conceivable, but the blow must have been an upwards thrust with what I suspect was a curved weapon.'

I frowned. To what could he possibly be referring? A sickle? It didn't seem likely.

'And do you have any idea of how long ago the death happened?'

'I would guess no more than a day before the body was found. There was minimal mortification.'

'Was there anything else about the body that you noticed?'

'Yes. There were clear signs that he had been close to a fire. Even after the overnight rain his hands and face had traces of smuts, and his hair was partially singed.'

'Do you recall that when you and I went to Clover Field looking unsuccessfully for Mr Turvey we found the smouldering remains of his beehives?'

'It was a sight difficult to forget.'

'Could the smuts on his face have been signs that he'd tried to put the fire out?'

'Yes, I suppose they might.'

His tone of voice suggested otherwise, however. Arsy-versy? I'd soon show him, I thought.

'You may quit the chair, Doctor, and I would like to hear now from Frederick Oldroyd.'

Oldroyd came up and took the stand, looking at me with the full square gaze of an honest and forthright man.

'Mr Oldroyd,' I said when I had sworn him, 'it's good of you to appear. You employ Harry Hawk, I believe? What is he like?'

'He is an honest and good worker. I don't much like looking at him, but I don't mind paying him.'

There was some suppressed laughter from the audience.

'Does he have outbursts of anger?'

'Aye, as we've just seen.'

'Did he tell you his feelings about the loss of his position as beekeeper to Mr Turvey?'

'He mentioned it. And, yes, he resented it.'

'Very well. Did you employ him on the day before yesterday, when we think Mr Turvey was killed?'

'I did. I gave him some tasks about the farmyard.'

'Until what time of day did he work?'

'I sent him home at midday, or thenabouts.'

'And would his path back from your place to Accrington have taken him past Mr Turvey's Clover Field?'

'Right past.'

I noticed a pair of hands raised in the air at the back of the room and realized they were those of Luke Fidelis. He was unmistakably miming the action of a hand writing on a piece of paper. My God! I thought. In all the excitement I had forgotten the paper containing his report.

I was forced briefly to pause my examination as I slipped it out of my pocket as surreptitiously as possible and opened it on the table in front of me. I believe my mouth may have dropped open to such a degree at this moment that, had there been a bee in the vicinity, it might have been tempted to land on my tongue and sting it. The report was brief indeed. It consisted of just eight words: *Old Nob killed Turvey. Oldroyd will tell you.*

I looked across the room at Fidelis. The teasing smile still played on his lips.

'Mr Oldroyd. Who, pray, is Old Nob?'

'That's my bull, Sir.'

'Your bull?'

'Yes.'

I remembered the animal – didn't someone say he was unusually sociable for a bull?

I looked down at the paper again. *Old Nob killed Turvey.*

'I have a difficulty, Mr Oldroyd. I've heard it said Old Nob is a particularly sweet-tempered and tractable beast. Is there any possibility that it was he that attacked Mr Turvey?'

'He is very tractable, you're right, Sir. But not when he's riled. Then he's like any other bull.'

'So what might rile him?'

'Frustration does it, if he wants to get at a cow. Or pain – I mean a sore head or summat of the kind. You wouldn't want to provoke him with a smack on the nose or anything.'

My God! All at once I saw how it must have been.

'And what would he do if you did so provoke him?'

'He would attack in a fit of rage. That is what bulls do. He would try and toss you with his horns.'

'And am I right in saying that Old Nob lives in a field adjacent to Clover Field?'

'Yes.'

'Could he have got into Clover Field itself if he saw someone there?'

'Happen, and he would try it more than likely.'

'So if there were a gate open or a gap in the hedge, he would go through it?'

'That's right.'

'And if he found someone setting fire to the beehives, what do you think would happen?'

'Well, as the doctor said to me this morning, the bees would have been going mad, wouldn't they? Likely as not the bull'd have got stung and had a fit of rage.'

'And attacked the person in front of him?'

'Yes, likely as not.'

'And have you seen the bull since the day Mr Turvey died?'

'Aye, I went to look at him with Dr Fidelis this morning.
That's when the doctor and I talked about the matter.'

'Were there any signs of blood on his horns and head?'

'There was nothing, but I reckon that's because it had rained
hard. Any blood had washed off. But Dr Fidelis pointed out
some marks on his nose. He said they were probably bee stings.'

'So, Mr Oldroyd, in sum, do you believe that Old Nob killed
Mr Thomas Turvey?'

'I do, Mr Cragg. I am sorry, but I do. I think he went up
to the little barn to join Mr Turvey by the burning bee skeps.
But he got stung, so he went mad and broke down the fence
between the field and the barn and gored Mr Turvey.'

'But something still puzzles me. How did the body of Mr
Turvey end up at the other lower end of the field, away from
the little barn?'

'If he got speared on the horns, Old Nob might have run
with him down the field and might not have shaken him off
until he reached the bottom.'

I felt a faint sickness in the pit of my stomach. I had been in
hot and wholly unjust pursuit of an innocent man, while attribu-
ting all sorts of convoluted motives to him. If it had been left to
me, Hawk would have been found responsible for two murders.
He would then have been taken to Lancaster Castle for the assize
and been hanged. How could I have been so foolish?

The truth! Hawk had told me I wouldn't know the truth
from a cow's arse. But all the time it had lain in a bull's horns.

I now gave my second summary of evidence, exonerating
Harry Hawk as best I could and direly warning the jurors not
to be swayed by any prejudice they might feel towards him.
I also reminded them of the strong evidence for a verdict of
death by bee sting in the first case, and by bull's horn in the
second. I then suggested they go into the Chamber Minor and
deliberate, and not take too long about it.

Ten minutes later, with the audience fidgeting and growing
impatient, Duckworth, the jury foreman, returned. Would I
come with him to the room? The jury had a question.

They were standing in two or three groups, talking quietly
together, some frowning and shaking their heads.

'So,' I said, 'what's the matter, Duckworth?'

The foreman insisted I sit at the table and he took the chair opposite. The rest of them gathered around him.

'Right,' said Duckworth. 'We catch on that Mr Turvey burned his beehives, which got him killed because the bull got stung. But why did he burn them? That's what we want to know.'

Another juryman thrust his hand towards me.

'He lived for them bees, Sir. Anyone who knew him knew that. He couldn't have destroyed them.'

'In the disturbed state of his mind, he could,' I said. 'You see, he was punishing the bees for what one of them had done – the killing of Flora Horntree.'

Duckworth waggled his head in dissent.

'But how did he know what the bee had done? As far as he knew, Mrs Horntree had upped and left his house with no trace. How could he know she'd been stung in the throat by that bee?'

'And she'd been buried,' said a third juror. 'Are you telling us he found her in the ground and found out about the bee and then reburied her?'

I closed my eyes for a moment. Patience, I told myself.

'No, he didn't dig her up and rebury her. He was the one that buried her in the first place. Because he was the one in the barn with her when she died.'

The jurors' mouths gaped, and one by one they voiced their astonishment.

'You're saying it was him that fucked her?'

'Tom Turvey? I knew him a bit and he'd never, Mr Cragg!'

'Well, by all! I can't credit that! I'll never believe that.'

'Yes! All of you, listen to me. You think you know somebody. But then they do something that makes you think you didn't really know them after all. Have you never met that kind of thing? Turvey was a big, strong man, but in society rather timid. He may not have been a good manager of his land, but most people respected and liked him and thought him virtuous. You have to remember, though, that for many years he'd been a lonely man in the prime of life with no woman to warm his bed. Now, Flora Horntree was an ex-whore – you've got that, haven't you?'

'Oh, aye. We got that.'

'She came unexpectedly into his house and she offered herself, and so he gave in to temptation. But he wouldn't do it in his house, not with his daughter there, so he took her up to the little barn.'

'When was this?'

It felt like a peculiar reversal. Usually it was me making the interrogation.

'On the morning she was missed,' I explained. 'He took her there clobbered up in bee armour, so everybody who saw them thought she was Seb Cook and took no notice. Surely all this was clear from the evidence?'

'So he never meant any harm to her?'

'Of course he didn't. Think of it as a transaction. She needed money, which he gave her – or rather, valuables from his wife's jewel box because he didn't have any actual cash. And in return, she let him . . . you know . . .'

One by one the clouds of doubt cleared from the men's visages. Now, radiant smiles beamed out at me, with expressions of satisfaction.

'That's tidy, is that. That's all in a teacup.'

'So it is,' I said. 'So shall you be able to agree your verdicts?'

'Oh, aye,' said the foreman. 'Is that right, lads?'

They nodded their heads as one.

'We'll come back with you now and give them out.'

'No, no,' I said hastily. 'Hang on here for a few minutes. Allow me to return to the court room, then come back up yourselves. That would be better.'

'Anything you say, Mr Cragg.'

I made a move towards the door, but Duckworth stopped me.

'Now, what was it again, Mr Cragg?' he said. 'The bee sting for Mrs Horntree and the bull's horn for Mr Turvey. Have I got that right?'

'Yes, Duckworth. When you return to the Chamber Major I will ask you formally, and then you will deliver the verdicts and Mrs Nightingale, my clerk, will record them. And that, I am glad to say, will be the end of this inquest.'

And so it was.

*   *   *

The next morning at the Dower House we began packing up. Belongings were boxed and baled. The rooms were swept. A carter was found who would transport us to Preston on the day following. Seeing all the activity, Suez became excited and ran around yapping and making a great nuisance. Elizabeth was singing as she went about her work, and even Hector seemed to sense the satisfaction in the air. He was more alive, laughing when he was spoken to and feeding vigorously. Only Matty was down in the mouth.

'Haven't you noticed?' said Elizabeth when I mentioned this. 'She's had that lad paying her attention, the boy at New Manor. He's turned the poor girl's head, so it's a good thing we're leaving.'

We had invited Mr Vaux and his mother, with Fidelis and Frances Nightingale, for a last dinner at the Dower House. We had also included Thomasina Turvey but she declined, saying she had a cold coming on.

'She doesn't yet feel like being in company,' said Elizabeth. 'But I have asked her to visit us in Preston and she has promised to come.'

We sat down to a jugged hare and huge Yorkshire puddings, washed down with the last of the ale I had got in from the Black Bull. We fed well and were tolerably merry, so that by the end of it all we were ready for some music. Mr Vaux had brought a lute, on which he played some antique music by William Byrd very prettily. He then proposed to accompany us in song. The first to perform was Fidelis, who had a rich and expressive voice. He picked up the volume of Shakespeare that I had just returned to Mr Vaux, leafed through the pages, and asked Vaux if he knew Bottom's Song *The Ousel Cock*. He did and we had it three times, laughing immoderately at the exaggerated ass's bray with which it ends.

It was after he had sung Ariel's song from *The Tempest* which begins 'Full fathom five thy father lies' that I thought again of Thomasina Turvey.

'What will become of poor Thomasina?' I asked.

'She has no relatives,' said Fidelis. 'She is alone in the world.'

'Well,' said Henry Vaux, in an exaggerated whisper, 'Mother and I have concocted a plan. Mother, tell them.'

'There is no need to sound like a conspirator, Henry,' said
Mrs Vaux. 'It's simple. There are two good Catholic households
in this village that have been sorely bereaved, and I think it
would be good to unite them. I mean, of course, Mr Gargrave
and Thomasina Turvey.'

'Oh, Mrs Vaux!' cried Elizabeth, 'You cannot mean them
to marry. She is still a child and he is fifty.'

Mrs Vaux laughed.

'Oh, no, my dear, nothing like that. But Gargrave lost his
daughter a few years ago and I mean for him to be a sort of
foster father to Thomasina. He shall live at New Manor and
manage the estate, at which he is skilled. The Turvey acres
badly need attention, as we know, but they are not to be
despaired of. They have promise, and in his hands I believe
New Accrington will have an excellent future.'

It seemed a good enough scheme and we drank a toast to
its success. This was followed by more singing, until finally
the Vauxes said they must leave before the light faded.

'One more song before you go,' insisted Frances Nightingale.
'I shall sing it. I know something highly appropriate and it
contains what we all want – a happy ending.'

She picked up the book we had been singing from.

'Where is *The Tempest*? Ah! Here it is, in the first place.'

She found the page and showed it to Henry Vaux, who
nodded and then struck up some introductory chords. Holding
the book in both hands, she stood beside him and began to
sing in a sweet, unaffected voice, the following words:

> *Where the bee sucks, there suck I*
> *In a cowslip's bell I lie;*
> *There I couch when owls do cry.*
> *On the bat's back I do fly*
> *After summer merrily.*
> *Merrily, merrily shall I live now*
> *Under the blossom that hangs on the bough.*

EPILOGUE

Since these events occurred I had no cause to return to Accrington, but in time Thomasina Turvey made the (for her) laborious cross-country journey to Preston to stay as our guest at Cheap Side. Then, and on subsequent visits, she brought us abreast of Accrington affairs. We heard how, following the disastrous loss of both squires in the same month, Lord Petre had taken a hand, after receiving a letter from Henry Vaux. In time, the peer made his first visit to the area and laid out a considerable sum in land purchases, which extended his holding to most of the New Manor and Hatchfly estates. All was entrusted to the management of John Gargrave, who took up residence – just as Vaux had suggested – at New Manor, becoming Miss Turvey's guardian and a figure of increased importance in the area. For the rest of his life the village would whisper about the stang ride he had to endure in the year '44, but no longer did anyone dare mention it in his presence.

Although I didn't go back to Accrington, I did return to Manchester the following September in order to dun the town for my coroner's expenses. Presenting Bower with the account in person at his house – he had ignored my repeated applications by letter – I was treated with a peculiar evasiveness. I took some pleasure in provoking this further by casually mentioning Cold Harbour Lane.

'I wonder what happened to the good Mrs Quinto,' I said.

'Mrs who?' said he.

'She lived in Cold Harbour Lane. She had the knack of reading fortunes, and was a great entertainer in the social way. Mr Grevel Horntree brought his wife, I do believe, from Mrs Quinto's to his house in Accrington. Many other gentlemen with business in the town frequented the house, no doubt, and many residents too. You yourself, perhaps, went there from time to time.'

Bower was sitting behind the writing table in his business room. Now he planted his arms on the tabletop and folded them, while matching my gaze with his own. I had his full attention.

'I am curious to know,' I went on, 'exactly what Horntree's interest was in the house. He was no mere customer, was he?'

Bower breathed deeply and seemed to make up his mind.

'Very well, Cragg, let us beat about the bush no more. I didn't know him as Horntree, but I did as Greenwood. And as Greenwood, he put up the money that launched Mrs Quinto's house.'

'Did he take profits from it?'

'Undoubtedly.'

'And these were considerable, I imagine.'

Bower smiled. He was beginning to be more at ease.

'Yes. Well, I am sure you understand the way of the world, Cragg. Mrs Quinto provided a place in which a man could enjoy his leisure in a number of unusual ways. Unusual ways of dressing, for instance. Mrs Q, as we called her, kept an extensive wardrobe, very extensive. Remarkable silks, she had.'

'Silks such as were the subject of the letter found in Mr Horntree's pocket?'

'Exactly so.'

'And was that letter written in your own hand?'

Bower smiled again.

'If it had been made public, I would quite plausibly have been able to say that I was enquiring about a dress for Mrs Bower.'

'Nevertheless, you destroyed the letter when it came back into your hands?'

Bower spread his hands wide.

'It had no bearing on Greenwood's unfortunate death, which was the result of a foolish action by a foolish boy. And I did not wish there to be any misinterpretation.'

He rose and, fetching a purse from a cupboard, placed it on the table in front of me.

'Allow me to leave the matter there, Mr Cragg. Here is your money. Shall we agree that our business is now concluded?'

It could be argued that he had committed perjury at the

inquest, but what did it matter now? I nodded my head, and in no time at all found myself being shown out of the house with the purse of money in my hand.

Back at the Swan Inn that evening, I fell into conversation with a portly, rubicund gentleman wearing a once smart and now shabby suit of clothes, who spoke in West Country accents. He was sitting at the fire in the reading room with the London papers and a large jug of punch by his side, which he helped himself to liberally and often, and generously helped me to when I took the chair on the other side of the fireplace.

From his wig I guessed I was in the presence of a fellow lawyer, and asked him if I was right.

'Partly, partly. I practise at the bar a little. I am here very briefly on a Chancery case, seeking evidence for a Writ of Ejectment being heard on the Western Circuit. We are trying to oust a dirty dog of a Jacobite from his estate. But I've made my living in other trades besides the law. I am no stranger to Grub Street. I wrote plays until the government shut down most of the theatres in '37, damn their eyes. They attacked me personally as seditious, because I called Walpole a coxcomb and a rogue – which he was – and something worse than a rogue, which he was too. I turned to writing novels after that.'

This perked up my interest extremely.

'You are a novelist? I am a reader myself, and have a pretty good library. Have you published?'

'Of course I've published. D'you think I'd write 'em and not print 'em? Making fun of Mr Samuel Richardson has been my stock-in-trade, and in particular his novel *Pamela: or, Virtue Rewarded*. You will know it. There were many parodies and by-products of that unaccountably successful book, and by common consent mine were the best. I did reasonably well out of them; but now sales have dried up, so I'm trying to think up a new story. It's damnably difficult to invent a story. Have you ever attempted it?'

I admitted that I had not and our conversation took a different turn for a while, away from the invention of stories and towards the operation of the law. I did not find him shy of voicing his opinions at considerable length.

'Crime, Sir, let us drink a toast to it, for it puts food on the tables of us lawyers. But in London robberies sorely increase year by year, and the law cannot tackle the evil as it lacks the men, let alone the legal power. This idea that the hue and cry can only go as far as the parish boundary, why it's a nonsense, a farce – and this I say as a playwright, so I know what I speak of. The constables are useless, too. Decrepit as well as lazy. We need a force of vigorous men who can run after the criminal and go on running until they catch him and drag him back to face justice. And we need to collect intelligence and keep records about the criminals, such as their description and habits. But conceivably you have fewer dealings with the criminal classes, Sir?'

I told him that as County Coroner I occasionally had to reckon with them.

'You are a coroner? That is excellent. Are you here on coroner's business?'

'Merely collecting my dues on an inquest I lately held in Manchester.'

'What case was that?'

'A very convoluted and remarkable one. And it occurs to me it might even furnish you with the bones of this new tale you mention.'

He leaned forward in his chair.

'Tell, then. I am all ears.'

For one who so evidently enjoyed holding forth I was surprised at how intently he listened, while continually drinking and smoking, and how well he absorbed the details of those fatally intermeshed events in Accrington and Manchester. He deplored the cruelty of the stang ride, laughed at the cocky young Ashton Lever, tut-tutted over Mrs Quinto's establishment, and shook his head sorrowfully at the plight of Thomas Turvey.

'I sympathize with both of the unfortunate widowers in the case.' He stared into the flames of the fire. 'My own wife is grievously sick.'

'I am very sorry to hear it.'

He drained his glass and filled it again. He was drinking twice as fast as I was.

'A man should have a woman in his bed,' he said, 'else he spends all his energies in the company of men. Men's affairs are just politics and money – dull stuff. Life must also contain a good amount of music, dancing and fucking, by God! No wonder he – what was his name? Turvey? – no wonder your Mr Turvey rogered that woman when the opportunity presented itself. Unfortunate about the bee getting her in the gullet in the throes of their pleasure. She was a pretty wench, you say?'

'She was, very.'

'I am glad, though I cannot approve of a woman giving herself to a man for money. Cash is no substitute for love, and whoring is a curse on society. It is only encouraged by the antics of men like Tom Coram and his Foundling Hospital. It is misguided charity. It merely rewards the getting of bastards. I do not agree with that type of charity, and even if I had the money I'd not contribute.'

'But is not the keeping of divided tokens in the hope a mother may claim back her child a touching matter, Sir?' I said.

'I doubt any child is ever claimed back. The degeneracy and persistent criminality of the poor must prevent it. No, I cannot see myself constructing a story for my novel on these foundations, my dear Sir. I could never have a gentleman, as you have described, bringing a whore into his house as a pretended servant or, so you allege, as his supposed wife. There is real scandal there, and it is too far from the common run of experience to be of use to a writer of novels. And then I must tell you the poor are not interesting either to me or my readers, nor are the maimed and crippled. I cannot abide a story with too much horror and deformity in it. Your old soldier's exploded face – now I could never put that into a book. My writings are known for their geniality, and their healthy good humour.'

'That fellow is better-looking now than he was,' I said. 'My excellent friend Dr Luke Fidelis has mended him to an extent. He called him to Preston, where he closed the open gash in his face by surgery. He still looks frightfully scarred, but it is an improvement.'

'I am happy for him, but I regret I can't put him in my story – for even if he were not disfigured, it is never decided

whether he is or is not who he says he is. I know you have
based this on an old French case of which (by the way) I am
cognizant. But that case was fully solved and legally concluded.
The man was shown to be a fraud. You, on the other hand,
have left your case up in the air!'

'That is simply how events shaped,' I protested. 'It was only
village suspicion and gossip, which I found I could neither
justify nor give the lie to.'

'And then there is, in your story, no solution to the death
of the shrewish wife. No one is found guilty. No one is
punished. We cannot have that.'

'The jury decided that for me. I had to defer to them, as
my power and responsibility had reached its limit. Matters
often fall out so.'

'And there you have the difference, my friend! The novelist
knows no limit to his power. Without blasphemy, I may say
his power is like God's. And for that very reason he must not
fail to use it to serve the good against the enemies of good
– by which I mean greed, hypocrisy, cruelty and lies. You will
take more punch?'

He filled my cup and again brimmed his own. Then, taking
a long gulp, sat back in his chair and mused for a while.

'There might, nevertheless, be something of use in your tale
after all,' he said at last. 'Some residual use, I might say. A
foundling raised in a gentleman's house, such as your Harry
Hawk was before he was ever a soldier. I say "before he was
a soldier" because I cannot abide soldiers: they are the most
dishonest, rough and pox-ridden villains in the world. However,
as I say, before he was a soldier he might come in handy. And
then, what was it? Ah yes! Neighbouring squires, very different
types and contending with each other – I might make something of them. I might very well make something of them.'

He fell silent again and his eyes again strayed towards the
flames. After a few moments, I saw his eyelids droop and
heard gentle snores. Leaning forward, I took the glass from
his fingers before it fell and placed it beside the punch jug.
And then I drained my own. It was late and I was tired. Quietly,
I stole away from him and went upstairs to bed.

Lightning Source UK Ltd.
Milton Keynes UK
UKHW010514200919
350097UK00004B/54/P